California's Over

California's
Over

⊙ ⊙ ⊙ ⊙

LOUIS B. JONES

PANTHEON BOOKS • NEW YORK

*Grateful acknowledgment is made to the following for
permission to reprint previously published material:*
Sony/ATV Music Publishing: Excerpts from the lyrics to "Bird on the
Wire" by Leonard Cohen. Copyright © 1968 by Sony /ATV Songs LLC.
All rights administered by Sony/ATV Music Publishing, 8 Music Square
West, Nashville, TN 37203. All rights reserved. Reprinted
by permission of Sony/ATV Music Publishing.
Stone Diamond Music Corporation: Excerpts from the lyrics to "Papa
Was a Rolling Stone" written by Norman J. Whitfield and Barrett
Strong. Copyright © 1972 by Stone Diamond Music Corporation.
All rights reserved. Reprinted by permission of
Stone Diamond Music Corporation.

Library of Congress Cataloging-in-Publication Data

Jones, Louis B.
California's over / Louis B. Jones.
p.   cm.
ISBN 0-679-42334-6
I. Title.
PS3560.O516C35   1997
813'.54—dc21   97-7284
CIP

Random House Web Address: http://www.randomhouse.com/

BOOK DESIGN BY FEARN CUTLER

Printed in the United States of America
First Edition
2 4 6 8 9 7 5 3 1

To Joy Harris and Dan Frank

And in memory of Don Carpenter

California's Over

◉ ◉ ◉ ◉

I nterstate 80—"America's Main Street" on the postcards—gets its first impulse way back on Manhattan Island, I believe at about 178th Street, where the George Washington Bridge connects New York City to land, and then it comes west through the Midwest, through Nebraska and Wyoming and Utah, very much along the route the pioneers first took, along the Platte River Valley and over the Wasatch. Through a rough section in Wyoming where the divided highway isn't finished yet, past the Huckleberry Finn Mystery Cave, past the concrete brontosaurus in Utah and the legendary colonies of stranded mermaids in the desert who sing to passing truckers over CB radio, past the casinos on the horizon, it climbs and climbs, toward the impassable Sierra, the spot nearest heaven, Donner Pass. Then in California it comes down the impossible stony mountains and crosses the agricultural valley in the haze, aiming straight at San Francisco on the flat, while the Coast Range looms, and then at last offers a westward exit ramp upon the northern arm of the Bay. At which point, to keep going straight west, you'd cross the Bay on the Richmond–San Rafael Bridge, into Marin County, where an exit ramp puts you down on Sir Francis Drake Boulevard—which halts at a few stoplights among shopping malls and subdivisions, then rises into the wind over the coastal mountains, into the dripping mist, through denser and denser redwood forest, still going west,

3

getting narrower and pot-holier among the tall trees, zigzag-ging in hairpin turns, its asphalt decaying in chunks, its double yellow line eventually erased, dropping over the last hill into the Pacific Ocean wind, to end finally at the lost beachy village of Seawall, preserved at the bottom of an ancient ocean of fog.

The last turn, off the coast highway, usually can't be found, because Seawall's citizens persist in tearing down the sign at the crossroads. Every few months, a Cal-Trans worker in an or-ange plastic vest will come out in a fresh orange truck to put up a new sign: the simple word SEAWALL in white letters on a green rectangle with an arrow pointing out toward the coast. But whenever a new sign appears, a band of local vigilantes comes out at night to cut it off at the base, by hatchet, by chain-saw, or by gently tapping it with the bumper of a pickup. At one point during the seventies, state highway workers planted a steel I-beam in concrete. To this the Seawall sign was bolted and welded. But the villagers used an acetylene torch to take it down during the night. Another time, high-impact reflective paint was applied to the road surface itself, to spell out SEAWALL with an arrow, but the locals came out and chiseled it off the pavement on hands and knees. Then the state put up a new sign and posted a guard to sit in his truck all night and watch over it. The guard was held captive at the point of a shotgun while the sign was taken down. After that incident, the guard—though his captors, he said, were polite and humor-ous—refused to go back to work. The Seawall Sign Wars con-tinue on and off to this day. If you want to get there, you just have to *know* which turn leads there off the coast highway, dis-tinguished by a stretch of deep oak woods on the left, then a dip and a long lull, a growing sense of distance from anywhere, a willow tree, a falling fence post.

If it's morning, the sun will be on your back, the fog bank ahead of you. After a mile or two, something will make you slow down—a potter's ware on shelves, a dog in the road. And

4

then Seawall will stand up through the fog as a string of salt-bleached shacks of silver wood, rusty hinges, flower boxes, the medieval-looking pennants on the Veritas Lost Wine Shop, Coast Feed and Hardware, Joan Baez's (supposedly) old Saab in Pete Rosenthal's front yard under a canvas dropcloth held down at the corners by firewood logs and pasted-down leaves, then the bookstore, then the grocery store, then the tiny public library with its wind sock tie-dyed in dark veins of beet and pumpkin, Alice's Lunch, The Quiet Woman Bakery and Cappuccino, Angelo Parinesi's Volkswagen bus stranded at the curb without wheels gaining poetry and illustrations by the year, Humper's Bar, the Bubble Gum Tree, the vacant lot for flea markets where the same collection of objects resurfaces every spring to be recirculated, then the General Store with the town bulletin board, then the automobile mechanic's barn, then the Soda Water Fountain with its gingham curtains and its sidewalk tables of immense rough cable-spools in the dripping fog, and its sharp scent of omelettes and bacon and coffee in the fresh tidal smell. All this was 1973. I can't bring back any of the people, nor any second chances for myself or anybody, but I can bring back every detail of the physical place, the boards and paint, the frizz of old staples in the telephone pole, the shade of the chestnut tree on gravel.

Around the last bend, a few shacks, some abandoned, are built out over the water on tarred stilts, where the road from New York trickles out in the pilings of the old wharf in the sand among the last few studios and galleries, padlocked and hostile to trade. Above and behind the last of these, on pitch-sticky pilings, there used to be a dark, quiet coffee house and used-bookstore, known as Little Tom's Round Table—at the farthest extension of New York's 178th Street, you might say. But out here, Little Tom wouldn't have paid much rent, if any. The door, at street level, was a swinging block of varnished rotten marine timber, on hinges of heavy brass powder-blistered by the weather. The walls of the inner staircase were painted black, shiny like fresh tar. That shine's faint starlight showed your way as you climbed.

Upstairs inside, the tomb of books, a few tables, a few morose figures in limbo at separate tables. It's all such a cliché. This was before the "bookstore" and the "coffee shop" were so successfully joined in a single business; Little Tom's inside had a very unmodern, mistaken kind of feeling, an atmosphere of miscellany and condemnedness like a storage room. The only sound was the *boink* in the pan under the ceiling leak, and at high tide the slap and kiss of waves beneath the floor, where marsh sand was massaged into long hard cold bars. Thousands of completely uninteresting old used books—dented round at the corners, cold from being nevermore touched—generated a murmurous twilight. To my knowledge, no one ever "bought" a book in Little Tom's but only grieved over them for a while and then wandered off. Or maybe walked away with one. Little Tom really wouldn't have cared. This was a time, and a place, when people's motives for doing things weren't economic.

At the end of the labyrinth of books in 1973 was a luminous white rectangle: a fresh 3 x 5 notecard was pinned to a bulletin board, headed, in the clear pica of an IBM Selectric, TEMPORARY WORK. I see myself standing there. I'm seventeen years old, and I'm crouching to unpin the card, which Dean Houlihan himself had just entered to post there. Dean was a local character who, supposedly, lived in a cave on the beach north of town. He spent most of his time in front of the General Store carrying his old antique surfboard, on which he'd carved illegible mottoes and scrimshaw diagrams; or else he would be out on the main road greeting strangers (frightening them, really) with the benediction "Only the pure of heart!" Other than that, he seldom spoke, but kept his peace, a vicar of the town. One year everybody pitched in and bought him some orthodontic work; and he kept being reelected as one of the several mayors. At the back doors of the local restaurants, he was given the day's leftover bread, or extra falafel, or soup, or a fondly prepared sandwich, and in the evenings a cup of wine at the Veritas. He tended to come around Little Tom's regularly in the mornings, and Little Tom would always crack two eggs in a paper cup and steam them with a burbling sound in the nozzle of his espresso machine, with a little salsa and cheese ("Esteemed Eggs" advertised the sign on the wall, in hand-drawn purple letters psychedelically swollen together), which then Dean would carry off steaming in the morning chill.

On this particular morning, he came up the front stairs in his usual deeply worried trudge and tacked the card on the board, and by the time he'd finished, Little Tom had already cracked his eggs in a cup and begun steaming them. The card read as follows:

TEMPORARY WORK
Lifting, Hauling, Sorting, Filing, various jobs.

One week only.
Call at Farmican house, Point Cuidad.

Seawall has always been a town where a few glamorous people live quietly. I had never read any of James Farmican's books, but it was enough in those days to touch the book jackets and receive excitement by conduction. I would have seen the movie in which Farmican makes an appearance onstage with The Doors, and then later backstage is treated with obsequious deference by Jim Morrison himself. I would have seen his caricatured, woolly, mocked image in magazines like *Saturday Review*. Possibly I would have heard of him when he got the Endicott Prize but then didn't show up to accept. His slender paperbacks had been printed and reprinted in large numbers during the sixties. He was The Poet of People's Park, the First Honest Writer. His suicide—by pistol, in the midst of the popular success that choked his work in a cloud of glory, in 1970—had provided a streak of dying light in the sky, at least for my generation, my quieter generation, who came along after the greater events. I was at that time sitting around doing nothing. All possible rebellion had already happened in the previous decade, so a sense of liberation had settled over everything everywhere. I mostly sat in cafés or restaurants in a happy state of eternal tourism. But I had a rented room in a nearby suburb of San Francisco, attached to the side of a house, which had once been its garage, with a square of carpet remnant, a rectangle of foam rubber from Foam Unlimited, a hotplate on the toilet tank, colorful packages of Sudafed and Contac littered around the floor beside the bed. It was to pay the rent on that room that I needed temporary work.

I unpinned the 3 x 5 card from the bulletin board, and I was still holding it when a man came up Little Tom's staircase with a government-issue vinyl briefcase, shiny black shoes, a suit and tie, a haircut. The few regular customers shifted guiltily in their shade. For such an apparition even to find the turn-off from the main road, he had to be implacable. Little Tom was pretending there was nothing unusual about the visitor.

"Hello. Excuse me. I'm looking for a Mr. Dean Houlihan."

A paper cup of Esteemed Eggs stood smoking on the counter.

Little Tom sucked back a corner of his lip: trying to place that name.

"I just saw him come in here," the man put in, saving Tom from perjuring himself. He was trying to keep his voice down, but in Little Tom's, especially if you've come in from the beach wind and its fever is on your cheeks, the silence was dramatically close. Tom admitted, "Yes, he does come in here sometimes."

"He gives this address as his residence."

"He does?" Tom was surprised but also, dawningly, honored.

"Is this . . ." The man held up his briefcase as a shield and began to rotate. "This is not the church."

"The church," Tom repeated.

The man saw his own defeat in Little Tom's confusion. The few regular customers in the room were averting their eyes and slouching in their chairs, by stillness blending into the general paisley. The modern coffee shop of the 1990s is made of bright washable surfaces designed to shed customers efficiently, but Little Tom's provided a sticky nap of varnish and velvet where these people like burrs could fade back toward habitation and its camouflage. Tom said helpfully, "You might try the Free Box. In front of the Food Co-op."

"The Free Box?"

"Just lift the lid. If he's in there, you'll see him. It's one of his places."

In the man's face, tiredness became visible. "Yes," he said, hiding his eyes from the room, "thanks very much." He turned to leave and ducked going downstairs, catching his briefcase, with a bang, on the frame of the too-narrow door. Tom waited for a minute, then put away the paper cup of Esteemed Eggs, and soon the usual blizzard of shared reverie rose again, to bury the room, its inmates separately.

As for me, I left. I had unpinned the white 3 x 5 card, and it lit my way down the tarred staircase. I inserted it in the foggy air before me as I climbed the drifting cobblestones toward Point Cuidad on the tectonically uptilted ground of Seawall, toward the great Farmican house that, today, emerges from memory only in glimpses, so bathed in fog it showed only a fluke here, a broad flank there. That house is gone today. Now there's just a flat area, of redwood splinters and bits of old masonry. If you went up there today and kicked around in the dirt, you'd turn up rubble of plaster and lath, a sequin winking underfoot in the rich gravel of ruin, a half-buried nylon-tipped drumstick printed "Remo Rhythm King®," a broken-off knob

reading "Balance." Almost a quarter-century later in an unimaginable 1997, in this immense suburb, I sit here every night
in the glow of my computer screen, peacefully in the closing
red velvet throat of Sebastiani, the balm of nicotine, reaching
every half-minute for the cigarette that provides the good kick-
in-the-face. *Click-click-click* the plastic Chiclets of my computer
keyboard within this old tract house, q w e r t y u i o p a s d f g
h j k l ; you reach a point where you realize it doesn't matter
what you say. In fact it really doesn't. Everything I'm describing was twenty-five years ago. What I really ought to be writing about is this neighborhood I live in, Terra Linda, all these
tract homes with identical shallow-peaked roofs: how all these
men can have wives, families! The mystery of it! A mystery as
deep as money! It always looked all-too-easy. You wind up
alone and inconsequential at forty, not by design but merely
through a kind of inattention, through distraction by joy, or
perhaps by not being very brave. Or through faithlessness.
One's own faithlessness or others'; it's the same thing. And, too,
bachelorhood is not such an unhappy state. The bathrobe, the
Wheat Chex, keeping up with *The New Yorker* and *The Nation*
and a few modern poets, masturbation's practicality, the freedom to pour an extra glass of wine in the evening, freedom in
general. At my age the usual pleasant shallow courtship becomes too, too negotiative, self-conscious—if not a little bit preposterous, me with now hair in my ears, this chest-fur, my
farts—and like a pirate in retirement I think back mostly on
lost chances for goodness. The guys who get the women are
the superficial ones, the users, the assholes. Everyone knows
that. Women know it too, but they pretend it's not happening. And then they *complain*. What they seem to want despite
their protests is someone strong who will tell them what to do
and what to think. Whereas, in my case, I seem not to have
been strong. I write because I love chain-smoking cigarettes.
In these California suburbs all around, every house-front, with

its closed door, seems to say, This is what someone wants, and he's got it. Satisfied desire is the only story of this town.

But on these streets (my street is Idylberry; between Alderberry and Mountainberry; my address is "555 Idylberry Lane"), on these streets I feel like a teenager or an idiot or a satyr or a rootless impostor. Last week, Wendy Farmican appeared in the doorway of the new Starbucks Café looking different of course—after the passage of almost twenty-five years—but yet exactly the same. When I saw her, I knew I was seeing again what I lost. I will always have been nothing more than the person who carried her on a mistaken adventure in her immaturity, before she was reabsorbed again into her family. And so our first conversation after twenty-five years began with the same old blurring ointment in the eye, the origin of all disappointment: the unwillingness to quite *look*, full-on, at another human being.

The last time we saw each other it was 1974 in a motel parking lot in Nevada. She was barefoot. The wind lifted her hair. And then later I went up to our campsite in the hills above Reno and waited all night, but she never came. The dead campfire, the polyethylene tarp, the toilet paper, the tape player: that campsite always looked like a plane-crash across the desert floor. The broken-down old Mercedes-Benz on the slope. Its doors hanging open. Judy Collins on the tape player. It was 1973, and the four of us were traveling through the Nevada desert. She and I and her two brothers were searching for a casino they thought they'd inherited. It was called The Cornucopia. But there was no casino there, there was nothing but dust, Nevada dust like pulverized concrete, all of Nevada looking eroded, looking already-mined-out, the whole state made of still-radioactive mat-

ter discarded at the Creation as waste, over the rim of the Interstate 80 guardrail. Still today, much of Nevada retains the
priceless value of being unwanted by anybody. We lived on the
other side of that guardrail. That incredibly heavy mahogany
roulette table is probably still lying out there today, right now,
in the desert under slow-growing branches of sage or man-
zanita, its wafers of inlaid wood shrinking in the sun, its green
felt nibbled by elk and rabbit. The craps table too, huge as a
rescue boat, round-bottomed, will be stranded on the hard
ground. The mysterious Sephirah-map of fate I never understood (PASS LINE, DON'T COME BAR, HARDWAY BETS) will be fading
on the green felt surface where empires might have grown
mosaically and then collapsed, and again grown and collapsed
in a single night. Flecks of Nevada snowflakes will collect inside during the mild high-desert winters. And then melt water-
lessly in that air. We left everything and scattered—I for the
Greyhound bus terminal, the two brothers for who-knows-
where (Peter for the army recruiting storefront on Virginia
Street in Reno, it turns out), Wendy for Ecstasy Ranch, where I
have imagined her with a lip lifted in feigned pleasure, in a
negligee of scratchy plastic lace. I went through a time, a year
or so during the eighties, when I went down to the Tenderloin
and paid for the embraces of those women who stand out there;
not out of desire, certainly; I think it was because I wanted to
look into their eyes. But I could never hold them and gaze deep
enough, as if into a prismatic place deep in a female where
practical love is separated from impractical love. They do seem
to be separable, and that is a frightening prism for a man to
look into because he has to consider how he may be divided
therein.

What else: The eternal sound of I-80, eighteen-wheelers
downshifting. The typewriter sitting on a rock, unplugged-in.
Ed's vinyl three-ring notebook lying on the ground, its spine
embossed with the words YOUR BUSINESS NAME HERE. The sign
"The Cornucopia Casino," made of twigs stitched to cardboard

with a shoelace. The blue-and-white tent, deflated and pooled among the rocks. The meals we made of Pringles or Slim Jims. Camping on the old scorched cement slab foundation of a burned-down gas station. My stupid cowboy boots. The cologne and chocolate I stole from casino gift shops for her. The theater of constant lust. That line kept jerking us on its embedded hook. The way the police—or highway patrol or the sheriff's deputies—would come around to chide us, with almost uncles' sad humorous care, moving us along. It was nearly twenty-five years ago, but I can still see her face, in the parking lot of the Starlite Motel. There's no judgment there but only disappointment, a falling look of trust.

◉　◉　◉

The warm sparkling light of a Starbucks franchise. The completely absolved, trust-free atmosphere of these more recent times. Her hair is cut shorter now and her face is fuller, and her body swings with a deeper comfort in flesh, very suburban and beige. But I'm the one who remembers the girl she was. I continue to feel entitled to her, like an adolescent, chafingly, because I'm the one who knows who she is, who she's always been, as if with a touch I could make her weak again. But I see who I am now, a forty-year-old tutor, who makes a living by grading essays for local colleges at my well-lit kitchen table, correcting grammatical errors, dangling modifiers, comma splices, sentence fragments, pronoun disagreements, subject-verb disagreements, the same crop of mistakes every year, a similar crowd of young people every year, so that I get the illusion of eternal youth in myself, falling naturally into temporary sexual stuckness with armor-plated coeds at the exact moment of their physical perfection, who will of course later move on to someone more serious.

Out here all Starbucks cafés, going for a Bohemian effect,

have cement floors and put caricatures of doleful-looking literary figures on the walls, Oscar Wilde, Shakespeare, Virginia
Woolf, Ernest Hemingway, Amy Tan, Stephen King. I sat
under Jane Austen, with a lostness that made me feel unfind-
able by Wendy in this confusion of malls off the Terra Linda
exit. We had exchanged directions on the phone, her familiar
voice easy to talk to, in an unreal kind of way. All these years
she has been living a few exits up, and I had no idea. I had no
idea. I can't remember what either of us said at first when she
appeared in the door. I remember my inability to stop looking
at her, the girl inside the woman, my mythological excuse for
not loving anyone all these years, the woman sketched over the
girl, my own radiant stupidity, the lostness of all the years in
between. And there was a dubbed-sounding exchange about
what she wanted to drink (decaf low-fat latte) while I rose as
she sat, and stood like a waiter beside the table. I get my hearing back only later, when the table between us holds some litter,
a bran muffin mostly undressed of its pleated skirt, and one
pink Sweet'N Low packet, which she picks up to start tinily
folding, and she says, "We're married, you and I. Do you remember?"

Her eyes flicked up and down, between me and the
Sweet'N Low packet.

"That's why we tried to find you and got in touch with you.
Maybe you and I could *pretend* we're married again, for a little
while, if it's all right with you, just for a little while. Because my
family is involved in a legal fight. If you and I are married, the
Farmican children can inherit a lot of money. I know this is all a
huge surprise. Yiikes." She dove for her latte. She hated this.

I said, "Can that marriage ceremony be legal? That church
was an imaginary church." I was quoting her words, spoken
twenty-five years ago in an embrace. "That church was his personal hallucination."

"That can be legal. You can file to have that be legal. It's
awkward, but it's worth a lot of money." She was ashamed of

the money motive, which wasn't her motive but her brothers', and she sighed. "It turns out my father did leave a will. He wrote it out before he died. The will says his estate skips a generation and goes to his grandchildren. This is *if* Dean's marriage ceremony is considered legally valid." She looked at me with apology and some distress. "This is all my brother Ed's idea. Ed is a lawyer now."

I didn't say anything, for a minute just picturing her dyslexic stubborn brother Ed as a lawyer. During the last minute, a kind of rind had grown on my skin. I wanted a cigarette, but the modern Starbucks is a smoke-free establishment.

"If we file a claim we've been married all these years"—she let her head nod softly aside along a row of falling dominoes—"then the money comes to—James Farmican's grandchild."

"Grandchild," I said.

She looked me in the eye and said, "You've been a father all this time."

He's twenty-four years old. His name is Gabriel. His last name is Farmican. He's tall, taller than I. His hair is cropped short like a mental patient's, which is fashionable now in San Francisco, and his body is fashionably mutilated: a metal grommet is installed in his earlobe and another one in a pinch of skin at his eyebrow. On these grommets he hangs unbent paper clips, fishing lures, flash cards portraying human anatomical features, a rabbit's foot, tampons, used-looking tampons, whatever strikes him as witty that morning. He's an artist. He's a walking trash-heap. At the San Francisco Art Institute, where he is a student, he has become a minor celebrity. His features are delicate and sensitive, but his manner is arrogant, if in a congested sort of way. He strikes you as almost *slinky* with a languor of inner self-confidence. A week after my meeting with Wendy, I drove into town and parked near the Art Institute, and I went poking around looking for him in the vandalized church that every art school is, or tries to be, feeling myself newly bourgeois and philistine in my new paternity, asking in

those spattered corridors where I might locate a Gabe Farmican. The first girl I asked told me with a yawn, "If you want to
see Heaven, it's forbidden. It's censored. Nobody can see it. You
have to find the October issue of *Art West*."

Heaven is the title of a work of art, created by my son,
which has made him slightly famous. It's a sculpture, made not
by chisel and mallet, but by computer programming. One of
his Art Institute classes gave him access to computers that com-
bine and manipulate photo images, which are then projected in
3-D, holographically, by laser light within a cone of dim space.
You can walk around it and it changes perspective as if it were
made of solid matter. Gabriel created this light-sculpture two
years ago. Since then, its fame has grown, and it has won him a
lot of treasure: a ten-thousand-dollar grant from a foundation,
gifts of computer and laser equipment from Hewlett-Packard
and the Beckman Institute, a scholarship to an art school in
Ohio. Life, to him, has been an unresistant medium so far. In a
public library, I found a copy of *Art West* magazine, which de-
votes a section to brief profiles of artists. Gabriel was the first
artist portrayed in the section. Unlike all the others', his art
wasn't illustrated in a photograph.

GABE FARMICAN

SAN FRANCISCO. Art can still shock. Maybe "photo-
realist sculpture" describes what Gabe Farmican is up to.
Thanks to hologram laser projections, Farmican's gross-
out catastrophes are right there in the room with you. He
feeds photographs into Apple Macintoshes, then com-
bines and recombines the images in appalling new ways.
When projected, his ugly little incidents appear big-
as-life and three-dimensional. The most notorious is
"Heaven," in which Nixon and Kennedy, quite *déshabillé*
except for one sagging sock, are frozen for eternity in
activities you'd rather not be present for. It's photo-

realist, all right: as you walk around it, you see every little vein and wrinkle and even the marvelous yellowed toenail-cuticles. All the details have been digitally sampled from pictures of elderly physiques of a not-too-Presidential sort. Farmican, who happens to be the grandson of Wild Poet James Farmican, received the Margaret and Orville Winnokur Award for 1997. Aikman Gallery.

He will be legally my son if we go through with this. The family lawyers' plan is that Wendy and Gabriel move in here—into my rented tract-house in "The Berries" section of Terra Linda—so that we may simulate a legal family, under the scrutiny of court-appointed lawyers. She described all this to me at Starbucks, and while she spoke, I knew immediately that it would happen. It is not easy picturing Wendy, the actual Wendy with her blue eyes always in repose—and tall, perforated Gabriel—specifically *here*, in this ugly Live-Rite Home from the fifties, on Idylberry Lane in a long curving row of Live-Rites, where I've got books and magazines stacked so high on my eating-nook table I can hardly fit my bowl of Tap Ramen in among them at night, and where the living room couch can't be sat on because it has served as a laundry bin for at least a decade, and where, too many nights, I end up in front of the television watching the Spice Channel's electronically garbled signal, in the old beanbag chair on the linoleum floor in my own all-too-efficient grip. I have not been very successful as a human being. I'll say that. When we went our separate ways in the desert, she had better hopes for me. It was one of our assumptions. Wendy will have to see the inside of this house, now, and it would be impossible, or else fodder for a stupid sitcom, for me to dress up my life as a success now. She and Gabriel can learn to tolerate the nicotine everywhere. I tried washing the windows once a few years ago and the varnish on the glass never came off, it just smeared around. I asked her, in the Starbucks, how long we were supposed to live together simulating marriage, and she answered, "Well, you see, Mom died. My mother."

Julia Farmican. The poet's widow. Her long black hair and mesmerizing gaze. I'd really only known her for four days, and it was two decades ago: the four days we were all together inside the Farmican house in Seawall. Yet it was surprising how, upon hearing she was dead, all my life felt mislaid. "When did she die?" Like an old husband hearing the news, I could feel, lifting into consciousness, the physical outline of my body in space, my existence, my survivorship. I picked up my coffee cup but didn't drink, and just set it down.

"She died last spring. And probate turns out to be unbelievably complicated. Because that artificial church still exists. I know it started as a joke, but now *it*, the *church*, has an automatic claim on all of James Farmican's legacy. Long ago all James Farmican's legacy was *donated* to it. Quote-unquote. I'm sorry about this. Truly, the money wouldn't matter to me. It's not even that much money. Or even if it is a lot of money . . ."

"Where was she living?"

"My mother?"

I could imagine her: with her big kimono sleeves, with her wooden ladle, still presiding over her great iron cauldron from the Japanese monastery, passing out stories of the great days in the fifties and sixties when there was still room everywhere, room to spread the wreckage. All the more, my lungs wanted a cigarette, my own little brush with death, but everything in a Starbucks—the touch of designer lighting on croissant flesh—seems too delicate a tissue. So I just sat there not smoking, with the encroaching familiar Wolfman-feeling in these days of popular sanctimony. Julia Farmican was dead and the world was emerging as a surprisingly empty knoll. "She was a whole . . . generation," I said, inarticulately.

"Yes?" Wendy was always very patient with adulation of her illustrious parents.

California's Over

I said, "But she divorced Faro. Didn't she? So there's no danger of her estate going to Faro."

"No, the estate would go to Faro's *church*. It was all donated to the church, long ago. The church is what has the power. Actually, the Open Foundation is the shell corporation that employs Faro's lawyers."

"The Open Foundation? The big philanthropic thing?"

"Yes. Museums, women's shelters, public broadcasting, computers for schools. They do a lot. They're wonderful."

"They're wonderful. They are. *That's* what happened to Faro Ness?"

"Nevertheless, there is a tenacious belief among Ed's lawyers—and lawyers seem to develop a momentum of their own, and of course Ed encourages it—there is a tenacious belief that Faro shouldn't have gotten the Farmican inheritance. Because we're married. You and I. If we're married, Gabe can inherit it. Gabe is the only grandson. My father's will said his estate should go to grandchildren. My brothers don't have any children."

"They're . . . unable."

"Biologically, yes, unable."

I said, "Cyanide?"

She looked at me while warily something melted around her eyes. I said, "Me too," happily with a nod toward my void testicles. In Nevada the ground around our campsite was saturated with cyanide. It's how mining corporations extract gold ore from rock. Sometimes in the far desert we'd see sprinkling systems doing their kick-turn pirouettes over acres of rubble, but didn't know they were casting cyanide about. Infertility is one hormonal result of prolonged exposure to cyanide. My brain lesion—my "necrotic tissue," as the doctors call it—is in the pituitary, where I imagine it as a tiny inner cave of brain cells looking shrunken and frosted. I suppose her brothers' neural damage would be just the same, or similar.

Louis B. Jones

I said, "Oh, but it's great. Not needing birth control. Makes seduction rather breezy." My standard joke. It does the dual job of conveying, lightly, that I'm never going to impregnate anyone but can still act out the merely dramatic parts. A tasteless remark now. I always had less class than she. Maybe that was my attraction, when she was sixteen. We smiled dimly across at each other over the lapse of years. She looks the same. I said, "How fortunate that *you've* had the problem of fertility. Remember Peter? *'LIFE is the Supreme Venereal Disease!'* " It was something her brother bellowed over the desert outside Reno, during the time we were planning our abortion. He was being funny.

She smiled. A soft tilt of the head. An inward-folding of the Sweet'N Low packet in her fingers. I'd still do anything. It's stupid. An intrepid kind of *waiting* is the main sensation of my life now. I did make an effort to start cleaning up around the house. Wendy and Gabriel will just have to get used to it. I'm afraid I will lose my peace of mind, which is embedded everywhere in this house. The mattress in the spare room is piled with books. I will have to go around cleaning up all the different things I use for ashtrays and rake all the laundry together and give up sorting laundry on floors, wash the windows in back with something stronger than Windex against the immortal Varathane, two packs a day for a quarter-century.

She said, from deep within her beige coat, behind the shield of her Sweet'N Low packet, "You'll like Gabe. I feel like I'm— like I'm glad—or honored—to be able to bring him to you. Do you know what I mean?" She leaned forward in a new fretful intimacy. "I've got a job. We won't be freeloaders."

"Oh?"

"I work at City Lights."

"At City Lights Books?"

"Distribution. Sales. But now I'm doing editorial upstairs in publishing, not down in the bookstore. I do keep sneaking down to stick the James Farmican books face-out on the

20

shelves. *The Green Conquistador* is the only one that still sells. *Anabasis* and *Begin Here* are still in print. But *Conquistador* will always be the steady seller."

She has a job. All these years, I had thought of her as going to a private college, traveling in Europe, having children and sending *them* on to college. I never did graduate and so have dwindled to this cramped autodidact who can never be a real teacher, in my polyester shirts, writing unpublishably late into the night. "I live in a Live-Rite," I said.

It came out as a warning. I meant it as an offer. I meant it as an agreement to live with her as her husband. My heart was actually pounding. I took a big breath but slowly, so she wouldn't notice.

◎   ◎   ◎

I'll say this. I'm not proud of myself in the way this stupid modern civilization scolds us to be "proud" of our "selves" or our "lifestyles," ideal self-presentation being the goal of all culture now in this century of gaudy twilight. Grading essays will turn out to be the high point of my career. Now it brings in $1,323.30 a month after taxes, with annual cost-of-living raises. At fifty-two, I'll be eligible to retire with one-third salary. That's only eleven years away. A decade can go fast, as I well know. I've made my choices and taken my risks. In fact, honestly, I've been pretty fortunate. I've had the luxury of all these nights with my writing, my red wine, my cigarettes, my all-but-metabolic need to coil up in a chair like a heap of bowels and sink for hours into the world of pure inward possibility, poetry, fiction, essays. A story in *The Kansas Quarterly*, another in *Fiction Reader*, a poem in the *Pacific Sun*. My choices in life had to do with certain obsolete, hard-to-explain old values, like the superiority of "non-material" as compared with "material" achievement, aiming *not* to own the big house on the hill and the fancy foreign car, but aiming rather for Beauty and Truth, art, integrity, blah blah blah. Fuck you, dear reader, dear judgmental reader. You're so smart and lucky, you'd never have such a limited life, would you. When I first met my son the Twenty-Four-Year-Old Successful Artist, he had hung a tiny plastic doll's-arm from his earlobe grommet. From his eyebrow grommet hung a nail-polish-daubed tampon, which banged against his cheek when he swung to lay his eyes on me—his father!—in immediate recognition. I had come upon him in the student café. Smell of turpentine, dust of kilns. "Hey" was his greeting, and he stood up. We met with not a hug but a handgrip, that good old symbolic male ceremony which is partly a joining but also a threat to wrestle. "You want to sit down?" he said, pulling out a chair whose seat was daubed with acrylic paint—it had served as somebody's palette. "Oops, nope, let's go out." He tucked the tampon back behind his ear where it wouldn't dangle, and he declared, "This is a good thing you're doing, making an honest woman of her. Giving the boy a name." He had some business involving an Audiovisual Activities Center, and then we walked outside and down the hill to a North Beach bar, a place I'd often visited over the past quarter-century, with women usually. While I got us beers, Gabriel waited in the corner with a *GQ* magazine, not reading it but just flipping through, slouching back, costumed as a person of color, a mestizo, as is fashionable now among Caucasians: khaki chinos; white T-shirt; high-top sneakers propped up on the chair opposite; oversized cloth jacket, baseball cap turned around backwards.

Before I had a chance even to sit down, carrying my two beers, he swung his high-tops off the chair and said, "First of all" (with a cocaine snuffle, closed eyes, an umpire's gesture of *safe-at-home*), "I want you to know I understand the whole thing, you know, like the whole history, know-what-I mean? And I want you to know: there's no hard feelings." He spoke in festooned rhythmic loops. I thought to myself: *subject-verb agreement.*

"You know, and secondly, this shit is all for career." He tapped his earring. "Here, have a seat. I know all this shit looks weird. But it's a angle. In the art world, everybody's got to have a angle. This is my angle. And it works. I'm a artist. Hey. So, like, you know. Just to put you at ease." In Nevada in 1973, a legal abortion was a hard thing to find. The Supreme Court in that year had legalized abortion for all the states. But in Nevada you still had to find an especially liberal doctor, in our case on C Street, off lower Virginia Street, in an all-but-invisible building that also contained the office of The Nevada Cosmetology Institute and a taxidermist. Certain things I remember. The building was fronted by a parking lot with six spaces. Dr. Tulip was the physician's name. Wendy was ambivalent about the operation, but I was all in favor of it, because I was an artist too, then, and I could see that artistic freedom and fatherhood wouldn't mix. Sitting now in this bar, across from the incarnation of my son looming up taller than I, a strange inner capsule broke: what would this Gabriel have been like when he was a small warm armful and he woke up frightened in the night? A few weeks ago I held the infant of a friend at school along the corridor, and the scalp's milky smell, the parsley breath, the radiant warmth of that little bag of groceries, its total faith in my embrace, came back now as something I could have had, something whose absence, in my life, explains the ground-temperature zero in my bones, my dug-up bones, when I awake alone in the tilted square of moonlight. The first meeting with Dr. Tulip took place on a sunny, cold Sunday morning in Reno when the streets were all empty. There was no receptionist at the front desk, which seemed strange. And then I remembered it was a Sunday, when the office was officially closed. The doctor, taking a serious professional risk, had come in alone to park his Cadillac and unlock the office with his jingling keys in the chilly sunshine and wait for us, and then greet us, standing beside the receptionist's desk in his white lab coat, with his strong, clean, empty hands.

So, sitting in the bar with Gabriel, I looked at him now amidst the spilled-around furniture of this bar in 1997, and I told him silently in my mind, I guess you're a survivor. I lifted a glass and said, "Congratulations on the success of your—is 'installation' the word? I've heard it's a success."

Gabriel shrugged and let his eyes drift aside. He had taken the remark as hostile—my toast had seemed a jeer, from within my own personal trench—and he replied, "You've turned out to be pretty ordinary." This insult was delivered to me in a tone almost congratulatory. I went on to make some noises about how I wasn't joking, I meant it, maybe it isn't exactly *my* taste in art but it's a good thing just to have made a dent in the world. I find I can't help looking for a flicker of my genes in him. No strong specific resemblances to me seem visible. Or maybe any resemblances in my sight would naturally vanish, bathed in the infrared inspection of a father. He caught me looking at him and said, "I have to take the grommets out. They get infected." There was, in fact, a pinkness at the rim.

He drank his beer. He sighed. And in a glad change of topic, while his forearm swung to wipe a moisture-ring off the tabletop, he said, "So! Hey! What do you think? Was it suicide or murder?"

"Pardon me? Who died?" I find myself delighted, or maybe *relieved*, by this boy, my son. It's a physical thing. He is in many ways already complete as a detestable person, but physically something in my body is fed by just being near him.

"Grandfather, The Great James Farmican. If it was murder, we get rich. If it was suicide, we stay poor. Oh! Ah! You don't know!" he said, and he tucked the swinging tampon behind his ear. Then with a furtive glance around the bar, he unhooked it from its grommet (he suspends it there by a wire hook from a Christmas-tree ornament) and slipped it into his pocket. "You haven't been filled in on this little plot," he gloated, and he sprawled forward over the table to give me the lowdown.

The money involved is half a million dollars in life insurance, a policy on James Farmican's life. In 1970, Farmican, at the height of his fame, was found dead in his study in Seawall with an unfinished manuscript on his desk. His gun was on the floor beside him. Because "suicide" was the coroner's description of his death, the insurance company wouldn't pay off. Insurance policies don't pay off on suicides. His widow, during her life, never allowed any other interpretation than suicide to be made. But now Julia Farmican is dead; and her second husband, Faro, is suing to have the case reopened. If he can prove it wasn't suicide, he can collect the half-million dollars in life insurance. He says that money belongs to his church, which owns all of James Farmican's estate. "He doesn't have to prove anything, he just has to raise a reasonable doubt," Gabriel finished. Ghoulishly, likably, he cozied up to all this as great gossip.

I was reminded of something mysterious Wendy said when we'd met in the Starbucks: "Remember there was no suicide note?" She had twisted her Sweet'N Low packet into a tight pink fuse. "Well, a sort of a note, of some kind, finally did turn up in all that stuff in the house. Remember all the old junk you were hired to move? It was amazing the incredible amount of stuff in that house. Well, do you remember noticing anything *weird* in all that stuff?"

Part
• 1 •

A hand-crank Victrola, missing its crank; a lot of first editions and rare bound-galley proofs by writers in Farmican's circle; a leather box filled with ivory sticks for casting the I Ching; orange crates of records from the fifties and sixties, "Odetta Sings," "Charlie Parker," "My Son the Nut," "A Child's Christmas in Wales," "Son of Word Jazz," "Flower Drum Song"; a box of old bent shoes; a trunk of dress-up materials like feather boas and top hats; a grand piano painted with purple housepaint and then varnished with a hundred peacock feathers; a box of reel-to-reel tapes of parties in the fifties and sixties, where it was customary to leave a tape recorder constantly running to record whatever happened (including songs sung in the Farmican kitchen by Tim Hardin, two members of The Weavers, and that woman folksinger with the flutter-strangle vibrato); a gold-encrusted medieval reliquary with crystal windows, like a lantern, which contained a wad of toilet paper bearing a streak of (purportedly) Rimbaud's shit; a potter's kickwheel; boxes and boxes of Farmican's correspondence, which I was to send off to the auction house's autograph-and-document appraiser; the actual heavy blue gun with which Farmican shot himself, still tagged with the Marin County Sheriff Department's cardboard disk on a string around the trigger; another, identical, gun, with the words "+ *Not This*

Louis B. Jones

One +" written on its barrel in White-Out erasure fluid; other now-archaic writing materials like carbon paper and onionskin; a bartender's towel, framed under glass and identified as the towel thrown into the toilet upstairs in Vesuvio's Saloon on June 10, 1960, by some discouraged writer named Ed Dunkel in a "Formal Throwing-in-the-Towel Procedure"; an elaborate HO-scale model railroad crushed under a ton of congealed *New Yorker* magazines; an ornate wooden table, later identified as a "Huerter" table, which the appraiser on the scene beheld with a weak-in-the-knees look, immediately shrouding it and standing guard beside it, unable to stop petting it and murmuring, "This is an important table"; scrapbooks, clipped book reviews and newspaper articles, especially archives of the publicity surrounding the battles with police and National Guardsmen over People's Park in Berkeley in 1969, in which James Farmican figures largely. It was only four days I spent at the Farmican house, in its basements and attics "Lifting, Hauling, Sorting, and Filing," under the direction of experts and appraisers from a San Francisco auction house. But in this inconsequential computer screen (with its blessed annihilating *delete* button, present always to add antimatter to this matter and, soundlessly, bring me back again to the original empty light-square, the infinite combination of all integers, positive and negative, equaling zero), inside this light-box I can reconstruct every molecule of those four days in 1973, with a saturating omniscience possible only decades later—as if a wrong turn might be found, or some error, before which my life was filled with all possibility fanning everywhere, after which I began to fuse into this single wrong man at 555 Idylberry.

The wrought-iron spearpoints along the front of the house conquered by vines, the cupola where Farmican shot himself, always erased by the fog it was thrust up into, the garage collapsing inward in tent-shapes, the old eczema paint on the doorframe, the urine-smell of rain on bricks where the sun never shone under the porte cochere, I can bring everything back, every possible perspective from all four corners of every room. When I first arrived, still holding up the white card I'd unpinned from Little Tom's bulletin board, I rang the doorbell and stood on the stair—out-of-breath from the climb out of Seawall to Point Cuidad, sweaty, wounded on the cheek by the thorny branch at the gate that swung up to attack all visitors. The big house on its promontory was impossible to *see* completely, because its facets tended to revolve out of view as you tried to approach it. It was Julia Farmican herself, James Farmican's actual wife, in person, who opened the front door: I was standing a step or two below, on stairs wrongly steep, like a temple's. And when she greeted me something immediately sexy happened, a sort of relaxation of her spine. She must have been in her forties then, but her waist and hip and thigh, in stiff new jeans, were a teenager's. A space of guilt opened in my gut. Her eyes fell closed and she smiled and told me, "You've come to rescue us," with an abrupt efficiency of communication, verging on clairvoyance, which I would become used to over the days to come: "All right then"; she turned away and showed me her narrow back and her stirring compact hips that mopped the air ahead of her as she walked into the dark foyer. I was already hired, and I was supposed to follow. I remembered then, stepping over the bar of bright moss on the doorsill, that I'd left my jacket at Little Tom's Round Table, hanging on a peg. I would have to go back and get it at the end of the day, which prospect would rescue *me*, from this place. So I thought. The front hall, as my eyes grew into the darkness, was a dusty paneled area where boxes had been stacked.

"That old doorknob will allegedly cost four hundred dollars to repair. Can you imagine?" She walked ahead, rinsing her fingers in air above her shoulder. "We never use this entrance."

"Oh, I'm sorry."

"Don't apologize," she said. She stopped and turned. Again

her body shamed me so that I wanted to back up a step, though I didn't. "*'Never apologize, never explain.'* Do you know who said that?"

"No," I said. The wish to back up made me taller.

"Satchel Paige."

By the sound of it, Satchel Paige would be a French philosopher. I said, urbanely, "Ah."

She reached to hold my head—to adjust its angle, to set it up straighter on my spine—and she said, "There," and brushed my hair back away from my face, petted epaulets on my shoulders while I stood numbly at attention. "It's a good thing you're not in that terrible war." She turned away. "We can work out a rate of compensation and so on. All that . . ." she shuddered ". . . *stuff*," as she went on ahead—and I followed—through a cathedral of shadows toward the back of the house, via a doorway that opened into a sunlit room. It was the kitchen. It hadn't been renovated since the nineteenth century. A high ceiling gave it a garage's chill. On a far wall stood the basin of a deep stone sink, like the sink in a potting shed. Many layers of overlapping oriental carpets, cemented together by ancient food debris, lay across the floor. A large central table was actually a barn door laid out on heavy legs. These carpets, the next day, I would be gently unpeeling from each other, while the rug appraiser looked on with greed and incredulity. Mrs. Farmican walked into the open space where the sunlight fell through motes as in an empty silo, and she swung to face me again, scarves of light flying away from her as she lifted both hands through the falling storm of my regard. "All this"—her arms rose so that her shoulders swiveled against the turn of her hips, one knee cocked, implying a fresh kink in her torso, like the grapefruit-built dancing goddesses of the Kama-sutra illustrations—"is to be dismantled."

The field between us seemed charged by the magnetic difference in our genders. Ashamed, I bulked up as if I were ready at that moment to seize something and start dismantling it. "Everything?" I said.

"Everything, the whole house, all four stories. Seven days from now, there will be absolutely nothing. We're moving to Oregon."

"You're moving?"

"Everybody knows California's over," she said, turning to lead me on. She passed through a door—and I followed—down a flagstone staircase so broken it was like a waterfall, where below was a sound of buried music. She explained with a wave, "My son." The music was a popular acid-rock song—called, I think, "Time"—that started fast and then slowed gradually, dilating toward the pulse-rate dirge of Timelessness Itself, while an echoing voice shouted the word *"Time!"* at lengthening intervals and the slap of a drumstick measured lagging seconds, taking forever to, like a heavy train, slow to a halt's lurch. The staircase wound improbably to the right, which must have been *into* the hillside, and I grew clumsily gigantic as the ceiling dropped and we made another right turn at the bottom of the stairs, into a long flagstone-floored corridor, where the wall on one side was simply a bank of dirt. The foundation had been, where sagging, propped up by makeshift piers: coffee cans filled with concrete. In other places, the old redwood timbers had sagged to rest on the soil, where they were crushed in decomposing. A shovel and a pick leaned among cobwebs. The corridor took another right turn, and the music sharpened. A doorway in the wall blasted light and sound.

Inside the furnace of noise, seated in a swivel chair with his back turned, was a long-haired blond shirtless boy, strumming, with passion, an imaginary guitar in his lap.

"Peter?" said his mother, raising her voice against the music, "This nice young man"—she turned to me—"whose name I don't yet know . . ."

He wriggled to sit up. "I wish you would learn to knock."

"Peter is working on the Great American Epic Poem. It's about the Donner Family expedition. They got stranded in the Sierra on the way here? Darling? Didn't they? And ate each other? And not only does he have the cutest *body* in the San Francisco literary scene, he was the major *star* of the Stanford Poetry Conference. The Stanford Poetry Conference meets every year, and Peter was a special fellowship participant. And now one of his poems is published!" She beamed on him. "Anyway, Peter, this is . . ." She touched my elbow.

My mouth filled with the balloon of a name, which was "Baelthon," a name I had adopted in California that summer in a literary impulse.

". . . *Baelthon*," she repeated, with, it now seems in memory, the faintest twinkle of skepticism. Peter had slipped his arms through the sleeves of a shirt, and he stood up to reach and cut the volume on the music. He was that era's ideal of male beauty. Golden hair hung in straight curtains beside his narrow, female face, and his bare belly had the emaciation of Christ's sexy crucifixion. His bedroom, down here, had no door at all, only empty hinges on the doorframe. A porcelain basin in the corner was plumbed with a green rubber garden hose. Fabric was tacked to the ceiling and hung down in billows, printed with an ornate thorny-sperm-cell design. Cinderblock-and-plank bookshelves. A poster of the movie *Easy Rider*. An expensive new IBM typewriter, the huge kind with the small silver meteor of letters inside, sat on an unmade bed, plugged in. A large rolltop desk, painted red, was heaped with books, papers, and a filthy glass coffee beaker, hourglass-shaped with a wooden girdle. Books lay open facedown stacked in towers like pagoda roofs. Unsleeved records were piled on a guitar case with old magazines and empty paper album-sleeves and a Strathmore sketch pad, all surmounted by a half-eaten pizza on a cardboard disk. My eye kept wandering to harvest the top bloom, while his mother explained, "'*Baelthon*' has answered

California's Over

the ad in the café. He's going to help us stir up the bottom
around here. Sometimes it's really time to face the music,
honey." She shimmered in my direction, "Peter plans to go on
living in this place after the rest of us have gone. It's quixotic,
don't you think? But an unrealistic quality of mind is allowed
in the case of genius. How else will a genius change the world
if he's not unrealistic?"

We both looked at Peter, who was lighting a cigarette,
squinting. He dropped the match among the twisted butts in a
stone bowl held up by a floor-standing stone cherub spray-
painted gold. He inhaled, winced in a gorgon's-wreath of
smoke, exhaled, and said, ". . . Whatever."

"Sweetheart, the auction-house people are coming tomorrow. In a few days they'll take everything. It's really *time*."

He scraped a flake of tobacco from his tongue and scowled
at it.

She looked at him in loving defeat, drew breath, turned and
sang, "Baelthon, tell us, what do you do?"

"I'm a novelist," I lied, off the top of my head, specifically,
confidently. In the new, more weightless feeling, I almost
shrugged. I was far from home. Far, that is, from Kaseburg,
Wisconsin, where my parents had divorced and so recovered a
youth equal to mine. The trite old white frame house in Kaseburg in a cloud of elm boughs—now already a dreamy old back-
water in American history, like a misty view of a plantation
mansion—had been replaced by, on the one hand, my mother's
basement apartment near the Madison campus, where a card
table held a stack of heavy textbooks, an electronic calculator, a
bowl for beans and rice, a bottle of soy sauce; and on the other
hand, across town, my father's bed-sitter by the railroad tracks,
where he drank gin and watched TV, lying down already beneath undiagnosed cancer and admitting open-mindedly, "You
know, some of these shows are pretty good, for television.
They're finally getting some good writers these days." My parents were growing and changing with the times. In the Farmi-

cans' basement, my calling myself a novelist felt heroic, and it wasn't completely a lie. Sitting in cafés all day in California, I did generally have a pencil in my hand making sketchy taps. And indeed I had been writing (then folding away forever, with the nervous suet-stains of composition) pages describing bad weather, or squalor, or weird states of the soul.

"In that case, you two will have plenty to talk about," said Mrs. Farmican. "This Poetry Conference was *ultra* prestigious. It involved an entire week at Stanford hobnobbing with the *major major people*"—I had begun to detect a tickling quality to everything Julia Farmican said, as if she thought everything slightly absurd and an irony almost erotic was everywhere magnetizing things—"and now they've all been published! In a book! You may have heard of it: *The New Voices*. It's published by Farrar, Straus. It's an anthology of all the hot new literary figures. Including Peter!"

We both looked at him. Under his mother's praise, looking pilloried, he blew out cigarette smoke.

"So come along, Baelthon. I'll show you all the skeletons in our closets." She was already gone, down the corridor. Left together, Peter and I looked at each other. He gave me a toss of the chin, simultaneously a greeting and an admonition that I'd better keep up with his mother.

The corridor out there was dark. ". . . which it will be your job to disinter," she said, her voice running ahead in the shadows of the passageway, its walls made untouchable by their being sooted by the blast that was the life they'd led here. It was dawning on me now as I followed, how little I knew, how stuporous I was with healthiness, a healthiness Wisconsonian and sleepy. "Pardon me?" I said. The passageway took another right turn.

"The skeletons. I've been in contact with an auction house, and they've scheduled a tent to arrive tomorrow. They'll set it up on the lawn out front, and then we can spread all this stuff out there for appraisal. *Supposedly!*

California's Over

"... And here ... we ... are!" We turned right again. We had come to a big dark bag of a room, where the passageway ended and the floor fell away in a new slant, the ceiling sloping up to vanish. It was lit by the inchworm filament of one dim bulb at my shoulder. The whole area was filled with perfectly undigested treasure. Tables and chairs were stacked upside-down on each other, towers of trunks receded into the distance, chandeliers lay stranded on shrouded tabletops, carpets had been rolled and piled, boxes were filled with crumpled balls of newsprint, objects attacked the eye from every surface, every-thing evenly coated with Brie dust, the whole empire spreading farther than the light of the bulb could penetrate. We looked at it all without speaking, in the grip of air cold as soil. Peter's music was too far off to be audible.

Then something moved among the boxes—a pale face.

"Wendy?" said Mrs. Farmican. "Why aren't you in school?"

It was a girl, in the deep shadows, with (my eyes lingered to confirm it) a spiderweb tattooed to her forearm. No, not tat-tooed; inscribed by a ballpoint pen. The dark outline of a hip in bell-bottom jeans, the lift of a shoulder against straight-falling hair, the brown hair of that shadowy greasy gold-to-green that can still be seen on album covers of the time, the light catching a puffy lower eyelid, the welt of sleeplessness or malcontent which has, ever since, been a sexual signal to me, her body's sil-houette exactly the template of my lack—all I saw of her then was a dark gesture, a cradling line of shoulder and arm, that old jacket of hers, made of worn-shiny suede in patchwork dia-monds dyed in alternating purple-green-brown, a stencil of hip and narrow thigh in the shadow, a full lip. I was passing through a once-in-a-lifetime door, all unwitting, with the easy force of innocence. Within a few days, in the desert, my own tongue would write there. We would find isolated places to-gether, go off over a ridgetop together, lie down on the cement soil of Nevada and begin the slow rehearsal that always led to the same void trophy. When we first crossed the border into

37

Nevada and we had to stop to put in a quart of oil, the first place we came to was a former gas station with an old painted-plywood sign half conquered by sagebrush announcing FIRST LUCKY SLOTS HERE. But now the gas station had been occupied by an immigrant Arab, a manufacturer and retailer of garden statuary, its rooms and courts populated by a crowd of concrete cupids and deer and armless Aphrodites and male torsos and frozen cement bunnies. He was a Muslim from someplace in the Middle East where it was a sin to represent the human image in any way. So, he said, he had emigrated with his wife and children, all the way to the Nevada desert, to the middle of nowhere, far from the sky of Islam, to set up his garden-statuary business, and sculpt and cast fawns and nudes and cherubs and squirrels and discus throwers, in the desert with not a tree or a shadow in sight. And something about *that* actually made Wendy feel sexy, something about a self-granted license to sin, obscenely by art, in the open desert. And while the others waited for the engine to cool and put oil in the car, she led me, by my little finger, into the bathroom to lock the door and liberate the improbably appended humorous hard penis, to take over my body again by mouth like a voodoo priestess; she loved to raise her eyes to *see* my face slain in trust, and get again the primary taste, the swallows, the coins of proof in one long, prolongable minute. She loved everything about it, the shared underwater dream of polishing, in which people almost become strangers to each other in their bodies, loved it all with a specificity that, ten years later when she was living with a periodontist in a ten-room house in the suburbs of Marin County, would seem a little regrettable, incomprehensible, or even demeaning, certainly unhygienic, all passion being forgettable, even ridiculous, only for the young really. And then I sank to my knees on the floor of the gas-station bathroom, to unbutton her shorts, easy to let fall, and I knelt while she leaned back on the rim of the sink and I closed my eyes to better see within, the few grams of up-stitched flesh where the entire soul can be sucked down to concentration, if only for a minute before amnesiac daylight floods back again. It was amazing then, how she held her breath, then held her breath again, because I could salve an inner sore. She got to be proud of her body in Nevada, as she had never been in her life at home in the Farmican house. Her hair lightened in the desert, and her skin browned, and her appetite changed, so that she became as slender as she desired, and she dressed from the trashy clothes in thrift shops. But when I first saw her, on that first day in Seawall, she was a pale shadow in the basement guarding her body with the spinal hunch of a freak in the dark. "Mother?" she said. "Is this what I think it is?"

She was holding a small cardboard box. The word McGuf-fin was printed in red letters on its side.

"Wendy, I'd like you to meet—I'm sorry, you'll have to tell me your name again. It's such an interesting name."

"Baelthon."

"Baelthon, this is my daughter Wendy."

◉   ◉   ◉

When Wendy first met me, she found me dislikable simply as a block against the light. I was the first of many intruders she was expecting, in an already humiliated time. Not only was she under the peculiar humiliation of having to leave the only home she'd ever known, but, too, at that moment, she believed the box in her hands contained her father's cremated ashes. They had been stashed here and simply forgotten, under a folded old tie-dyed silk parachute on the billiard table. McGuffin was printed on all four sides of the box—it was the name of a funeral home over the hill in the suburbs. On a top flap of the box, in Magic Marker script, the name *J. Farmican* was written—the name of the occupant.

"Is this . . ." she couldn't say it (*Is this . . . Dad?*), prevented by the unfair comedy of it. But she could see she'd guessed right, by her mother's characteristic humorous, stabbed drop of the shoulders as she moved into the depths of the storeroom. "Wendy, isn't today a school day?"

Involuntarily she drew the—remarkably light!—box closer in her arms. "I thought these were"—she lowered her voice— "scattered."

"We have been remiss. Wendy, if you'd like to take them and devise a sort of—a sort of disposition for them, then go ahead, dear. I have to show this nice person over our whole acre of rotten old *stuff*"; she was moving out into the stacks with a paddling motion of her forearms, clearly in one of her operatic moods, Wendy could see. "Oh, Baelthon," she moaned as she vanished, "I'm so materialistic, it's so embarrassing."

Wendy said, "In that case, what did you scatter? Mother?"

She didn't answer. Wendy just stood there. At last she answered from the dark somewhere, "If you recall, sweetheart, that was an incredibly complicated week and we couldn't *get* over the hill to that *place*." Meaning, by her tone, the crematorium. She reappeared beside some shrouded trunks. "We substituted some dirt or something and scattered *that*. If you *have* strong feelings about the symbolism of it, then go ahead. Do something. It sounds fun. Though I'm sure *he* wouldn't have cared. He was Mister Iconoclast, if you recall. Now, Baelthon, just be brave and stalwart and follow me. I want to show you this upright piano. It might be possible to save it. It got rather cemented in place." She was disappearing again into a crack of darkness. "Actually, it got literally cemented in place. You'll see. Ick. Lao-tzu says in The Book of Tao, 'The eye is blinded by the Ten Thousand Things.' So I just put them all down here. Ha-ha-ha."

Wendy put the box under one arm—and she picked up the guitar case, which was what she had come down for in the first place. And she left, heading for daylight, striding up the incline of the corridor with a gait that, she could never forget, was so graceless she seemed totally unrelated to her mother. She hadn't once even raised her eyes to look at the employee, out of a numbness that must be fatigue, just fatigue, the inexplicable fatigue that kept accumulating in fine webs, boredom in the midst of a scary time. In the long basement tunnel, the stone floor's upward incline, Egyptian-feeling, made her bow her head, against the strap of a headache. Carrying her father's earthly remains was too electrifying to think specifically about. She had a completely unwise wish to show Peter. But he would have laughed. He was the one who had inherited their father's brilliance. He was probably in there now, working on his epic poem about the Donner Family, snowbound in their gory ice cave in the Sierra sadly picking off pieces of the already-dead. She ought to be packing for the move, but all she wanted to do —all she ever liked doing—was mourn in paralysis. Buy a pack of cigarettes and sit somewhere smoking.

She took the back way upstairs to her bedroom and stood in the middle of the room holding the McGUFFIN box level like a hamster cage. The idea of calling Rachel had crossed her mind. She and Rachel Feinman were the only two girls in school who wore never-washed jeans and shapeless sweaters and *didn't* shampoo their hair every day, and in general botched themselves sarcastically, as a way of making war against superficiality everywhere, against boys everywhere. But Rachel had lately shown signs of betraying their, peculiarly ethical, friendship— by flirting, in the most simpering way, with Jeff DeBono, the guitarist for a stupid Terra Linda garage band. Who, for his part, ignored her completely. Which is how males make themselves attractive.

"... the poor piano being bulldozed in along with the rest of it ..." Her mother's voice rose up the main staircase. They were coming this way. Now all these appraisers and movers would arrive, their bodies blocky in the corridors, their big hands hanging. The worst thing would be the blindness of their glance, an efficient, trowel-like glance. Her mother's voice was coming up the north corridor. They were coming this way, but she had time to get out the back door.

She put the McGuffin box down exactly in the middle of the pillow—where it hardly made a dent, its weight was on another planet—and she popped the buckles on the heavy armored guitar case. But the case was empty. The crushed velvet lining, imprinted by the body's shape, made a corpse of the guitar. Or rather a resurrection. Where could it be? It had been her father's. Would Peter have taken it?

In any case, she had to get away before they came down her corridor. She made it to the top of the stairs, but her mother's voice caught her.

"Wendy?"

She stopped at the top stair with her shoulders high. Her mother could see her through an alignment of empty doorways.

"Wendy, my consciousness-raising group is here this afternoon, and it would be nice if you looked presentable in case you *deign* to pass through the room. Those jeans are all inky. Oh, just listen to me, Baelthon"—she turned and *touched* the mover's shoulder, in that simulation of nymphomania Wendy was starting to find absolutely slimy and contaminating. "I sound like *my* mother. I take it back, Wendy, you can look any way you want." She confided aside, "I've never been a very satisfying parent to rebel against"—one of her favorite boasts. Wendy waited, aiming down the staircase, looking at the old radiator on the landing—just the sort of thing that wouldn't be exactly *visible* to the blind eyes of the new intruders here: the radiator that had stung *her* cute bottom when she got dressed before it on cold mornings, that had melted *her* Silly Putty once, with its stashed peanut-butter-sandwich crusts, little stale brackets on the floor behind, with its penciled graffiti only she could find, tiny asterisks, which used to be her favorite doodles, until her older brother pointed out, crowing, that they looked like little anuses, which ruined asterisks forever, so that her pen with its inch of black venom hovered unable to doodle, until later in life she discovered spiderwebs. "Wendy is an enormous help. Our consciousness-raising group supports everything— peace and ecology and anti-nuke and so on—and last year Wendy helped us make some beautiful posters!" she went on, providing in her usual way a thirty-second ad for each child. "Wendy, we don't mean to detain you. You have the attitude of someone who wants to leave. You look like a racehorse."

"Nice to meet you," she said.

As she poured down the staircase, her sneakers made an unfortunate heavy pounding. And when she burst out into the backyard, she let the screen door slam far behind her as she galumphed like a fat girl, her stupid small breasts a-flop, her belly patted by a new pad of female fat as she jogged, down the increasingly steep slope toward the edge of the bluff, where the path ran diagonally along the face of the cliff. She might as well be honest: it wasn't that she had *decided* to botch herself. Rather, it was destined in her flesh that she not even enter the competition, her belly so ill defined, her breasts so sadly pointy, face so flat and round, hair so warped. A girl like Rachel Feinman by contrast *couldn't help* but betray their friendship. With her tiny mouth and her tiny seed-shaped nostrils, with her long thighs, Rachel's *body* had betrayed the friendship, emerging with all the lifts and hollows that hold a male's eye and somehow wake him up, make him immediately grow up, stop being a jerk, for the first time in his life. The hallways at that suburban school were filled with girls whose bodies seemed buoyed up in contradiction of Earth's pull, lifting them into a whole different mysterious sort of *economy*. You just hit a point when you have to admit you'll never have that. Don't want it, really, to be honest.

She sat down on the bottom step at beach level, tired by the idea of walking all the way to town, on sand that spills underfoot and subtracts progress. The long-journeying ocean waves were falling on the shore without fame or notice, just as they had done before she was born and just as they would do long after she was gone, until global warming cooked the sea dry and the ugly floor showed. She took her Bic pen out. Its inner hemorrhage of ink, a stuck blot darting in the prism of plastic, made her decide to throw it away in the dune grass. But there it would have remained as litter, non-biodegradable. So she hung onto it and instead began sketching on her thumbnail, blackening it in. Her hand like a little boy's hand. Her English teacher last week had taunted her by saying, in front of the whole class, that Wendy was a "women's libber," which really just meant ugly and argumentative, and it was possible that she was right, she *could* end up a women's libber, like a female doctor or lawyer or something, ineligible for love. It was so obvious everywhere that all romantic success depends on what's only skin-deep, on pure fakery, which makes womanhood itself weak, greedy, strategic, she hated it, she was frequently guilty of thinking a dark thought (*that her mother didn't love her new husband, that she was just being practical*), a thought poisonously nourishing to think, at the same time as it made *her* smaller and meaner, and shrank the world to a mean anecdote of predation, the whole planet like one of those museum dioramas showing a group of animals tending toward extinction on a concrete slope.

His name was Faro Ness, an Ivy League–educated psychotherapist from a really rich family back East. He was handsome, too. He was the perfect new husband and stepfather, he was basically wonderful, but still she couldn't help but feel he was a helpless spreader of doomed good-intentions. You felt guilty around him. He was innocent somehow. He once even said (with a weird look, toward Wendy, of sharing a joke), "Preserving my innocence has been my life's highest aspiration. That is what Open Ranch is *for*."

The Open Ranch was a location he had found by using a compass to draw circles around possible targets of nuclear attack. Goshen Valley, in Oregon, lay outside all the penciled rings, so he had bought creek-fed land and built a fence to contain a space that would eventually be filled with windmills and waterwheels. And hydroponic greenhouses and a potter's wheel and art studios and gardens and solar collectors: she'd started to picture it as crowded as a miniature-golf course, so that you could be saved on that acre, saved by the lack of spaces between things. After dinner he drew everybody around to his side of the table, to show them the spot on the big map unfolded by candlelight. Penciled rings isolated Seattle, Boise, Salt Lake City, San Francisco, zones where unthinking people would always be dependent on supermarkets for their food, iron pipes for their water. "I thought I might bring up some Louis Armstrong? And Ella Fitzgerald? And Stravinsky and stuff, *along* with a big library. If a sort-of Dark Ages is coming around, why not go ahead and *preserve* a little civilization?" He was asking Peter. "You're the resident Visigoth here. We can be like monks keeping the Arts and Sciences alive, eh? When the infrastructure starts to break down . . ." His shoulder nudged Peter's, which in turn jostled Wendy, and he placed his finger on the chosen spot outside all the circles—Goshen Valley—and he said (with a tug, and a piercing buttonhook wink that pulled the knit of his plan tight around the three of them), "Mark my words: Civilization is the first luxury to be dispensed with. Civilization is a veneer," and he tapped the map.

By the time she came up from the beach into Seawall, she had faced the fact that she would go ahead and eat at the General Store, eat to the point of mental dimness, and then smoke a cigarette. The one sensation of filching a reward from the world is when, sitting out behind the store against the wall, her vision dulled by fat, she struggles over the new boulder of food in her stomach to fellate the unaccustomed cigarette, drawing smoke into her lungs that, by stunning her, absents her from this world. Friday afternoon, the main street was quiet when she came up from the beach road. Nobody she knew, in fact nobody at all, was in the General Store, fortunately. And the counter was manned by the long-haired nerd, instead of Mr. Pucci, who would have noticed that the Farmican girl was in here again buying a lot of food. She moved with a bandit's suave economy of motion and got a bag of Doritos and a can of Tab—and she put them on the counter beside the cash register. "Can I have a pack of Camel non-filters?" she said to the boy— whose habit was never to respond to anybody, or even lift his eyes—and she took a package of Hostess Twinkies from the rack. Behind the eternally hot plate-glass gummed with amber fat was the bed of roast chicken halves on foil trays under heat-shrunken cellophane. She raised the smallest yet raunchiest one. In the cash register's window, numbered tin cards popped up and sank, concluding at "$4.29" with tax—and she paid and got out of the store into the thin foggy sunshine and went around the corner onto the gravel behind the row of parked cars. On a quiet weekday when she should have been in school, the only sound was—from the auto mechanics' barn—the occasional whirring popple of the pneumatic gun that unscrews lugs. She sat, as always, facing the bumpers of parked cars, and with the usual half-thought prayer of remorse, tore the cellophane. The leg, its truncated white end-knuckle, was the obvious handle, and she bent the whole thing up. But rather than breaking off neatly at the knee, the entire shin pulled free. A few shreds of meat clung at the ankle where the sauce and skin are cooked together to a sticky caramel, salty glue between the snarl-exposed teeth. On the offered body, salt-dry skin tore like papyrus, revealing at the breast an expanse of white, and at the thigh, gray meat wetter and slipperier. By pinching off morsels with her fingers and probing into hollows against the bone to pry off cloves of meat, she ate until—all too soon—the revolving carcass had no more secrets, unweighted now. It's amazing how little meat there is on a chicken. You very soon come to the end of it.

Which is why it's smart to buy, also, a bag of Doritos. She used her teeth, and when it tore, the bag exhaled a salt-and-cheese breath in her face. The chips spilling in her hands were worthless currency, where does all this appetite come from? It's bottomless. It comes from a cosmic indebtedness, beneath and beyond herself, she's merely the open trumpet of it, merely the mouth, paint-fingered and paint-lipped, far now from the talcum of her father's perfected remains, which fire in the kiln has purified of all loyalty to this earth, this flesh, this dirt. In a minute of gluttony she can *join* with the forces of pollution and grease that are going to win anyway. She popped the pop-top on the can of Tab letting out the burp of commercial stomach-smell from the aluminum hole, hungry as much for such commercial effects as for the drink itself. Which amounts to pornography, in a way, but everybody's got the same perversion, everybody's mind is tuned-in to the same commercial. And then open the cigarettes, tearing through layers of litter, down to the ripping foil, freeing a single Camel non-filter, whose fine paper was delicately watermarked, as if to be non-counterfeitable, but then became printed with the personal oil-stains of *her* fingers, and she lit up to wait while the food began to hit her stomach. The sudden whirl of smoke sped her head against the wall. The two dreadful Twinkies were still in the immediate future, the next five minutes. Which was the limit of how far ahead she could think.

A boy, or rather a young man, came into view on the sidewalk in front of The Quiet Woman. He set down two suitcases and then looked up and down the street.

He was wrongly dressed for Seawall. His pants, definitely polyester—of a Sanka shade possible only in the chemistry of polyester—had been creased at the thigh horizontally by a wire coat hanger. His sports coat was actually plaid. He was from someplace far away where they had plaid. He might have been dropped off by a Christian evangelical organization to proselytize: his stance implied he had something to sell, something in which he was utterly confident. It was sad, to see utter confidence. He noticed her, sitting as she was on the fallen telephone pole with her back against the wall, and he picked up his suitcases and—audaciously—crossed the gravel to talk to her, with an attitude of sureness that she would be perfectly glad to talk to him. His walk, his way of using space, was not a Seawaller's; Seawallers tended, Indian-like, to slip through air with a more tentative and respectful motion, whereas this was a suburbanite's walk, the walk of one who conquers space freely. He said, "Hello. Maybe you can help me." He would have just stepped off the Golden Gate Transit bus, which now made two stops each day here despite the efforts of the Town Council to prevent it. He was exactly the sort of thing the Town Council was trying to prevent. "I'm looking for the Farmican house." Maybe he had seen the bulletin board in Little Tom's. Of course, he wouldn't get the job.

But if she told him that, it would mean revealing that she was a Farmican herself. She simply said, "It's down the road. Turn left at the stop sign by the big trees; it's at the end of that road."

He was already handing her a pad of paper and a pen. "If you could just draw me a little map."

Despite the adhesive of the chicken on her fingers, she took the pen and drew a knight's-move L: "This part here is the road out of town. There's the stop sign. It's up there at the top of a hill. You can't miss it."

"Super. Thanks. Excellent. Have a nice day." He pocketed the pad, picked up his suitcases, and walked off. He'd forgotten his pen, jauntily. It was a retractable ballpoint with an ad etched in the barrel:

California's Over

"A Penny Saved is a Penny Earned" — *Ben Franklin.*
First Federal Savings and Loan
Modesto, California.

With the pen from Modesto she began to work on the knee of her jeans, adding to a web she'd begun in the denim earlier that day in P.E.—the scalloped net climbing the curvature of her sometimes overlarge thigh toward the incredible planet of her knee—while she contemplated, in the pleasant malice of omniscience, the peril of the newcomer. His first disappointment will be in not getting the job. Unless her mother finds him cute. Which she won't. He looked like he had enough energy to walk all the way to her house without setting down his suitcases once.

⊚　　⊚　　⊚

At that point, "Ed Farmican" literally wasn't anybody yet, walking up the main street with all his possessions in two suitcases. He had been Ed "Pease" all his life, in Modesto in a green aluminum house, but when he got a letter informing him that his biological father had died some years ago and that his estate was now being split up, he traded in "Pease" for "Farmican," so as to inherit the deed to a genuine Nevada casino. That's what was promised in the letter from the lawyers. On our long trip through the desert, Ed was the one who took the promise of a casino literally—and then kept on believing, despite the evidence everywhere—leading us through the desert to find the place to pitch the tent of the Cornucopia. None of us had faith and we grumbled against him the whole time, yet went along with him, I suppose because the rest of us were only teenagers and he was twenty-four. But also because Ed made the idea of a roadside casino plausible. He knew how to talk to the bureaucrats in Carson City. He knew how to practice the legal principle of acquiring land by squatting. He knew how to sweeten poisonous alkali-water in the desert, by soaking a branch in it. At the lowest point in our trip, while 1973 dragged on into 1974 in a dirty Reno Christmas and President Nixon was subpoenaed and Patty Hearst adopted her captors as her liberators, when all of us but Ed had given up trying to establish a site for the casino, when I was drunk all the time on beer and cigarettes in a Reno motel room pretending to write a novel, when Wendy was pregnant and Peter was sleeping on the sidewalk behind the Circus Circus casino, his thumb broken by gangsters and wrapped in dirty mummy-bandages, hanging around at the pinball arcade giving tourists winsome looks—in other words, when everything had spun out into debris around Reno—it was then that Ed showed up like General Patton in the motel parking lot, in his gleaming chrome *Cornucopia Chuckwagon!* He was the only one still living out at the desert campsite then. The *Cornucopia Chuckwagon!* was a trailer he had made a down payment on, a two-wheeled cube of mirror-bright quilted aluminum with lift-window sides, which would display apples and bananas and Baby Ruths and Butterfingers and laminated baloney-and-cheese sandwiches in cellophane, all on a bed of crushed ice. It had two spigots on the side, one for hot coffee and one for cold lemonade, which he pointed to as if they were miraculous inexhaustible teats. He brought it to our motel in town to store it in our parking place. And soon he was dragging it to the fairgrounds and rodeos, returning it to the parking spot late at night, carrying in his pocket as much as $150 in ones and fives and twenties. That was a lot of money then.

The *Cornucopia Chuckwagon!* was the beginning of Ed's Nevada empire, according to Wendy. Now he owns a lot of land and business interests in northern Nevada, and he has a legal practice in Reno. I wasn't surprised when Wendy told me that, last week at Starbucks. Ed was always a born lawyer. Innocent selfishness was always his driving force. He has the

right combination of beliefs, in justice, and in his own justifia-
bility. And he has singlemindedness. When he first walked up
the main street of Seawall in the fog, carrying his two suitcases,
all he wanted was to collect his inheritance and then leave. A
blindfold of righteousness would save him, so he felt, would
save him from having to comprehend anything about this dim
place, Seawall, which he didn't like. To him at that moment, it
was slightly satisfying to dislike Seawall, slightly gladdening, to
see how impoverished it was, to keep turning up evidence that
James Farmican was a failed writer. No Farmican books had
been visible at the immense long paperback racks in the Lucky
Market in Modesto, nor at PayLess, nor at Walgreen's. He
wouldn't have read them anyway. Dyslexia had always felt like
a consequence of being ill-born, yet also a source of inborn
power. It isolated him but it also lifted him to a predatory vantage in clearer air than everyone else in the world whose eyes
were pulled down to printed words everywhere, whereas his
own glance was forever unsheathed. He'd taken only one college course—"Personal Investment Goals" at Modesto Junior
College—and despite his reading difficulties, he earned a solid
A, that tiny alp of a letter printed faintly but unmistakably on
his grade report. Now he knew about no-load mutual funds,
which is really all you need to know, and at this point he had
more than four thousand dollars saved. And now this inheritance was coming. The letter from the Farmican estate had
said unmistakably: "The Cornucopia Resort/Casino, Void,
Nevada." Right away he got in touch with an inexpensive
lawyer, secretly, and soon then found himself dialing the
lawyer's phone number perhaps too often, just because he simply liked those seven digits, with a new loyalty, as if that lawyer
were his real family, his first outside contact. He kept getting
clumsier around the Peases' house, among the Peases' cold-
vinyl furniture, tripping over the carpet-protecting strips of
grooved rubber in the living room and dining room, or in the
kitchen where an ironing board was always set up in the center

of the floor waiting to be knocked over. His clumsiness was like a repressed talent. Every fumble, every clank at the dinner table was an insult to "Frank Pease," the soft pink-and-gold man who read the *Modesto Bee* every evening in his underwear, who worked as a color adjuster at Gallo all day adding drops of red and blue dyes to vats of Hearty Burgundy, breakfasting every morning on ham with butter. Ed found the circumcision of the name "Pease" completely painless. All you had to do was decide inwardly, and then say it to yourself: *Ed Farmican.* His lawyer, one of those inexpensive, probably-Jewish young lawyers with a social conscience at a Legal Aid Society, interpreted the letter for him, basically for free. Its only important phrase was that all property bequeathable under California law was listed on an attached page. The attached page showed only one item: "Cornucopia Resort/Casino Establishment," in a place called Void, Nevada. The lawyer had sent a letter to an address in Void. But no response ever came.

So he came straight to Seawall, walking up the main street, where the whole amputated idea of "Ed Farmican" was still nothing more than a tingle of absence. His new jacket was making him prickle and perspire clammily in the foggy sunshine. The street curved as it left town: he could see the stop sign.

Ahead on the right, a big man was crashing up through the weeds from the marsh below the road. He was dragging something six feet long and stiff. When he had climbed up to the level of the pavement, he hoisted it—it was a surfboard—and he started walking. He was a large person. His feet had a splayed way of slapping the pavement. His hair stuck together in dusty pads and ropes. Ed focused his eyes on the distance ahead. As they neared each other, the man raised a palm. "Only the pure of heart," he called. Obviously it was his way of greeting folks on the road. Ed didn't let his eyes swerve or his mouth compress.

"If you're going to Jim Farmican's place, the job's been filled."

"I'm not looking for a job."

"Oh, you're not." He reversed direction, fighting the momentum of his surfboard. "You just arrived." He limped to jog up and walk alongside, examining Ed a little too closely, the hair of holy camel's-tails swinging, a heavy amulet's regular thump blessing his breastbone. Ed walked on without looking aside.

"My name is Dean, pleased to meet you, delighted to meet you," he started speaking in parody, the yawping whine of W. C. Fields. "You've come back to the right place. I'll tell you that. This is where you want to be when the comet hits."

"Fine," Ed said, picking up his pace. The village idiot (which apparently was what he was) fell back limping.

"You're certainly headed in the right direction. That's the road. It's a good thing to be saying hello to you. Welcome, welcome," he said as he hobbled to a stop. Ed rounded the corner at the stop sign, picked up his pace, and the surfer stayed behind holding his surfboard, on which he had apparently carved words and sentences. If he had kept tagging along, Ed could never have presented himself on the Farmicans' front step. "His family's" front step. He had foreseen his mother, Mrs. Julia Farmican, as a teapot-shaped person in an apron padded with batting like a pot holder, wringing her hands at her waist, standing in a doorway. He'd sent a letter ahead, but she didn't answer. She might be ashamed of his existence, or even afraid of him. That would make sense. He had thought all this out. His main job would be putting her at ease. They would be simple people. Because after all the father had only been a writer. And they lived in this place. It would be perfectly understandable if they distrusted him at first. Thus the new plaid sports coat. And the genuine Sansabelt slacks and the Bass Weejun penny loafers. Something as simple as a new pair of shoes can raise you in class immediately. Seeing now how backward the town was, he was almost afraid of intimidating them.

But when the road rose and a large roof started spilling

slowly into view, his heart heaved in the other direction. The many-pointed, many-gabled slate roof kept expanding over a mansion against a cliff. You could get lost in there. That was definitely the house. There was no other house around. The whole idea of wealth should be a cause for happiness, of course, but also now he felt himself like a con man almost. It seemed even a little bit rash now, to show up like this, on the doorstep with suitcases. Better to go back to Modesto, to his job in the dining room of a retirement home, bringing shallow dishes of consommé to people in steel chairs, and every week picking up that computer-printed paycheck with its little tab to tear off along the perforations. He had told the kitchen supervisor he was only taking a day off and would be back at work on Monday, as usual. But he'd brought his birth certificate, and his high school diploma, and his bankbook. And in the other suitcase was all his six-month revolving store of canned soup and Spam and ravioli and Spaghetti-O's, clanking together, along with the heavy *Financial Planning Today* textbook. He stopped at the gate to set down the suitcases.

Somebody was there. Many doors—forty or fifty doors—every door in the house—had been laid out on the front lawn. And somebody, a teenager, was moving among them with a measuring tape. He bent over and grasped a knob and pulled it up, like an entrance to a cellar in the earth, then lifted it up to a standing position and embraced it to waltz across the lawn toward the front steps.

Ed picked up his suitcases. A thorny whip of a branch at the gate rose toward his face, and he had to swing up a shoulder to fend it off. Plucking it from the fabric took a minute. Each thorn had a separate will of its own. "Excuse me," he said, and a spell was broken by the sound of his own voice. The teenager swung his door around. "Hi."

"I'm looking for Mrs. Farmican."

"She's in the basement. Go around back, and you'll see a

basement entrance. Just go down those stairs." He buried his face in the door and moved on.

Ed picked up his suitcases. The exchange had pushed him farther from feeling any ownership or entitlement here, this gravelly earth under his unscarred leather soles. He was still queasy from the bus ride, the lurch of the brakes on the steep winding road, the mentholated air that rose from the slot along the window, the vomit-smell of rubber, and picking his way through the gaps of grass between doors was a dizzying process. All their hinges were still attached, their knobs rusty. The boom of the ocean rose over the bluff as he got free of the labyrinth of doors and came around the corner carrying his suitcases. The shining watery horizon brimmed improbably high against the sky, actually overhead, a wall of water, held back by a mysterious command from flooding over us. The tall house kept unpleating beside him: maybe the teenage handyman had sent him around the long way. The ground underfoot sloped down and he rounded another corner to come upon the backyard, where a cellar door lay at the foundation of the house. It was propped open. On the grass beyond it, a woman's bare feet stuck out, lying on a beach towel. She was sunbathing in the shelter from the breeze against the house. Ed said "Excuse me" without thinking.

She sat up and looked around the edge of the door. It was her, he knew it. But she was beautiful.

"Hello," she said. "Are you answering the advertisement?"

"I'm Ed."

She stood up and showed her small naked breasts, nipples sucked taut in the cold air and goose-pimpled. Ed said "Oh" and he set down his suitcases, darkness embracing his skull.

"It's you," said his mother. "Just a minute. How marvelous, I can't believe it. Okay, turn around, I'm decent."

She was putting on—tugging up—a top as small as a handkerchief that bunched her breasts; her bathing suit bottom was

55

a string riding high over her hip carving out a bright pillar of ivory under his dilating eye. She shrugged her shoulders, fragile as a girl's, and tossed her loose arms out in the suggestion of a hug, a Playboy Playmate's hint of a smile, tilt of the head: "I knew you were coming."

Ed pointed behind him and said, "The bus." It came out as a whimper.

"Oh?" She nodded. "Well, we've all been hoping you'd turn up soon."

With no particular cause, he felt like crying. Smiled and rubbed his ear and said, "I'm twenty-three," with a gesture toward himself: his hand came up and pulled his own ear down.

"And you're so tall and handsome!"

Then she seemed to make a conscious revision of her stance, opened her arms with a cluck sound in her throat and let him in, despite the awkwardness of all the bare skin, and he bowed his face into her scent, of bread, in the hollow of her neck, her fine small back, its female braided planes. He was tall. His forearms held her, his palms flanged away in air on bent wrists.

She pulled back and looked at him and said, "You're twenty-three." She was as beautiful as a TV star. "Oh God, nineteen fifty," she said. "It was quite a time, you should have been there. I suppose you were! We certainly have some catching up to do! I received your letter." Her hands were holding both of his. "You've been living in Modesto."

"Yeah."

"With that family. Fred Pease."

"Frank."

"Frank and Irene, yes, we met long ago, when we were 'All Just Kids.' Well!" She threw his hands away. "Holy Smoke! Come on inside. Is that all you've got?" She turned. She was as ashamed as he. Some flutter was in her throat. "Let's go this way 'cause I'm barefoot. Do you want to bring those?"—his suitcases—"Or no, just leave them. You have to meet Peter and

Wendy. They're your brother and sister. Did the Peases tell you anything?"

A brother and a sister: the casino would be divided three ways. Fine. He had a brother and a sister. He was following her down the cellar stairs, into a cold smell like the Gallo distillery, something of winey mold in clay.

"You received a letter from those lawyers, didn't you?" At the bottom of the stairs she turned, looked, her eyes shining full. She was really beautiful. "You see, I've remarried"—she gestured at her own unpeeled body. She was gazing with absolute satisfaction upon him, but then she shied again. "Oh, but wait, first why don't you meet your brother. This is a little bit mind-blowing. My *new* husband is coming over for dinner tonight. We have all the wonderful work of getting reacquainted."

She called down the dark passageway, "Peter?" while holding Ed's eyes in hers. "Come here, Peter. I want you to meet someone."

Nobody answered. They looked at each other. Her shoulders lifted and dropped. For a moment, the stream of time had hit an unmoving stone and purled there. "So," her voice said softly in a strange intimacy almost of contact-resonance in his skull-bone, "Am I much different than the imaginary me would have been?"

Peter's voice said, "I'm up here, Mom." He stood above them in the daylight at the top of the stairs, leaning across the space of the doorframe canceling the light, shirtless, looking like the sort of leopard-hipped rock star who gets arrested for public indecency onstage. "Fucking fridge." He licked his fingers. "'S fucking empty." Ed faded back in the smell of clay. His suitcases were still outside in the backyard, but his mother was going upstairs toward the kitchen.

"There's an entire *jambe d'homme*, dear, and there's a lot of the linguini. You're not looking." She made a hand-offering gesture to urge Ed along upstairs.

"*Jambe d'homme*," Peter moaned.

"Peter, get ready. Do you remember my telling you about your older brother?"

He said, "Oh, wow," and looked past her into the dark, making a visor of his hands. "Hey. Whoa."

"Your father and I abandoned him back in the bad old days, when I was just too self-centered and wild and I would have made a terrible mother anyway I was such a slut. But *now*"— they reached the top of the stairs and she stood aside to present him—"he's forgiven us! He's come back to us! This is Edward! Edward, Male, Live Birth!"

Peter said, "Far out," a depressing expression that always seemed to fill the room with marijuana fumes. He looked about eighteen or nineteen, college age, but at home on a weekday afternoon.

Ed offered his hand. But Peter closed his eyes, set aside a bottle of ketchup, and bent his knees. "*Papa was a rollin' stone/Wherever he laid his hat was his home . . .*" A guitar, sculpted of air in his hands, trembled under the jab of his finger and the bang of his hip. "Peter is musical," his mother said, as she began watching with tired admiration. Ed folded his arms and installed his unaccepted handshake in his armpit. ". . . *And when he DIED . . .*" Ed kept trying to end the song, by catching Peter's eye, with a flicker of an unconvinced smile. ". . . *All he left us was a loan, whoa-whoa-whoa . . .*"

"So tell us, Ed. What do you do?"

"Do?" His job at Modesto Hillhaven Convalescent—or "Heaven's Little Waiting Room," as the kitchen staff called it—involved tying terry-cloth bibs on cadavers in steel chairs and setting a dark mirror of consommé before each one. He didn't know whether to say that was his present job or to say instead, *Actually, I thought I might look for work around here.*

But she spun away, "Whew, golly, I'm cold," kindling her forearms together between her breasts. "Let me just go upstairs and put something *on* and you two get to *know* each other." She ran away on tiptoe. "You're brothers!" she reminded them. "Imagine that!"

"Mrs. Farmican?" came a voice from somewhere in the house as she vanished. "Mrs. Farmican?"

"Yes, Baelthon," she shouted while she ran up the stairs.

"Is it possible these doors have expanded? Or shrunk?"

"Anything's possible, Baelthon." Her voice was lost, and Ed was left alone with his younger brother.

◎　◎　◎

They looked at each other.

Peter threw open his arms, parted his knees wide, and thrust his crotch straight at Ed. "Brother!"

"I left my," Ed said, with a backward gesture, "suitcases outside." He almost bumped the doorframe, but didn't. He had so far not *touched* anything in this mansion, his hands haloed like a thief's, stuck now in his pockets.

"Want a beer? I've got some cold pizza downstairs, *and* have you ever seen a microwave oven? It's the latest diabolical deviation from the industrial magnets. My mom bought it, but she gave it to me 'cause it cooks her ovaries at a distance."

"Maybe I should . . . ," Ed said with a gesture, thinking of his suitcase as he followed Peter down. But he gave up. They would be safe outside. "Your bedroom is in the basement?" he asked, going down the treacherous stairs, still not touching anything, forbidden by some fairy-tale logic in this castle.

Peter stopped on a stair and turned to speak: "The muses here are chthonic," he said in a leering Dracula yawn, "the vapors rise"—his finger wriggled upward while one eye peered, then hc swung back down the stairs. This might mean that there was some problem with the upper house, like with the furnace or the ventilation. Ed said, "I noticed all these pictures

59

on the walls." At the bottom of the stairs were some scratchy chalky images like cave drawings.

"That's a genuine Karl Boronovska. He did those," said Peter as he went on down. "Do you know who he is? Or rather was? I'll show you. I'm so used to them, I hardly notice them anymore. They're supposed to retell the story of the battle for People's Park. In Berkeley? You know? Like in my father's poem *Anabasis*? See, these are all the police. And here these are the National Guard. And these are all the students and protesters. It starts here. This is the Free Speech Movement guy with a bullhorn . . ."

Ed stood aside to let light in, his shadow an archaeologist's. The mural was tiered: the narrative read from the upper-left corner to the lower-right. The National Guard were phalanxes of stick figures in profile, their feet and elbows in profile too. The students were similarly flattened but they faced in the opposite direction, and they were more variously colored and dressed. "This is where they go down Telegraph Avenue smashing store windows"—Peter followed the story with a rather longish fingernail, a boy-Pharaoh's fingernail. "And this is where he stood on a car and read a poem when they all got chased up Dwight Way. And this part here is the park. This is People's Park." It was a green rectangle in the center, the size of a playing card. "This is the Free Space. This is the country of blamelessness, where the world was reborn pure. Have you read that poem?"

Ed pretended not to hear. This whole town was starting to add up together in his mind. When he first got off the bus in town there was another mural, in those socialistic, Mexican colors, all sweaty and wounded, portraying a dragon whose two heads were Johnson and Nixon, and whose tentacles crushed a mass of perfectly nice-looking people of various racial hues, yam and lemon and eggplant. A muscular woman like a giant green waitress was doing battle with it, bursting free of its tentacles. And the girl sitting on the ground beneath the mural, who gave him directions, she had a recognizable tone of voice, the left-wing nun voice, both patient and unforgiving, that makes livelier people somehow guilty. This whole place was like a preserve. Peter was looking at him in happy expectation. So he asked, "What does this part say?" There was writing between panels, which his dyslexia prevented him from conning, producing instead only the familiar old cramp, loneliness. And from within that loneliness, he took a short realistic look out into the future and purely *guessed* that the Cornucopia Casino, out there in the desert, had not been producing a lot of income for this family. It was defunct. He just got that feeling, looking around, yet it was a partly triumphant thought, the idea of his returning to a ruin.

"All this?" said Peter, "It tells what's happening. This one says, *'The Siege of the Administration Building.'* And this one says, *'Interlude with a Tear Gas Cannister.'* And this says, *'Blocked by the National Guard, the Crowd Surges up Haste Street.'* "

"Who's this?" A recurrent figure: it was a long-haired green doll, whose arms were crooked in a flattened embrace. He faced a phalanx of black mummies holding sticks.

"That's . . . *Dad! Our* Dad." He threw open his arms, and again thrust his pubis at Ed. Ed touched the wall, cowering. "What's he doing?"

"Him? He's seceding! People's Park is a separate country. He and some other people declared it independent of the United States. It's still a separate country today. You could go visit it. He wrote the whole Constitution right then and there—about no more racism, no more sexism, no more injustice, no more violence. Just peace, fairness to all . . ." He looked eagerly at Ed. "Justice, charity, mercy . . ."

"Wow," Ed said, hiding his hands again. "Sounds great."

◉   ◉   ◉

Peter completely put the Donner Family poem out of his mind for the rest of the morning because he wanted to show Ed everything. He'd left him by himself for a minute in the library while he ran upstairs, virtually flew up the main staircase, a cigarette burning in hand like one sprained wing—to the cabinet in the upper sitting room where the specially-minted Endicott medal was kept, sliding around in a shallow basket with pennies and nickels and pesos, and even a brass token for a pornographic peep show. Baelthon the mover could be heard in the west corridor bumping and dragging one of his futile doors. The cozy disrepair everywhere had, with Ed here now, suddenly jumped up to be more obvious: the wood slats showing through the plaster, the oceanward slope in all the floors, the amputated section of bannister where, at midpoint, the trusting hand went to heaven—strange how he felt *responsible* for it all now with Ed. He kept finding himself stealing glances, in amazement, at Ed's large Farmican face, the eyes like Wendy's. He flew back down the stairs with the weighty medal in his hand, its senile Benjamin Franklin in profile, and in the library he found Ed standing around uncomfortably like a kleptomaniac, and he decided with satisfaction, *He's helpless.* The typical Farmican facial features were magnified and dazed, his father's great nose, fat lower lip and absent upper lip, shoulders mounded. "Here"—he handed him the six-ounce disk that still held the whole family down to earth. "See the inscription? They don't give a medal for the poetry category, but they had this specially minted. And Dad gave it as a gift to my mother— that is, to '*Mom*.' Heh."

Ed took it but didn't focus. He just held it, like weighing it.

"He was on the front page of the *New York Times*. And we went there for the ceremony, and Dad wore jeans at this big thing where you're supposed to wear a tuxedo. And then at the ceremony, he didn't even show up. He had it inscribed, see?" He was aware he was babbling. Ed's wall of silence made him shrill.

California's Over

"What does it say?" Ed handed it back.

"No, it's on this side." He held it up to the light. "It's a poem—or rather lyrics from a song —

> *"Like a baby stillborn,*
> *Like a beast with his horn,*
> *I have torn everyone who reached out for me.*

> *"Like a fish on a hook,*
> *Like a knight in an old-fashioned book,*
> *I have saved all my ribbons—for thee."*

"Great," Ed said, while his attention rose along the high shelves.

"Actually, I wrote that myself." It was a safe bet Ed had never seen those lines anywhere or probably wouldn't even know who Leonard Cohen was. He didn't seem to be paying attention. He had this way of retracting his head into his shoulders.

"Then there's this," Peter said, jumping to the desk. "The pen he used when he wrote *The Green Conquistador.*" He held up the cube of transparent Lucite with the pen thrust into it.

Ed took it and tried to pull the pen out.

"No, it's a paperweight."

He got a better grip and pulled hard.

"No no," Peter said, reaching.

"Oh, I see, it's stuck in there. I get it."

"When I was younger I used to try to pull it out."

Ed handed it back and started looking around grinding his shoulders. "I think I ought to return back to San Rafael for a minute. The only other bus leaves in half an hour, and I have a plan that's firmed up. I saw a car for sale at a used-car lot."

"Oh, don't buy a car."

Ed seemed insulted and looked him in the eye for the first time. "It's a Mercedes-Benz," he said. "It's four hundred dollars, for a genuine 1955 Mercedes-Benz. It said so on the windshield. And they can't sell a car that isn't in working order, or they'd open themselves up to the possibility of being sued."

It was the longest sentence he had spoken so far. Before Peter's eyes, while all the lost years exploded in atomized mist, Ed condensed into a lonely stunted person.

"Are you going to live here? Why don't you just move in? Just move in and stay. We're rich!" he said wildly. Not stopping to weigh the *accuracy* of every tiny little thing is really a kind of generosity, or at least a big sloppy expansiveness. In fact, they weren't rich at all. In fact, if Faro Ness hadn't come along, they probably would have had to get *jobs*. But they would certainly seem rich to Ed, who looked like he'd always had a job. His eyes had a restless, hurt, vitamin-deficient way of never settling, always moving. It's what an ordinary place like Modesto will do to you. "Don't buy a car. Cars are so *boring*," he said, the word boring distended by a special weight of ethical and aesthetic meaning, impossible to convey. His longing was to educate Ed because his hard travels were over, and kindness was here, and finer things, finer feelings. "Are you drinking your beer? This is considered the best beer in the world. Gourmets have taste tests where they soak the labels off the bottles, and this beer always wins. They have to *smuggle* it out of Czechoslovakia in oxcarts. Only about a hundred cases ever reach the outside world," he added, imaginatively, his body dwindling as he spoke, sensing in his lofty soul the burning toast smell of his old Lionel electric-train transformer as anxious love loaded his nerves.

"Who's that?" Ed said, looking out the window. Wendy was out there. She was taking the brick path to the side door, her face averted in the sinking fog.

"That! Is your sister! Come on, you want to meet her?"

"I saw her in town."

"She's always in town," he said with a tone alluding to her secret episodes of gluttony, which Edward wouldn't catch (there was so much for him to learn about this *family*!) and he grasped Edward's shoulder (the weird, surprising polyester under his fingers as cool as kerosene) to guide him to the hall, to present him to Wendy. "But really. Don't buy a car. Cars are ridiculous. They pollute and they make noise and they're stupid. And they're all ugly if you look at them. If you buy a car you're just the butt of a big joke, like everybody else in America. Plus, you won't be back in time for dinner, and my mother's new husband is coming over for dinner. He's *your* stepfather too, after all."

"I can meet him another time."

"He's a Harvard psychologist. And he's a genuine intellectual. He's the only person I know who's preserving the ideals of the sixties in this miserable decade. Doesn't it seem to you the seventies is going to be one of those in-between times when nothing decent will happen?" he blathered on, his cheerful voice vying with his heart. "Also, my mother will make her amazing cioppino tonight, from clams and mussels right out of the mud," though he knew his words were striking a shiny moving surface. Some people have a sort of deafness, which gives them power, making more generous people around them almost faggy-sounding, and Peter found himself simply getting tired talking to him, there's simply a kind of exhaustion in clowning to keep that ball up in the air. Wendy came in by the side door, in her usual furtive slouch, and he said, with an, almost, *pressure* in his voice intended somehow to poke up her posture, "Wendy. Listen. The greatest thing in the world has happened. This is your long-lost brother, Edward. Remember the letter?"

She lingered on the lower step. "*You're* Edward Pease?"

She was drooping. It was typical. Poor Edward. Faced immediately with Wendy's self-absorbed dismissal of the whole world around her.

Edward explained to Peter, "We met in town. She gave me directions to get here."

"I didn't know who you were," Wendy said, and then told Peter, "We didn't know who each other was."

"Oh! Well! This is who each other is!"

She was standing three steps down on the landing. All she did was bob her head, eyes downcast, and acknowledge the strangeness of the situation by saying, "Hm." Hands in pockets, she straightened her arms to dig her elbows into her ribs, her body prodded toward exit, such a self-centered girl, always struggling perversely away from everything. A meeting of one of their mother's committees was just starting and voices could be heard on the north steps.

The side door from outside opened. Baelthon the hired mover was hauling an unhinged door. ". . . Excuse me."

He separated everybody by dragging the door across their midst. On her side of the cut space, Wendy drifted away canceling them all with a wave as she grimaced to make a smile, and then she ran.

Ed was grinding his shoulders again. "I better get my suitcases. It's going to be raining out there, and I have to go get this car." So everybody scattered in different directions, leaving Peter holding both beer bottles, standing alone there like a circus strongman whose burden, an inflated planet, turns out to be weightless.

◉　◉　◉

"Everybody said his suicide was a mystery, because he was at the height of his career right then." Peter was almost *singing* up among the narrow staircase walls, carrying a beer in each hand, following Baelthon as he dragged his old door up the winding side stairs. Baelthon had agreed to drink the rest of Ed's beer. And at least he knew who James Farmican *was*; at least he was slightly literate; whereas Ed had started walking back down the road to the bus stop without even taking a second sip from his beer. The new brother might turn out to be not only uncultivated but, in that way of uncultivated people lacking in inner

66

resources, mysteriously pissed-off all the time. "... But there's a sense in which suicide was a logical inevitable thing for a man like him in this *society*. He was simply more ideal than the rest of us. It was like his nerve endings were more directly connected to everything."

He wouldn't even try to work any more on his poem today. In fact, the poem, ever since the Stanford Seminar, had collapsed into a mere inaccessible stomach ache, now even heavy to carry upstairs. It was that literally a weight. Yet in the floating wreckage of this house as it broke up, it would be his only rescue. "Nobody realizes," he said with a funneled anger Baelthon wouldn't detect, "nobody realizes anymore what James Farmican stood for. Have you ever seen People's Park? I mean the actual place? Have you ever seen it?"

"Is it a public park now?" Baelthon said, hauling his door.

"Well, you understand, it's a foreign country."

"What is? People's Park?"

"They formally broke off from America. It's in his poem. It's in the *Anabasis* cycle. But you should see it now."

"Who owns it?"

"Who owns it. The land used to belong to the university. But they won't touch it. It's holy. But you should see it now. It's fucked."

Bump went the heavy door against the wall. Some plaster fell, but Baelthon didn't notice.

"The old bandstand is still there. But now the park is just a place for drunk frat-boys to pee when the bars close. And a few bums sleep there. People's Park is *the* symbol for what happened to the idealism of that generation. That's why he committed suicide, essentially. You want to see where?"

Baelthon at the top of the stairs took a breather. "Where what?"

"Where he committed suicide. It's in the cupola. The bullet is still embedded in the barometer."

Baelthon's eyes shone. Peter was reminded, it was rather

lucky for a simple Midwesterner to arrive exactly *here* at what might as well be a national historic landmark, or maybe even possibly could be someday. He handed him his bottle of beer. "I'll show you. This is the tower. The cupola is just two flights up."

"What's going on with the floor right there?"

"Oh, that. That's always like that. The tower is sinking so the floor has a gap."

"You can see right down," Baelthon complained in awe as he peered through the slot in the floor. With a concluding shudder, the shudder by which a rather limited Midwesterner shakes off mystery, he handed his beer back to Peter and picked up the door again, saying, "You know, it's going to start raining pretty hard. And all those doors are all out there in the rain."

It was true, the wind was up, tossing everything. Outside the window, the single great willow on the cliff-top lumbered through gusts. Peter always found himself feeling loyally defensive of the climate here in his home, in the midst of rain-clouds always forming and bursting, mushrooms parting the fiber of doormats, fur growing on plates in the cabinets, buildings and cars decomposing, clouds of mold rising up and carrying things off. He was standing in front of—blocking—the aquarium-dim window, beyond which the lone willow tree of his childhood was climbing through the storm like a mastodon. Baelthon said, "Do you think I could use the big tarp in the garage? If all those doors get wet, they'll be ruined."

"Oh, who cares," Peter said. Unscrewing the doors from their hinges had been one of his father's strange solitary jokes, during those last weeks when he was here by himself; and Peter had always inexplicably *liked* living inside a petrified joke, inside a heart without valves. He honestly knew it wasn't very realistic, his idea of staying on here after everybody had moved to Oregon, writing alone by candlelight, while gaps opened in the house's joints in the wrenching weather. But he was going to do it anyway.

California's Over

Baelthon was kneeling before the doorframe, to wiggle the door into place with a screwdriver. "Doesn't fit?" Peter said, with dismissal for the whole project. He sneaked a swallow from Baelthon's beer. He'd never notice. "Did you measure?"

"Everything measures. But the doorframes are the wrong *shape*. They're all, like, parallelograms instead of squares."

"Well, the house did settle. Come on, man, this is boring. Come on up to the cupola. Everything is precisely the way he left it. His pen is lying right exactly where it fell."

Baelthon got to his feet. "I'll just leave this one here," he said. He embraced the door and swung it around toward the landing of the stairs—where its swinging mass hit the oaken sphere atop the newel post, breaking the sphere off at the neck. It hit the floor and rolled like a bowling ball against the wall.

Baelthon said, "Uh-oh."

"Don't give it a second thought. Nobody cares. It's only a material object." Peter picked up the wooden ball: it was dreamily light. The wood inside looked like stale bread. He showed it to Baelthon. "Powder-post beetles."

"—Powder-post beetles," Baelthon repeated, looking in.

"Don't worry about it. I'm sure the Mother Superior doesn't give a shit. They're all leaving anyway." He set the ball back on the floor, his face descending through strata of private grief in his rotten house. Staying on here, his typewriter would need electricity. In a daydream, he'd seen a string of extension cords running across the rainy heath from town into his basement window. Faro Ness said there would always be a bunk for him on the self-sufficient Oregon ranch; but he also implied life in Oregon would be harsh, virtuous, in a summer-camp sort of way. His only other alternative was to move over the hill into suburbia. Which was nothing more than a collection of all-alike houses on straight streets. Having James Farmican for a father was like inheriting a fortune in Confederate currency. You feel like you're lying when you talk about him. Even if you stick strictly to the factual truth, still you feel, if you watch people's responses, like there's a slight change-of-angle at the refracting surface. He stepped across the gap in the floor. "Come on, man, let's go up to the tower."

Baelthon, cradling the sphere and picking at the broken wood, looked up absentmindedly.

He started up the stairs. "I've got your beer."

Baelthon followed, stepping over the gap in the floor. "You know, a dowel would fix that."

"These here are actual bongo drums from the Six Gallery reading in 1956 or whatever, where Ginsberg read *Howl*. And this is a mandala some poet made. The cupola is two more flights up. You live in the suburbs, don't you? Baelthon?"

"Me?"

"What do people *do* there?"

"Do?"

"Like, do you rent something?"

"I rent a room. It's actually the garage, but I live there."

It was incomprehensible, the ability of most people to sign a "lease" and then start paying out hundreds of dollars every month. It was unimaginable. They all work. They all have jobs, covering up their entire lives, and then they lose whatever had been special about them. Or else there never was anything special about them in the first place, and so they experience no sense of loss when they turn over their lives to working and paying rent.

Peter said, "Here it is." They had come to the top, the round room, flooded with witnessing daylight.

Baelthon stood there and looked around, his collarbone lifting.

"There's the bullet hole right up there. The police went over the room and the blood was cleaned up, but mostly everything is just the way it was. See, there's his pen. Here's the ashtray. Still with butts. This would have been coffee here. The radio is tuned to K-JAZZ. He was halfway through this pack of cigarettes. They'd be pretty stale by now. Go ahead. Smoke a genuine James Farmican cigarette. Maybe whatever's in the to-bacco will give you genius. Or check this out—"

A cardboard Almadén Mountain Chablis box stood on the floor. He untucked the lid to reveal a stack of typed pages. "Flip through the Great Unpublished James Farmican Novel. This manuscript has been bid on by all the important literary agents," he went on, stretching the truth again. "They come around literally begging. They say they'll pay any amount of money for this little stack of pages. But we just don't feel like selling it. You know? We just don't feel like it."

Baelthon looked hung on a peg. He was too impressed to speak. At last he whispered, "I really should cover those doors. They'll get ruined in this rain." So Peter let up on him. The whole world reentered his lungs in a big cold breath, while he followed Baelthon back down the tower stairs, still holding both beer bottles. This world his father had scorned and risen from was a bare space, and he had a steely thought: he would have to go back down and write.

> *insanity blood squish*
> *Vietnam bite the muscle*
> *kill the indian*
> *America*
> *play golf*
> *the picnic at Donner Pass*
> *look whats between your teeth*

Peter was alone in the basement at his desk staring at the most recent verses of the Donner Family poem, unable to add a single line, lying in a slouch, his body trickling glacially off the chair, his extremities cold, his eyes scumming over peacefully, growing ever more distant from it. It was like seeing a peak he had once stood on but couldn't now regain. There was some connection he wasn't making, some secret of living he didn't get. In the far mirror, he watched his honestly sometimes incredibly good-looking doomed face, the narrow jaw defined by a lucky biased slice of light, the silky hair falling beside a straight brow, the lipless mouth, the clear eye, a face under a magic spell of eternal youth, the same spell his mother was under, he liked to think. In fact, he was right, his image would always chime in mirrors as supernaturally young. Today in his forties, living in an oceanfront condominium in La Jolla, the owner of a successful swimming pool–cleaning service with five locations in the San Diego area, Peter Farmican still looks magically young, and he leads a completely satisfying social life centered in the Vic Tanny health club in Pacific Beach, where he is locally famous as the host of a community-access cable-TV talk show called *Peter!* with two swivel chairs and a coffee table on a spot-lit dais, discussing local politics or cultural events; and even more famous as the star of his own ten-second commercials on late-night television for his swimming pool–cleaning service.

But at this moment, with no such knowledge of his future, he looked at the few lines on the page and hated them, or even feared them for their mysterious insufficiency. At the Stanford Conference, people had seemed to systematically exclude him, at first perhaps only because his name was Farmican, which is always a sort of embarrassment. But also, at this Conference you had to be East-Coast and exclusive and, basically, boring. He would never tell his mother how he spent most of the time standing by the coffee urn, looking profound, or how they averted their eyes from him when he crossed the room, how he overheard ironic references to his clothes, how people completely ignored his (he almost choked on them) declarations of aesthetic principles—his rule that every line be spontaneous, unanticipated, unrevisable, still in a state of innocence. He lifted his head. He set his fingers on the keyboard, and angrily—ignoring the dreamy roaring psychotic sensation right on his skin—he took another stab at it and rose up straighter in his chair to type, in a faint sit-up posture like a corpse. ". . . Insanity of Ameriac," he wrote, and then he dropped back, wounded by a typo, a typo that some scholar of the future might analyze for symbolic content. It was all too depressing.

Then an idea came to him. He could call it an opera. But really an opera. A *real* opera. Songs. A full orchestra. Purple shadows. Heavy costumes. You don't realize how brilliant something is until, sneakily, you touch it with the wand of ambition. He could picture a stage set. Snowy white papier-mâché. The walls were smeared with blood. And the members of the Donner Family would stagger over the set in bloody rags, delivering his poetry as *songs, while* swinging a severed leg or an elbow joint. The Donner father would hold up a dripping thigh bone, singing, center-stage.

He wanted to tell someone. Baelthon the mover was upstairs taking a bath and changing into some dry clothes. He stood up to go tell him. Or rather not tell him but just gloat.

"Genius at work," said a voice behind him in the doorway, applying that terrible old word like a dunce cap. It was Faro. Hands-in-pockets, concave, his body had a sweet way of, like a half-parentheses, standing aside from the role of "father" as if it were a target. His thick curly hair graying at the temples, his complexion heightened by ruddiness, he always looked *famous*. Peter thought of it as the look imparted by Harvard.

"Hi." He stood with his back to the typewriter. Faro wouldn't be able to see anything. In fact no one, not even the Stanford people, had ever seen this poem. But now it wasn't a poem, it was an opera. He couldn't have been interrupted at a better moment, in midair, before he would have to—inevitably— lower a perfect idea into the usual specific disappointments.

"Dinner," Faro confided as he shuffled in, barefoot in jeans, with a shrug upstairs meaning there was no hurry. He was a godsend. The unlikely combination, rich *and* liberal, seemed a matter almost of good genes, like physical health, like good nutrition, along with the spring in his step and the sharp humorous light in his eye. His huge complex of family businesses, and the meshing of its gears with other gears, which in turn meshed with the distant machinery of an axiomatic foreign war, was operated and lubricated by lawyers, so he remained obviously free to lead the life of an intellectual, hands in pockets, his benign teacherly stoop, fern-like, defining the base-curve of a greater arc of protectiveness. He was decently ashamed of all the wealth, and then even subversive of it. Just this year, from the glacier of money, an immense hunk had naturally fallen off, which his family lawyers had released to him. And that was how the Oregon ranch was being financed. "Is this"—he nodded toward the typewriter—"the Donner Family thing?"

"Oh, yes, yeah, but I never talk about what I'm working on. It releases the—" he rubbed his fingertips together, pinching escaping fumes.

"Wup. Yep. Gotcha. Profanes the inspiration." He sat on a stereo speaker and lifted his shoulders high and dropped them, looking around. "Where's your guitar?"

"Oh, it's someplace." Peter frowned, because the implication was he wouldn't mind hearing him play sometime. When he did play, it was always alone by himself. It was probably stupid. By turning up the fuzztone, the phase shifter, the tremolo and the reverb, all at once, he could tease from the amp an eerie snake of white-noise in whose inward-spiraling cone his head could be stuck for hours at a time until his brain was rubbed sore and he came upstairs at mealtime in a pallor. Faro, gazing at his own knee almost cross-eyed in personal concentration, said, "Great album. I love this album."

It was only a Joni Mitchell album. He was getting around to something. This flanking remark gave Peter the old schoolboy feeling of, like, being "in trouble," who-knows-why—maybe for not packing up yet, for not being realistic about the evacuation of the house. Faro lifted one ankle up on his knee and started massaging his instep in both hands. Peter's gaze dribbled around the floor guiltily, then up to a big slop-and-slash painting he had done. Which no gallery would ever display, let alone sell for fifty thousand dollars. Be realistic.

"So tell me, Peter," he began. He gave his thighs a slap and rub, and stood up and started ambling toward the door. Peter followed.

"I wanna ask you about something. You're going to stay on here alone in the house. I say great. Wonderful. Pacing the parapets. Frightening neighborhood children. Writing the Great American Epic Poem. I say excellent." He was standing at the door caving inward to let Peter pass, and then as they started walking up the passageway, put one arm around Peter and squeezed his scapulae together and got to the point: "Nevertheless, poets ought to have a few experiences besides inside-their-own-head. Do you know anything about trigonometry?"

"Trigonometry?"

"This would require you to come up to the Ranch. I've been thinking a lot about clocksprings. Huge clocksprings. Now listen, don't scoff. I think clocksprings are a way to store energy." His free hand swung: "Big, big, huge clocksprings."

Peter had no response.

"I'm into the *post*-petroleum era. See, a windmill—or else a waterwheel, say—can charge up a great big clockspring by winding it up tight. Many little gears for leverage. Then later it can unwind to run a generator to make electricity. You store energy indefinitely. A clockspring would be like a battery. But it's a mechanical battery rather than an electrochemical battery. It's very *low*-tech."

"Why trigonometry?"

"Oh shoof, you need to figure out how many pounds of torque you get per degree of arc. Or something like that. I'm not good at technical stuff. You could just *hire* somebody to do the math if you want." A vague, flushed-out-of-hiding sensation: Faro and his mother would have been discussing this: What To Do About Peter, Peter's Not Packing His Things.

They were climbing the stairs toward the kitchen, Faro's arm still around him. Above, they could hear the clack of shellfish being stirred in his mother's giant broth. "Are you willing to help with that? Does it all sound too fantastical? It would mean you'd have to come up to the Ranch sometimes." They reached the top and Faro stood aside.

"Sure, yeah, I guess," he assented easily in the familiar general gravity-free environment and, heightened by Faro's arm-squeeze about the shoulders, he was released into the steamy brilliant light of the kitchen, confused and happy and blind. This kitchen would always be heaven, the future unthinkable.

"Peter agrees he'll help with the clocksprings. More or less enthusiastically."

"But I'm still going to go on living here," Peter said. "I am. They can go ahead and disconnect the phone and the utilities." His mother's and Faro's eyes were tipping toward glazing over, and he went on perhaps a little too sharply, "I'll use candles. And I'll bring that wood-burning stove down there. The manual typewriter will be fine. I've figured it all out. I'll just be here by myself. Because I'm *working*. On my *writing*."

Faro set a hand on his shoulder, yet spoke toward his mother. "But do come up to the Ranch *sometimes* to help with this clockspring project. Or at least give it some thought. Tonight I just wanted to plant the seed of an idea."

For a second they both looked at him, fondly, then his mother turned back to her iron cauldron and said, "Is Edward around? Did he go somewhere?"

"Edward," said Peter—emphasizing the name—"went over the hill to San Rafael. He says he wants to buy a used Mercedes-Benz."

There came a great avalanche of descent on the servants' back stairs, recognizable as his sister. "*Mom!*" Wendy sang angrily from the staircase. "Mo-*ther!*" Her voice gained vibrato in the pounding of her heels on the steps.

"Yes, Wendy."

"Mom." She appeared in the doorway, pale and angry. "Where's the—" She looked at the two males, then back at her mother, and lowered her voice. "Where's the *thing?*" she hissed.

"What thing, dear? You used to have such a wonderful vocabulary."

"The *thing* . . . the *McGuffin.*"

◉   ◉   ◉

Wendy's job was always to set the table and light the dining room candles, tall wax drums her mother bought in a Zen monastery in Japan whose sooty wicks had receded into forearm-deep wells, so deep that, on the first try, holding the lit match in her two longest fingers like tweezers, she burned her fingertips and dropped the match and the pain of it traveled up along nerves to flash briefly against the *general* futility of things. She struck another match and (in the smell of a snuffed wick, the lightning-struck, party's-over smell that, to her alone, was so sad) she tilted the candle to tap the droplet of new flame against the little black pimple where a wick was supposed to be in the polluted ivory well. Her heart was a small animal making unsuccessful burrowing motions. *Her* role now, on this stage, was to go through the motions of comedy generated by a box of her father's remains.

Which she had only narrowly saved. Her mother had found the box on her bed and taken it downstairs and set it on—of all places—the edge of the washing machine, where anything could have happened to it. *Then* she suggested, in her usual sarcastic way, maybe they should donate it to the Seawall Historical Society Museum—which was really just an eternally locked storefront with a collection of old photos and a few rusty nails and Indian artifacts, like twisty little turds in glass cases, in the storefront that used to be the laundromat. Faro had then remarked, *Wouldn't some grander museum be interested?* leaning arms-folded beside the stove with the impertinent kingliness of an idle man in a busy kitchen.

But she had quickly, smoothly, faded back in the doorway, to lift the McGuffin box from the washing machine; and she had slipped upstairs to her room—bringing, too, a large-size jar of Tang from the pantry—because its powder would have equal weight and density to the ashes'. Sitting on her bed, she paused to try to summon up some sacramental emotion, and then she opened the McGuffin box. Inside was a can of shiny thin metal, amazing how cheap, like one of those noisy bonking cookie tins. She lifted the lid, to find a plastic lining, choked shut by a twist-em tie, printed with this surprising admonition from the netherworld: NOT A TOY. KEEP THIS AND ALL OTHER PLASTIC BAGS AWAY FROM CHILDREN. And while kitchen sounds went on innocently below, she switched the Tang and the ashes, first pouring the orange powder into the funerary tin. Then she lifted the plastic bag, carefully as a transplanted organ, and gently kneaded it to make it fit into the empty Tang jar. (It wasn't powdery—it felt like old chunky clay—like a fermented paste—and its color, in contact with the white-plastic membrane, looked mud-grey.)

The guitar case was the nearest coffin. But the jar would have had to lie down inside, which seemed wrong. She found herself drifting out in the hall, holding the Tang jar ahead like a lamp, and she decided to put it in a place where no one ever went: the empty servants' linen closet. On the center of the eye-level shelf, she stood it up, ever-so-gently without a click of contact: James Farmican. Then in the minutes before she had to set the table, she put the tin urn back in the funeral-home box and tiptoed fast down the rear staircase and replaced it on the washing machine. The Tang powder inside had just the right weight. Let her mother do whatever she wanted with it now.

78

"*Ora pro nobis*," Faro's voice chanted behind her in the dining room doorway.

It was some joke pertaining to candle-lighting. She didn't turn to face him but moved on to the next candle. His going barefoot around the house made her inexplicably mean-souled, as did the light he shed, the light of a degree in psychology. "How dexterous!" he marveled at her candle-lighting; he was trying so hard in this family, dodging from place to place to support every collapse. "Folks like me are amazed by any dexterity. I'm all thumbs"—he held his palms open: in fact his hands were beautifully shaped, strong, and they held a bowl of light. She averted her eyes and turned to the next candle. His white shirt, by some ultraviolet chemistry of bleach or detergent, luminesced bluely in the candlelight against his suntanned throat, and in Wendy's bewitched vision, the members of his other family by a first marriage (an accident-prone ex-wife now in an alcoholism-recovery program, a son working as a busboy and selling cocaine, a daughter who died piecemeal in a series of automobile crashes) all seemed to revolve in the pantheon of enhancing darkness around his head. They were a sort of wreckage behind him constituting his shadow, an absorbent, purifying shadow. He said, "Anyway, listen. The time will soon come when we ascend to Oregon. And I know you of course want to finish high school. But I wonder if those schools aren't just put-down factories. You know? Conspiracies of the mediocre? I have a theory that people are generally more wonderful than they realize." His voice had narrowed. She looked at him. She didn't know what he meant. She was caught in a beam from deep in his eye—or else it was only her imagination—a gem tilted in the dark.

Her mother called from the kitchen, *Wendy, I'm putting the tureen on the table. Is the heat-protecting thing on?*

"Yes, Mom." Her own voice startled her. She turned away, while Faro sauntered off in another direction, as if they'd been interrupted in kissing.

Her mother flew into the room with the tureen, blinking in

its storm of steam. "Ah, Baelthon! Baelthon is staying for dinner too," she said. "Has everyone met Baelthon? Baelthon is a RENOWNED NOVELIST." Her mother loved to crowd the stage with mute actors. The mover entered, in the embrace of a puff of novels he had supposedly written. He was wearing borrowed dry clothes, and he came in tugging his cuffs, obviously beginning to feel shruggingly comfortable among Julia Farmican's attitudes condensing everywhere on everything. Wendy grumbled (with new disgust: for he had seemed a simple-enough person, but now his being a "novelist" would involve additional layers of pretentiousness, a thickening of the plot, of a sort she'd seen a lot of in this house), speaking down into her candle's bowl, "Yes, we all know *Bael*thon." She couldn't resist putting a long sarcastic pressure on the name. He was obviously a big self-confident specimen of male averageness, but his name, when spoken aloud, involved a completely subversive lisp, on the tongue more like a flap of skin than a name, so that she almost laughed, being cruel innately. He seemed dimly aware of the web he'd walked into, and he stopped behind his chair with the unsure, stung smile of suspecting treachery.

"*Baelthon*," her mother yodeled in her way, canceling out Wendy's manner of pronouncing it (while the soup rotated in the tureen under her big ladle, shells clicking and grinding sandily) "—has the *Augean* job of digging out all this crap in this house. Isn't he *brave?*" A defeating wave rose against Wendy's heart. In an audience of guests, this dining room—its dark walls falling away in twitching candle-shadows—always rose into a Kabuki-like space, in which, flattened behind her mask, her own character was limited to grimaces and deaf shows of violence, unnoticed, in the open-ended time of injustice left by a father's death. She sat down. Her place was at the northwest corner, with the dark house-creaks and the cold draft at her back, and the ocean beyond. "Are we all here?" said her mother. "Where's Peter?—*Peter?*" she called upward into her occult horn of air.

Faro, in the head position, stroked his edge of the table. "So!" he said. "How was the consciousness-raising group? I'm sorry I couldn't make it."

Her mother sighed, lifting her spoon. "Lisa told us about her friend on a lesbian commune in Tennessee, where they're working on parthenogenesis."

"Mmm, parthenogenesis," Faro repeated with a smile. "Yum. My favorite thing."

Her mother explained, "They join two ovums. Someday we won't need sperm anymore at all."

"Imagine that."

Julia Farmican cultivated ridiculousness all around and beneath herself. She was presenting this as another of her perfect orchids of irony. She observed, "And then the human race wouldn't have men, unfortunately, dear."

"But still boy babies would pop out half the time," said Faro. "Wouldn't they?"

"No, there would be only X-chromosomes. We ladies are XX. You gentlemen are XY." She smiled at him, ladling soup into a bowl. "Only XXs would mate. All the Y-chromosomes would die out in one generation and we'd have an Amazon planet."

Faro thought about this and then he actually said piously in all seriousness, "Well, it would certainly be a better planet." He would sink in Wendy's esteem if he started pretending to be a women's libber. It was all very well for her mother to be mindblowingly beautiful *and* a women's libber. After all, this was the house where we all pretend we're not materialistic. In one second the phoniness of it all piled up on her, and in the atmosphere, her body throbbed—physically throbbed—and Faro, sensing her nastiness, laid the bough of one arm across the table on her side (it was the gesture of one of those people in *The Last Supper* painting), and he addressed everybody, "Wendy and I were just talking, about the idea of home-schooling on the Ranch. I would like to offer up, to be kicked around, the general proposition that there's a difference between training and true education. And that, in this society, schools only *train* people. Anybody wanting an actual 'education' is shamed and penalized."

Spoons clinked quietly on bowls' rims. In initiating a Topic of Discussion, he had lifted a fatherly scepter. He clasped his hands and stretched his neck to sit up taller, walking his buns in his chair. Imagining people's genitals—especially superior people's genitals—had always provided a happy irrelevancy, a sort of secret leak of justice in the world, and she supposed at this moment Faro's asshole had tightened and climbed like a spider up between his buns. His sex organ would be not one of those great gray weapons displayed in pornography, but rather a small clean bullet, cherubic, like on old statues. They're obviously made of flippity-floppy boneless stuff like earlobe-flesh that would jiggle if you filliped it. The one time she'd been close to one it was Bobby Grimaldi's, in his parents' old Thunderbird, but the glimpse she got was too shadowy and stashed-away. Faro put his elbows on the table looking expensive in the candlelight: his gray temples and kind piercing eyes. Nobody in this family was taking him up—so with patience he leaned forward and prayed with his hands and said, "Wendy, do the students have to sit in orderly rows at that public school? Are the desks arranged in rows or in a circle? Just for example."

"Rows."

He always said family dinner-table conversation was the greatest institution in society. He would never let anybody leave the table—if she got a phone call; or if *Kung Fu* was on and Peter wanted to go watch it while twink-twanking on his unamplified guitar. Dinner discussion was sacred. According to Faro, families didn't eat dinner together anymore and "communicate on the ethical matters of their day," but rather left notes for each other on the fridge or on the "goddamn infernal microwave": she knew most of the lecture by heart.

Peter, sitting down across from her, gloated, "That's why *I* went to Shambhala Academy."

Faro picked up a mussel shell from the bowl before him and began to exercise its hinge, opening it gently with two thumbs. "Training people for obedience in the work world. Lining 'em up in straight lines. Filling 'em up with what they call facts. Actually *preventing* creativity."

"At Shambhala, we didn't *have* desks. We could do anything we wanted. It was chaos."

With a faint compression between his brows, Faro, admirably, hid his opinion of the private school Peter went to. Only Wendy saw it. He ducked, as his lips kissed between the inner halves of a lifted mussel shell and his tongue started scooping upward in the valve. His eyes fell shut. She couldn't look.

"You know what my senior thesis was?" her brother asked Baelthon the mover. "The Lost Chord. There's a chord where, if you hit it, you have like an orgasm or something. But they lost it. I think they lost it in the Middle Ages."

"Peter! What a half-baked idea!" cried their mother with joy. "You never mentioned this."

Stimulated, Peter went on, "It's like, there's this one note on the bass guitar. If it's loud enough and low enough, it'll make you void your large intestine. It'll make whole audiences void their large intestines, all at once." He was aiming this information at the mover, who, for his part, smiled worriedly. "It'll make your whole anus just . . ." Peter shimmied ". . . bluagh."

"So this was just an idea I had," Faro said, as he chewed, trying to be genially deaf. "If you want to start your own private school, you know the government's one big legal requirement? Keep daily attendance! That's all! Indicating, I think, the one imperative of state-funded education: Hold 'em. Keep 'em off the streets. Baby-sit 'em. Keep 'em stupid." He picked up another mussel. "It's very easy to charter a school. If you keep attendance, do phys ed and California history, and have a driver's ed class, you can do pretty much what you want. Like Peter's Shambhala School. Require yoga or whatever."

"Nobody did *yoga*," Peter chuckled softly.

"It would be easy to charter our own school on the Open Ranch. Design our own curriculum." He scanned the table. Wendy kept her eyes down, exactly like a student trying not to get called on.

Her mother turned aside and said in a quiet melody, "Baelthon? Faro is building a new living space in the mountains, as I told you. He's calling it Open Ranch, because he wants it to have no purpose or agenda at all."

"Like for example. Wendy, you don't know anything about architecture, so *you* be the architect and *you* design the structures for the Ranch and learn all the necessary physics and mechanics and whatever. Do whatever you want. Go beyond the average suburban, roof-and-wall, post-and-beam, square houses. Why does everything have to be square? It's a learning experience. Innovate! Make mistakes! Go ahead! The little square *house* unit, you could say, is what sets up the social structure and the family structure, and then keeps us all dishonest!" He had wound up at a surprising thought, surprising to himself, and felt encouraged to go on. "Like, how about the American Indians? They all lived together in big hogans! It's hard to keep up all the social hypocrisies when you all live together like that. Am I being stupid about this? Am I being totally naive?" To his wife he lifted his wineglass, looking a little happily hopeless about the eyes.

"Of course you are, dear," she said, but with pride, teasing him larger, lifting her own wineglass in reflection of him. Wendy could see wifeliness there, in all its mysterious complexity.

"People *want* to buy a square little house, and then get a thirty-year mortgage. The whole middle class thinks it's smart. Cut up the land into parcels and say you 'own' one. So the unpropertied class can pretend they own property. It's actually a massive swindle." He bit some bread and munched, looking handsome and worried. "And then, look at the position of women inside that box: the housewife. They literally call her the 'house'-wife. So hell, you could design a habitation that completely shatters that social unit." He glanced around the table and then, because maybe he was talking in a vacuum, shrugged and began poking around for another mussel.

Baelthon, the novelist and furniture mover, spoke up, phlegm in his unused voice. "My mom divorced my father." He was offering this as an example of social progress. He was the only one at the table listening with pure belief, like dry tinder, someone very earnest and serious about everything.

"Good for her," Faro said, and he made a little swing of a fist like catching a tossed lucky coin.

The table fell silent. She couldn't eat. She'd eaten too much in town. Not participating in dinner would somehow help to excuse her from the Open Ranch, where she was too lazy and selfish and untalented to go. Her brother across the table had picked up a clam. He slanted the axis of his head before bringing his mouth, teeth-first, into the shell. Meanwhile, Baelthon had begun prodding a mussel with the points of a fork, holding it far from his eye, as if he expected to be squirted. Her very flesh tingled with the nauseous desire not to be present here; to be all alone by herself; or, ideally, to leave her body and fly invisibly free in the night as a friendless immortal goblin, from now until the end of time, and never again touch anyone or anything. Her inner wealth of hatefulness could make her skin a membrane of aches, all hectic.

Faro said, "Can I engage you all in some discussion of this? The family dinner used to be a cultural institution. Conversation is a philosophical exercise. It's an exercise in ethical evaluation of our common daily lives. But unfortunately it's a dying art, especially in California, *especially* in Marin County." He lifted another mussel shell and gloomily toasted everybody with it.

"Ah," said her brother across the table. His face had lifted into the smirk that Wendy recognized as his Inscrutable Poetry Smirk, signifying that he was about to disgorge a profound remark. He said:

"A conversation is a brick in the insane cosmic ocean."

This meaningless comment would halt all talk for a minute. He was showing off for the benefit of this novelistic Baelthon.

Faro murmured, "Yes. Good." And then he inhaled and tried again, with his hands joined and lifted, "I suppose all I'm saying, Wendy for example, is that the *unit* of the modern economy is the heterosexual monogamous 'marriage,' which in fact is a totally arbitrary convention. It's a necessary social fiction. So we live separated by houses and walls, and we learn to be ashamed of our bodies. Especially women are taught to be ashamed of their bodies. And sex is supposed to be hidden in a separate room."

"Eating is obscene," Peter quipped, keeping a sly eye on Baelthon, then addressing him more directly with a gagging leer, "People should eat alone in private, in little bathrooms. It's a bodily function," he gurgled. All of which seemed to make Baelthon feel pleasantly uncomfortable.

"Wendy, say if you designed the buildings on the Ranch and broke every rule in the book? Just say. What about that? Wouldn't that be more educational than this public school, where everybody gets out of real classes by being in the Drama Department?"

"Wendy's looking sick," Peter snerfled. "She doesn't *want* to have group nudity and all live in a hogan."

Faro glanced at his wife in complaint and surrender, and started troweling his soup, grumbling, "Socrates' guest appearance on *Laugh-In*." The smile sent back by his wife, in response, came vaguely through mists. It was strange how the Mother Superior, as Peter called her, never even seemed to quite *notice* Faro specifically, her eyelids perpetually half-lowered in a smile

86

against the sad predictability of everything, having already *had* James Farmican for a husband.

"What's that?" Peter said. There was a noise outside like a car pulling up on the gravel. Then Peter answered his own question. "It's Ed. He took the bus into San Rafael to buy a '*car*.' Now he's back with his '*car*'."

Her mother stood up. "I'll get him. I'm so glad he wasn't a minute later."

She left, and Peter started slipping down in his chair, onto his back, bringing his eyes down under the lid of Wendy's vision. He said, "Just try to get Fat Bubbula here to take her clothes off and be a free spirit. Hah! Disgust-oh-matic! She'd have to shave her navel."

"Shut up," she said quietly, even with civility, but her voice was strangely seized from within. In fact she wasn't fat. She knew she wasn't. But saying the word aloud made it stick to her in front of everybody.

"Spread the ole Gillette Foamy."

"Hey Peter, is that how you talk to your sister?"

"Go ahead, stab me with your spoon," Peter said. For indeed her hand had gripped the spoon in a fist. "Go ahead. '*Fat Girl On Rampage. Multiple Spoon-Stabbings In Seawall. Sits On Guest, Crushes Head.*'"

She flipped her bowl of soup at him. But through bad luck, all the soup landed on stupid Baelthon, who smiled.

"Okay okay okay," said Faro, usurping the role of father. His hands floated heavily out on the turbulence. "Give Belson a napkin. Here, Belson, dry yourself off."

"You're such a fucking"—her mind was suspended flailing in an empty space—"vagina dick," she came up with at last.

That made Peter think. But it also made his lips compress a dawning smile.

"I hate you," she clarified.

"I'm sorry," Peter said. "Sincerely. Please accept my apology.

I mean it. I'm sorry. You're right. I am a vagina dick sometimes."

"You are a fucking asshole."

"I'm truly sorry," Peter said, "I was only trying to humor you, I didn't mean to hurt your feelings. Don't say you hate people. That's a terrible thing to say."

"It's not funny!"

Faro said, "Peter is apologizing, Wendy."

"He doesn't mean it. He's such a phony."

"All right, this is an object lesson in exactly what I'm saying. You both love each other more than this."

Faro was directing this lecture at *her!* "*I* didn't do anything."

"What are you feeling in your heart right now?" He held an open embrace in her direction. "Honestly, honestly."

She folded her arms. She couldn't believe it. He was on Peter's side.

"In a more *conversant* environment, people wouldn't be able to hurt each other's feelings by recourse to bad values. Peter? I'm talking about bad values. Values imposed by society. Wendy, *he* shouldn't be able to make you feel bad about your body. You've internalized the belief that you have to be perfect-looking. Supposedly, you have to look like some sort of a bloody *perfect Barbie doll* to deserve love. But think about it. Barbie dolls were invented by some *man!* You lose all self-esteem if you're at all," he gestured, "unique or individual."

The devil's voice spoke in her hard neck: "I don't accept you as a guru. You're just . . . rich, that's all. You're just rich," she repeated, unable to find a better word. But that somehow summed it up, fatally. Faro's eyes went unfocused: bluer in sorrow. She had directly hurt him. She just sat still while the stain spread. Probably there was justice in her being humiliated in front of their guest, regular-featured Baelthon, whose emotional life is perfectly uncomplicated—you can tell by looking at him, he's terrified.

Lowering his eyes, Faro started to speak, slowly. "I think I do see what you mean." He laid a hand over his male heart-attack zone. "You'd be surprised." His eyes went to hers, and she looked away. "But Wendy—" A silence created a frame around his voice. It lifted the four paneled walls into consciousness. Her wish to be elsewhere right now was so intense it could almost generate a field like microwaves that would vaporize her on the spot. The arrival of Ed could be heard now in the kitchen.

Faro said, "If we could just be *honest* with each other."

"Really," her brother put in, his voice soft. "I'm sorry, Wendy. I didn't mean it. Please accept my sincere apology."

"Civilization . . . ," Faro said, leaning back, with a gesture of sadness at the civilization all around.

Peter finished for him, quoting him, "—is a veneer."

He caught Peter's eye and he winked.

◉　◉　◉

Ed had indeed bought the Mercedes-Benz, and in sitting down at the Farmican dinner table, he felt like a sweaty Technicolor actor superimposed on a black-and-white melodrama, his breath audible, his shirt sticking to his back damp from rain: he'd spent a minute checking the oil before coming inside. The engine *seemed* to have lost a little oil in the short drive over the mountain. It might have a tiny leak. But still it was a genuine Mercedes. A Mercedes' armrests and seat ask a certain posture of the driver's spine, which he recognized in himself right away, nothing like the surly slouch behind the wheel of the Peases' Ford Gremlin. On the road back, the windshield wipers had tick-tocked with a European motion over the classy old lantern-like windshield, and the upholstery, of red leather biscuits, though cracked, smelled rich. Just knowing it was sitting outside added elbow-room to his entitled space, even in here, as he shook Faro Ness's hand across the table.

He sat. Things got quiet. This dinner, its ring of pale flickering faces around the long bier, was an interrupted seance. Mrs. Farmican resettled herself at the table with the strange remark, "Baelthon looks cute in soup." To which nobody responded. Ed didn't say anything, a visitor from another aeon, in this nest of pterodactyls all differently evolved together in their isolation. The whole place, from the moment he got off the bus in town, had started right away to creep up around him feeling like one of those isolated lochs where the rumor of a foggy monster still swims. Just sitting down, he had cleaved some silence, some mysterious local hostility: he tried not to bristle too happily with the cold air he'd brought in around him—as if the knowledge of his father's suicide was invigorating. Which, in a way, it almost was. He almost climbed upon it. The man's downfall made *room* for the bastard to inherit. Or so it was possible to propose to himself inconsequentially, with an indulgence of common evil, here in this family where he would probably never be fully accepted; face it, new shoes didn't mean anything here.

Unfortunately, seafood was something he always disliked. He knew he wouldn't get far into it, put off by the smell, and by the look of it, the little yawns of death on an exposed reef. Others' spoons worked busily. After a long period of general silence—in which the room seemed almost to sway and plummet in incredible new bursts of the ocean gale outside (though the candle flames stood perfectly still), Ed, with a dutiful feeling, like trying to seize a wandering tiller, raised his voice and said loudly, making a generous fake shudder, "Boy! Whew!" And when no one quite got the import of that, he said, "It's really raining out there," and added, "It's like cats and dogs."

He was an unheard ghost. He picked up his spoon in defeat. "Great weather for ducks."

"I knew you were going to say that," said Peter with a happy sneer.

"What."

"Great weather for ducks."

"You did?"

"Oh! Say! Everybody!" Mrs. Farmican set her spoon down. "Guess what Wendy found. Some of us haven't heard this." People just kept eating. Ed at least *looked* at her. His strenuous polite attention alone was propping up a sag in this family that must have existed long before he got here.

"Wendy? Tell everybody what you found. She found her father's remains!"

"Oh, in the basement," said Peter, bored by the news. Ed had paused for a minute—but then he knew immediately it wasn't the dead body itself but rather some memorial remnant, like his ashes. It had been three years since his death.

Wendy was looking at Peter. "You knew it was there? All this time?"

"So!" said her mother, a self-blinding twinkle in her eye. "Now that we're all together again"—she slightly moved a salt-shaker, like a pawn in tribute in Ed's vicinity—"we might discuss what to do with them. If we feel sentimental about them, we could bury them in the garden and say some . . . *words*. Or Faro thought a museum might want them. The little historical society museum in town might put them on a pedestal. He would have loved that."

"Great," said Peter. He turned toward Ed to share a joke. "Put him on a pedestal. With recorded harp music. Or Muzak! Let Dad spend eternity in Muzak. On a pedestal."

Wendy had begun looking with revulsion upon Peter. Her mother laid her arm out on the table, her fingertips touching Wendy's forearm. "Well in any case, they're in the pantry now. Before we leave the old house, we might want to have a private little ceremony in the garden, for example, and bury them out there beside Flubber. Would that be the right thing?"

Peter hadn't stopped grinning, his face swimming forward, focusing his humor on Ed. "Or couldn't we suspend them over a pit of fire?"

"Peter? Certain people take things seriously. And certain people are sensitive." She turned to Wendy. "He might be very happy out there with Flubber, and that snail named Curt. Remember that snail?" She turned to Ed, apparently warming to a story of the burial of household pets. "It was the funniest thing, Edward. May I call you Edward? That's how I'll always think of you: 'Edward, male, live birth.' That's what it said on the little card at the hospital."

"Don't embarrass him," Faro said. "After a certain point in life, our mothers are forbidden cutesy comments. Isn't that right, Edward?"

"I'm not being cutesy, I'm truly sentimental. We were all living in this terrific basement in North Beach. We *invented* selfishness and irresponsibility. I do hope you forgive us, Edward. Civilization was so medieval in those days, we didn't *have* abortions then, if you can imagine, and we were just babies ourselves!"

Peter said, "How about People's Park? We could bury him in People's Park. In Berkeley." He looked around the table. He was serious.

"In public?" said Wendy. "In broad daylight?"

"We could sneak in there at night."

"You jerk," sang Wendy in a rapture of dismay.

"I'm not kidding. I'm serious."

"It's disgusting there. You yourself are always saying that's where bums pee."

"He'd love that. He'd be down there underground saying, 'Piss on me O thy bum.'" Peter opened his hands to the ceiling. "'Piss on me all the urine of thou cheap wine. For I have changeth the course of literature and wonneth the Endicott Prize, and now I'm down here getting pissed on.'"

"Peter," his mother scolded happily.

His eyes lost focus. His center of consciousness seemed to be slipping down his vertebrae toward his pelvis. "O thou bum of American insanity . . ."

Wendy said, "Mom, make him stop. He's such a fraud."

That remark snapped him back to consciousness and he looked at his sister and told her, "You don't know anything. You don't know . . ." Unable to describe everything she didn't know, he summed her up by saying simply—with a loosely affixed new grin—"Just look at you."

Faro lifted his arms. "Our two guests come from places where politeness and good taste prevail, farther east. Especially Belson. He's from Wisconsin! Edward, Belson is a novelist. Unpublished but not for long." He was directing all this information at Ed, not knowing it was a wasted effort.

"I don't read," he said.

Faro—this news seemed to make him sleepy—said, "Really."

"I'm dyslexic." He might as well plant himself centrally in the family by saying everything right off.

Wendy cried, "Hey." She was looking at the hired installer of doors. "Where'd you get those clothes?"

He didn't know he was being spoken to. Everybody looked at him, but he just kept lifting his spoon to his lips, ducking.

Then he looked up and said, "Me?"

Peter, too, leaned out to see the jeans and plaid flannel shirt. He turned on his mother: "Mom!"

"Oh, you guys, they're not sacred garments. Baelthon was *wet*."

"Did you just go in and get them out of his closet?"

"Peter, don't be so materialistic. Our very flesh is raiment to be put off." She smiled across at her new husband. Ed looked down at the low-tide pool in his bowl. Bread and butter were on the table, but he hadn't reached out and taken any, like a gentile at a meal of some religion where it was impolite to ask about their weird customs and you had to learn by watching. It was partly their own fault, in a way, if he'd come back as such a dead weight. He decided to simply be abrupt and jump right in again: "Tell me. Just for my own information. Who has"—

with a gesture upward at the house above them, he lifted his eyes to see (and for a moment the sight stopped his sentence) a timber sagging around a lengthwise crack, suspended in a mist of cobwebs—"who has *bought* the house?"

His mother said, "Oh, the poor house. Are you looking at that broken beam? It's been that way for years."

Faro looked up. "Julie! Look at that! What's it like in the room above? Is the floor depressed?" At the mention of the name "Julie," Ed found himself looking at his mother, at her profile, from a photographic hiding-place: all the years in Modesto, working at the Hillhaven Home or, before that, the Pizza Hut, eating the deep-dish pepperoni-and-mushrooms after work, picking up softball games on the weekends, which he played only angrily, unskilled at all sports—all those years suddenly collapsed to nothing. A fairy-tale feeling had begun congealing around him here, a cobwebby tickle he rubbed his face to clear. She said, "It's only a little saggy," with a tickled girlish rise in one shoulder, that mocking sequin in her eye again.

"Isn't it dangerous?" Faro was flirting with his wife. He found the dilapidation of her house sexy.

"That's the room Peter had his pottery studio in. Remember? Peter? With the wheel and the kiln that caused the little fire? That's where you made it to second base with Alison Tennis."

" 'Second base'?" asked Faro.

"Heavy petting," she explained to him. "The girl takes off her brassiere."

"I know that. I'm just pleased by your saying it." They gazed at each other and then they started lifting their soup spoons again, in unison. Ed woke up with the unsure feeling that they were evading his question. So he asked it again. "But who is *purchasing* the house? The house has been sold, right?"

She said, "A church is buying it."

Peter looked up through the curtain of blond hair and said, "A church?" The girl, too, had a swindled expression. Obviously no one had yet asked or even bothered to wonder.

Faro said, after a sigh and a soft jab at his soup, "It's really just a tax arrangement. It's all very technical. It's still our house. This church will own it only on paper. This church *exists* only on paper. It's all an elaborate ruse." He smiled.

Of course, anybody who bought this house would tear it down, Ed could see that. And then develop ocean-view condominiums—it was obvious, the place was crying out for it. For that matter, the whole town had unexploited possibilities. It could be another Malibu or someplace.

Peter said, "How much are they paying? A lot?"

His mother said, "Oh, ick, Peter, we don't discuss money. Let's get back to the topic of James's purloined holy vestments. That was a happy discussion."

Faro reached over and softly rapped on Peter's wrist. "It'll be a preserve for poets," he said with a wink. He met his wife's eyes again. "A sort of rookery. Or what do they call those things where doves live? A columbarium? For poets."

"Well!" said Mrs. Julia Farmican Ness, in a new tone. Her thin, bare arms glided out over the tablecloth on either side, ironing. "We have a third member of the younger generation to cast his vote. Isn't it interesting having a newly discovered brother? Isn't it interesting *being* a newly discovered brother?" her voice rose to soprano, her arms levitated.

Ed looked around. They were looking at him. Resolving to get off on the right foot, he said, perfectly amicably, "I hope it doesn't put anybody's nose out of joint that I'll be inheriting a third of Farmican's estate, because of the remarriage."

His mother laughed, and Ed loved the sound of it, it made him magically sleepy. "Oh, Edward, rest assured, you've fallen in with a very metaphysical group. We concentrate more on philosophy," she gestured to herself, "and poetry," she gestured to Peter, "and . . . ," gesturing to Wendy but unable to think of a distinguishing vocation for her, she let her fingers make a general sprinkling motion over her.

". . . Eating," her brother said. She laid on him a distilled pissy expression.

"However, as you all might already know," Faro said, straightening up taller and pulling on a cuff (he was about to say something portentous), "it may turn out that there's not much money left to distribute. Net estate value." He was speaking to his wife, but the words were intended for the children. Ed looked at him and decided, in an instant, that he was rich. Some sort of suntan lay upon him.

"How do you mean?" Ed said. "I got a letter from her lawyer."

"Those were my lawyers, actually. But you see, there may not be much left." He gestured slightly around at all the broken junk. "There've been a lot of years of what you'd have to call negative cash flow."

Mrs. Farmican put down her spoon, closed her eyes, and began to sing, tunelessly, "Hmm, hmm-*hmmm*, HMM-Hummm! Ommmm. Om Mani Padme Hum, Om Mani Padme Hum . . ."

"It's complicated," Faro said, nodding toward the humming woman. "Finance companies were foreclosing on the house to recover their losses. But the house has gone so far, it proved impossible to sell. Impossible to put on the market at all. We'd have to *pay* somebody to take it. It's in a hole. The realtors' euphemism was 'deferred maintenance.'" He tilted his head. "So you see."

Mrs. Farmican stopped chanting, opened her eyes and looked around blinking, refreshed. It was distinctly aphrodisiac, her way of constantly adjusting veils around herself. Within the many veils, the light in her eye was *self*-mocking.

Faro said, in love with her, "Because certain people prefer to live in cloud-cuckoo land, certain other people have to watch cash flow, down here on the degrading Wheel of Karma. The Wheel of Meat, as the late Mr. Farmican put it."

Her lids half-sank. "Oh but my third eye sees everything, and knows all." She twinkled at Ed, in some way without looking directly at him.

"However, Edward, nobody is going to go hungry. For example, I'm buying the land for the Open Ranch in the name of the Farmican children. Your name, now too, will go on the deed."

"What ranch?"

"Ah! It's called Open Ranch. It's up in Oregon. We were just talking about it. It's going to be a kind of a community, but that's the wrong word because even *it* has Orwellian connotations these days. Ranch is really the word. Or just *place* is really the best word. It's just a *place*. Briefly, your sister was just making the point that I'm too wealthy, which I am, and it just seems to me that the world is going to hell in a handbasket, so I'm trying to plant a seed. A place of creativity outside the goddamn cruel marketplace." He lifted his shoulders to make a gentle cone of his arms funneling down to his cupped hands. "A seed."

"Is there a large quantity of acreage involved?"

"No. A few thousand. It's in Oregon in the Goshen Valley. It's going to be a very *open* space."

"Open," said Ed.

Faro spoke as he chewed. "Let me explain it. Want to hear my speech? I plan to support it but never rule it. Be more like a janitor. Or be like God, everywhere at work but nowhere visible. Let creativity manifest itself. Don't let the marketplace nexus penalize people right away. For example, look. Here's somebody" (in the palm of his hand) "who might want to work on developing elegant technologies. By elegant I mean working with rather than against nature. Or here's somebody else who might want to write an essay about it first! Or a poem! Maybe the poem naturally has to come first! Give people resources!

And stop judging!" Ed felt himself stretched thin under Faro's maniacal gaze. He suddenly, unwillingly, liked Faro: creative types are so tender and vulnerable, and they get this light in their eye. Faro broke off and flopped back in his chair. "I look around and I see people living with artificial crap. I see no shared ethic. Everything comes vacuum-sealed in plastic"—his fingers stiffened and wiggled—"and people just say in resignation, *Oh, well, I guess that's how it comes.* It seems to me that right now we're in a historical *moment.* We're at this peak of affluence. So before everything slips back down to the usual greed, here's this *moment,* to be *seized.*"

"Oh!" Wendy said. She slid her chair back with a scrape. "I think I just heard the tower move." She looked around at each face. "Excuse me for interrupting, but I think the tower's moving."

Everybody listened. Peter said, "I didn't hear anything."

"I'm sure I heard it. It is raining pretty hard out there."

"You people go check it out," said Faro, subsiding in his chair. "Your mother and I will sit here and drink while the whole place slowly sinks in the west."

◉ ◉ ◉

So they went outside, and when they got around under the tower, the problem was obvious. Three big iron house-jacks were supposed to hold up the corner of the house; but one of them, the largest, had long ago lost its footing in the slope and fallen over, which was gladdening to Ed: he took off his jacket and rolled up his sleeves and decided to go ahead and get a badge of mud on each knee of his genuine Sansabelt slacks. "I need the flashlight on this."

Wendy said, "Wait, shine it up there."

The light flipped up under the house foundation on a dry inner slope of dirt. There was a slew of miscellaneous objects.

An unzipped sleeping bag, a twisted blanket, a pair of maracas, binoculars, some muddy magazines, a foil tray lidded as "Pepperidge Farm Carrot Cake," plastic bags that would hold granola and dried fruit, two surfboards stacked in a sandwich, a jar of vitamin C pills, books. Somebody had been living here, some homeless person, and Ed got angry, angry on behalf of the family, to the point of physical sickness. Human nests like this are so obscene in the exposure of a twitching flashlight. "Let's just rake all that shit out of there." He weeded out, first of all, a cardboard box printed GENUINE FRYE BOOTS as he started scrambling up.

"No, don't," said Wendy, "it's Merlin."

They *knew* this homeless person.

"Shine it up there." She grabbed to guide the flashlight beam. It shone on an electric guitar lying facedown. "It's the Stratocaster."

"Wow," said Peter. "It's probably ruined." Peter and Wendy had briefly looked at each other in some extrasensory communication. Ed just waited. In Modesto all his life he had always taken control by talking, by using his own obnoxious *voice* to hold things down in place around him; but he was starting to see that this family, its dreamlike logic, would shut him up for a while. He stood there holding the FRYE BOOTS box, its lid lifting. Inside was a rubber stamp, a few papers, miscellaneous junk. He closed it back up.

"The neck is warped," Peter said, of the guitar.

A moment of silence. The rain was letting up, which made the rivulets louder.

Baelthon the mover cleared his throat and asked, "This tower isn't . . . " and he made a feeble gesture imitating its fall.

"No, no, it's just settling. The slope goes down to the ocean from here and the rain runs off."

The roar of runoff was mounting louder everywhere in a quiet gap in the storm when the bright moon came out. All the other siblings were cowering slender and small, unwilling to come near the big rusty jack in the mud. So Ed stepped forward, readiness to work enlarging his body. "If you'll put the light in there, I'll get this jack back up on its stand. Is there a shovel?" He handed the box aside to Wendy.

"I don't think there's a shovel," said Peter.

A flinty plate of rock was lying right there, which would work fine, and he picked it up and started scraping at the ground to make a flat footing. The house-jack had spikes on its underside to stab and hold the ground. This would actually make a good solid footing. This earth was rocky and hard-packed. The rest of them were spectators. He tipped the house-jack back upright and dug its one great cleat into the tough soil, this blue clay-and-flint soil he'd have to get used to now it was where he came from. To get in close, he had to scramble around to the far side and get his elbows in the mud, and he put his foot down in a swampy area of gathered water. The muck sucked the good new lustrous loafer off his foot and—off-balance—his stockinged foot swung out away and then landed in the deep puddle.

Baelthon said, "Do you raise this part?" He was picking at the jack with a finger.

"Damn." He couldn't help putting his weight on his unshod foot, which sank in the mud. There was a half-second delay before cold water flooded the knit of his sock. But the jack was upright. A heavy steel ring could be turned to climb a central core of screw threads. A hole was there to insert a pole for leverage. Crouching lower and grasping a handful of weed-tops on the slope, he pulled out his painted foot and swung it around, dripping, into the toe of the cemented-down loafer. "Damn."

"What," said Peter.

"I lost my shoe for a second. We have to turn that big screw thing." Baelthon and Peter moved in and took a turn at revolving the threaded iron ring. Ed stepped back outside the circle of work. His forearms were muddy, and he held them up surgeon-wise, as in supplication. And then, with a stab of inner warmth, as the rain started to fall again, watching them work, he realized something: It was true, he was somebody's brother. The idea filled him secretly in the dark, so that he found himself almost liking the feeling of rainwater dripping under his shirt collar. He just stood there, too happy to move. Others' hands crowded to grapple the rusty jack in the shadow, screwing it upward to the point of making contact with the big timber of the foundation, and Ed, speaking in the throat's grip of his happiness, said, "You need a board or something, to distribute the weight"— because the jack, rising, would have merely punctured the house's mushy timber.

Peter said, "There's that surfboard. Why not?" he told Wendy. "It's not his. It's some other old board."

"What's it made of?"

"It's the old-fashioned kind. They weigh a ton."

Baelthon started crawling in under the house to wrestle the—obviously heavy—surfboard out into the open.

Wendy said to Peter softly, "This is where he gets in." When Peter didn't answer, she added, "I wonder if there's some kind of trouble."

Peter hugged himself in the cold. "It's ironic, supporting this old house with a surfboard. Isn't it ironic? Or symbolic?"

He was asking Ed, his head weaving in amusement over those slippery concepts, beloved of English teachers at Modesto High School, where all the corridors were ruled by the sweaty steel smell of lockers, which was also the smell of the mysterious, unremovable mask blocking Ed "Pease's" big face from ever understanding anything.

Baelthon was cranking the jack, and he told him, "That's enough. We just want to support it. If it's making contact, it's fine."

Baelthon stood up, and then everybody was just standing there.

Peter told Wendy, "We should leave everything the way it was."

"We have to bring the guitar, though."

"I'll get it," Baelthon said, and he ducked.

"Shine the light," Peter said. "Oh, it's wrecked. The pickups are all rusty. Let's get it inside." It was handed across to Wendy, who cradled it in her arms, and they all began to mill and re-group on the slippery slope. And then in single file they trudged around the corner—Ed last of all—beneath the tall house in the rain, a cortege attending a corpse. Over his shoulder, Peter spoke to Ed in his clever tone: "Electrified musicality: the bane of our resident gnome's existence." He seemed to indicate the guitar.

"Mm," said Ed. An education: that was the most important thing he'd missed, not being here in this family. In the second grade, under the chalk-dusted claws of Miss Deercoop, when he was struggling with the first signs of dyslexia, he developed the mythological idea that his reading ability had been taken away from him as a sort of punishment. And so it was his as-signment in life to go forth and find out what he was being punished for, a strange boy already, already suspicious of every-thing, even before he learned he was adopted, on the play-ground his arms clamped to his sides in a stealthy hunchback. Wendy, ahead, was obviously related to him. Her motions made sense to him, her long, low-crotched stride across the lawn, her hip held still at the center of her body's motion, her one shoulder more knitted-up than the other: it was *his* body carrying the guitar into the house. Every Christmas at the Pease house in Modesto, Frank Pease would go out to the garage, where the Christmas tree was stored behind the spare tires, and he would assemble it quietly, with little clanking sounds, sometimes picking a moment when nobody else was home. It happened to be around Christmas that his wife, Irene, had the last of her several miscarriages; and Ed, about four then, began secretly bestowing offerings to The True Pease Child at the base of the tree every night, slices of Wonder Bread he had pressed and rolled into little sweaty pills, gray with palm-grime, as gifts to the floating fetus who, at night while the family slept, nosed through the Christmas tree's shining steely branches, foraging, its motions in air like a seahorse's, moving in squirts through space, its ears and eyes never closing throughout eternity, indeed gazing into an oceanic eternity in total omniscience, an unborn fetus's eyes being lidless. Then later his offerings were found under the tree, and Ed was in trouble for wasting perfectly good food. His father told his mother, "Don't ask *me* where these ideas come from."

Well, they came from his flesh. That was always the problem, his flesh. It was some other family's flesh, olive-greener and firmer than the Peases' ham-pink tissue. But now he was here. In single file, guitar in the lead, they entered the side door, and Baelthon drifted to one side, while Ed followed them, limping politely for the mud on one hoof, into the warm, dry library, where his sister sat on the couch with the guitar lying across her lap. So, then, when she said, "I'm sorry, you guys, but I have to give it a decent burial," the strange idea made some sense to him. It, too, was in his flesh. "I can't see this guitar go in a smelly old garbage can," she added.

For an isolated minute nobody spoke—the three suspended souls swung slowly in the room—until Wendy and Peter came around telepathically to the same thought. "He's been doing so well, lately," she said. She was referring to the Merlin who had built a nest under the house. "There must be some kind of trouble."

Peter swung on Ed. "Let's smoke some pot."

◉　◉　◉

And so Ed found himself in Peter's basement room, crept over by the ugly khaki smell of marijuana, the smell of lostness, the cloud God temporarily can't see you through. He'd always hated marijuana, the feeling of surging stupidity. The few times he'd tried it, it invariably made him sit in the corner puzzling over some single idea like a handful of wet grout in his palm. But tonight, just this once, only because saying no would have seemed unfriendly, he came downstairs and dipped his head and sat on the bed cross-legged with Peter and—barefoot now, his muddy loafers upstairs on the kitchen floor—he watched as the flakes, sliding around in the bottom of a shoebox, were pinched together and drizzled over the rolling paper (Peter talking all the while), crouching with him under the feeling of a hut, and he started accepting the wrinkled-up little marijuana cigarette as it was passed to him, the little cosmic kiss, and immediately the sinking feeling began in his spine, it was hourglass-sand, trickling vertebra-to-vertebra in stacked dimples. Peter was trying to say something. His hand was making a dice-shaking gesture as he tried to cough up a thought while holding the smoke in his lungs, and he said at last, "You know," speaking in the withheld belch that would release almost no smoke, "I wrote this." He was pointing toward the song on the radio. "Dylan copyrighted it under his own name. But I wrote it. I told him he could have it. I believe in being generous about artistic creations."

Ed dug his shoulders around in a shivery feeling. A shudder just from *thinking* of dustballs made him hunch and move nearer to the electric space heater with its six fat bars glowing red and buzzing. Wendy had gone to bed, declining any pot, which made *him* all the more mistaken and entrapped here. Upstairs, his suitcases were still standing in the corner of the kitchen, seeming to hold zipped-up the big uncouth question *What is the Cornucopia Resort/Casino of Void, Nevada, and how much is it worth.*

"Who is Dylan?" Ed said, the words strangely clotted. A whole feathery chandelier of light clashed in his eyelashes. Peter didn't answer for a long time. Ed began to wonder if he had actually voiced the question, or if instead it was reverberating in that echo chamber where unspoken thoughts are churned and churned in rehearsal.

Peter said at last, "You don't know *Bob Dylan?*" And then, in the way of stoned conversations, the exchange was suddenly over, with a shrug and a grin.

But then it wasn't over: Peter hoisted his smiling face into range and said, "You don't know Bob Dylan." He leaned forward off the bed and drew a floor-standing ashtray nearer. On its rim he sculpted the ash of the marijuana cigarette—all the while smiling fondly over an inward thought.

Ed looked at his own foot. Drowned-looking ankle skin.

Peter handed him the cigarette again. "Dylan wears these wild shirts," he said, and he stuck out his belly and swung his arms to embody a wild shirt. "I wrote most of the songs on that one big album. But naturally that's a secret. You have to promise not to tell anybody. That's a major secret. A million copyright lawyers would *shit.*"

Ed was smiling rather generally out at Peter, his smile veering. He knew he ought to respond somehow to this story. But ages had passed and still he hadn't said anything. He wasn't holding up his end of the conversation. The last thing he'd said was *Who is Dylan,* which felt like ten minutes ago, so many strobe replications of the world had intervened in the meantime. Fortunately Peter was forgiving of his paralysis—or unnoticing of it—chuckling and smiling to himself over a memory, scratching at a freckle of fallen marijuana on his knee. He lit a match, lifted the cigarette, and made of his face a fierce mask, to draw in smoke. He was fascinating to watch. At the pinnacle of his lungs he said, in strangulation, "I inherited my father's genius," then expelled air. "There's a natural tendency for the survivor to blame themselves. But *we* didn't. You know who's to blame? Truly? Society is to blame. I'm not coming out. I'm going to go on living here. I don't care what they say." He offered the smoldering little twig to Ed.

Ed accepted it. In general probably, most people who kill themselves have some good reason, like because they were weak and they honestly knew it. Ed stood up, impatiently. And in rising he'd reached a new altitude where the air is clear.

"Anyway, you have to keep the Dylan thing a secret," said Peter. "Probably a million lawyers would come around and sue me"—he gestured backward at the hosts of lawyers, and his hand fanned out like a deck of cards, spilled and scooped. "Where are you going?" he said, looking up at Ed.

Ed didn't know. But he knew one thing: he had made it here, to the profound 415 area code. He'd been unfaithful to the casino for this one night, but in the morning he'd be fine again, having passed this night of confusion and dark germinations, fallen into a sweaty pouch. Where would his bed be? He could picture it as lamp-lit, a soft raft. This house kept unfolding. Everything here smelled like inside an accordion. The basement corridor led only into deeper cold, further exhalations of darkness, this house itself a deck of cards spilled-and-scooped, where no one had asked him what his plans were, no one seemed to *have* any plans, no one had even asked him whether he was staying the night, or told him where there was a spare bedroom, or (as Irene Pease would have done) laid out a fresh towel on a crisply new-sheeted, lamp-lit bed.

The stairs were easy to find. Also, they were so steep they allowed him to use his hands too on the treads. And then upstairs, there was a right turn, into the sensation (though not the reality) of a warm surface against his right cheek, and the general feeling that his mind had oozed into an upholstery crease, taking on the stain of the fabric, his cheek dented by the print of lost crumbs. It was shameful, to have gotten stoned in this house and groped face-first into this feed-bag dead-end.

"Hello, I'd like to speak to Harris Carlisle. Harris! You'll never guess who this is."

It was Faro Ness, across a hallway. His voice reached Ed by being bounced in a Z, off two walls. He had to stand perfectly still to appreciate the wonderful clarity in everything. From a vantage point outside the river of time, Ed himself had been expecting this conversation; his ears had already been shaped to the sound of this voice, the whole world cupped, all of time-space contracted in a dewdrop, to optically focus this voice. "... *It's Lansford Ness*," said Faro. "*Yes! My lawn chair at net position! We're all entitled to a second chance. What time is it? It's still a decent hour there, isn't it? Well, I've got something for you. Are you still in the book business? Great, great. Congratulations. It was predicted by the auspex.*"

Ed's knees had met with the edge of a coffee table. They had been pressed against it for some time, actually. Then he was obeying, inwardly, an unavoidable gyroscopic tilt, revolving to sit down on it. He had faced the fact that he was lost. He was barefoot. And at this moment the job assigned to him by fate was to eavesdrop on a telephone conversation. It would be a part of his education: How the Rich Talk.

"*Do you think you'd be interested in some poetry by the son of James Farmican? Farmican's son writes poetry. Actually, I just recently married Farmican's widow, Julia Buckley. Yes, great, thank you. Oh, a quiet life. Early bedtime. I'm old now. Gray hair. Pot belly. We all look a little better on the West Coast. It's a bed of crimson joy, Harris. But tell me now, what can you do with this? I don't know much about publishing. Oh, I see. And you take a percentage of course. So what do you think? His name is 'Farmican,' so it would say 'Farmican' on the dust jacket. Isn't that a million book sales right there? As I say, I'll understand entirely. He's a great young person, he could use a kick, and I just thought I'd ask. Kids need help getting started, especially artists. I haven't seen any poems, but I assume. Great. In that case, I'll get back to you. I appreciate this, Harris. Nice to talk to you again. Again, congratulations. Is that your office number? Okay. Of course. Yes. It's a pleasure. Thanks. Night.*" He hung up and walked away down a corridor.

The ancient feeling, that he didn't belong anywhere on earth, swept over Ed again from its corner of dark irrelevancy.

His forehead had come to rest in his hands. Through an upward chute he sent up his usual fill-in-the-blanks prayer, *trapping* "God" in the usual vague covenant, whatever-it-is. And then he stood up, entitled to hope again.

And then his mother appeared out there in the hallway. Not Irene Pease but the mythical goddess. She held a bunched-up quilt in her arms, and a pillow. "I've been looking for you. Come on. I'll show you your room." She turned.

While his face quickly gelled behind her back, she led him through the house, through a misplaced parlor that, surprisingly, connected to the living room. All this time, he hadn't been lost. His arms and legs swung normally. His body had reassembled itself under her vision. She was saying, "The room that would have been yours all these years, I suppose."

His suitcases were at the foot of the stairs. They had been moved. Now somebody knew, how heavy one of them was with canned goods. They would think it was stupid.

She stopped and stood. Hugging the quilt, she faced him. He had to look off to one side. Bringing his eyebrows down lowered a barrier against the headache of possible emotions. She said, "There's so much to say, it'll take years. You won't believe this but I've missed you. Does that sound strange? Can you see how that might be? When you've given a child up for adoption, you mustn't interfere with the child's new life. Now we have a lot of work to do. We've lost a lot of time."

She seemed to be talking in zigzags. Or maybe that was an effect of the marijuana. She was unbelievably pretty. He looked away again. She went on, "Memory becomes a more important force as you get older. Memory becomes more of a substantial reality. So-called 'reality' becomes less substantial. When you came along, I was very popular and happy and lucky, and all *that* can seem important. All the Ten Thousand Things. Even 'happiness' is just one more of the Ten Thousand Things."

He scowled and shrugged, pooling his mind to the smallest disk possible because the only way to get through these first en-

counters was without thinking too much about the consequences of everything and then panicking. She was looking at
him, thinking about him.

"Would you say . . ." She touched him on the shoulder and
turned and started leading the way up the stairs. He picked up
his suitcases. "Would you say that life has been good for you?
With Frank and Irene Pease? I know that's a rather large, sim-
plistic question, but."

". . . Yes," he said, as he followed her. "Yes it has." And then
the truth entered him easily, that it *had* been good. He missed
Irene Pease. He actually wanted to call her, babyishly, but of
course wouldn't. At least the Peases were normal. He wouldn't
have *wanted* to grow up here, where everything was like a big
cold stage set, the scene of a suicide.

"I suppose you know how your father died," she said. Her
mind had slid to cover his thought.

"Yes," he said. And then he added—because it would be
best to speak the words aloud, early, among these walls—"He
shot himself."

She looked over her shoulder at him as she moved on. They
got to the top of the stairs.

Then he remembered. He did hear something once about a
famous idealistic poet who died by his own gun in a coastal
cupola. It was a few years ago. His father had been famous. His
father had been in *Time* and *Newsweek*. How can glory look so
squalid? With its broken furniture held together by bungee
cords, with its cheap fish soup like Mexicans eat?

At the top of the stairs she turned left, then left again. In the
wall was a door, where there seemed only room for a closet. But
it led to a large bedroom with a window and a fireplace: a small
fire was already burning. "I've been thinking a lot, Edward," she
said. "And I suppose you have to learn to forgive me. But there's
also self-forgiveness. I have to forgive myself. I can be objective
and *see* that. You know, lost time is the only real waste. You
might have the totally wrong idea that we gave you up for some

good reason. Do you suppose—" She dumped the quilt on the bare mattress; she was standing before the fire and it lit a golden frizz on her hair. "Do you suppose a mother's love can go *back* in time?" She was so distant, she was talking more to herself. "Do you know what I mean? How time can be broken up and reconstructed in memory? To have more useful memories? I mean I'm talking about how time is basically unreal."

She was looking at him. It made his gaze fall to one side again.

He would have to go on saying as little as possible for a while, to conceal how slow he was, compared with these people. They didn't know that about him yet. But he was stubborn, too. And he was honest. They didn't know that yet, either. And those two qualities are all you need, honesty and stubbornness.

She sighed, it seemed happily. "We all pass before each other's eyes. It's too bad, how we only get some things by looking back. Oh, I'm talking silly." She put her hands on his shoulders. "I want us all to work on building memories. When you get older you'll see about memory: there isn't much difference between things you do experience and the things you wished. We've got some time." She gave him a priestess's kiss on the forehead and left.

◉　◉　◉

The jar of ashes couldn't stay in the hall closet. Wendy knew that. The space under the bed might be better, if still not permanent. Nothing was permanent anymore. In her bedroom she got down on her knees and started pulling things out, a box of mismatched socks with a hair band; magazines; half a roll of Wild Cherry Life Savers giving off the scent of Rachel Feinman's entire personality so ruthless; an ancient stale paperback *Everything You Always Wanted to Know About Sex** covered with lint-halos and page-embedded granules, spread-eagled wide open in rigor mortis at "The Butterfly Flick"; her guilt-creating old zither; the checkers game she and her father had been playing before he died, its red and black pieces still lying exactly where they'd left them, a testament to the law of inertia and her own delicate maladjustment in the world. As she levitated it out, she kept it level. Not one piece slid. Farther back was her sleeping bag held together by safety pins with hunters and dogs on its crappy flannel lining. She was beginning to get the necessary migrant feeling. She'd eaten almost nothing at dinner. The pang of virtue was in her stomach. She rolled on her hip to stand up and go out in the hallway for the jar of ashes. To carry the vessel, one empties the mortal body of feeling.

The jar was gone. The closet shelf held nothing. Somebody had taken it.

This could be a deliberate act of mischief. Or, more likely, it was somebody's mistake. Somebody had thought the jar was worthless and thrown it out: it looked like just a Tang jar. In that case, it could still be recovered. It would be in a trash can somewhere.

That should have been a calming explanation, yet her voice climbed like a tarantula in her throat as she shouted, from the top of the main stairs, *"Who was here?"* then held herself perfectly still in the web of suspicions. She could hardly go around asking people point-blank, it was too absurd, the way she'd taken personal custody of it. Its very existence, a grail of burned remnants, was too completely surrealistic to even mention.

She stood at the top of the stairs just listening, to the historical silence of the house with no doors—and then turned back to her room—where she kicked off her waxy old clothes and, naked in the cold, in a quick convulsion like Houdini underwater, she pulled on the thermal long-underwear she used for pajamas. She could see herself in the windowglass. Too edgy to go to bed, too robbed-feeling, she was instead outfitted now to climb out the window and down the drainpipe barefoot in the rain. Her reflection appeared full-length, her body covered entirely in the waffle-texture from wrists to ankles. Turning in the light, she saw Venus de Milo's curves on her behind, helped by her standing on tiptoe, the single lightbulb casting a planetary shadow over its curves, curves men would sacrifice to touch. Or so it was interesting to imagine, alone standing on tiptoe, the erotic seraph under her baggy clothes was always so surprising to release, a jackknife: she watched her body fold and dive, out of sight, to crouch with the checkers-board on the floor.

Where she began Scotch-taping the pieces to the board. The whole thing would have to be transported within a few days. Taped down, the pieces wouldn't slide. To make doubly sure, she was fastening them under *crosses* of tape. Her father (red) was in a position to jump her; but that same red piece—a doubled-up "king"—could then be jumped by her own black piece, which would then itself be kinged. He always arranged to lose, strategically always in retreat, sitting across from her squinting and munching, tossing in his waltz of tics amidst cigarette smoke, clearing his throat every thirty seconds. In her memory the specific features were decaying. Soon all that remained would be the choreographic diagram of the tics, the wisps of smoke, the strategy of the checkers game, his way of losing to rebalance the universe. She used to wish, childishly, that a message today might be read in the board, something crucial he could tell her across the barrier of time and death.

"Wendy?"

It was Faro. She slid the board under the bed.

"I hope I'm not disturbing you. Is it okay if I come in?"

She got to her feet and hung her head.

"This must be the unfortunate guitar."

"That's just the case. We put the guitar in the ballroom."

"The 'ballroom,'" he said with a chuckle of wonder. He'd brought his glass of red wine to hold defensively before him, his maleness bulking obscene in her bedroom, the froggy spring in his thigh muscles sheathed in tight jeans, the very masculine armored belly above his groin, gray hair showing in his shirt-collar where the sprigs lifted his shirt away with the force of fizz. Her eyes were driven away. It was obvious what was happening. They'd been sitting around over their wine talking about her; about her insulting behavior at dinner. And they had decided that, as her stepfather now, *he* should be the one to go up and have a talk with her, about "her attitude." She *liked* sitting in straight rows in class and not getting called on, she didn't want to be a genius, she liked her friends at that school where mediocrity was encouraged. When everybody went to Oregon, she could stay and finish the semester, living in Rachel Feinman's garage, where there was a couch to sleep on. Karma Johnstone had stayed there when she ran away from home for a while. Last week, just as a test, she mentioned the idea to her mother. But her only response had been to mutter, drowsily in distraction, *Oh how fun*, which made the whole idea more possible than she'd meant. She couldn't imagine herself living on Faro's ranch. She couldn't picture herself sitting at a huge slanty drafting table on a tall stool, making sketches in blue pencil. Or whatever his picture of it was. She didn't want to be intellectual or brave or liberated; she didn't want to be anything. "Hm," he said in approval of her room. His wineglass went out from his chest to make a helicopter trip over the constantly churning plot. "Very comfortable." She drifted back farther from him in her waffle-leotard, in this breaking-up world where floes separate and carry people off in different directions. The weak or unlucky ones—that is, the obstinate, the dull, the faithful—end up on a couch in Rachel Feinman's garage, where the concrete floor is so cold at night you can't set a bare toe on it, beside Rachel's mother's BMW or, more often, beside its intimate oilstain. The couch cushions there, made not of batting but of big foam-rubber sandwiches, had a treacherous way of compressing during the night and slowly tilting to dump you off; but you could lodge a hand and an ankle in the crack, to stay on. Rachel's mother was a rep for several different wineries, so she was never home, gone with her clinking canvas bag. When Karma was living there it was fun, the TV was always on, the phone was constantly off the hook, and popcorn was popped every night, the Jiffy-Pop foil moon rising huge.

"So listen, can I sit down?" Faro was circulating backward. She too had backed up, against her desk, lifting her bottom to hook it over the desk-edge. She looked down, forming inwardly a question about the jar of ashes with a Tang label, but then she put the idea away.

He said, "I've come up here because—I think I was pretty thoughtless and insulting at dinner."

Of course *she* was the insulting one. His reversing the blame was, typically, infinitely strategic.

"This thing about my being 'merely rich.' Well, I have to hand it to you, Wendy. Money can be stultifying. You obviously know that. But I want your help, rather than your judgment. You see? It's hard for me to squirm out of the role of authority figure around here. Obviously in some way I'm supposed to be playing the role of 'Father' in this space." He poked his shoulders around. It was true, everything he said within these walls was a sort of audition—and so now he shrank in her sight, as he lowered his head and took a big gulp of his wine, shrank as he had been shrinking in her mother's sight, gradually to dwarf-size. He couldn't lift his eyes to her. Wendy's revealed *body* was forcing his eyes away, in thermal underwear an undressed mannequin, her breasts a shelf. He said, glowering at the floor, "You have to see that you're an authority figure, too."

She looked offstage and rolled her eyes in fake agony and shifted, tied to this stake. Her hands supported her behind her back. He had started addressing a space next to the supernatural form of her, unable to face her body. She pitied him and enjoyed it: that's how nasty she was turning out to be. Strangest of all, her nipples hardened with this ascendancy above him. In self-revision, she folded her arms again. One waffle-textured thigh crossed over the other. He would have no idea that she was watching him fishily through the Instamatic-viewfinder of inconsequential fantasy, that her new *body* wanted to swim up to his regard.

"Anyway . . ." He took a curious poke at a dirty old plaster-and-gauze cast on the table, in the shape of her elbow, which had always floated around her room ever since she broke her arm in fourth grade, frayed and dirty, illustrated by all her fourth-grade friends in colored pen. "Anyway, I just wanted to let you know. That I'm aware I've been caught in one of my usual conceits. Patronizing people from on top of my big pedestal. Because, see"—his hands flubbed in embracing this idea, and he dropped them—"the psychosexual dynamic I want here in this family is *not* for me to be the father figure. *Not* for me to have a parent-child relationship with you. But to have a sibling relationship. These are new times." He looked at her for a second and smiled: he was handsome. He was simple-hearted. He meant all this. That was what her mother saw. "This is what my Ranch is all about. At a certain phase of life, you want to stop being so selfish and give a gift." His hands delivered air out toward her, in almost an embrace. A withering embrace. Because what he couldn't have known was how peculiarly undeserving *she* was. She *liked* all the barriers, the walls, the selfishness. Something had gone nicely wrong in her, and the spinal chi energy of her mother's Buddhism that was supposed to flow up from the earth got stuck in her: the congestion of fat around her mysterious groin, the dense little headache behind her eyes, the buildup of tissue under her weird conical nipples now smothered by her forearms, the anger that could clog her very flesh, everything about her stood before him as evidence of negativity in creation, accumulating matter as if by some electrical rule. Men are different. They seem totally different. They're just camels.

He was waiting. She said at last, "I'll try designing buildings if you want, but I don't think I can live there. I've been thinking about it."

"You don't think you can live there?"

"I don't know." Now she'd stepped in it.

"Wendy, why not?" Now he was hurt.

"I just really don't think I'm the type. And I have to finish school. I'm only a sophomore!" for some reason her voice rose up almost weepy on this stupid subject of finishing school. She shifted her weight to the other foot.

"Oh, that school is the essence of this whole system. What they call an English class involves nothing more than watching old movies. They're just marking time baby-sitting you, waiting for you all to get out and start in the labor force."

"Movies are a significant cultural artifact." The words came by inspiration, quoted from somewhere. Clichés are the infallible coins adults pass around. Defeated by it, he sighed.

He was thinking, trying to come up with a new angle of attack. He shook his head. Then he said, "Wendy, you say you're 'not the type.' That just seems so sad. It's so self- . . . self-*diminishing*!"

"Oh no. It's not self-diminishing." In fact it was the opposite, it was a profound kind of selfish egotism, truly invisible to somebody like him, of his generation.

"We can be any 'type' we want," he said, innocent as a Christian, straightening his spine and getting a little taller. "Don't you see?" When he grinned, a hard dimple delved into one cheek, and his eye was gripped by a very nice knuckle of tanned creases. She could see how her mother was attracted to him. She refolded her arms. He was her suitor in this room, struggling toward deserving her.

"I can't design any buildings. I don't know anything about that. It's all so contrived. You're just thinking things up."

"Thinking things up?"

"For us to do."

He looked at her, then looked away. He admitted, "I suppose I am. Partly. In a way."

She said, but too quietly, "Your Ranch will be fine," and then she was swept by a wave of self-pity. If she went to live in Rachel's garage she knew what would happen: her mother would send along helpful newspaper clippings, ugly clothes she didn't want, books about Eastern religions, chipped cooking utensils missing their handles.

Faro was frowning. He seemed to be deciding she was right, she was never meant to be free-spirited or creative or any of that. He said, "Well . . ." He was going back downstairs. "Let's call it a night, for now."

They would have to embrace. She kept her face down and shuffled against him, her body swaying limp, her head stuck at a neck-breaking angle against his chest. "Tomorrow's another day," he murmured. "Tomorrow let's see if we can't fix that guitar." He would have no way of knowing it was beyond fixing. She put her arms around him. The interesting, sloping terrain of a male body was mappable by contact, curious, inevitable terrain, peculiarly *beneath* male consciousness, so that it seems naturally to fall more to the female's department of consideration. If he wore briefs, the soft cord of his sex would be—is this how they do it?—crumpled or folded to one side, with those pitiful eyelid-skin creases, like the genital equipment photographed in *Playgirl*, an audacious new magazine Rachel's mother actually subscribed to, which she left out on the coffee table in plain sight. Once, when Karma was staying there, Rachel had produced from her mother's room a pair of pornographic videos for them to jeer at and perhaps secretly study—one was called something like "Fantasies," the other "Big Butt Babes"—in which women evinced bliss that looked like agony or sank in happy slavery to an exposed erection. But those were pale shiny *boys,* whereas Faro at his more priestly age had a solid oaken warmth. He released her and picked up his glass, standing back. "Sleep tight," he said, looking down at his shoes. He was pinching the back of his neck. Then with a little noise in the throat, he turned and left. She went on standing on the same spot, unclothed by the embrace, the house's cold air creeping against her, listening, as she could hear him reentering her mother's museum of broken sacred objects, where his footsteps sounded lost and valiant, vanquished. Somehow, the encounter felt like a triumph of her body physically: the words had all been Faro's, but the dialogue was all muted to silence—or at least meaningless—and *she* had controlled the encounter of their physical bodies in space, as well as the final repulsion, like a wrestling match where she'd burst his hold. And so she stood alone, in the loneliness of the victor, in the victor's cleared space.

Part
⦿ 2 ⦿

So night fell on Point Cuidad while the great house pushed on through the storm. As for me, I lay awake on a cold futon in an upper, inner room with no windows, unable to sleep. It was the end of the first of the four days I would spend in that house, and I had met Wendy four times— in the basement, the corridor, the landing, and then the dining room—and each time my vision was cut off by a blaze from my own cheeks. I was in the presence of an alien, a girl, bearing her unearthly characteristics with utter casual disregard, the distribution of her shirt-front, the strange moths of a girl's eyes, the different mound of hip, the forbidding austere slope of her jeans' front, the unearthly self-possession, the female supremacy of the soul in the body. Love then took the form purely of a dutiful sensation of my own unworthiness. I thought I would lie awake all night like a stowaway, too excited to sleep. But the antihistamines swallowed me and I fell into a deep, cold sleep of enchantment. In my room somewhere near the center of the house, I could hear the wooden structure creak and groan in the wind. During the night I was aware of having an unworthy dream, in which not Wendy but *Mrs.* Farmican came to my room, with a ring of keys and a candle, an unworthy dream indeed, involving the exchange of a brass hashish pipe, and then her clambering to kneel over my laid-out body with frank avidity like a boy scout kindling a fire, and

121

her lying against me whispering (I remember being worried by the past tense), "It was good that you came to this house," while her hand made frosting-spreading motions over my bare chest, sealing me away, immuring me like a treasure in stucco. Such dream-states are also half-waking, and I could hear, too, the house twist in the storm, feeling my own body as a strand braided into a heavy cable being stretched to creaking, my sheets trussing my thighs. I didn't completely regain consciousness until morning, when it turned out my room did have a window—or a window had appeared overnight—through which daylight came indirectly. It was quiet. The storm was over. The house had run aground. I was far from home.

From home in Wisconsin, that is. In Kaseburg, Wisconsin, there were two places to get a job—at the AMC automobile plant in Kenosha, where assembly-line workers were building a now-discontinued model called the American Condor; or else in the Kraft Foods factory outside Burlington, where all Kraft's aerosol products—cheese, ham spread, and fish spread to be tinted either salmon or trout—were canned in colloid suspension in pressurized gas with plastic nozzles. At both the Kraft and the AMC factories, I would have received a permanent locker of my own and an employment contract describing gradual upward steps in salary and benefits to take effect over the decades, accumulating vacation days, sick time, early-retirement credit, death benefits. My father had spent his life avoiding such work, and had therefore been a good example of a local failure, by turns an ad salesman, a bartender, a snowmobile dealer, a music store owner, a restaurant manager. His only enjoyment in life seemed to be music. In the basement rec room paneled in creamy plastic wood, in winter overheated by the furnace, he had a big wood-cabineted Hammond organ with two keyboards in parallel steps, a row of foot-pedals on the floor like a marimba underfoot, and dozens of sliding tone-control levers labeled *clarinet, viola, trombone, claves, cowbell*. He would tap the "bossa nova" rhythm and then, seated on the organ's high bench in the posture of a chariot driver, he would vanish over a landscape of his own imagining, actually leaning into the turns as he took them. It was never any other rhythm than bossa nova, lewd and strange in Wisconsin. When I watched his big soft back as he played, I was ashamed of him— or seeing him at the restaurant behind the bar screwing a luminous towel in a series of shotglasses—or even just seeing him leave for work, foolishly optimistic in his green Plymouth Satellite station wagon. I was ashamed of my father's fidelity to the ordinariness of everything. But now I had a chance to overcome my origins. That seemed to me to be what people do in their lives. The night before, Faro had elevated me to service, by casually inviting me to come to Oregon: *Help out? Anything? Come on. Do. It'll be fun.* I had gone outside after dinner because I could hear the tarp slapping in the wind—it was supposed to be staked down covering all the old doors on the lawn—so I found a rubber jacket in the kitchen mudroom and went out a side door, there to find Faro sitting on the step under the north porte cochere, sneaking a cigarette. He looked at me guiltily and said, "The Dalai Lama smokes." I hopped and shrugged to make this whopping rubber jacket spill evenly around my shoulders, and I explained why I'd come outside, to cover the doors.

"Oh, those doors. You know something? What is the point of putting all those doors back?"

The project had always felt futile, but until now I had no permission to think so. "Well, but in the rain," I said, ". . . some of that inlaid wood . . ."

He said—sincerely—"Shame," having inhaled and exhaled cigarette smoke. It laid the question to rest. "But listen. This is an assignment. Tomorrow the auction house is coming, and I want you to keep an eye out for some documents: anything that seems to pertain to taxes or church contributions. There's something called the Church of Bread and Wine. Just hang on to any kind of documents. Can you do that?" He drew on his cigarette and together for a minute we looked out over the cemetery of doors in the rain.

"Here's something," he said. "Look at this. This used to be a big turntable for turning the car around." His finger was dialing in air above a big disk in the pavement. "Is that Victorian or what? Just drive your big-ole Duesenberg up on here? And fwoop? Abracadabra?"

From his cigarette, smoke spun in the light breeze and I lusted for it, on the brink of bumming one. I said, "Yeah." In my clogged head, my voice had nowhere to drain. I had taken another brace of antihistamines, and so felt all the more enclosed in parentheses, dully.

"Tell me. Forgive me. I never got how to pronounce your name." I told him *Baelthon*, in a phonetically instructive grimace. He sipped his wine. "So Baelthon, describe your novel for me. You're working on a novel."

"Oh, it's still . . ." My hand stirred vaguely to indicate a nebula about heart-height.

"I see, of course. Hm." He frowned. "Baelthon? I'm sincere. Would you like to come to the Ranch? Help out? Anything? Come on. Do. It'll be fun."

So the next morning as I lay on my cold futon, I was thinking about never sleeping in my rented room again, letting my landlord keep the damage deposit, leaving behind my few possessions, leaving my car, too, which was still parked in Seawall, a Volkswagen Bug with no headlights. I'd left it in town because it was so hard to start. I had bought it for fifty dollars, without a receipt, and it still wasn't registered: it would be easy to abandon it right there in town, on a side street whose end was buried in a sand dune of the Pacific Ocean.

And soon, as I lay in the morning light, I heard—or rather I realized I had been hearing for some while—sounds from outside: the irregular chop of a shovel in soil. The window looked straight across at a blank wall of the house's other wing. Fog drifted across the property. The outer grounds were partly visible on one side—a slope led down to the edge of the cliff—and as I looked, shovelfuls of dirt flopped onto a growing pile, tossed there by someone just around the corner of the wall. Somebody was digging in the garden.

I crept into my clothes: my doorway had no door and anybody might have walked past. Somewhere in this house was Wendy. I came down the front staircase with the lightest possible pressure of my feet on the steps, expecting creaks.

But on the landing, I was stopped by fear. A big man was coming down behind me. His hair was immense, and he was dressed in overlapping layers of thrift-shop rags. It was Dean Houlihan. He had let himself into the house. It was Dean who nested under the foundation. I remembered now, once at Little Tom's coffee house, a pair of graduate students from Columbia had shown up carrying a reel-to-reel tape recorder, wanting to interview Dean. They were treated as tourists and cheerfully misdirected. It mystified me at the time, but now I realized Dean Houlihan had been a friend of James Farmican.

We were both stopped at the landing. It was like encountering a yak on a staircase. He told me I had slept well, and then he said, "You've taken this job." He looked at me as if judging my weight. "Good luck," he said, but then he didn't move on: he was going to speak further to me. He gave off a musty smell of long storage and campfire hotdogs. "As you do this," he said, his voice compressed to occupy a nut of time-space we stood within, "keep an eye peeled for an end to all war. Can you remember that? That will be your job." Red threads wandered through his parched eye. He aged mortally in close-up. A quilt hung beneath each eye. One lid had a salty scab. One nostril had a fold like a deformed strawberry. "It's in a box," he said. His face was not symmetrical. He sharpened his gaze to pierce through my fog, and then with a deeper crease in his brow he turned and went on down the stairs. Maybe he was little more than a trespasser, but I felt tapped now by a distinguishment: I was supposed to look for a box containing an end to all war. I didn't understand. I stood still and watched him go. His footsteps sounded along the corridor to the kitchen, and I heard him leave by the back door. I stayed there on the stair trying to interpret what had just happened. In a way, I didn't want to be responsible for having seen Dean in the house.

Or, maybe it hadn't been a strange encounter at all. He was obviously a friend of the family. He came and went as he pleased. It wasn't trespassing. He was concerned about a box of, maybe, his own possessions. That was an explanation. I went downstairs to the first floor, on the boards' creaks and snaps. Everyone else but me in that house could travel over the floors without making the boards creak.

Downstairs, no one seemed to be around.

"Good morning, Baelthon," sang out Mrs. Farmican, coming along the hallway from the side door, cold weather around her, shedding a sheepskin coat. She was wearing the same black sweater and jeans as yesterday. It seems to me now in memory that everyone in those days wore the same clothes every day, though that can't be right. "Where is everybody?" she asked me, and she lifted her voice, *"Peter?"*

Peter answered, "I'm right here," from the direction of the big cold hall they referred to as the ballroom.

"Not many days left, Baelthon!" she sang as she walked off. I followed, always in this opera a silent player. I'd missed my chance and hadn't immediately mentioned Dean, there was something so imaginary about having seen him on the stairs, and all these events were swinging past me in muting slow-motion. "Baelthon, you really have to give up on that misbegotten project of installing doors," she trilled in walking offstage. "My former husband would be unhappy if he knew. Besides, the appraisers come today, and you'll have to help *them.* Peter? I want to talk about something but we must wait till Wendy gets here."

In the ballroom, Peter was kneeling on the floor beside the warped guitar, unzipping an old wardrobe-suitcase. He seemed to be preparing food for the guitar in the netherworld—a handful of picks, a package of guitar strings labeled "Super Slinky" in zingy-looking letters, songbooks with chords.

I had been in this ballroom the night before, but it had been too dark to see, holding sounds like a big hangar, and so cold it might have been outdoors. Now, in daylight, it turned out to be small, a little bigger than a tennis court. Its walls had been painted in overlapping designs of Day-Glo paint—which the eye quickly deciphered into writhing body-parts. People had taken off their clothes, sloshed themselves with paint, and rolled themselves on the walls to print their breasts and buttocks and genitals and arms and legs, now faded and powdering off. That whole decade was pervaded by a general sense of having missed a party. I supposed the seal of James Farmican's authentic penis was printed somewhere around me in fluorescent colors fading to sad Pompeian hues as some wet flour oozed from the walls. At the far end of the room, the carpet had swelled in a mound, on which blades of grass grew, and bright evidence of moss: an old window had broken, exposing the floor below to wind and rain, and the carpet itself had thickened in a shallow dome of chlorophyll.

Mrs. Farmican said, "Where's Edward? Is he around?"

"He went off in his Mercedes-Benz. People will think the middle class moved in." Peter was lining the bottom of the suitcase with songbooks—*Complete Sounds of Silence*, Mel Bay's *Easy Guitar Licks*, *Eric Clapton Teaches You Lead Scales with Free Giant Fold-Out Poster*. Beside me in the corner, where wind had chased them, were a whiffle ball, a strand of shining tinsel, a baseball card washed blank.

"Okay, I'm here," Wendy said, entering the ballroom wearing her suede jacket. In her presence, I narrowed where I stood. She seemed breathless, her cheeks were roughened healthily, her hair was thickened by outdoor air, and the immediate heartbreak, in the cold-snap of that autumn morning, turned my solid flesh to vapor distilled, where I stood outside a circle now closing. Since the moment of first putting on James Farmican's stiff denim armor, I had begun fading to invisibility, already the omniscient narrator. "We have to discuss something, Lovies," said their mother. "I was just in town and Merlin is in some kind of trouble. A man from the government is looking for him."

"What kind of trouble?"

"Little Tom says the sheriff and a man from the Internal Revenue Service are looking for him."

"The Internal Revenue Service? *He* doesn't have any income."

"He won't stay here," said Wendy. "He hates being cooped up."

"We'll insist."

"He's probably in his cave," Peter said.

"I just saw him," I said. I cleared my throat. My own voice was always an intrusion from the fourth dimension. "I just saw him on the stairs."

"You did?" Peter and Wendy said in unison.

"He came down the front stairs and went outside."

"How long ago?"

"Just now."

Peter told his mother, "The north attic."

She said, "He'll be on the beach now."

"Where will we put him?"

His mother didn't answer but turned away and started wandering—arms folded, a sway in her hips—out over the ballroom floor. She stopped at the damp hump in the carpet beneath the broken window, and she prodded it with her toe. A species of delicate groundcover thrives along the north coast, called baby's-tears, like heaps of fresh parsley. She set her foot lightly on it and then let it spring back up again. "We could put him in that room nobody can ever find, with the dirt floor behind the old washer and dryer. He refuses to come to Oregon. He's so funny."

I watched Wendy. She hugged herself, her eyes bright with worry. Seeing her in distress changed me. Thereafter I would be erect with duty, awakened and immortal, willing to do anything—though I knew I didn't have the right yet, not even secretly to hope. It was only in the Nevada desert that I was filled tight with the blood of being her protector, her knight, among dangers real and imaginary. My protection took the form of training her to prefer Jeff Beck to Led Zeppelin, and to forsake her Motown soul music altogether. Also, I cajoled her into taking up cigarettes—Salem became her brand, though I couldn't help feeling she was only a temporary smoker, disloyally. I remember standing beside her in the hills above Reno, keeping an arm tight around her, at the edge of an old grave as it was being dug up. We'd found it near our campsite and gone for the police. The four of us—Peter and Ed, too—stood around the rim where this woman was being unearthed. The exhumation, with a plain shovel, was unceremonious, like a building contractor's probing for a buried pipe: no cordon around the site, no police photographer, no painstaking collection of clues. It was a woman, dead a few years judging by the vintage of her miniskirt. Along with the shovel man, a Nevada sheriff's homicide investigator was there to watch, his stainless-steel clipboard's page flipping in the wind, his Wallaby-shod feet at the edge of the hole. Somebody asked him who she would have been, and his answer was, "Oh, the hills are full of these young women." Meaning she would have been a refugee of the Died-and-Gone-to-Heaven Ranch, or Edna Bane's Desert Rose Garden, or Ecstasy or, he said, more likely some house farther away in Winnemucca or Pahrump. She could have died by her own hand, or by another's: in his tone, they amounted to the same thing essentially. He summed her up, "Nobody would have missed her," which was also the obstacle making police work futile. "Some of these girls will've reached a point where there's nobody they can call anymore." In his voice was some surprising, unprofessional sadness, which made Wendy, beside me, drift into plaint, "Well, but who knows? Maybe she was a horrible person." The cop shrugged in concession, and she went on, "Like, how do people *reach* a point where nobody accepts their phone calls anymore? Maybe plenty of people *tried* with her, but she was completely hard-to-handle. Who knows?" The cop didn't try to argue. The shovel kept working, and eventually we all started to mill, and shoulder aside, and sift back down the slope, especially Ed, who was the queasiest, while Wendy proved the strongest-stomached and went on watching steadily. The woman was half-covered by a sheet of old Masonite pegboard with a pile of white dirt on it. The rotting process had passed and left only cleanness, but three things remained intact: her pink plastic dental retainer, some bits of foil confetti still twinkling in her dusted hair, and a pair of lustrous breast implants lying on her ribcage like shining undestroyable jellyfish. Where we stood at the rim, I hardened my arm around Wendy's waist, feeling vindicated by this perilous place. But also, I was afraid. The old grave was a first painful sign that I wouldn't be able to protect Wendy, as I like to think, in the few bright weeks in Nevada like a series of overexposed beige photos.

None of us could have known how, migrating from California, the iridescent coral of the soul would be exposed to air and come out grey. Things started going bad right away, on the first day in Nevada, when we pulled up at the "casino" in our Mercedes, swallowed by the whirl of white dust that always caught up with us when we stopped. The Cornucopia Casino, in its entirety, turned out to be three old gaming tables under a tarp in a rancher's barn: a blackjack table, a big round-bottomed craps table missing its legs, and a roulette wheel with a tendency to get stuck. The rancher, at first suspicious of us, was then glad to get all that old stuff out of his barn. The rest of us had been murmuring against Ed during the entire trip, but now we openly, zestily, grieved. Wendy and I sat on hay bales in the barn. In this shipwreck I was taking pleasure, which I censored in myself. Peter, who also seemed to thrive on disappointments, was fooling around with the old roulette wheel and found it had a tendency to get stuck at one point, so that, as he noted, one could devise a clever way to cheat.

Ed, humorless in his role as entrepreneur, was made lofty by this trouble. He rose taller like Moses in the sunny doorway of the barn, holding up his papers, printed *STATE OF NEVADA License for Gaming Franchise, CLASS A*, and perforated with the braille of a notary's seal. He brandished the pages at us and said, "Nevertheless," and walked straight out into the desert, where for a long time we could see his flea-sized form hopping against the horizon, walking in little circles. He had the car keys. Also, it was his car. When he came back, he was still holding the official pages, and he said, "Do you know how valuable this is?" He rattled the papers. "This is grandfathered-in."

So we dragged the tables, legs detached, atilt on their hulls, out into the sun. In a town called Minden, Ed bought a two-wheel trailer-hitch wagon that could carry all this equipment. In a suburban subdivision in Sparks, we bought an old sideshow tent left over from the Reno Rodeo. It was blue-and-white-striped, and it had a rip, but we could staple the rip together with unbent paper clips. In Carson City we bought, at a discount, some of the necessities of the casino business: racks and trays for chips; an official Nevada-approved "drop box" for cash to collect in; a "counting gown" which the Gaming Control Board required for the bimonthly "hard counts" of cash: it was a seamless, pocketless vestment of canvas that tied in back like a hospital gown. And of course we invested in chips, real chips, the good kind, heavy ceramic-clay chips with brass centers and sheathed rims, whose click together sounded like solvency itself.

That was how we began looking for a place to set up the dark tabernacle, getting kicked off a series of carefully chosen places. Ed's plan was to establish a roadside casino that, with almost no overhead, would pull in three or four hundred dollars a day from passing tourists. It might seem today like a bad idea, but at the time, if you squinted right, you could see it clearly. "Just wait till we count the difference between the drop and the take," Ed would say, rapping the *Casino Gambling Business* book that lay on the dashboard. The scheme grew to be more and more plausible as we experienced small victories. The first goal was to find an unwanted piece of land, of which there seemed to be plenty, and at last we did succeed in taking over a spot of waste earth just off I-80, above Reno, which no one would bother to kick us off of. I'm sure it's still there, exactly as desolate. Get off at the Wild Horse exit and turn left, go under the Interstate and follow the road—not far—to the point over the hill, where the pavement ends in an area of scraped dirt. I remember a sign on the empty horizon reading CONGESTED AREA: DISCHARGE OF FIREARMS PROHIBITED, which of course was shot through with rusty bullet holes. We got our tent up, and then immediately Ed began filing documents in Carson City claiming legal ownership of the property. He was tireless. To mark boundaries, he drove firewood sticks into the ground in the sagebrush. He rented a P.O. box in Reno. He began the process of registering the casino with government agencies, paying reinstatement fees, which were low because the assessed value of the Cornucopia Casino, in 1943, was low. He stayed up at night studying by flashlight, murmuring aloud to himself while he read from an oversized paperback called *How to Form Your Own Legal Corporation for Under $50**. He received, by mail order, a kit containing ledgers and legal forms and twenty genuine stock certificates that read "The Cornucopia Casino, Inc." in ornate embossed printing. Countless mornings he woke up early and drove to Carson City, wearing a coat and tie, to apply for restaurant licenses and liquor licenses and business permits and construction permits. But most of his applications failed. Every government bureaucrat detected unsoundness in the project.

But then he finally did succeed in getting a picnic permit, renewable by the week, which would allow us to sell soft drinks. This miracle was accomplishable because the Nevada Department of Parks and Recreation didn't communicate with the Gaming Control Board, and neither communicated with the County Planning Department. He really almost succeeded in setting up a roadside casino. "Wait till you guys count the difference between the drop and the take," he taunted us again as we rode in his car toward celebratory ice cream cones in Reno. And then he sang out into the road-wind, "The Four Ps of Marketing: Place, Price, Promotion, and something else. I forget." In Nevada, he was changed. He was happy. Ed was happy and Wendy grew slender and tanned.

We never did get a single customer inside the dark tent. For one thing, we were badly positioned, just over a ridge from I-80, not wanting to be too conspicuous to the authorities. In the end, it wasn't the gangsters or the police that defeated the Cornucopia Casino, or even the Gaming Control Board. It was red tape. It was Title Nine of the new Humboldt Basin Environmental Integrity Code, and it was the Restaurant Safety Inspector and the building inspector and the Nevada Irrigation District. It was the new energy regulations and the Sanitation District and the Employee Health Act requirements and the state insurance commission regulations. They just wore Ed down. The one thing he did succeed with was claiming ownership of the real estate. His claim to that slope of sagebrush was never contested. Part of his fortune today is built on Nevada land holdings. Wendy says he owns hundreds of thousands of acres north of I-80. And his fleet of, eventually, fifteen *Cornucopia Chuckwagon!* trailers provides sandwiches and Cokes, these days, for basketball games and rodeos and conventions and tourist attractions all over northern Nevada. He seems to have faith. Where did he get it? Is it just stupidity? Whatever it is, he always had it. He still has it today. Three days ago at the San Francisco Airport, I met him again, and it was immediately clear that the lapse of twenty-five years has rebuilt him as a permanently happy, generous man, looming one step above

me at the airport restaurant, arms outspread, with a threat of
such positive attitude that I cringed within the dim cage of my
hangover. He's so successful now, he flew his own plane from
Reno to meet us in the airport, and then bragged that he'd
made the trip from Nevada faster than it would have taken me
to drive from Terra Linda in morning rush-hour traffic. Peter
Farmican flew up for the meeting, too, from Southern California. He's forty-something, his golden hair now wavy, striding
up the airport's H Concourse, just off the San Diego plane, not
so skinny anymore, permanently suntanned, carrying himself
like a bodybuilder, like a stack of cutlets. Wendy was already
there when I arrived, sitting alone at the airport bar, though I
didn't quite look at her. She was wearing a sweater and a long
skirt, a muffling disguise, but her body keeps coming forth, a
pulse at the edge of my vision. I'm just the same as ever. My
hangover was something I could use to shorten my sight
against seeing her. I didn't want to be there. I didn't think
my presence was really necessary. This was a meeting we'd
arranged—we four desert sojourners, reunited—in order to
discuss this legal stratagem: pretending to be married. It took
place in an overpriced airport restaurant called A Taste of Old
Frisco. I supposed at first that the meeting would accomplish
exactly nothing: merely to reaffirm everything we had already
agreed on: that Wendy and I would live together until a court
hearing established the historical fact of our "marriage," at
which point we would get a brisk, unsentimental divorce.

But Ed turned to me, aimed a swizzlestick at my heart, and
said, "Here is an initial reason we called this meeting. We think
you ought to be compensated too. You are tantamount to a
member of the family after all. And you're being so cooperative
in this delicate legal situation. We have discussed this between
ourselves, and we want you to have two-point-five percent of
all net proceeds from the James Farmican estate, if we succeed
in getting it back."

I'm afraid I may have alienated them at that meeting. It was probably my hangover. I stood up from my seat because right away I felt physically germy from the mention of money. Also—here is how well I know myself—I was performing for Wendy's spectatorship. Such is gallantry. Show her what a waste I am. And will persist in being. I said (standing over their table without looking at her), "I don't want your money. I have no doubt that all of this money was collected in the dubious ways of all businessmen and lawyers." I was speaking with surprising eloquence somehow abetted by my hangover, causing me to close my eyes against the heavenly airport—yes, heavenly: all airports are heavenly, with heaven's glassy acoustics, heaven's constant echo of mysterious permanent departures and arrivals, heaven's wash of fresh anonymity, heaven's atmosphere of being always under renovation and construction (in my wine-headache I was dimly aware of a plywood wall to one side, a plywood ramp, a dust of Sheetrock)—as I went on, "I'm willing to suffer through this charade for the sake of your good fortune. You're the ones interested in the money, whereas in my poverty I can see that a calm heart is worth more than a treasure." It sounded like something from the Book of Proverbs. "As far as I'm concerned, the deal is still on and we're still married. That is, I'll go through with this—despite the fact that I have no sure way of knowing whether the child," I said recklessly, referring to Gabriel, "is in fact the child of one of her customers." I turned and walked down the reverberating H Concourse toward LUGGAGE—PICKUP—PARKING—TERMINAL. Those last—regrettable, preposterous—remarks had put, on Ed's face, a confident smile of dim tolerance. His arms were folded.

I don't believe I was the ruination of Wendy. No guilt belongs to me. People are responsible for themselves. When I left Reno on a Greyhound bus, I thought she would get the operation. I took with me the eight hundred dollars meant for that purpose. But I thought her mother had plenty of money and could easily pay for the operation. We had made an appointment with the doctor. We had had long conversations about how much smarter it would be. I could see that I was not very good for her, and I believed fundamentally she would be glad to be free of me.

It was Breece who influenced her, Dexter Breece, with his heavy gold necklace on his bumpy old iguana chest, with his sports coats in Cadillac colors, with his snakeskin boots coming unstitched at one seam. Breece who could hold a card up between two fingers and revolve it slowly so that it vanished edgewise but then never reappeared. It was gone. His hands remained in air, scrubbed-looking like a doctor's. Then later reach out in air and pull the card back from some gash in space where he'd slipped it. He could throw a card across a room to make it stick under an ashtray; or throw it straight down into the cuff of his pants. It was Breece who became a moral counselor to her after I was gone, or even while I was still there.

I first saw him when I was working at the Silver City Swap, a pawn shop across the street from the big casinos on Virginia Street. This was when things were starting to be bad. Peter had started sleeping sometimes behind the Circus Circus casino on a square of corrugated cardboard, wearing his fancy velour jacket inside-out as he slept, to preserve it from wear, showing thready seams and pocket-linings. Wendy was pregnant. She and I were living in the Starlite Motel on Virginia Street, and I had taken a job in the pawn shop next door, belonging to the same man who also owned our motel, Abner Kind. I'll always remember Abner Kind with gratitude. He's probably dead by now. He was an old man then, bald, his eyes parenthetically omniscient in the alkali-blue of desert air. He used to give me paperback books—set them on my worktable and rap them with a knuckle and shuffle away saying, "Required reading." It was mostly existentialist theologians, Bultmann and Tillich and Niebuhr, who were popular at the time. I never read them.

One morning I was working in the back room of the shop

when I heard the sleighbells on the front door. Mr. Kind's voice said, guardedly, "Hello, Breece."

"Abner," said the visitor. Nobody said anything for a while. The rhythmic sound of Mr. Kind's old-fashioned adding machine had stopped. Through my back-room door, all I could see of this Breece was a dusty boot, split open at the heel and worn round-heeled. At last he said, "Been visiting your hippie friends next door. That girl there."

That was us. The paradox of entering the "wilderness" is that you may feel like you're vanishing but in fact you become immediately, locally, comically conspicuous. This was still the old Nevada: the whole northern part of the state probably had a total resident population of a few thousand. The blue-and-white tent of The Cornucopia Casino, pitched over a ridge just off I-80, would have made the entire network of communication tremble, among the loners and retirees in their desert trailers, the colonies of prostitutes behind security fences, the few concrete-block structures of law enforcement, the sad casinos in town like giant vertical motels. Breece referred to us "hippies" so casually, I got a quick sense of our fame.

I slowly—soundlessly—set down the X-acto knife and the bear's prostate gland I had been slicing into oval wafers. Mr. Kind's pawn shop was a diversified business, and rapidly he had started trusting me with jobs other than shopkeeping up front. A bear had been hit by a car in Yosemite that week; one of the usual bounty hunters had brought it in, parceled up in plastic bags of slippery giblets, all labeled, its glands and integuments to be variously prepared and sent away to San Francisco's Chinatown. The job had to be done quickly and the worktable wiped clean before it came to the attention of the Department of Fish and Game officers, who sometimes came around posing as taxidermists. Therefore, that day I had let myself in early to work on it before Mr. Kind arrived. He didn't know I was there to eavesdrop.

His teacup made a sound of being set down on his glass desktop. Through the doorway's slice of vision, I could see Mr. Kind's old blotchy fingers pinching the teabag down to a hard cold almond in the bowl of his spoon to get the last drop. He said to Breece, "I understand you have a protégé in the younger brother of that family."

Breece didn't answer. I heard the clink of his heavy bracelet on the countertop. He was browsing over the glass cases, where lay displayed the jewelry men discarded before crossing the street to wade into that jingling surf-sound in the always-open, wide doors of the El Dorado or Harrah's Club or the Flamingo—wristwatches, tie-pins, cuff links, all their silver still smudged by the breath of ownership, a personal sheen that, I found as an employee, no polish can ever completely remove. Once, in a reverie, Mr. Kind had stared off at the casinos outside, his palms gliding over the display case, and said faintly, in his European accent, *This countertop: it's a sort of cliff, sometimes I think.*

Breece wasn't talking, so Mr. Kind went on, "They are a group of children, and I hope you're not taking advantage of them."

"Oh, for pity's sake, Abner. We're both too old."

Through a section of doorway, I could see Breece pass: a burgundy fishnet shirt showed a chest hard and bumpy and mummy-brown, between the lapels of a creamy eggnog polyester jacket, filthy at the seams. A hawk-like face, lizard mouth. Wavy hair of a yellow shine, grown long to the need-a-haircut length. And his hands: it was the first time I saw the fan of skilled talons, spread at rest now on the countertop.

Mr. Kind's tilt-back chair creaked. Then I heard him say, "Forgive me, Breece. I'm a prejudiced old man. Tell me, how is your life out in the desert."

"Aww. As you have observed, that Farmican younger *boy* has been staying out at my other trailer, and he keeps bugging me to teach him card tricks, which now I realize will only get him into trouble. I just kicked him out. You're about to have an extra tenant in that ground-floor unit. Did you know the girl's pregnant?"

"Mm?" said Mr. Kind noncommittally. In fact he did know. In fact, he was financing the abortion. We couldn't afford the doctor's fee—which was high because an abortion was a nefarious thing in Nevada then—and I had asked Mr. Kind if he would let me go into debt to him for a few weeks' salary. It was fatherly of him: he sat me down and tried to talk me out of the operation. He and his wife were childless, yet he tried to persuade me that changing dirty diapers at 4 A.M. was a most ennobling occupation. I was able to convince him that the real horror was in the loss of freedom, paying the mortgage, being a steady husband and father, keeping up a house, having the same job for years, being gradually buried in the world. His sadness increased as I spoke, and he relented at last and agreed to loan me eight hundred dollars. And he said he knew a doctor. But that marked a change in our relationship. I felt at the time that he had shown an uncharacteristic narrow-mindedness. At any rate, he stopped recommending reading for me.

Breece said, "The boy is in debt. Peter is his name. He's been playing at the hundred-dollar tables and signing bad chits. I think he wants to be a card mucker when he grows up. That is his aspiration. He's got me teaching him tricks, bottom-dealing, Greek-dealing, hop-and-crimp. Shit like that. Strictly for mucking. He's fascinated by it. Why I kicked him out."

"I didn't know that."

"He's into 'em for four thousand dollars."

Mr. Kind took longer to answer. "I didn't know that," he repeated, his voice muffled by the rim of his teacup.

"Fuckin' San Francisco." Breece shook his head and moved idly away, out of my line of vision. He slowly turned a revolving rack of postcards, I could hear its squeak. "You knew the girl was pregnant, didn't you. Are you helping them, Abner, in any way? Something tells me you are."

Mr. Kind made a dismissive cough.

"Are you loaning her money? Because I just spent the last two days telling that *brother* in no uncertain terms that I would *not* reach into my own pocket on something risky like a bunch of goddamn suburban hippies. They're basically good kids. Nothing wrong with 'em. That's the problem."

Mr. Kind's chairspring clanged in tilting farther back. "Why are you here, Dexter?"

"Aw, I just wanted to ask you. About those kids. I'm just meddling. They're nice kids, but they have no idea. The Guardian Angel of Stupid Damn Ignorance is still guarding over them right now, but that won't last forever. Where are their parents?"

"The father is dead, the mother is irresponsible. That's the impression I have."

"Still, they could phone home. I feel like the family has money. Why don't they phone home?"

"Ach. Pff. Children these days."

Breece moved around the store, dawdling. His hands rose and raked through his nicotine-blond hair and gathered its short ends in a fist in back. "You *are* taking her to a good place, Abner."

"The girl? Yes. Yes."

"A practicing M.D."

"Ach. Breece, you underestimate me. Perhaps you underestimate the whole world." He brought up his handkerchief, pinched and nipped it up into a blossom like a hand of cards, and then noisily blew his nose. It was a long time then before anyone spoke. "Did you come here to moralize? You know I can't be saved."

"Me? I'm just snooping, Abner. I'm just being a busybody. Old enough, nothing else to do."

"The boy is in love with her. Eight hundred dollars he can work off in a few weeks."

"Yes. Perhaps. But the brother. He's a fuck-up. I think

maybe those gangsters have seen that boy to be devious. That is what the gamblers will sense. Mendacity. It's a defect of character leading to other weaknesses, so that he is susceptible to the squeeze. I believe the gamblers' collectors assume that boy is my chicken."

Mr. Kind made no reply. He just generated his meditative sinus-clearing click sounds, folding away his handkerchief, and picked up his teacup.

Breece went on, "I'd like to help them, Abner, but it is *strictly* against my principles to loan four thousand dollars to an amalgamation of hippies on a lark, however innocent they may seem. Innocence is exactly the difficulty, don't you see."

"Would you like some coffee, Dexter? Or tea? I'm having tea."

"No. But thank you. Thanks anyway. It's been a while since I was in here. You expanded."

Through my doorway, I could see him wander toward the window and look out at the palisades of the Flamingo and the El Dorado across the street, his hands gripping his hipbones. His gold hair had crusty waves. He said, "You know what those gamblers' collectors are like. They're not going to put the boy on some sort of weekly installment plan. He's in trouble. And if he's in trouble, they're all in trouble. She's a nice young woman, not the kind of girl who should end up down in some whorehouse in Nye County in captivity. You know they're not fair, those people down there. They *keep* 'em in those double-wides. She won't get out of those double-wides until they decide they're done with her. And she's smart. She's got the big picture."

Mr. Kind thought about this. At last he said, "I agree with you that four thousand dollars is too much money for a personal loan on a gambling debt. But that girl. She is sixteen. For a girl of her background, sixteen can be childhood. I'm not so sure she has 'the big picture,' as you say."

Breece plucked distractedly at postcards on the revolving

rack, then at last said, "We're a couple of old men now. We've reached an age of detachment. Sixty-two I am. I don't know about you."

"Dexter, you are sixty-two! Only yesterday you were coming up Virginia Street in your Packard."

"My Packard, oh!" He put his knuckles to his heart.

"Your Packard Carribean, red and white, with a soft-top. And picking up girls. I'll say one thing for you. Your adventures have preserved your youth and your yellow hair."

"Now, don't make fun of my good fortune, Abner, you fuckin' Hebrew, I know what *you* think of yellow hair. You and your wife, you continue to think I'm immoral. I understand that."

"No, no, again you underestimate. I've lived enough to see morality is merely . . . morality is just a popular melodrama. I must be fair to you and say I understand completely. With this girl. I understand that you feel we together should weave a basket—to *catch* her." From my doorway, I saw Mr. Kind's hands rise, the fingers laced in a cradle. "But I predict that this girl will decline your notion. The girl is educated in the ethics of liberal middle class. She is educated by the popular melodrama."

"But you agree with me that this basket is weavable?"

"Weavable, yes." A smile could be heard in his voice, a peculiarly unhappy smile I knew well, lips pursed. It was the same smile I'd seen when he consented, reluctantly, to pay for the operation.

Breece sighed. "Guess I'll go back to walking to and fro in the earth, and up and down in it." That was some kind of a joke. It made Mr. Kind chuckle. Breece was leaving. I kept quiet. I had understood most of this exchange, but certain parts I did not. I didn't know what double-wides were. The one thing that was very clear was the part about Peter being in debt. Wendy and I had suspected it. But four thousand dollars was a towering sum of money. Listening to this person Breece,

I experienced a renewal of faith in human nature. Even the reptilian creatures of the desert were looking out for our welfare. "You are underestimating that girl," Breece said, "I seen her around, and it's pretty clear she is the prize in that particular box o' Crackerjack. Forgive me, but you know what I think, Abner. It is very Jewish of you, to be giving those kids money for the purpose of eliminating that baby. You know how I feel about that. Abner, deep in your heart where you don't examine, you know the spiritual truth about that."

Mr. Kind said, "Go ahead, my friend. But this girl, she is, as you would say, a smart cookie. The basket is weavable, yes, but it will not catch her. Go ahead and try."

We had already known Peter was in some kind of trouble. We also knew he had been sleeping sometimes in a spare trailer belonging to an old cardsharp outside town. Ed had seen Breece's place and told us about it, because one night he drove Peter out there. He described the ranch as looking like an old massacre spread around a gulch, woodsmoke indicating there was habitation, Peter's trailer a tilting Sundowner, its hitch resting on a cement block, a flattened Marlboro carton for a windowpane.

Evicted from there, Peter showed up at our motel room door that same night. Wendy and I were at home. I had told her about the conversation I overheard in the pawn shop, about the locals who seemed to be watching out for our interests, and about their admiration in particular for her, a pretty girl in all the moral dangers of Nevada. I told her, too, about Peter's four-thousand-dollar debt. She was heating soup with Sterno in the bathroom, while I answered Peter's knock on the door.

He was standing there wobbling. One platform heel folded aside. He actually fell, but he caught himself in a little curtsey and he smiled, his eyes fever-bright with apology, and he confided, "You have to take care of me." He was holding a huge, industrial-sized can of Accent meat tenderizer, as big as a baton, which he handed into my keeping: "Here," he said.

He started to move past me, exalted on his gold shoes in his immense elephant-bell velvet pants. He'd bought them on our first day in Reno, with a hundred dollars in slot-machine winnings. These pants swayed like heavy drapes, so that he had a way of moving with the hesitant grace of a giraffe, or rather like a small *herd* of giraffes, on the sidewalks of Reno. Having passed to me the inexplicable can of Accent, he stopped and turned, gave me an apologetic look, and vomited exactly toward me, a gallon of clear liquid. His eyes looked bruised. It was mascara. Cocaine was usually, as now, visible in his face, the sinuses' magnesium drip feeding a steady flare. "I took three hits of mescaline all at once," he admitted, coyly, wiping his chin, and in a shrug he began smiling, with a shrug worming his way up in space, smiling beatifically *down* on all this trouble from a wedged-up vantage point on his platform shoes. He closed his eyes and lifted his arms toward crucifixion and hung himself in bliss before us, one hip dropped, as if he could rise skinnily up through his clothes, bowing his head and hanging his arms out limp in blessing us all: *I'm your problem.*

I looked at Wendy. Holding a spatula, she rolled her eyes. I set down the big sixty-four-ounce can of Accent, not knowing what I was supposed to do with it. I had dodged the vomit. Outside in the parking space, there was an immense new, dusty Cadillac. Breece was there, tossing his brimmed hat in on the passenger seat. "Evening," he said through the doorway, "this would be the Farmican residence, I think." He opened the rear door of his car, where, on the backseat, I could see Peter's electric guitar, along with a couple of cardboard boxes that would be clothes and books. He pulled out Peter's heavy typewriter. "My name is Dexter Breece. I'm a friend of Peter's. Peter is having a tough time now and I thought I should bring him by here and discuss his . . . *maintenance* with you all."

He put the typewriter on the floor inside the door. Wendy was there, and on seeing her he grew taller and bowed. He said softly and deeply, "Ma'am." It was courtly of him. It made her tug her robe sash tighter and press a tress of hair back, in an instinct of vanity, so that I began to be, unconsciously, annoyed. Bowing, he'd slightly pressed together the heels of his shoes— not boots now but Adidas, dirty Adidas with beige pants. There was something regal in Dexter Breece that shone through his clothes. It was easy to picture him coming into a small town and getting up a friendly card game among retirees, at the Kiwanis or a country club or a sports bar or a community barbecue, and then leaving town with a few thousand dollars. That was how he'd made his living for years, all over Arizona and New Mexico and Southern California. According to Peter, he never went out anymore, but lived royally off Ziploc bags of cash buried all over the desert, and Tupperware containers full of Krugerrands. He'd had to stop card mucking because, supposedly, he got too well known. I had never seen Wendy glow in quite this way, with an authority of womanliness he conferred. It was an instant that excluded me where I stood, made me feel again that I was only seventeen years old, which was something I could ordinarily try to forget. There was nothing for me to do but start bringing in the rest of Peter's belongings, the guitar and the boxes. Breece said, "I apologize for all this. I think it's time for me to tell you about Peter's gambling trouble, because I want to be what help I can. He's been staying out at my place."

Wendy said, "We understand he's in debt."

Sorrily, Breece mopped about the floor with his eyes. "It's possible that I am partly responsible for his activities. And now he is in this predicament of debt. Gamblers like these fellows his creditors, they are generally unreasonable people. There is no way to placate them sometimes. I can't put myself in the position of *harboring* this weasel. Yet I would like to be helpful."

Peter was still looking sick, but he had picked up his electric guitar and begun to pluck it, his head weaving, as he followed the discussion with his eyes.

"He can stay here," Wendy said, meaning on the layers of cardboard and torn-down shower curtain on the floor that served as our spare bed.

"Well, yes, ma'am, but he's going to need some looking after. May I be frank? I know who you kids are. You're the kids who were going to start your own casino. Quite an idea. But I have to be honest with you. You're in a different environment here." At a loss for words, Breece's hands came together to form a little chapel over his heart. "For one thing, your brother has a gambling *addiction,* I believe."

Peter sat on the bed with a dewy-eyed interest in the outcome, still squanking quietly on the guitar. I got down on my knees to mop up vomit with pages of the Reno *Gazette* that piled up by the door: we were perhaps the only people in Nevada in 1973 who had a "newspaper recycling pile," but with of course no place to take it.

Breece walked over and laid a hand on Peter's shoulder. He said to Wendy, "Gambling is profound. It's profound but it's also the most superficial thing in the world. I don't know anything about your family, but this boy has had no spiritual training. You see? That would be a necessary condition to a gambling problem. What you have to realize in your soul, son"—he shook Peter's limp shoulder, and then began to detach the guitar from him—"is that games of hazard do not have anything to do with First and Last Things. Games of hazard are strictly the province of science or the devil." He watched Peter, holding the now-freed guitar by its neck, and he scratched his crotch thoughtfully. "I want to tell you-all something about gambling. Do you have coffee, dear?"

"We have Yuban." She went into the bathroom to relight the Sterno.

"Now, you-all live in high-desert here." He leaned the guitar in the corner. "If you look around, you don't see a great number of life forms being supported." When he spoke, he had a mannerism of letting his eyes flutter and fall shut. His lipless mouth flattened, his spine stretched, and his talented fingers spread in fans over his hipbones. Once he had wound up into a speech, his eyes were locked shut, tight almost in a wince, preventing interruption. "This sparsity here is like a *metaphor*. Y'all know what a metaphor is. Society here has different rules than what you may be accustomed to. Here you have to choose your friends carefully, and with an eye to *their* interests. And that goes for me too, by the way." He opened one eye to look straight at Wendy. "You must trust me only insofar as you see my interests being served. Now a young man like this one with a spiritual weakness, the gamblers can see him coming a mile away. I'll tell you the sign by which you recognize this weakness." He turned to focus on Peter. "You don't care about the money anymore, especially when you win. The pile of winnings feels like just a burden, like a responsibility, like something that'll just keep you at the table longer. When money is valueless, then you are in a spiritually transfigured condition. Now. I am a Christian. Is that tap water, dear?"

"This?"

"Peter, you stand up now and go out in my car and bring your sister a whole case of that bottled water I got. Go now."

While he skated away, Breece went on, "This is the Great Basin, dear. You're in it. It's all around you. You must be careful what you put in your body. Particularly in view of the condition you are in, which is a blessed condition. I'll drink that now. Don't bother to reheat some other water. But don't you kids be using tap water anymore." He looked at her, at me, smacked his lips in sadness over the ecology of the situation, and went on. "As I say, I'm a Christian. And from what-all I understand, I suppose you children are influenced by this bullshit Buddhism, which is an inferior religion in any form, because it is based on the bedrock premise that life is suffering—which is fine, *that's*

147

Christian, *that's* fine, that's the truth!—but then it adds the idea that suffering can be overcome. Well, it can't. And of course it shouldn't. That's the bullshit for popular consumption. This boy, what he's going to have to do, is go straight into things, rather than going around them. He's going to have to talk to Julian Satis, who is really the issuer of Peter's debt, and he's going to have to ask Mr. Satis what he must do."

"Yeah well those *ass*holes," Peter whined. He had come back in the door with a box of Calistoga Water.

Breece's eyelids fluttered closed again. "Then after that, because he is a compulsive gambler, he's got to get out of Nevada and not come back. I'm telling you how things are. But he can't get out without first getting straight with Mr. Satis. Mr. Satis will track people down."

He paused. All this was addressed to Wendy. She said, "Cream? Or sugar?"

"Nothing. Thanks. Black. Now Peter, listen here. What you have to get straight is, gambling has nothing to do with your true fate. This here is a business. The casinos' actuaries have got it figured where you'll just go on losing at an average rate of three-point-six percent in blackjack, eleven-point-five in poker, and so on. God does not breathe on the dice or any such magic shit. Nor does he even care whether you win or lose. Instead the Lord is adding things up very differently in your soul. Winning and losing isn't the point. Surely you've noticed *that* phenomenon. Surely you've been deep enough in, to notice that it doesn't matter whether you win or lose."

Thinking about it, Peter shuddered and picked his nose.

"You have to go straight into a great deal of pain, boy. Pain and trouble is planned for people in the world, but that's a *good* plan."

Wendy came up stirring the coffee carefully so as not to make a tink of the spoon, trying not to intrude on whatever exorcism was taking place. She set the coffee still spinning on the windowsill.

"You got anyone at home you could borrow the money from?"

"Out of the question," said Peter with his angry smile.

Breece looked at Wendy, who affirmed softly, "Out of the question."

He spread his claws on his hips and lengthened his already long spine and let his eyes fall shut, and he grimaced. "Well, that's the best news possible. We are all in the Lord's workshop. You can call Mr. Satis and walk directly through the doorway yourself."

The next day, Peter rose up from his bed of cardboard squares early in the morning and left the motel room before Wendy or I was awake. He was gone all day, and then came back around sundown with his thumb bandaged and his face badly sunburned. The door was open, and he came in saying, "They broke my thumb," in amazement and, almost, pride.

"Peter!" said his sister. She fluttered but didn't touch him. "Who did?"

"Can I use the phone? They said I have to have the money tonight." He was carrying a cardboard box under his arm, with the word "McGuffin" printed on all four sides in red, which he clutched as if it contained a treasure.

"Tonight? Who? Peter, who did this?"

"The collectors. It's what they do to real card manipulators. They took me out in the desert. They were actually sort of cool about it."

They had driven him out and left him, telling him he was not supposed to die out there, he was just supposed to get scared and have a lot of trouble finding his way home. Which is what he did. He followed a dry riverbed because he thought that, as a rule, rivers always lead downstream to some sort of civilization; and he rejoiced as the riverbed grew mossy and pits of standing water appeared. But then this *Nevada* riverbed, running eastward, dried out scummily and ended in a sinkhole. He had to retrace his path back uphill.

"Where did you get the bandage?" I said. It looked well applied, with a professional-looking metal closure clipping the end of the gauze. Wendy had come to hold his wrist gently in her two hands.

"Washoe County Memorial. It's great. You just go to the emergency room and tell them you're indigent. But really, could you just let me be alone while I use your phone? I need to make some calls."

"Wait a minute, relax, just wait a minute," said Wendy and she stood back. She shifted uncomfortably inside her shirt, and then she bowed her head and put her fingers to her eyes. She needed a minute.

At the moment when Peter arrived, she and I had been having an important disagreement: I had come back from Mr. Kind's shop with the necessary eight hundred dollars in cash. Our appointment was for the following morning at Dr. Tulip's office, where the whole procedure would require only an hour. But when I came home and presented her with Mr. Kind's money, rolled into a cylinder, she'd started crying, then stopped crying, and then told me with a firm soft grip on her voice, that she wanted to go ahead and have the baby. This she knew was a betrayal. She knew it would reduce our lives to hard work and missed opportunities and mediocre expectations. We'd only had a minute to talk about it when Peter came in. At that moment I was standing far in the corner, at an odd distance, shrunken and revised.

She said, "Peter, can you just relax for a minute and sit down? You're all keyed up." She had begun gripping her little finger in one fist, something she did sometimes. "Can we just all sit down for a minute," she said but didn't sit down. She started toward the door, to close it. Then she saw the McGuffin box he'd put on the bed. "Peter! What are you doing with this?"

"This . . ." He went for it. "*This* is going to save us." He lifted one flap. Inside was the title page of a typescript. "It's Dad's novel. It's probably worth a fortune."

Wendy looked at him, watching him dissolve to bits and then reconstitute himself before her eyes.

He gave a little impatient whimper. "Please would you guys just leave me alone for a minute so I can make some calls."

Neither Wendy nor I spoke, each of us perhaps stunned in our own different ways.

Peter took the silence as a requirement of more explanation. "I'm doing as Breece says. I'm calling Mr. Satis. But I want to be alone when I do it."

Wendy said, of the novel in the box, "You just *took* it?"

"You guys. Please. I have to make these calls."

Wendy and I looked at each other, agreeing by glance that he must be in earnest.

"As Breece says, 'The only way out is through.' Did you know he got a master's degree? He went to Purdue University? Did I already tell you that?"

"Ugh," Wendy told me. "Let's let him be alone here."

She went out of the room into the sun, and I followed.

But when we got outside, we lingered in our parking space beside the half-barrel of dry dirt that always stood there: the window was open, and we could hear Peter inside. The first thing he did was dial long-distance information and ask for a Manhattan number: a literary agency, any agency. He said, "Just any literary agency. Pick one." Obviously, the operator told him he needed to ask for a specific name, so he produced the name "William Morris," and then dialed a number. When he got through to a bonafide literary agent, he said, "My name is Peter Farmican. I'm the son of James Farmican."

Outside, Wendy and I were standing apart from each other.

"I'm calling because I'm holding in my hand here an un-published novel by my father, James Farmican. This novel has never seen the light of day. I want to discuss bringing it to market at this time. I've heard a number of good things about the William Morris agency so I figured I would bring it to you. James Farmican. Farmican. He was a poet. He died. He was a poet. Well, yes, but this is a novel. It's not finished, but it's brilliant. He got the Endicott. In California. I see, well, in that case, who *would* be interested in that period. What agency does handle . . . No, James Farmican. Farmican. He wrote *The Green Conquistador*. He wrote the *Anabasis Cycle*. He got the Endicott. A university press! No, you don't understand. This is a potential blockbuster. A university press doesn't have the, you know, the *size*, the *prestige*. This is a novel by James Farmican. Don't you remember *The Green Conquistador*? A university press is for pissy little fuck-ass shitty books," he said and hung up.

Wendy and I, soundlessly, were distancing ourselves from the window, a few parking places down. "Let's take him out to the campsite," I said. "Ed is there. Nobody'll look for him there."

"They *know* the Cornucopia is there. Everybody knows it's there. That's the first place they'll look."

"Still," I said. "It's a start. Then we can find a better place."

She assented by not saying anything, then adding, "Also, let's find his friend Breece and ask him what to do."

I looked at the ground for a minute. I said, "Wendy? We still have an appointment tomorrow. We need more time to talk about this." She looked at me with hope and trust. She looked at me as one looks up at someone who will pull them out of the water. I told her, "We're both young. You're too young to be a mother. Think about it. It's unfair to the child. It's not only material things you need, with a child. It's like, lessons. Music lessons or whatever. And braces. And they break their arm and need a doctor, which costs money. But it's more than that. You have to be stable. You can *say* you won't go to your parents for help, but—"

"I'm simply not. I'm not going back there."

I just looked down, unwilling to show my skepticism. It

was a basic doubt of mine, so deep I couldn't say it, or even quite admit it to myself. That I was too young and too poor and too lower-class to play this role of husband. That this whole trip was purely fantastical. That her mother and Faro would one day rescue her from me.

Peter's voice, inside, was talking on the phone again. She looked, but I got her attention by taking her hand. "Wendy. It's not a human being yet. It's like a finger. It's like you're cutting off a tiny tip of a finger. That's all. You know that. It's a scientific fact."

"I know," she said.

"You know that as well as I."

"I know."

"And you're just too young and irresponsible. So am I. We both are. You've got your whole life ahead of you. I promise I'll go with you tomorrow and help you every step of the way. I love you."

She leaned into me and put her arms around me and said, "Okay."

"I'll take care of you. It'll be easy." She laid her temple against my heart, and for a little while we were together like that. I thought I was already helping her mourn. Who knows what she was actually mourning. Her mind may have begun, even then, to move independently and mistrust me. Without wanting to mistrust me, she might have yet begun.

Then we could hear Peter's voice inside. I drew back. He was sounding insistent. She gave me a little look of weary dread, and we went back closer to the window. "Will he be in later?" Peter was saying. "No, I'd rather speak to him personally. All right, if you'll convey the following information to him. My name is Peter Farmican. I would like to sell Mr. Satis part ownership in a casino. Yes. One-third ownership. It's called the Cornucopia Casino, and it's been in existence since, like, the thirties. It has no capital assets, and it has no real

estate. It doesn't have a lot of equipment. It hasn't been operating. But it's registered with the state, and it actually *is* chartered
as a casino. I think Mr. Satis will know the value of that. So if
he wants it . . . Because I'm in debt to him . . . Peter Farmican.
You just tell him 'Peter Farmican.' Tell him I've got something
he'll be interested in. Tell him I'm willing to negotiate."

I whispered to Wendy, "You take him out there. Out there
to the Cornucopia. Just take a cab. I'll go find Breece. Breece
will have an idea. And then I'll meet you out in the desert." She
agreed, with a softened hopeless look about the eyes. That was
the last time I saw her. It's hard for a man to know exactly
when a woman doesn't trust him anymore. Maybe it's because a
woman goes on trying to have faith, knowing her faith is important, and so she tries not to identify a particular moment she
stops respecting him. Only later can she look back and see a
time when something inside her decided.

She and Peter got into a taxi to drive out to the campsite in
the hills, where Ed was still living, alone now with his car and
his tent, and his card table covered with paperwork. I was supposed to find Breece and then meet them out there. After I
watched the taxi disappear up Virginia Street (then turn right
at the gas station to enter eastbound I-80, a last flicker of the
taxi's red fender among the gas pumps in the snapshot colors of
memory, the commercial reds and yellows of 1973, the decade
when, it almost seems now, the general popular aesthetic was a
crucial part of the mystery of unhappiness and cruelty), I went
inside the motel room to find the phone ringing on the bedside
table. It was their mother. It was Julia Farmican. She said, "Is
this *Bael-thon?*" Hearing her voice, the squalor of the room
rose around me: I was like a felon answering a phone call at the
scene of the crime. She was in Lake Tahoe, only an hour from
Reno, calling from a pay phone. She wanted to know where

this motel of ours was, exactly. She did have some old friends in Lake Tahoe, but she didn't want to bother them in this situation. Those were her words. "I don't want to bother them in this situation."

I didn't ask what situation, I simply told her how to get here. But the words came back to me during the rest of the day: I decided Wendy might have told her. Or else Peter had called and told her. Told her about the pregnancy, and now she was coming out to rescue her daughter. It was understandable. My masquerading as her protector had always been absurd. I asked Mrs. Farmican if Faro was with her, and she said, "No, Faro is going to stay in Oregon." I thought I could hear something hard in her voice. When I hung up, I walked out the door, down the street, not looking back. In an hour, she would be knocking on the door there.

Then I couldn't find Breece. I tried looking in a bar where he was reputed to spend time. The bartender said he would be either at home or at a casino called the Golden Bubble, where he liked to have dinner, far outside town.

I hired a cab to take me out to Breece's littered gulch. No one was there. Not even stovesmoke. Then the cab driver—who had waited for me, his meter running—took me on toward The Golden Bubble. We had driven for ten minutes when I learned The Golden Bubble was an hour's drive away. So I told him to turn around and take me back to town. When we got back to Reno, he waited at the curb with the meter running, while I checked inside Harrah's Club. The meter at this point read forty-some dollars, which was a lot of money then, especially in my scale of expense. I went in the front door, through the shining loud gamut of slot machines on the carpet, and out the back door, where I ran down the alley and toward Interstate 80, toward the campsite on foot. I ran most of the way, in my cowboy boots along the I-80 guardrail in the sunset.

Nobody was at the old Cornucopia campsite. The deflated tent lay on the ground. The campfire was cold. The old gaming tables were there, legless, tilting on their keels. But everything else was gone, and all around, in sunset's still air, the dry ocean bed of the Ordovician period was perfectly silent. Darkness was falling, and I just stayed there all night, hoping someone would show up, squatting by the cold firespot, or standing up and pacing. Nobody came. Toward dawn, I swept an edge of the canvas tent up around myself and sat up on the ground in its folds, dozing upright. Nobody ever came.

This is all so boring. Who cares about the specifics? Everybody has a story like this. Youth is all made of mistakes, when love seems real and substantial. Today I came home to find Richard Nixon and John Kennedy, life-size, disporting in my living room, Nixon in agony, a lock of thin hair falling over his eyes, Kennedy standing behind him, his lip lifted in a handsome snarl of pleasure. HEAVEN reads the placard at their feet. I was going to unplug the projection equipment, but then didn't. It's art. That would be censorship. Instead I just avoid the living room. It isn't really visible during the daytime, because the sunlight from the living room windows washes it out. At first I didn't even see it. I noticed only the projection equipment: a big black Kodak box and the "Coherent Holographic" machine with two small glass wands of light, the hum of its fan; and on the coffee table an oval mirror mounted slantwise in calibrated orbit-hoops; and on the floor under my old work desk was a computer whose screen drifted lazily through its screen-saver designs. Later, as dusk came on, the presidents became more visible, in thin air.

It's the first sign of Gabriel and Wendy, along with a pair of suitcases and some art textbooks in the spare bedroom. But Gabriel himself hasn't shown up. They are supposed to move in next week. I mailed Wendy a house key; obviously she has given the key to Gabriel so he can get a start moving in. It seems an amusing misfortune that, because my own living room has become a den of trysting for spectral presidents, I can't keep my nightly rendezvous with the Spice Channel, to peer through the headachey images electronically garbled like a rack of neckties in a windstorm, searching for a glimpse of a breast or a hip, or, on the sound track, the sweet gasp of a woman in thrall, because now I prefer the televised effigy of woman to the actual practical reality of her presence in flesh, the threat of mistrust which is the edgy center of love. Alcohol 12 percent by volume. Contains sulfites. Surgeon General's Warning: Cigarette Smoke Contains Carbon Monoxide.

My "Wife and Child" may have to live here for as much as a year. So says Ed. To satisfy Faro Ness's probate lawyers, we must literally live together. Can't just say we did. Wendy is as ashamed of this project as I am, ashamed on my behalf too. Ashamed of how diminished are all possibilities. It's not just that I personally am diminished, at forty-one, but the whole world has grown small and hard and stupid now, and I'm not joking. To call *that* "art," for example. To praise it and award it money. It is so ugly. It's really sickening. This has always been a stupid land but now it's getting worse, not better. Nixon's sparse hair is flopped forward. Kennedy, at the thighs, has been provided with the faintest suggestion of under-skin cottage cheese and a paunch including stretch marks. There's more. It is unbelievably graphic. I almost had a heart attack when I turned the corner and found it there in its halo of unearthly light among the dimmed-down lamps. Haven't been in the living room since. Haven't even approached that doorway, turned back by the glow. For the first time in years I left my dinner dishes in the sink unwashed. Camel Light butts are floating in the blue milk of Wheat Chex. It's too late for us. We've been preserved as grown-ups in this unimaginable decade, we aren't young anymore, the kiss would be dentally cement-flavored, the skin is numb, the blush of blood has retreated to the core of the body, to irrigate the intestines, the liver, the fart-factory. I don't blame anyone. When I left her behind in Reno, I chose freedom. Freedom was supposed to be a good thing. I thought it would be best for both of us. When I got back to the motel that morning, Breece was in our room. He was collecting Wendy's belongings. There was a woman with him. He introduced her as Dana, and she said to me, "That's a hardheaded girlfriend you've got there." I'd been feeling sick, having spent the night sitting up dozing on the cold ground, wrapped in the old canvas circus tent. I said, "Where is she?"

Breece put a hand on the woman's spine and said, "Dana, could you leave us? We want to have a private talk."

She said, "I'll go next door and visit with Abner Kind," but then she stood smiling upon me for a minute. "You be nice to this boy, Dex. He's a good boy." She was dressed with the quiet force of a rich businesswoman. I realized the heavy white BMW in the parking lot was hers. She said, "I'll be next door," and she left. Breece sat down on the bed.

"Where is she," I said.

He stared down at his big hands clasped together. "Right now she's at Ecstasy."

"Where is she?" I repeated. I had heard what he said, but my voice went on asking again anyway.

"It's where the gamblers' collectors won't think to look. I'm taking a considerable risk, putting you-all up there. Her mother came out."

"Her mother is at Ecstasy?" I had a hard time imagining this, Wendy and her mother among the, as I pictured it, Spanish-style walled gardens enclosing fountains and trees and lawns in the desert, the grounds roamed by perfectly desirable women like hinds in a preserve.

"Wendy asked me to give you a message. She says to tell you she loves you and she's sorry."

"She's sorry?" I had gone unnaturally calm and objective.

"She is going to go ahead and have that baby. I understand you believe she should have it aborted. But she is a girl not impervious to instruction. You boys have been fortunate to be tagged onto such a person. You're too young to understand. You get old and wise, like us old bastards . . ."

His friend Dana appeared in the doorway. "Abner's not open yet. It's only eight-thirty, Breece. Let's buy this young man a breakfast. He looks hungry. Get you off your sermon."

Then nobody said anything, and I repeated, just to establish it as fact, "She's with her mom."

"Well, now, this might seem hard. You're in love. But, son, it looks like you're not a good influence on Wendy. I have offered her a very short career in that entertainment business there, to pay off her brother's gambling debt."

Dana told me, "A girl like her could earn that in a few nights. Come on, Dex, I want to go and get some food in this young man. Look at him, he's exhausted, and you're scaring him. He's going through an emotional trauma." She punched Breece's arm. "Let's go to the Hick'ry Pit."

He ignored her. "Now, I know this can all seem hard. A woman who has labored that way is"—his clasped hands struggled together in a two-backed turtle—"held in disgrace in the world. The whole prospect would naturally make you jealous and disturbed, the position you're in. But I'll tell you something. Some certain kinds of difficulties can only be solved by thinking of the long term. I want you to try to have some perspective. Heaven's ways are mysterious." He stopped and watched me. "They're all perfectly safe. Nobody's going to do anything against anybody's will."

"What did her mother do?"

"Just now her mother has gone back to Lake Tahoe, 'cause she's driving some kind of rent-a-car she can't afford no more."

I made a brave laugh, or rather my face toughened in a way that was supposed to indicate scorn, and told him, "Her mother will pay for everything. She'll pay Peter's gambling debt. Wendy doesn't need your help. Her mother is a good person."

He lowered his eyes. "I am not convinced her mother is a good person. Her mother tells her, too, to abort the baby. Son,

I'm sorry but I have to at least influence things. I can't just stand by. The flesh is a mystery. The flesh is a mystery, boy. You know who that unborn child is? Really? That child is you and me." He made a grin like a twinge of pain, and turned half toward Dana. "But you ain't a crazy mystical old coot like me living out there in the desert without any fuckin' toilet paper." That was a remark aimed at Dana, who was idly grazing the room and was above responding. "Also"—he started refastening a cuff link—"in fact, her mother claims she has no money. She claims her rent-a-car is on a canceled credit card."

I told him with complete confidence, "Oh, her mother has money."

"Her husband does seem to have been rich. But she is divorcing him. None of that is completely clear to me."

"She's getting divorced? Wendy's mother?" This unthought-of idea fit perfectly.

"Her husband got her money locked up in some kind of fi-nancial arrangement," he said, putting a hinge in the word *financial*, where Nevadan skepticism detected a weak spot. I looked at Breece. His form, its edges, had a just-rinsed distinctness in my sight. I was seeing him for the first time now as my active enemy. "Did you really get a master's degree?" I said, in an insane irrelevancy.

He puffed through his nose, smiling. "My checkered past. Peter exaggerates, of course." He glanced at Dana, who was trying to be patient, poking around the room.

"Hon, really," she said.

"Yes, let's go. You need some real breakfast. This will all start to look better when you got a full stomach."

"No thanks," I said, and turned away from the hand on my shoulder. I walked out the door. I already knew I had to go to Ecstasy.

"Wait a minute, son, this is all a very delicate situation and you mustn't go about fucking it up with heroics based on misunderstandings." He followed me out into the parking lot. "Wait, now. Wendy has made agreements that don't include you, unfortunately. You have to think about that."

I was around the corner and out of sight. With complete clarity of mind, I knew what to do. I circled the block and went through the alley, to the back door of Mr. Kind's pawn shop. I let myself in with the key he'd trusted me with. In a top drawer, he kept a key to the old Volvo that stayed in the alley behind the shop. It had been his wife's car, but now it spent all its time parked in the alley providing long-term storage for pawn shop miscellany. On the front seat was a box of elk hooves, which I pulled out and set on the ground. The engine started easily. Sacrums and pelvises and wishbones of various animals—reptiles, birds—lay on the peculiarly table-like dashboard, where they were supposed to whiten in the sun.

They teetered and rocked when I pulled out of the alley on to the street. The morning sun was blinding. I remember how sunlight covered the dusty windshield while I drove straight into it, east on I-80, toward Ecstasy. Everyone knew generally the locations of these places. Ecstasy was down among a stand of trees in a low spot in the desert, east of town, and I parked in the lot out front. It was surrounded by a barbed-wire-topped fence. Inside the gate was a set of linked boxes with trailer hitches protruding through foundation shrubs. It had a parking lot of old asphalt hoary from the ages of desert sun—with a few customers' cars, even at this hour of the morning. I pushed an outer doorbell. After I was buzzed in through the door (my bootheels on a ramp of plywood covered with indoor-outdoor green carpeting), five girls blocked my entrance, by swinging out limply like carcasses on a butcher's ceiling-hooks. They were presenting themselves in a row, for my choice, on their morning shift. I could only say, "I'm looking for someone," which broke up the formation and they sauntered back to a lounge, or to the bar, or to a white vinyl couch where a paperback *The Thorn Birds* lay splayed open. One girl spoke in bored despondency to an open office door, "It's a boyfriend."

Then nothing happened. Nobody threw me out. Nobody even addressed me. One girl went back to reading *The Thorn Birds*. Another picked up the receiver of a pay phone which had been lying atop the cigarette machine, and, wearing a black bikini, started talking softly. It was a cheaper-looking place than I'd pictured. There was a temporary-looking bar, like from a furniture-rental store, with a bartender, who I assumed acted as a sort of peacekeeper, probably armed. But he wasn't interested in me and went on washing glasses in a sink while talking to a girl in a blue negligee. There was an adjoining small office, like the office in a gas station, with just a metal desk and a metal chair; but I couldn't see anybody in there. I could see down a short corridor of rooms, where one bedroom door stood open showing a Fleetwood Mac poster and a pink nightstand with a room deodorizer and a box of Kleenexes. I was standing in the middle of the open floor. I didn't have a plan, now that I was there. The red wall-to-wall carpet was wrinkled, laid out without a carpet pad.

I went over to the bar and asked for a Coke. The bartender lifted his eyes to the window that looked out on the parking lot, through the tall chain-link fence. Two cars pulled up and parked in the morning sun out there. First was Mr. Kind's new Volvo. It was immediately followed by Breece's Cadillac.

The bartender never did bring me a Coke. We both watched the two men coming up to the door. Breece let Mr. Kind enter first. I told Mr. Kind as he came in, "I'm sorry, sir." I was referring to my theft of his spare car. "I was in a hurry."

"Don't even think of it. I understand. A detail."

"Why don't we go in here," said Breece. He was heading for a door, around the corner from the juke box.

Mr. Kind smiled unhappily and told me, "She is not here. They've all been moved." I said something like *What do you mean she's not here,* not expecting an answer. Now my hearing and sight were going to fail me for a minute. I think it was at this point I started to realize how large a web had been woven. Mr. Kind gestured to the door Breece had gone through. "You must realize, Mr. Breece has put himself in considerable risk, helping you and your friends."

The room—Mr. Kind came in after me and closed the door—looked like an employee lounge. There was a big folding table, and there was a microwave oven and a few vending machines, a stainless steel sink and a Mr. Coffee machine. Breece watched me come in, his big hands spread over his hipbones. I sat down in a folding chair as if I were under arrest. A failure of bravery never identifies itself under the name "cowardice," not then in the midst of events. I suppose cowards usually think they're only being reasonable. I said, "Where's Wendy?"

"First, you've got to have some food," Breece said, facing the vending machines, fishing in his pocket. "All we seem to have available to us here is these microwave burritos."

Mr. Kind, older and more fragile outside his shop, had folded his arms, standing on the opposite side of the room. He was watching Breece prepare a dollar bill to feed it to the slot in the change machine. "Breece," he said, "is it Julian Satis?"

Breece didn't answer. It amounted to an affirmative response.

"The girl's mother is . . . ?"

". . . Taking a rent-a-car back to Tahoe. Then she's coming back here on the train. I am supposed to meet the train. I'm also supposed to keep the mother in the dark about this. Imagine that." This element of the scheme annoyed him. "Supposedly, her mother will be living over at the lake, and they'll all tell her the girl got a temporary housekeeping job in a Winnemucca casino."

The change machine rejected Breece's dollar bill, gliding it right back out at him. He went back to carefully unpleating the wrinkled bill on his lifted hip, ironing it. "These goddamn things. Do you have a decent dollar, Abner? Or some quarters?"

"That girl has every right to an operation, Breece. What you're doing is wrong. I understand you have this great certainty. But certainty is not a virtue. You have to consider the consequences of this in people's lives."

"She doesn't want an abortion. That's the truth, Abner." The machine accepted his dollar, and a handful of coins clinked in the cup below. "I think you fail to grant her enough respect."

"The child, when it's born, will grow up with all the disadvantages. And think about the girl's life, too. She can be something. She's not ready for motherhood."

Breece turned, with his handful of change, and got a little taller. "Abner, none of us is ready for anything."

"That is *your* Christian philosophy. *Your* Christian philosophy won't help her when she can't feed the child."

"We're fed by faith."

". . . and has lost so much of her life, because she could have been something."

"'*Be* something'?" Breece turned to regard the vending machine and push its buttons. She already *is* something. That baby of hers is something. Trouble with you, Abner, is you think people can get what they want, or even know what they want." He started consulting the fine print on the burrito's plastic sleeve, then stooped, squinting, to press buttons on the microwave. "Whereas what the Lord may want for us . . ." he said, and then didn't finish the thought. He looked up at Mr. Kind. "Do you think I am forcing the girl in any way? Abner? Do you think it's anything but her own decision? You know I would never have offered this protection if it were not her own free will."

Mr. Kind gave me a comradely look, of powerlessness. For some reason he went on having confidence in me, even though

California's Over

I had stolen his spare car, and even though I already knew, somewhere in my folded, shadowy heart, that I would leave town that day with the eight hundred dollars he had given us for the operation. I'd always known in the end Wendy would be better off without me, especially with her mother here now. It seemed a manly thing to do, to forsake what I loved, because all I had to offer her was love. I was seventeen, and I had begun to have a feeling that love might not be really enough, that some other profound mysterious resource is required in a grown man, that for love to be enough in life is a kind of effeminacy, in the eyes of woman too. I thought I was doing the right thing. At that moment, my mind was very clear and shallow, and almost elated. The only evidence of shock was that I had begun to tremble in my spine. It was something that continued for a few days on and off, a constant hint of tremor, like the threat of a chill, that reduces my posture, makes me look elderly, makes me bring out the old air force parka I've had for years and wear it around the house, even on summer evenings. It's not very warm anymore, the goosedown inside has thinned to nothing. With its orange lining and rags of rabbit-fur around the hood, it will be another thing Gabriel and Wendy will be have to get used to, when they're living here: me in my old duffel coat.

The burrito was cooking in the microwave. The two men on opposing walls of the room mourned silently over an intractable situation. Outside in the corridor, a woman's voice shouted happily, "Check it out. They got Patty Hearst. It's on TV. The whole SLA is in Los Angeles and they've got the house surrounded. It's on two different channels. I'm in my room."

The oven's timer was making a scratchy hum. Breece leaned back on a vending machine, folded his arms, and hung his head thinking. "She won't be doing it long," he said. "She won't even be very good at it. She's one of the few girls I believe can get in and out of it." He added, "Maybe it's the old absent-father situation. But I agree with you, she ain't one of these girls by nature."

"You have some sense of the hypocrisy? To prevent an abortion, you will lead the girl to sin."

"This ain't a sin. You sophist. You know it ain't sin. These women surely have sinned *else*where"—he gripped his own throat, making an ascot of his big hand—"and they've sinned in more important ways, more deeper ways, beginning way back I'm sure. These girls have plenty of troubles worse than Wendy. But this sad copulation in this house, it's not necessarily sin. Sometimes it's grace, Abner. One could never know. This is the Lord's workshop, this house, just like anyplace else. And now, I'll tell you, Abner, in the Lord's workshop there is a baby coming."

"You could let us talk with her by phone."

Breece closed his eyes. His head sleepily dropped so that his chin was on his chest. His hands hung by thumbs from his belt. The burrito finished cooking, with a *ching* from the oven, and he shuffled around to lift it out of the chamber and set it before me, where I sat at the table. It looked like an artificial display specimen of molded vinyl. At last he answered Mr. Kind, "Abner, I know you would try to influence the girl if you talked to her at all. I ain't holding her captive in any sense, but I've got to encourage any little glimmer of strength. I am sure that you would try to bend her into weakness and worldliness. The gate is wide and the way is easy."

Mr. Kind told me, stirring, "We'll find a way to reach her. Don't worry."

But it was too late. Wendy's mother had come for her, and that changed everything. Already I had begun picturing the Reno bus depot in sharp morning light. And I still remember it today, a big empty room with two benches, the ticket window of heavy bullet-proof glass that tinted an inner world, the lockers, the shut-up candy stand, the chrome trim around the ticket counter. When I was sitting on that hard public pew there, later that day, with my duffel bag, I knew I was not brave, and in a way I suppose I saw my life stretch before me then: I was someone who wouldn't get what he loved. But I thought at the time, plenty of people don't get what they love, it's part of a man's life, especially if you're still young, you get over it, that's what I thought.

So the day was over for me. It was only nine or ten in the morning. "Let's go," Mr. Kind said, putting a hand on my shoulder. "He is a procurer."

"No I ain't. You know as well as I, how these girls happen. These girls are all just heedless children who are playing next to a cliff. They come running through the tall grass and somebody has to be here to catch them. You're just a Jew, Abner, so you never take on the real duty."

Mr. Kind turned on him. "Dexter, sometimes faith is the great cause of damage. Only *un*certainty can save you. I am not a Jew—"

"Oh no, you're a Jew all right. You think you can leave all that behind. You *wish* you could leave all that behind. Abner, listen to me. Every minute of every day and night, in the darkest hour of midnight and in the hot noontime in the sun, Jesus is holding out for you, saying it don't matter what you been . . ."

Mr. Kind led me out the door. The front room was empty. Even the bartender had left his post. Mr. Kind found a phone book and dialed a number, moving with a lot of speed and decision. Breece's insults had taken years off him. He said into the phone, "This is Abner Kind. I think Millie has some guests of Dexter Breece staying there. Yes, that would be fine."

He looked at me and said "Bingo," then handed the phone to me.

I wasn't sure I wanted to be having this conversation.

The person who came on the line was Peter, who whispered, "Baelthon! Is this weird? Are you watching?"

"What?"

"The whole fuckin' Symbionese Liberation Army is surrounded. It's like Custer's Last Stand."

"Are you watching television?"

"They got Tania."

"Who?"

"Patty Hearst. They've been firing into the building, but nobody is sure whether *she's* inside. You should be watching this. This is a spectacle. This is the total American spectacle. They even stop for commercial breaks. They advertise laundry detergent, and then it's back to *pow! pow!* They're inside this little house, and the whole National Guard is surrounding them. Remember what that comedian used to say, *The Revolution Will Not Be Televised! The Revolution Will Not Be Brought to You by the 3-M Corporation or the Makers of Hallmark Cards!*"

"Is Wendy with you?"

"I'm sorry about this, man. This is weird. She wanted it to be a clean break like this. It's just me and Ed here. Did Breece get to you? Did Breece talk to you?"

"Is your mother here?"

"She'll be back soon. Wendy said, you know, it would be better if you guys didn't communicate. She's crazy. She's going to have the baby. And I'm going to be guilty forever. Guilty guilty guilty."

"Couldn't your mom help? Couldn't she just . . . *pay?*"

"She doesn't even have a checkbook. It's Faro and his church. All their money is totally tied up. Nobody can get to it. Not even Faro."

"Are they getting a divorce? Is that true?"

Peter, rather than answering, gave one of his stoned sniffs.

"Peter? Is your mother really divorcing Faro?"

"Divorcing the *church*, more like. The house got demolished. Did you know? It's demolished. It was just a black hole of mortgages. All we had was debts, so we gave our *debts* to the church. But hey," he concluded lamely, glad to be helpless.

There I stood. Many of life's decisions are made before we stand at the crossroad, already implicit in our bones, in a hunch of the shoulder. I said, "Maybe they're divorced, but Faro will help."

"He can't, man. The government has to basically approve every check he writes."

"Doesn't he have any other resources?"

"This whole family is under constant audit. Everything is impounded. It's like the CIA or something. The government has to *see* every check he writes."

"Yes, but he can borrow from a friend. He couldn't've tied everything up so tight."

"It's tied up so tight, *he* can't untie himself. You have no idea of the scale of Faro's whole thing."

◉　◉　◉

"Wendy? May I invite you to be my partner in crime? I want your help in hiding all my filthy old money."

That was how Faro first introduced Wendy to the church, in a smiling growl parodying piracy with a greedy hand-washing motion, as he stood outside the door of the ballroom, while the rest of them were gathered around the rusty guitar on the floor. Everyone else was staring at him. He happened to be standing beside the wall where paint-sloshed bodies had printed themselves, and he edged away from that. He straightened up, and gained some dignity. "I'd like a word with you. This is actually a serious proposal I want to make."

Her brother zipped his jacket up. "Mom and I can find Merlin. He'll be on the beach. You stay here. You've got your guitar to bury."

It lay at her feet.

She said, "*Baelthon* can bury it. He's paid to work here."

"It's a ceremony, Wen," Peter spoke as he walked out the door, following his mother, past Faro. "Somebody has to be there besides the gravedigger."

She had suddenly outgrown the idea of having a burial ceremony.

Faro said (with an undertaker's somberness, respectful of the lifeless guitar on the floor), "Wendy? When you're done? I'll be in the kitchen." He turned and went down the rear hall, humming a musical refrain from the *Addams Family* TV show, which was one of his standard jokes around the house.

Outside, a car door slammed. Wendy went to the window. A truck was in the drive. *Butterfield & Butterfield, Auctioneers and Appraisers Since 1865.* The driver was walking up the path, calling in a tough accent she could hear through the pane: "If this is where the tent goes, somebody will have to move all those *doors.*" He was irritated. And he was about to be more irritated because he was coming to the front gate where the thorn-branch would catch him.

Alone in the room now with the hired mover—who again today was wearing her father's old clothes—she looked down at the guitar, showing him a profile in which a temporary rash rose and fell, she could feel it in her collar. He was just standing there. Then he surprised her by saying, "'Merlin' is Dean, isn't he." He was so confident in his right to be curious. She turned away toward the window. "The guy with the surfboard," he clarified.

Now Merlin was only the guy with the surfboard. The glances of newcomers will bury everything. Nobody will ever *see* that the guy with the surfboard cooked French toast on mornings when everybody was still passed-out or missing, and made sure she got to school, packed her lunch box, spent hours lying out on the big brown couch making changes in her father's manuscripts, took her out for ice cream at Baskin-Robbins the time her father was arrested for drunk driving and Wendy watched from the passenger seat as he let himself be handcuffed and then when he got to the jail made his one phone call not to a lawyer but to his publicity agent. How strange all those days seemed now. It all made her feel painfully open-ended.

"I like Dean" was Baelthon's next comment.

He had an inert way of gradually soaking in, wherever he was. He added, "I see him at Little Tom's."

"Listen to me, Baelthon. Can you move a mattress? You have to help me make a guest room ready for Dean. I'm going to go talk to Faro now. You wait here. There's a mattress we can put in a basement room."

She knew the room. It was in the rear cellar, under the kitchen, to be entered only by slipping sideways behind the defunct washing machine in the old laundry room, through a gap that had always been covered by a big sign leaning there reading "UNGRY I." It would be cozy with a few carpets, plenty of lamps. Nobody would find him there, not even the auctioneers' movers—who were outside unpacking on the lawn, hauling a tremendous green-canvas afterbirth out of the back of their panel truck, tossing out crowbars and grappling hooks and ropes and tarps and blankets, all the tools of burglary.

"You stay here. Don't move. I'll be right back," she said, and she left to talk to Faro.

◉　◉　◉

"This 'church,'" he began, gesturing around at the house, "is perfectly legal. My lawyers are turning me into a 501(c)(3). This whole thing will be safe from the government."

She said, "I don't know what that is—a 501(c)(3)."

They were standing beside the big kitchen table. He had been out for his daily swim in the ocean, and now he was wearing a bulky white turtleneck sweater and corduroy pants, his hair still wet from having taken a shower.

"It means we're all going to be non-profit. *Everything* is going to be non-profit. It's a little bit ambitious. And there's one part I'm hoping you'll play. Do you remember your father's Free Store in People's Park? It had the famous Infinite Soup, a magic pot, never empty. And then the Free Store was a similar kind of thing: take what you need without paying. Subvert the economy. Remember all that? It was all in People's Park?"

He paused. She didn't respond but only shifted, warily; she was starting to get the feeling she was about to be a disappointment to him again.

"All the Ness family holdings will be broken up. As much as possible will come into church ownership. There will be a lot of flotsam and jetsam. Many thousands of dollars' worth of miscellaneous stuff. I want to set up a way of giving it to the church. And then distributing it to needy people. I thought we'd call the operation a Free Store." He was looking at her with embarrassed pride.

She said, "There's already a Free Box in town."

"Oh, I'm talking about something on a much larger scale. Just let me explain. I haven't talked about this with anyone yet, other than the Ness accountants."

He sighed. His arms lifted and dropped. "I'm totally reorganizing my assets. Sometimes you have not cash but property. Which you *don't* want. A lot of it is residential and office. And there's two hotels, for instance. There are people called liquidators, who sell stuff off for you. But a huge amount is below-the-line stuff, stuff that's not valuable enough to sell, but too valuable to throw away. Now, Goodwill and the Salvation Army can't accept donations over ten thousand dollars' worth. They can, but if they do they have to report it. It begins to look like a tax scam. So here's what I'm asking."

"Over ten thousand dollars?"

"Oh, easily. In junk alone. You have no idea. Just the two hotels in California will generate tremendous amounts of cast-off stuff. Which would ordinarily just be junked! Just tossed in landfill! Because a liquidator doesn't want to bother with it. Used but perfectly good carpeting. Kitchen stuff. Lamps. Appliances. Tables and chairs. See what I mean? And there are some other properties. Houses and apartment buildings. There's *this* place, for a start. All this stuff around here. So here's what I'm asking. You would have the job of disposing this stuff. All kinds of stuff. Miscellaneous stuff. It would be a giveaway. That's the point. But you could do it any way you want. You'd have to find a home for lots of valuable stuff. It would be entirely your bailiwick. And it would turn into a real job. Lasting maybe six months. For example, you'd have to rent warehouse space."

"What stuff?" she said—fakily because she had started to feel trapped. Her shoulder always rose toward her ear when she was dissembling.

"What stuff! Shoof! Just look." He lifted the nearest thing—a stump of a homemade sand-candle that had been on the windowsill for years. "You can't *sell* this stuff." A rain of loose sand made him put it right back. He brushed off his palms, saying, "Yet this stuff is a resource. For somebody."

"I'd be in charge of giving it away?"

"Well, first it would be donated to the church. You'd have to keep detailed records. You'd come up with a plan. Identify recipients. Identify needs to be filled. Whatever. Then distributing the stuff too. I'd have to approve your plan. You'd have to know in advance, Wendy, I wouldn't pay you for any of this. This is strictly the goodness of your heart. You'd have to keep records for the tax people. I don't want any profit coming back to the Open Ranch or the church. That's the whole point. I don't want to *make* money. We're all going to be a 501(c)(3). This creates negative flow for my accountants. What you'd get to do, is you'd get to be an angel." His eyes in their earnestness looked parched and far-seeing. Between his eyebrows a single hair reached straight out, as dark as a beetle's leg. She wanted, cosmetically, to pluck it. Her mother should have plucked it for him.

It must have made him self-conscious, her staring at him. He turned away. "Like this table right here." He sat down and put his elbows on it, showing that it worked just fine as a table. "Who's going to 'buy' a table like this? Nobody. But it's perfectly good."

"Well, this table is historical, it's definitely not for sale," she said, taking perhaps comfort in his mistakenness. "My dad wrote *The Green Conquistador* at this table. And the underside has a Karl Boronovska drawing, and all my dad's friends scratched things into it when they sat here—"

"Okay, fine, but you get my point. Maybe you have some old clothes for instance. Or, maybe Peter has his—I don't know— his potter's wheel. Butterfield's doesn't want to auction that. And a liquidator doesn't want to bother with it. But somebody could *use* that potter's wheel. For all we know, somebody could make a living with it. What you'd be doing here is altruism."

She said nothing.

"You can work around your school schedule."

Hopelessness overtook her, and of course Faro sensed it.

"Any businessman would advise that I simply junk this stuff. Either way, I could call it a tax loss. It makes no material difference to me. It's up to *you* whether a bunch of perfectly good stuff gets recycled to benefit somebody or ends up in landfill polluting the environment. We live in the most affluent society in history. The average American family's *garbage* can is like a *treasure*-chest for ninety percent of the rest of the world."

She knew good faith is simply a habit some people have; and anybody can develop the habit. And she knew people like her actually do make the world colder and more unfair. She thought of all her wasted sad time, her empty hours, her strange non-specific appetite for everything, anything—and she surprised herself by saying, "Okay, I'll do it," in a limp moment of, like, turning herself inside-out. She couldn't believe it. "Well, fine. Marvelous." He stared downward. "I thought you would. But then"—he stood up from his chair and turned half-away, and his voice sharpened—". . . I could see I had you trapped. Am I such a jerk? Jesus Christ, Wendy. You have no idea." He hung his head and lingered and made fists with both hands. He said, "Sorry," and walked out of the room fast. She didn't know what had happened, what she'd done.

◉　◉　◉

Meanwhile Peter was sitting out on a sand dune, while the figure of Dean Houlihan grew larger in the distance coming up the beach. Actually, he'd begun by trying to *avoid* finding Dean, simply because, when he faced it more specifically, he changed his mind and didn't want the awkward duty of it. Instead he'd been walking in the opposite direction, trying—even to the point of closing his eyes—to invite in his mind the personal migraine of poetic inspiration, but failing, finding himself forced back upon such original conjuring-ceremonies as lighting a cigarette, in his Marlboro Man method, the way his father always lit cigarettes, cupping the match in his palms against the wind, with a toss of hair: maybe your home is being broken up, maybe they're selling off the furniture and the specially minted Endicott Medal and everything else; maybe your education was, face it, lazy and pretentious and your entire *vocabulary* is a trite little self-obscuring paisley cloud the color of Santana's *Abraxas* album cover; maybe it's peculiarly unthinkable for you to ever have a "job"—but sometimes just lighting a cigarette the right way will get you through life. With an exhalation of smoke whipped away by wind, he moved on down the shore and his spirit soared and leveled off again at the height of judgment, to look down upon a kind of small map of the USA. Which is how wishing for inspiration always felt.

But the sand sucked each footstep back in pockets. And walking while smoking is tiring. So he changed direction, uphill toward the shelter of the bluff, to find a place to sit, with a literary infirmity now. The poet's eye ought to be sharp and merciless, but his eyes had been rubbed by the lotion of comfort all his life. He sat down. And then there was Dean, far down the beach. It was definitely Dean. The characteristic walk. Unbalanced by his surfboard. A tyrannosaurus rex. The tassel of hair. Peter drew on his cigarette and decided he would pretend to know nothing about the sleeping bag under the house or the electric guitar. It was all too embarrassing. Let Wendy or his mother bring it up. Dean's figure grew larger and developed a self-conscious limp coming toward him. Peter dragged on his cigarette and raised his voice over the ocean's applause, "Merlin."

"Young Farmican!" His bunched fingertips kissed his forehead and made a flourish. He was climbing the beach toward Peter. "Peace."

"How's everything?"

He arrived and stood above Peter, laid his surfboard down and then stood there, scratching his buttocks with both hands, looking up the far beach. "Heard about the comet yet?" In the bagged-out pocket of a fluorescent crocheted-yarn vest, he had a paperback book, which he pulled out and tossed at Peter's feet. The cover had been torn off, but the title-page said: *Worlds in Collision*. The author was Immanuel Velikovsky.

"Heard about that?" He gripped his knees and lowered himself onto the sand beside Peter. "That fellow Velikovsky is not held in very high esteem by the scientific community. He is considered marginal, to use a euphemism. This book is about one particular comet that came around in fourteen-something B.C. The next one is coming this Christmas. They're calling the new one Kohoutek. This is a big year, Farmican. '73. Astrologically the biggest cataclysm since '68. This energy crisis is only the first in a series. Ain't heard much about the energy crisis yet, I suppose. Ah, but you will."

In talking Dean had a style of self-ridicule, while behind his mask an eye seemed to watch you. He had steadfastly declined to come to Oregon. Maybe the whole town would go on taking care of him forever, keep designating him one of the several simultaneous mayors of Seawall, keep offering him shelter during the rainy months, a paper cup of wine out the back door of the Veritas in the evenings. Peter sighed, discovering more of his cigarette-headache, squeezing escaping pages under his thumbnail. That depressing yellow dye they use on paperbacks' edges. On the inner pages, pocks marked where grains of sand had been trapped. The book flopped open to an S.S.I. check, *Department of the Treasury, $119.00*, on stiff green card-paper punched with computer holes.

"New comet'll be a humdinger," Dean said. "Might want to be ready." He made an elbow-in-the-ribs gesture.

Peter closed the book and lightly weighed it. "Is it going to hit Earth? Is that it?"

Dean didn't answer. Just looked out at the ocean horizon. On his surfboard's top surface, a sticker said "Zildjian Cymbals." Another said "Grande Hotel Marrakesh." Cutting over both stickers were lines of carved inscription, Babylonian-looking in their cuneiform uniformity: +THE+FIVE+COL-ORS+BLIND+THE+EYE, one of them seemed to say.

"The Farmicans have been looking for me," he said, without taking his vision from the horizon. His eyes were increasingly attacked by crow's-feet now, the inner ivory stained orange: it was multiplying capillaries if you looked close. Yet he was also eternally young-looking, as the insane can be. He dug with a fingernail at something between his teeth, and then he spoke again. "Trouble with all you people is you're afraid of taking the plunge. Ah, but then most people are."

The many *layers* of him were always baffling, tiring. "How

do you mean?" Peter said, but weakly. His father had, in his life, taken the plunge. Peter certainly hadn't. Wouldn't. Destined for poetry merely by being so perfectly handsome, living suspended in his room under the house where he kept the space heater up to a dull fever. What he could never face was—his father's secret—that the path of art leads, through the truth, straight toward death, an algebraic equation toward zero. But that very zero was really a kind of money, an *infinite* zero. By spending it, you purchase all this cheap world, this unreasonable world, where a brass doorknob for the front door costs more than *he* could earn in a *month* at any job out there. Four hundred dollars, his mother had said, for a mere doorknob. His decision to stay on in the house alone had given him a new autobiographical or even suicidal detachment, so even the sound of the waves grew small and tinny, as in a seashell.

Dean grasped his ankles and pulled his legs into the lotus position, and started explaining. "I'll consent to you folks— oh—protecting me from myself—even though I'd be just as happy in the Civic Center jail as anywhere else. A truly organized man can be happy anywhere." He fingered his Day-Glo vest, as if it were evidence of what an organized man he was. "However, I'm interested in the state of affairs in your household right now. You have a house guest."

"You mean Ed? Did you know about that? You knew they had another child?"

"Young man, I married your parents. I presided over the sacrament."

"So you knew about Ed? All this time? All these years?"

He didn't answer. He had a thoughtful way of sucking on a tooth. "Tell me. What is Ed's attitude toward things? How does he conduct himself?"

"He's . . ." Peter turned away, searching for a word, ". . . straight."

"Ah!" said Dean, still looking out to sea. "Meaning 'square.'" They sat side by side for a time. Sitting beside Dean was as close as he would ever come again to his father. His father once said all his ideas were plagiarized, originally Dean's. *The Green Conquistador* was dedicated to Dean.

"Perhaps you'd like to escort me back to your house. I'll go peacefully. I surrender."

"Were they married when Ed was born?"

Dean frowned, but didn't answer. He hugged his knees. At last he said, "We were all living under this church in North Beach. There was a place in the basement where a lot of extremely beat individuals made these little pads. We called them pads." He seemed to find that sad, fondly. "First Congregational Church. The minister was very cool. The scene had already started to get phony, people with their Jean-Paul Sartre and their red wine and their burlap and their college educations. The bourgeois suburbs came in, like they always do, but I don't blame 'em. You can't blame anybody. It was nice, really. The bourgeois suburbs is peace and love." He stood up, stretched, grabbed his own ass. "Let's go, Farmican. I'm a fugitive from justice."

He and Dean climbed up from the beach to see an immense new green tent rising on his own lawn, first its peak, then the whole thing, pulsing and swaying semi-erect, newer-looking and better constructed than anything ever in the whole town of Seawall. The estate auctioneer's shining-clean van was parked in the drive. One of their employees was moving around with some stakes, tugging on guy wires, making the heavy canvas heave in throbbing up taut. Everybody was gathered out there—his mother, Wendy, Faro, Baelthon, and a fat man holding a steel clipboard—all standing around in a circle discussing an object: it was a leather drum from Africa that had always hung on the wall in the library, now exposed outside in daylight looking dusty and pale and mummified, its flesh-stretches and wrinkles burnished golden. In a movie's subliminal flash-frame, Peter's tired mind glimpsed it as some kind of dug-up old human *piece* being bargained over. The nauseating wall of canvas was swaying in a heavy, dreamy new motion he couldn't shake off. He heard his mother saying, "I could see it either way," her hands tucked high under her arms.

"What is this?" Peter said as he came across the lawn.

Wendy, seeing Dean, cried, "Merlin!"

His mother said, "Dean, we were looking for you." Dean's rolling hand tapped his forehead, chin, and breast, closing his eyes. He started accepting people's embraces. "What is this?" Peter asked again.

And then his sister did a strange thing: she seemed to grin with happiness. "Oh! Peter! There's going to be a Free Store again! Remember Dad's Free Store?" He had never seen Wendy's eyebrows lift quite like that. As her brother, he was suspicious. She explained, "Where you give stuff away?"

Faro said, "Well? Isn't this just exactly the kind of thing?"

"Honey, it's a genuine Watusi marriage drum," his wife said. "If we sell something like this, we could use the money to *employ* some poor person."

It was the sort of suggestion his mother would never have made before. Their lives now, outside this house, would look meaner and duller. He knew he should be ashamed of her standing here and suggesting they exploit the unemployed poor, but he said nothing to oppose her, and his cowardly heart shrank within the sound of her voice. Which must be something families do, too: preserve the weak and the hypocritical. She said, "Besides, there's already the Free Box in front of the Co-op. I don't get this Free Store project. Why don't you just give it all to the Salvation Army and take that write-off?"

"Julie, *we're* a non-profit. Everything is going through our non-profit number now."

"How much is it worth?" she asked the man with the clip-board.

He hugged his clipboard in a slouch. "The ethnographic appraiser isn't here. But if it's old? I'd say, oh, three hundred."

The figure was a defeat to Faro, who rolled his eyes.

Dean spoke up, "Folks don't put things in the Free Box." With the fingernails of both hands, he was scratching his cheeks and neck. "They think they'll hit me on the head."

The appraiser just looked at the ground. Nobody spoke. A low spot had rolled them together. Faro started up again, "Maybe this drum is a bad example, but we have to draw the line somewhere where we're making *some* sacrifices, or else we'll only be giving the poor a lot of worthless shit. Like how about that old car in there? Does it run?"

"The Ford? Sure it runs. But the same principle holds. We could sell it and use the money."

"I know that's how the *economy* works. But Wendy and I are setting up a whole new kind of accountancy. Aren't we. It's supposed to put fertilizer at the bottom of the food chain."

"I don't know, Fare. I suppose we could give the Ford away," she said.

Faro was a saint, Peter found it almost unbelievable. The world could be made new. If it were *him* in charge, he would have wanted to keep the car for himself, and he looked down at the ground in almost fear, a feeling of free fall, a child's lonely disappointment in getting *exactly* what he wanted, the administration of a heavenly economy. It gave him the idea he'd probably end up in Oregon eventually.

A man in shirtsleeves was edging in from the driveway. He had been standing there for some while, holding a square of bright-orange cardboard: it was a sign, with the word DANGER at the center in large type. "Excuse me, is this the church? I'm from the County. Are you Lansford Ness?"

"What can I do for you?"

At that moment, Dean dropped his surfboard to the ground, where it flopped like a porpoise. He seemed slugged backward. Everyone looked at him. He looked straight at Peter's mother, narrowing his eyes. "Julia. Are you married?" His astonishment was stagy, his knees had buckled and his arms flung wide to embrace the whole planet of her marriedness.

She sighed.

"Why wasn't I told? Julia!"

"I'm sorry, Dean, I know we ought to have asked you."

Faro asked the man from the County, "What can I do for you?" and he put out a hand to lead him away.

Unsuccessfully. The man stood his ground, taking his attention from Dean and reapplying it to Faro. "I'm from the County, and I've come out here to post this property with a red tag. But I can't do that until you have a surrounding barrier against ingress. You have to have it within four days."

"I don't understand."

"Escrow is supposed to close on this property in four days. At that time it changes hands. But the building inspector's report indicates it is unsafe for habitation: I got faulty foundation, wiring, sub-flooring at failure level, unheated living areas, illegal heating and ventilation and drainage. If you want to close escrow, you have to have the red tag. It's the law. And the red tag requires a continuous surrounding barrier against ingress."

"Right at this point I wonder if I oughtn't to ask you to leave the property. You understand, this is something for my lawyers."

"I understand, sir, and that's fine. It just has to be legally posted. When the property changes hands, it has to be posted condemned."

"The County wants me to put up a *fence* in four days?"

"It could be a temporary cyclone fence. It could be anything. But right now it's illegal for me to post the property until there is a surrounding barrier against ingress."

"Condemned?" Peter spoke up in disbelief.

"It's a technicality," Faro told everybody. "We still have every right to use the house."

"Here's my card. This number is the Planning Department. I can come back out to post it, but if you don't have a barrier, escrow can't close. We'll have to notify the title company, and escrow can't close."

"I'm sorry you had to come all the way out here," Faro said. The man turned to his car. Faro went drifting after him. "I can promise to have a fence up, even within a day or two . . ."

"Condemned," Peter said again, trying to send up the word in public space, with maybe almost a thrill in the catastrophe, because in a legendary way, it fit: that he should dig in alone and begin writing here in a condemned structure. He warned his mother, testing happiness inwardly, "This is *my* house. I'm going to *be* here." As he spoke, righteousness mounted inside to the point of plugging his ears. He knew he'd always be hearing his own voice speak inwardly, against even his own unbelief. "This house is sacred. They can't touch it."

"It's just a technicality," Faro came back interrupting. The building inspector had tossed his orange DANGER sign in on the car seat and had sat inside to start the engine. "These bureaucrats just need to put their sign up. We can still do whatever we want. Let 'em call it condemned. It doesn't mean anything."

Dean laid a big hand on Peter's shoulder and closed his masseur's grip, pleasantly stunning. "Julia?" he said. "What kind of ceremony did you use?"

She looked at him and then looked down. Dean's graveness came over everyone, even the poor appraiser, stranded here now. She said, "We really didn't think you'd disapprove. It doesn't make that much difference, does it?"

"I consider myself as having certain historical responsibilities. Now I see it's getting harder for me to discharge them." His W. C. Fields imitation was coming on. The appraiser, with his clipboard, started edging away, but Dean reached over and stopped him with his molding grip: "Hold on, here, my good man, stay here for just a moment. You're going to be a witness. And you too," he told Baelthon. Baelthon's open mouth closed.

He turned to her again. "What kind of ceremony did you use?"

She smiled at her new husband Faro. "We didn't use a ceremony at all. We just decided. We wanted to keep it free. You know how I feel about clap-trap."

"'Free'? Is that the word you counter-culture types use?"

Faro made a chuckle, his arms folded. "Hell, Dean, I should think you, of all people . . ." His hand flipped out, at Dean's outfit, the Day-Glo-yarn vest, the pants with purple stripes. "The Beatniks! The original anarchists! Hey!" It was sad, Faro didn't know any better. Dean wouldn't even stand aside to *look* at Faro, who had sunk to doing the Twist almost.

He said, "Julia Buckley Farmican, do you take this man, Faro Ness, to be your lawful wedded husband?"

"Oh, Merlin!"

"This is the actual moment, Jule. All you have to say is I do."

It was strange, her face unclouded and went back in years. Peter actually felt a shiver. She said, "I do," unable to repress a flutter of a grin that made her look like a teenager.

"Faro Ness," said Dean, "do you take this woman to be your lawful wedded wife?"

Faro had fixed Dean in an evaluative look, then he smiled sadly. Even the ocean seemed to fall silent. The appraiser with his clipboard was keeping his eyes off to one side. "I do," Faro said. It was like a poker game.

"By the power vested in me, I now pronounce you man and wife."

Faro breathed and spread his arms wide, then let them drop. "Dean, it's an honor. Truly. If I'd known you could marry us we could have had a ceremony long before. But listen. More of this anon." He started touching people's shoulders. "People, get cracking. Why don't you and Baelthon here, why don't you start bringing *all* the stuff out. Let's get it all out where we can look at it. Dean should check out his room in the basement. See if you like it. It took us forever to reach a decision about this one little drum, and it's only the first object to come out."

Dean said, "Yess, yess," high up in the loftiest trajectory of his W. C. Fields voice. "Let us do go. Show me to my room." He hoisted his surfboard about, and he put one arm around Peter's shoulders and swung to lead him away, up the stretch of bumpy lawn. Under Dean's arm, Peter felt scooped into the confidence that he could actually be a real poet. Behind them Faro was revolving on an axis and swinging his arms in windmills. "Bring it all out. Just bring everything. We can make decisions when we've got it all in one big pile. And then set aside a great big *tithe*. Right, Wendy? A great big *flow* of economic *goods,* right?"

◉ ◉ ◉

That afternoon Wendy found herself kissed on the lips, by Baelthon the hired mover, and her left breast hefted by him, exploratively, thoughtfully, like a water balloon as she rediscovered its peculiar weight in his objective palm, in the semi-darkness of the basement room where they were fixing up Merlin's hiding-place—which contained so far only a bare mattress, a metal milk-crate for a night table, a dormant Lava Lamp whose blob of cosmic semen had sunk to a cold dark plug at the bottom, and an extension cord, whose distant pronged end was inserted into an electrical outlet in the outer room. She held its other end behind herself, tight in the small of her back while he kissed her.

She allowed it because it was interesting of course, but also with a feeling that she wished to suffer generally under the *duty* of it. She wasn't sure how she had disappointed Faro in the kitchen, or what in general her fault was. Or else maybe it was perfectly clear: Faro had seen her selfishness and cynicism and wanted to give up on her. Now she felt wary around the house, everywhere scalded, and during the first moment of being arrested under Baelthon's mouth she realized behind her eyelids this was the beginning of a new responsibility. It would probably happen again while he was here, probably more than once, and she would permit it, because anyway it would supposedly get more enjoyable after the first layer of strangeness is rubbed off and she could touch her instincts the way most girls do and dive through it all like a totally self-assured movie actress, an otter among bedsheets in a sex scene.

Meanwhile she just held still to make herself an easy target. Lifting the face, closing the eyes, parting the lips, it felt like the preliminary sacrament of all female duty. With her in particular it would always be strange and difficult, because her father had deserted her, via the ultimate act of self-preservation. Unlike other girls, she would always have a third, never-closeable eye recessed in a niche watching. At least she wasn't a virgin. She had suffered complete penetration, painless and meaningless, with poor Bobby Grimaldi last winter in his parents' Thunderbird parked permanently up on blocks behind the Grimaldis' garage. Bobby Grimaldi was an example of ideal perfection, the handsomest boy in the school, the handsomest boy imaginable in any possible universe, though totally unpopular, even friendless. Unfortunately, she didn't even like him. It was his first time too, totally silent except when it came to discussing how to clean up, and they hadn't spoken since, avoiding each other at school. Sometimes she wondered with a twinge of guilt if she'd ruined Bobby Grimaldi's sex life, he'd seemed forever after so scared. As a temporary, local experience, Baelthon was perfect, less pathetic than Bobby, more insensitive, and even quite arrogant. She had known when it was going to happen. He kept standing too near, blocking, swelling, and then he blurred, his mouth came forward and covered hers. She kept her eyes closed, because if she looked she might find *his* eye open an inch from hers photographing her cornea. His grip on her breast really held her *away*. She was wearing an underwire bra and his thumb first hooked on *it*, following its metal arc curiously, his mouth on hers going slack.

She took the initiative, hostess-like, of guiding them both backwards to sit down on the mattress, where she kept her arms out to offer a lot of surface-area. He at last reached the underwire's sharp far end, almost under her armpit, where the tip protruded because it was an old bra. His finger tested it with a prick. Then, releasing breath through his nose, he left off from the interesting construction of her brassiere and started searching, by pinches, for her nipple, which he couldn't find through the fabric.

She sent up a sigh. She also put one hand on his shoulder. Her breasts she knew would be disappointing. His hand-honks began to grow wider, and even annoyed, as if he felt, dawningly, swindled, which *is* how boys think. He was staring over her shoulder into the dark with, probably, a pissed-off look, because they expect all breasts to be like movie stars', or like the girls' in Archie comic books, eye-knocking-out dirigibles that are never, ever mentioned but are the true, central subject of each comic-frame. Then he surprised her by speaking, tenderly.

"I don't believe in marriage either."

"Pardon me? You don't?"

"As your mom was saying. It takes away your freedom. If society sanctions it, it's artificial."

This was a philosophical discussion. She said, tentatively, ". . . Me too."

All this had to do with his disappointment in her body, her exclusion from normal pleasure. In an efficient inward contraction, she decided she was less vulnerable than she'd thought, and her voice toughened happily. "My real dad didn't really *'marry'* her either."

"They were never married?"

"They were married by Dean. Dean has a church. But it's an imaginary church. It's his delusion."

Baelthon thought about this, and said, "Mm." And then he loomed up to start kissing her again. She kept herself loosely parted waiting for the pleasure, but pleasure was ruled out, by the strangeness of the situation, by the fact that anybody could come barging in at any minute, by her lacking the right instincts. Her mistake with Bobby Grimaldi had hardened inwardly into an inhibition, permanent gristle in the heart. The fact is, none of this is enjoyable if you don't have a beautiful body. She could have her breasts surgically augmented, like a famous stripper in San Francisco whose notorious bosom contained bombs of plastic gel automatically attractive of men's hands. Baelthon's large tongue had come in to swab behind her teeth and even at the root of her own tongue, which in books drove women wild; but in her case, she couldn't help but open her eyes like a victim of smothering, holding the electrical cord behind her. At last, he took his mouth away and put his chin on her head. He was an expert at this. He would have had plenty of actual sex before.

"It's so exploitive," he said.

He was still on the topic of marriage. She didn't answer for a minute, then she said, "Mm-hm."

"And not only exploitive for the woman. For the man too." He drew his head back to look at her.

"I agree," she said. In a way, it was a relief: Baelthon could talk. It was an aspect of this she hadn't considered. She added, "The female has to be a housewife. But he has to be a hubby."

"Yeah, and get a job. Then he spends his whole life working for a corporation. While his wife is stuck at home. With her whole *identity* taken away."

"And then kids."

"Yeah."

" 'Good-bye identity.' "

California's Over

He embraced her with a formality as if they had exchanged vows. His chest felt nice: he had claimed he was a "novelist" so supposedly he would have actually written a novel, or at least tried. The complexity of a whole novel, its many branching inner tunnels and chambers, added an interesting chill to his silence. Even if it wasn't a very good novel. Which it probably wasn't, he was so young. It was strange, thinking of him that way, she could see how sad he was, how fragrant like something new, how bumbling and short-sighted, and, too, how desirable she herself was in his arms, how temporary everything is, how doomed, and in order to put both hands around his back and complete the embrace, she let go of the electrical cord.

"What's a Varda?" he asked, clomping along the narrow upstairs corridor after her, really swarming too close behind. As repellently as she could, she told him, "Varda is a person, not a thing," keeping a lid on his ignorance, peculiarly accountable for his behavior on these premises now that she'd kissed him. When they were down in the basement and he pressed her down on the mattress, her leg had accidentally knocked over the Lava Lamp, breaking the glass, mixing its two cosmic fluids, which on the floor had collapsed to an egg-yolk slime impossible to clean up except with towels; but when they went upstairs for towels, her mother was there saying, "Oh! Good! Wendy! Right this minute, would you show Baelthon where the Varda is? The appraisers are interested in it. It's in the attic above the guest rooms. Would you just help Baelthon bring it down?"

And so a mistake of alchemy went unremedied and became permanent on the basement floor, while they climbed to the far attic. At the end of the corridor, a doorless doorframe led up a steep staircase, where he kept bumping her amorously from behind like a sleepwalker, led into contact by his own unwieldy bat. He had no such dividedness-of-mind as she did. This wasn't his house. Everything was simple for him. She dodged at the top of the stairs among the attic's shadows, the cello case, the boxes of books, the zip-vinyl wardrobe bags, the stack of empty metal movie reels, the hanged marionettes of Jane Fonda and Ho Chi Minh, the raccoon cage, boxes of papers.

The Varda—of lumberyard scraps and driftwood, nailed together and spray-painted Rust-Oleum-black—was in the back corner by itself, and she knelt before it to slip her fingers under its base and test its weight. It was weightless. From below in the house rose a sound that must have been an electric saw, vibrating the house's timbers. The auctioneers were dismantling something. She didn't want to think specifically about it. It affected her like a dentist's drill.

Baelthon had stayed back in the doorway. "Do you know something about 'an end to all war'?" he said.

"No. I don't understand."

"When I saw Dean on the stairs, he said I should look for an end to all war. I didn't know what he meant. He said it like 'an end to all war' was *something* somewhere in this house. Something in a box, like."

"Dean is very rational, in fact"; she heard her own voice as peevish. Everything she said now would be shattered and diffused. She took her eyes from his and looked away at the world that had always held her—at the hanging clothes, the empty cello case, the beanbag ashtray that was always sitting on the Smith-Corona case under the window here, choked with the old filter-tipped butts of another decade, Tareytons, with lipstick marks. She was sitting on a box of books.

Baelthon offered the remark, generally, "Sure is a lot of stuff."

Her toe strummed the corner of the cello case.

Idly he picked up a trophy from the fifties, actually a dildo that had been painted glitter-gold and mounted on a block inscribed *The Honorary Homo Award*. Seeing what it was, he put it back down. A rain of hard little seeds fell from a dried-out sunflower hanging on a nail in the corner. He remarked, on the topic of Dean, "All he said was, it's in a box."

He sat down beside her. He had dark clear eyes, and his eyebrows met in the center. His chest was ample, suggesting almost a tendency to excess weight. Karma and Rachel would think he was cute, until the moment when he opened his mouth and the Wisconsin voice came out, the vowel-tone that hit a frugal limit in the sinus. He moved closer. She said, to repel him, "That's the Varda right there," but he was enveloping her, with more confidence this time, his hands glomming upward, his tongue moving into the groove behind her ear where she always got pimples and a paraffin feeling. She shuddered. "We have to take this sculpture."

Studiously he put his nose in her ear, where it breathed. His two index fingers began to etch concentric spirals, and then to press her nipples like doorbells, against her ribs through the inner mammary jam. He mistook her shrug for a sign of pleasure. The general, diffuse guilt in this house now swarmed together to collapse upon a specific memory: that jar of ashes. It was still unaccounted-for, still somewhere in this house. She turned out of his grasp and took both his hands in hers and said, "We have to get this sculpture downstairs."

He grinned, narrowed his eyes with debonair sexual languor. It was alarming. She turned away and twittered, transparently, "Wow, gosh, look at that fog coming in again already." She crawled to the Varda sculpture and slid it across the floor in a single easy pull without effort, it was so light, it was worthless-feeling. In only a few days, she would have to leave this house, and still she hadn't called Rachel to ask if she could sleep in her garage.

He said, responding to the fog's arrival, "What time is it," groggily.

Ed's black Mercedes was down there. Through the window

she could see it coming up the road to the house. He had been gone all day. Ed was lonely: she shared that with him. He, too, didn't fit here. But that was easier for him, because he hadn't grown up here: he hadn't *lived* here, in the ringing, post-gun-shot silence of three years, tiptoeing around Peter's huge invisible epic poem, as if *it* would rescue them. Then waiting to be rescued by Faro Ness. Instead, Ed had Modesto. What had he been doing all day? He was a total stranger. Yet he was her brother. She told Baelthon, with a sadness in contact with the thought of Ed Pease, "This isn't heavy, it's just awkward."

He stood up—"Here, let me get it. I'll get it"—obviously wanting to demonstrate his strength. So she wilted admiringly, and he picked it up. "If the fog is coming back, I should go soon. My car doesn't have any headlights."

"You mean go home?"

He put down the sculpture in the doorway at the top of the stairs, and he turned around, hands on hips, approaching with a confident embrace, a swagger really. "One thing you have to know about me: I'm a wandering kind of guy." He enveloped her in his arms speaking down into her hair, his masculine larynx widening to a pipe in his chest: "Never let a female tie you down. Freedom is the one requirement in life."

"Ah," she said.

"My car doesn't have any headlights. So I might get stranded here again for another night."

He *wanted* to get stranded. And so immediately she was pleased. She climbed free of him saying, "Let's get this thing downstairs." But again he came up behind her, again holding that *fact* against the cheek of her jeans, wrapping his forearms around her waist, and she found she liked it more all the time, in the sense that she was *curious,* and felt the inward giving-way, almost like the have-to-pee-in-your-pants urgency but pleasantly allowed. That was it, it was curiosity, curiosity would provide a path inward, simple curiosity, about the anatomy and mechanics of it all, about the amazing gravity-defiance of that famous original organ. Simple curiosity can be the beginning, the plucking through clothes toward inquiry. Curiosity about herself too, about the technology of it, the blood-hydraulics that cause levitation, the discolorations and seizures and spasms, the dimming of the mind in the body. To magically, by stroking, turn sweet bumbling Baelthon temporarily into a monster would be like a kind of healing—for herself too—so she actually did turn and put her arms up around him, herself to embody the downward sluice, all the trouble in the world.

But it couldn't happen exactly here, here in this house where she was paralyzed in the old daughterly web. Even her mother's feminist duty to be sexually free, even that seemed like an assignment here. She had to get out. And Baelthon could help with that. She spun and knelt at the sculpture, confusing him, pleasantly. "Let's go. My mother's waiting."

◉   ◉   ◉

Ed knew one thing at this point; he knew he would never spend another morning like today, with no *reason* for getting up and showing himself in the hallways, lying in bed motionless as a thief. Driving up the long driveway in the dusk, it was like being a breadwinner now, bringing back a crucial piece of information. He had spent the day at the legal library in the Civic Center, and he was carrying home a very important three-part sentence, unfolded and held down flat in his dyslexic mind under constant pressure:

Certain property is by force excluded from a subsequent marriage and passes directly to natural heirs if: (1), the property was acquired *in toto* before the time of the first

marriage; and (2), it exists outside the geographical
boundaries of California; and (3) it is not chartered as a
California Corporation.

In which case, the three Farmican children would indeed be
the sole owners of a Nevada casino, a real casino, where crowds
of people come in every day and throw away hundreds of dollars apiece on a huge acre of carpet like a threshing-floor, men
in tuxedos reaching with little hockey-stick-things to rake in
people's money across green felt tables into slots that feed, via
vacuum tubes, down into a central counting-room in the basement. Where there'd be like a big central sink. He knew of
course the actual Cornucopia might not be in such great shape.
But if it needed some work, fine! All the better! He would
enjoy putting some effort into something, into making it jingle
and clink and ding again. He stopped the car beside the garage
and punched the gearshift and sat there in the Mercedes' tick-
ing silence on the breath of old leather upholstery. This morning his mother had told him a casino did exist, "though of
course nobody ever *saw* it," and the legal deed of transfer was
"probably" in a strongbox in the medicine cabinet. That piece
of paper was what he needed to see now. That was the next
thing. Getting his hands physically on the paper.

He got out of the car and slammed the door, a forlorn sound
against the house's tall wall. He stood still. In the fog, the far
boom of the ocean established the location of the cliff beyond
the lawn, where the material world pulled away fatally into
aerosol droplets, cold comfort. A clank came from the house.
Wendy and the hired-hand Baelthon were, together, carrying a
little structure of spray-painted scrap wood. It was art. He
knew art when he saw it. They set it down and hung their
heads in talk. They were aware he was there. Everything was
so furtive in this place.

He said, "Wendy?" and the sound of his own voice lifted
him from jealousy, dispelled all the years of injustice, and in an

instant he was her brother again, carried into worry by his own voice. It's not the heart that decides, or still less the brain, but rather it's the voice in the throat that goes ahead into all these risks. "I have some news."

She and Baelthon said something to each other. He picked up the painted wooden thing and carried it off toward the tent. As she came on across the lawn to him, Ed said, "There's something I want to discuss with you." She drifted to a stop and anchored at an over-polite distance. "I went to the Civic Center library, and I learned something today." The magnitude of this gift, a genuine casino to share out among themselves, was suddenly for some reason an anticlimax; something inconsolable in her eyes belittled it. "First I spent most of the day *looking* for the Civic Center. And then I found the law library and did a lot of research on property law. And that took some effort too. Like I said at dinner, I'm dyslexic."

She didn't answer but tossed her hair.

"What dyslexia is"—he was starting to get talkative, which was his dumb way of putting people at ease, turning himself into a ninny before them. "It's an inability to read written things. My verbal capacities are excellent, but my written capacities are extremely drastic. When I look at words, they appear unreadable. Because of that factor, I tend to always have the *executive* function in any given situation. In any given situation, I'm the decision-making factor, rather than the—you know—the research-and-development factor."

She had hooded her vision again. When they first met in town, why didn't she *tell* him she was a Farmican? What sort of complicated insult is involved with keeping yourself a secret? She was so grave, so serious, already grieving for the world, expecting bigotry and corruption and exploitation, expecting annihilation by nuclear blast, in her tie-dyed T-shirt a big bright target.

"Anyway, so I had to get the librarians to help me. And these *books*. They're like big heavy *things*."

"Property law?" she said, keeping him on track.

"Well, to make a long story short" (his hunchback had come back), "the reason I want to talk to you is that I have reason to believe that you and I and Peter might be wealthy. Because this is the situation. Whenever people get married in California, automatically all of everybody's property goes to the other person. But in this case, there was no Last Will and Testament"— he made a glance upward to the cupola vanished in the fog somewhere on the decapitated house. "But three legal conditions are satisfied. California has laws about community property, but they don't apply to not-California areas . . ." She was beginning to contemplate *him* rather than his explanation, her eyes flicking over his hair, his haircut, his clothes, then away to the horizon. "Therefore, some of James Farmican's property goes straight to us." She looked at him. That word *us*, already regrettable.

"What property?"

"We have to find your mother and ask her to get it out of her strongbox. She said it's there."

"What's there?"

"A deed. It says James Farmican is the owner of a *casino!* In *Nevada!*"

Her eyes had already flipped away. "Oh, that."

"Wait, Wendy," he said, using her name, impolitely it felt, like a door-to-door salesman reaching in and petting people's tender names. "Do you know what a profitable concern a casino has the potential for? Hasn't anybody mentioned it exists?"

"Oh, that casino is part of the family . . . mythology."

"What if it's an actual big casino? It might be. You never know."

Looking down, one corner of her mouth crept sideways.

He said, "Come on, let's go find her and ask. Where is she?"

"She's somewhere." Her tone was hopeless but she started to lead the way up toward the house. He shouldn't have brought this up so fast. It was premature. Now he's the *scheming* orphan. Now he's being taken inside so she can tell her mother: he hasn't been here for even twenty-four hours and already he wants to grope around for legal documents in strongboxes.

◎ ◎ ◎

Holding his powerful new secret, Ed looked down at his bowl and he recognized some of the same shellfish as last night, in particular an oyster with a familiar chip on its rim. And the same black meat ruffles in its lips. It was the exact same oyster. He wouldn't be able to eat. At least there was bread again. Peter, sitting down opposite, said, "Where's Merlin? Isn't he eating with us?"

"Merlin," said his mother at the head of the table, her eyes closed and her palms lifted, always transcendent in her surrounding shining mist of sarcasm, "prefers to eat in his . . . cell."

"Completes a nice gothic atmosphere," Faro grumbled, stirring around in his broth.

"Did somebody bring him food?" said Peter.

"Wendy was good. She brought him a bowl of soup."

Faro said, of the soup, "Always better the second night," toasting everybody with a spoonful and then looking at his talented wife.

"I stretched it," she said. "I found a mysterious jar of old black miso paste and added it. Miso is like *instant* soup stock. I didn't know I had it. It was sitting on the lavabo in the pantry in an old glass jar."

There was a distinguishable new mud in the bottom of the bowl. Everyone's face fell to look at it.

"Don't worry, Edward," she patronized him by instructing him. "Miso is only fermented soybean paste."

197

Ed said, "Who is Merlin?" And then he remembered. "He's
not the *person*"—he pointed behind himself toward last night's
pitiful nest, the sleeping bag under the house.

Peter told him, "Yeah, but he's not so bad."

They all seemed inordinately calm about the prospect of
having a mentally imbalanced man in the house.

"You'll understand when you get to know him"—his
mother turned her smile upon him, adding—"Edward male
live birth."

Wendy said, "I just have this question."

"Wendy has a question."

"Has anyone seen a jar of Tang? It was in the closet by my
room."

"Tang the orange-juice drink?"

"I thought maybe somebody might have moved it."

"Dear, it might have gone back to the pantry."

"I looked there."

Peter said, his mouth full, "Probably Merlin."

That seemed to end that discussion, and in a lull, everybody
ate. Ed lacked any defenses against feeling swamped by it all.
He straightened up in his seat. This was the time to go ahead
and bring up the casino. Before dinner, his mother had taken
him to the medicine cabinet, where she kept her unlocked
strongbox. Together, he and Wendy—candy-smelling, sister-
fragrant, dark Wendy—had read the Deed of Transfer of The
Cornucopia Casino, Void, Nevada: it did "consign over" to
James Farmican, in 1947, "all property and equipment and fix-
tures and furniture and premises and keys and other indicia of
possession, all stock in trade, accounts and bills receivable, con-
tracts and debts due or owing, including the goodwill as a
going concern"—a likable, lively phrase in a legal contract.
Then in the minutes before dinner, he went ahead and actually
phoned Nevada. He found the little room with a telephone and
called the Nevada Gaming Commission in Carson City: a
casino called Cornucopia was still registered, though its "gross

revenues tax" hadn't been paid for thirty years; nor its quarterly "game fees." But it was there. Yet now, sitting at the dinner table, all his good news felt like connivance, and he found himself unable to bring it up, sunken on his spine.

Faro lowered his voice: ". . . How does he get in here and"—he raised his shoulders around his lifted spoon—"creep around?"

In answer, his wife only smiled, eyes closed, luminous.

Faro said, "Why does he consent to stay here? I thought he was such a free spirit."

"I asked him that," said Wendy.

"You did? What did he say?"

"He just went into one of his things."

"What thing did he go into?"

"About the Israelites. About 'they should never have gone down into Egypt.'"

"Israelites!" Faro said in glad despair.

"It's one of his things."

A thoughtfulness had come over Julia Farmican, which got people's attention. She elevated her chin and started explaining, as if thinking out loud, dim-eyed, "Dean thinks Jim was too successful. He doesn't believe in success. He believes in failure. He's a beatnik."

"He's a Taoist," Peter corrected her.

"Dean thinks failure is great," Wendy went on. "He says, 'This country was made great by failure.'"

All this family's talk rushing together made confusion, but yet, too, flotation. In the little green Pease house on Larch Avenue in Modesto, with every front window blocked off by its own air-conditioning unit, there'd been little talk at dinner, just the clink of knife on plate, because everything was obvious in Modesto, sitting plumb in the middle of its unwrapped explanations. Whereas here, far from the uniform light of the Peases' fluorescent kitchen, his own personal shadow was sharpened and deepened, he himself more raised and mobile.

Louis B. Jones

He'd changed. He could never go to Nevada alone. Without them, now, any trip would be meaningless. It was a new weakness, he could feel it, literally as a new emptiness in his side.

Faro said, "Tell me," and then for a minute, he ate, "what's so great about failure?"

Nobody answered and then Wendy swung gloomily into it, "He *loves* failure, he wants to *be* a failure, he says the country *belongs* to failures, he loves the *word* failure, he says *he's* a failure in his *soul*, and failure is what made this country *great*." Her voice fell into a tired rhythm. Ed had missed all these years of her. ". . . And Negroes are the *ultimate*. It's always American Negro *this*, American Negro *that* . . ."

"Why," said Faro, with a show of surprise, "he's not crazy."

"Has he told you about the comet yet?" said Peter.

"What comet?"

"It's coming this Christmas. Kohoutek's comet. It's an Old Testament comet. It's the end of the world."

Ed spoke up, "I'd like to talk about something. Can I bring this up?"

"Wait. Before you get into Nevada—" Wendy said—and Ed was silenced. Because she knew what he was going to say. He was predictable. He had never been predictable to anybody before. "—I really want to settle this about the jar of Tang. It was about this big. Like a normal jar. Somebody must have seen it, because I remember exactly where I left it."

Peter set his spoon in his soup and chanted primly, "Wendy, your older brother Edward would like to make a point."

"He just wants to talk about that casino."

"What casino?"

"I've already looked in the garbage, so I assume nobody threw it out."

"What casino?"

"Dear?" her mother said. "This way of keeping *prêt-à-manger* in your bedroom is never a good idea. It provides too

200

ready a temptation. It's bad for your figure. It invites mice as well as other vermin. And it just isn't done. People eat at the table. People eat at mealtime."

This advice from her mother had the effect of silencing Wendy. She just sat there looking drenched. So Ed with perfect justice started right in, after a decent pause, gripping the table edge. "As a matter of fact, I did want to inquire about this casino."

Now people were listening.

"I've ascertained a certain amount about it. And I've ascertained it actually exists. It's located in Void, Nevada, and it's called the Cornucopia, and," he addressed Peter, "it has been legally inherited to the children of James Farmican. The existing Cornucopia doesn't presently have a phone number in the Nevada phone book, but I wrote them a letter. Or that is, a letter was written by my attorney in Modesto before I left," he said, impressively, *not* glancing toward Faro. "But that was three weeks ago and nobody answered. Additionally, just now I called a Nevada government-thing-place. And *they* said there still is a casino. It's on their records. So we have to go out there. Some of us do. That's what I think." His heart was beating.

"Julie?" Faro demanded.

She lifted both palms and held them up beside her face, smiled, and closed her eyes.

Faro said, "Have you ever *heard* of a casino?"

"James won it in a poker game. The deed has been in the strongbox ever since. I've always assumed it no longer existed. Apparently I was wrong."

"Have you ever had any income from it? Or paid any taxes to the state of Nevada? Or done *anything* about it?"

"Our family has experienced only utter silence from," she smiled, "the Cornucopia."

Ed went on, "According to California law, us three children can inherit it. It doesn't count as community property in your marriage. I and Wendy and Peter can go out anytime with the deed and take possession. Or we can contest possession if somebody else is running it right now."

Spoons went on clinking on the rims of bowls. Faro said, "What if it's a real casino?"

"It *is* a real casino. It has a license in the State of Nevada. Those licenses are worth their weight in gold."

"But what if it's a big . . ." he kept his hand rolling, "business?"

"Heh." Ed looked around the table. "What if it's not? If it's *not*, I'll build it up."

"Oh, I see," said Faro, folding his hands. He leaned back at a comfortable remove, and his face slanted off: there was now a prism between himself and the topic, which obviously pleased him. He said to his wife, "Sounds like an interesting plan."

Ed said, "I think it's an interesting plan." He lowered his brow and ate bread.

"Edward would like to get a visor and some sleeve-garters and be a croupier," said his mother. "I think it sounds like fun."

Faro said, "Is it legal for something like that to be managed by minors?"

"I'm not a minor. I agree it might be inoperable momentarily. The Office of Gambling-Whatever in Nevada said it hasn't reported income since 1943. But still."

"Julie?" Faro asked his wife.

She said absentmindedly, "Sorry?"

"I don't want to actively oppose this—"

"It'll make money," Ed said. He knew he would come off sounding stupid in this discussion. But a year from now, if they could look back on this argument, *then* who would seem stupid?

Faro had paused, squinting, lifting his hands to frame a square of air before him. "Here's my attitude, I guess, toward owning and operating a casino. Everybody here is still young. A casino is a business. It's dedicated to this purpose, shearing the sheep. If there *is* a casino out there, it must be based on . . . well, on the profit motive, not to put too fine a point on it. Do we want a whole new generation getting involved with *that?*" He kept talking to his wife rather than Ed. "I say let them go on pretending to be poets and whatever, because hell, dreams tend to come true. Dreams are tricky that way. You're only young once. You know the thing John Adams said, about how *he* had to practice commerce so that his *grandchildren* could study poetry and philosophy. Julie, I fail to detect what's so amusing."

She had been smiling downward, and dabbed her mouth with a napkin. "I'm sorry, it's just that they have to choose between a Ranch and a Cornucopia. I'd say there's no contest."

"*I don't have to choose,*" Peter grumbled—murderously, softly—but no one paid attention. Ed was the only one keeping an eye on him: he had suddenly begun staring angrily before him at nothingness, cross-eyed, under a mysterious concussion. Poet.

"Julie, a casino is all about profit. There's no business that worships the Almighty Dollar *more*. Or is *more* exploitive of the underclasses. Or is *more* exploitive of women. Have you ever been to one of those places?"

Ed spoke up, "I was in Terra Linda at the Civic Center today looking it up. The law is really clearly specific. It doesn't count as community property. It's ours. Because there was a remarriage."

"Our marriage isn't applicable here. And Julie, your levity is not helping. I'm trying to exert a little influence but I'm just sounding like the Bad Guy. Hell, okay, maybe I'm wrong. Maybe they should take over a casino. And sit out there in the desert raking in money. Fine."

Ed said, "What do you mean your marriage isn't applicable?"

"I accede, Ed. I give up," Faro said, folding his arms. "Indeed I may be wrong. Maybe a casino will be fun." And then he answered Ed's question. "I just mean we didn't sign a piece of paper at city hall."

"Either you're married or not," Ed said. He wanted to catch Faro on this point because the widow's remarriage was one of the three legal conditions that would allow the casino to go directly to the children.

Faro sighed before explaining. "Ed? Marriage is a civic institution. It exists so the middle class can keep the faith. And it exists as an economic unit, and to cultivate certain middle-class virtues, like consumerism, and boredom. And that's the kind of relationship your mother and I *don't* have." He turned to his wife. "If you and I are unmarried, the casino remains your property. In the eyes of the government, in legal fact, we're *not* married."

Wendy said, "Merlin married you today, ha ha."

Faro sagged affectionately: "Merlin, fuff. Poor Merlin."

Suddenly Peter, who had been quiet for a minute, lifted a fork high and stabbed the back of his own hand. His left hand was lying palm-down on the table, and his right hand brought the fork down hard. At the back of Ed's mind a little switch was flipped: a conclusion was reached—or he'd been on the brink of this idea all along—that there was real mental trouble in this family. But it didn't scare him at all. In a way, it was almost gladdening, it opened up the rules of the game, it was a sore he could enter by.

Peter stood up and hopped and spun and gripped his wrist and said, "Shit! Fuck!" While, like a bicyclist, one foot kept lifting and sinking. No blood flowed. Apparently he hadn't even broken the skin; that web of tendons and bones is very tough. And then, pedaling this unicycle beside the table, at the moment when his humiliation and anger were most revved up, in an inspiration (you could see it in his face), his calm inner gremlin, from deep within an inner pit of reconnaissance behind his eyes, commanded him to reach through a quiet, open slot in whirling space and seize the serrated bread-knife.

He held it up, with the smile of a threat. Ed didn't like this.

Then without hesitating, grimly merry, he drew its blade once across the bony side of his wrist, not the soft inner face. He didn't hit an artery. No blood came out. But then, as he looked, it started to ooze. He stood up taller and held up the cup of his wound and said, "This isn't even a metaphor." The dove of a napkin flew up as his mother rose in the swift angelic motion, while his sister crouched for the knife that had clattered to the floor. And towering in this ballet, a kind of triumph shone in Peter's eyes, a kind of limpness and relief and afterglow.

That night in her room, Wendy got into her closet where the wrinkled old Lucky Market paper bag was, now as soft as chamois, filled with snacks and their litter, Ding Dongs, a stack of Oreos, licorice, a couple of weightless softballs of popcorn stuck together by caramel, Ritz crackers, Sugar Babies, cellophane and foil, chocolate kisses.

Which *is* a way of responding to a problem—in this case Peter, among all the other problems now, like the theft of the Tang jar, her own lack of a future, the thousand farewells to small objects drifting out to the big green tent—but mostly Peter, in the midst of all this. It was a clever kind of disloyalty, his desertion by escape to a more exalted realm. It's a way of cashing in, leaving others' investments devalued, like in the family Monopoly games he used to win ruthlessly and then walk away from. Why wasn't *she* allowed to be over-sensitive too? She had problems too. She had the problem of the lost ashes, the inescapable reality that someone here at the house had taken them and wouldn't admit it. Plus, she had allowed Baelthon that earnest gripping in the basement, in memory now as awkward as a swimming lesson, struggling toward shore. Maybe sex is all very interesting and inevitable in itself, but then afterward there's the problem of the boy's "personality," an attached dialogue-balloon. In the case of Baelthon, he's so inert, he's like a heavier-than-air gas everywhere, presuming his own relevance everywhere. Eventually she would have to introduce him to Rachel and everybody. Which would be one more reason for never going back to high school, its empty stairwells and terrible corridor intersections, its sad parking lots in the sun. She felt a place in her stomach as the grinding-point of larger masses outside herself. Hostess Cupcakes, caramel drops, cream puffs, they're all medicine in the throat, sedative butter in the aorta. Her lucky metabolism, by worrying, had always burned up the excess food: she never got fat like some girls, like unfortunate Karma, who stayed fat even when her parents made her eat only algae pellets and bran husks.

As a matter of fact, she had no real friends now, her one friend Karma too unpopular to call, her other friend Rachel now perhaps too popular. But friendlessness was almost a sort of blessing, in this temporary time of disgrace when she had to leave home, crouching in the tunnel of it. She sat on the edge of the bed chewing, biting off more of her licorice vine, resting her elbows on her knees, poking around in the bag.

Floorboards creaked in the corridor, somebody was coming. She bit off the red licorice cord and stuffed the rest of its coils into the old paper placenta and pushed it in the closet—such secrecy hopeless in this house whose doorways had not a single door, all removed by her father on a weird night when he was alone here. Nevertheless, she hid the bag far away behind the Beefeater's Gin box that held all her Troll dolls and her old *Josie and the Pussycats* comic books and her childish Danskins, all to be bequeathed to the Free Store perhaps, or else to float on the scummy surface of this shipwreck. Anything that isn't set aside will be packed off carelessly by movers. All unreal!

Her clothes still hanging in the closet! Her shoes lying cast aside in the corner exactly where she always tossed them!

It was Faro. She knew it would be him. In the doorframe, he cried, "Oh!" as if he'd found an intruder. "Somebody who's not a crazy artist! How did you get in here?"

She made a blurred grin of appreciation. She felt weak. She was sitting on her hands.

"May I join you? Share a little self-pity?"

She said, "Where's Peter."

"Peter. Out on the beach still. Your mom went after him. I just looked at the Free Store stuff. That coffeemaker needs a beaker. But there are those eight-track tapes. And the car radio. Your mom says it works. There's actually some good things."

"Yeah. Except some of it."

"Like what?"

"I don't know. Old mayonnaise jars." Right away, she was being negative again. "Or a Bic pen cap."

"Plastic. There'll be recycling *centers* in a few decades maybe."

"Yeah but who's going to want a cap to a Bic pen?" she said, though she was wrong, she knew. It's plastic. Those are all non-renewable petrochemicals in there. Faro could have, but didn't, prosecute her on the point. He put his hands in his pockets and shuffled around. "C'I come in? Hang out?" He was one of those men whose hopes for people keep springing back up, despite people's unsoundness, even here in Julia Buckley Farmican's museum of broken souvenirs—where she herself—strange!—had maybe always been one of the souvenirs, chilled by admiration.

He sat down. "Tell me. I hope you're not worried about Peter." Having sat, he married his palms and sank behind them.

"No, he's just showing off, getting attention."

"Well, listen, about this Free Store, we'll just wait and see how it works. If it works, that's fine. If not, that's fine too. See how much stuff accumulates. We needn't feel any big pressure."

He was planning for her failure, considerately, and she sat there petted down into a sick slouch. She sneaked a glimpse under her eyebrows. He was looking at the floor, with his legs crossed. He recrossed his legs in the opposite direction. Reclasped his hands. A man sitting in a trap. Her mother was so tired from her past life as James Farmican's wife, she could scarcely *see* her new husband. Picturing them in the sex act, she could only imagine her mother as largely impassive, the male waspily smaller than the female in the picture.

Just for something to say, she asked, "Is somebody going to go look at the"—with disgust—"casino?" She felt flimsy, chilly.

"Mm!" he smiled. "Isn't that funny? I suppose somebody should go and look. Something that valuable. But listen. Speaking of all the different various pressures. I want to talk about something." He breathed. "This is really why I came up here. This morning I lost my cool when we were talking in the kitchen. I don't want to be *persecuting* you with all my, quote, Good Intentions."

"It's not you," she moaned, but couldn't go any further into the work of telling him *he* wasn't the problem, *he* didn't have to go around taking blame for everything.

"But I am persecuting you, Wendy." He looked away. "I believe it's best for people to be honest with each other. I want to tell you what's going on. Male psychology is very Jekyll-and-Hyde. This is . . . ," he said, holding his eyes down, "this is hard to talk about. But you're very much a grown-up, Wendy. Believe me. It's a dangerous idea, this concept of 'dispensing with hypocrisy.' People have perfectly natural feelings. People get all . . ." he made a gesture as if gripping breasts on his own chest and wrenching them.

"Don't worry. I'll do it. I'm not persecuted."

"Do what? The Free Store thing? Jesus, Wendy. Sometimes

you seem to me like the one person most unspoiled and innocent for this Ranch."

"'Innocent'?" He had no notion. *He* was innocent. It almost
seemed a generational thing. His generation remembered integrity, from before the sixties, whereas she'd been born into
the new era of unashamed sexiness and ambitiousness, the
planet shrinking, while everyone wants to be famous.

He stood up, one hand holding the other wrist. "Within
myself," he said, "the ratio between Hyde and Jekyll gets out of
proportion, tipped off-center," and then he sat down beside her
on the bed. His weight made a trough that unbalanced her, so
that now they were too close.

And then she knew what he was getting at. In a way, she
should have always known what he was getting at, it was obvious. And while of course a tingle of shame covered her, she felt
at the same time an inward collapse, simply because it was flattering. She was observing herself as if she were a character in a
movie. This was all dangerous and utterly wrong. It trans-
formed her mother into, rather than a good witch, a hag. Herself into Faro's young bride, third wife, callous young toy, using
his money to start her own career or get her education. All too
complicated to think of. Someone else's life, not hers.

"It's an emotional reality"—his hand flicked toward their
two bodies. The gesture made her body feel offered to him,
such was his power.

"I only say all this because I believe in principle that your
age makes no difference, in terms of your own judgment. Your
own moral authority. And even if an impulse goes unacted-
upon"—his fist softly knocked back his own heart—"still it en-
dangers . . . everything."

"Yes," she said. The world had plunged into a photographic
negative.

"It's not that there'd *be* anything immoral. I'm not somebody who worries about conventional morality," he went on,

and she knew then it would never happen. With excess words he was papering over the possibility. She was cut off from him by a transparent wall, watching him suffer. And while of course that was a relief, yet she was also a little bit insulted.

"Here I am, see. I don't want you to fall into the *trap* women fall into just because you're beautiful. Don't make faces, I'm being honest. Being beautiful, you'll find, is a terrific distorter of things. It ends up being female oppression. Beauty is how oppression appears in the world. All these suburban housewives, I see them in my practice, they're supposed to be in paradise, with their dishwashers and their tennis and their ceramics classes, or their graduate-school work. Or whatever. But they just end up going crazy, the halfway intelligent ones."

She could only stare downward allowing a completely unashamed part of herself to blaze out of control because it was interesting to be desired by him, if only just for the way it would ruin everything, like a big gradual slow-motion trainwreck. That's how evil she was.

"See, I'm the 'Step-Father'"—with a sarcastic, grossed-out leer, rounding his shoulders feebly—"the new theory is that, actually, the constant threat of rape is what underlies *all* male-female relationships. *All.* But listen, Wendy. Wendy?" She looked. His gaze penetrated hers, but tenderly, prophylactically. "I don't want to be like that. I'm not like that"—he touched her knee, denim-numb, then took his hand away. "I don't want the world to be all about only power plays. So . . . ," he said.

For a second then, when he thought she wasn't noticing, he had a truly scared look. It was a man-before-a-firing-squad look, and she could have loved him for it. He believed he was revealing to her the frailty of men, which he thought might be a terrible revelation.

"When we're up on the Ranch . . ." He shrugged, in a helpless gesture of casting about him the wealth of all Creation.

Now there was no question. She would have to live in Rachel's garage.

California's Over

He stood up. The mattress righted itself. She took a breath. Their bodies had been arranged for a fall. And high up within her divided soul, she was partly pleased by this discovery of her own corruption. Of course nothing would ever happen between them. But from now on she would begin to pity her mother. That was a new responsibility. She straightened her spine, taking a photograph of herself at this last peak of childhood: remarkably pretty, wide-awake. She would never tell her mother about this. And so she was growing up and taking on—it was rather bracing—a very adult responsibility: duplicity.

The next morning the doorbell rang. Nobody ever rang the doorbell. Then it rang again. Whoever it was, wasn't going away. Footsteps crossed the floor upstairs, answering it. They were Wendy's footsteps. Peter listened as he lay in bed. His X-ray vision watched the fabric tacked to his ceiling. He'd been fine at first, wakening slowly into the usual dull enfeeblement of being home, in home's dense air, safe in his old stillborn imprint. But gradually a few thoughts got a hold on him, especially about last night, and an ache identified itself. He would never be such a child anymore after last night, or such a phony anymore. After the knife hit the floor, he had walked out of the dining room and walked straight out of the house and up the beach, in the moonless dark holding up his trophied hand, alone in a whole new world of responsibility. It was time to start writing poetry that was actually *good*, made with dedication, rather than with immaturity and ignorance and pretentiousness cherished within this family. The beach was totally black, but like a drunk his path in the dark was lit by his own personal light. His whole future as a poet glittered before him, foreordained, in its terrible grinding symmetry a view into a kaleidoscope. There was no going back. There was a short papery scab on his wrist now this morning. The scene at dinner was indeed a public self-murder. He was willing to be famous even among his family. He had actually run away from his mother. She had followed him outside into the dark, not dressed warmly enough. But when he stopped, she could only say, in a voice made strange by the high wind, "I just want you to be happy." Everybody always knew he had no talent. Now, since Stanford, there was proof. It held him down in bed in the morning, motionless in his own sweaty fossil on the sheets, a painfully *half*-evolved creature. This is how families kill artists.

Well, now he would get talent. He would get it by work, by ardor, by not being so treasured anymore. He turned away from her but she stopped him with a sharp hand on his arm, her hair crazy in the beach wind, her face sharpening weirdly. "It's not interesting, it's contemptible. Do you think *that improved* him?" Her hand lifted toward the cupola. "You are never to hurt yourself. Not ever. Oh, you're my baby, oh." He ran from her tentacles, in panic but also in a strange joy, his breast in advance. She was a goblin in the dark. He had never before seen her as ugly. At the moment when she said, "Oh, you're my baby," incipient cartilage lifted her face into old-age.

And then later when he was sneaking back into the house, all ear-achey and fevered from the beach wind, he stopped to listen because he heard her voice in the kitchen speaking from a sybil's tired old shriveled lung he'd never heard before: "None of them were serious writers, they were just playing. They were just playing. After that, it was all publicity. It was all the American celebrity machine. Everybody pretends to be revolutionary. To have the wit to be revolutionary."

A silence, then a scrape of a glass on the countertop. It was Faro. He said, "Julie, you're not that cynical." He ran water at the sink for a second. They seemed to be leaving the kitchen and going upstairs. He was putting his arm around her.

She drank from her glass, and said, "They're just like flowers in the spring."

"Who is?"

She pushed her chair back. "Nobody cares to distinguish anymore. Well they succeeded. Now it's all mistrust and cynicism everywhere. And I feel like . . ." She was going to say something self-accusing, but didn't. She stood up and left the kitchen. Faro put something in the sink and followed her, leaving by the front hallway. "Jule?" his voice faded up the main staircase. Peter was left alone, a witness onstage in his niche of Shakespearean shadows. She didn't respect her own husband, James Farmican. She never had. Like all news that would change his life forever, it at first caused only a healthy unthinkingness, a blank spot to be filled in later. But the next morning as he lay in bed, her words were still in his ear. She clearly implied James Farmican wasn't a good writer. It gave him a confused joyful sickness-at-heart.

Then he heard Wendy's flip-flop sandals on the flagstones of the basement corridor. She was running. When she came into his room she was flushed, bright-eyed, in an accidental snapshot beautiful. "Some guy is at the front door. With that sheriff's deputy Sammy. *And* nobody's home."

"Where's Mom?"

"I said nobody's home."

"Who is it?"

"Sammy and some guy wearing a *suit*."

"Lots of people wear suits, Wendy." This morning Peter saw her as beautiful. She was beautiful. Just during the last year, something had happened. "It's probably a fan looking for Dad. It's probably an English teacher."

"This is like a *Dragnet* suit, and he flashed identification in his wallet." Finding herself near the microwave, she backed out the door.

"Get out of here, I'm not wearing any pajamas."

"Maybe he's a narc and they'll find flakes of pot."

So he scared her back upstairs, saying, "Fuck off, you gross bitch," in an overflow of irrelevant love, sitting up within the bedclothes, rising into a sort of gratitude. Because this is what would happen: people would not mention his pantomime of last night. It's how a family is made of scar tissue, forever forming, forever re-sketching each other over erasures. He'd always had certain memories of his father that sharpened by going unspoken—of him passed out on the back lawn, naked in the cold rain exactly like a corpse; or passed out halfway-out of the parked car; always during his "creative periods" when his mother kept taking the children away to foreign countries and they saw him less and less; toward the end increasingly stringy-haired, fragrant like a Zippo lighter; and once holding the infant Wendy by an ankle over the railing of an overpass in San Francisco (this was the only context in which he ever remembered the famous purple Jaguar; it was crashed against a lamppost; they'd just been ejected from The Coffee Gallery), while he said with a clenched grin, *Here I am, the happy clown of my generation.* And his mother, unable to reach the dangling child, wearing a lacy dress that the wind on this bridge pressed against her body, said in soft disbelief, *You've become inhuman.* Wendy wouldn't remember. He himself pictures it only in the twilight of half-plausible dreams. Because those times were not the real truth of James Farmican's life. Families accomplish this tireless, vigilant work of erasure, forgetfulness, actually ignoring each other, forgetting each other. Blind spots float through these rooms like ball-lightning, healing. It made him wonder what he was blind to in his sister: how pretty she was getting to be, how generous and unthinking. As for himself, being a real poet, at first, would require of him almost a certain, like, psychosis in the world, a blindness to his own obvious mediocrity. It had been strangely beautiful, that whole six seconds, the six seconds of his rise from the dinner table with a knife, the slant red cut, the clatter of the knife on the floor, the upward flight of the linen of the women, it was a beautiful interlude, like a slow-motion instant-replay of graceful TV-violence, or like that magical moment, that crowning moment in history, when the president's shining forehead

flies away in a red spray, jerkily, frame-by-frame in the Za-
pruder film.

◉ ◉ ◉

In fact, the suit was ominous, cheap and governmental-
looking, constructed of a dark shiny material, maybe called
"sharkskin," muddy brown but revealing mouths of irides-
cence in its folds. Sammy was there too, in his deputy's uniform, fatter than ever, eyes smaller, mouth sweeter. He seemed
to have come along more as guide than as law officer, standing
aside on the doorstep while the man introduced himself: Mr.
Murrain, of the Internal Revenue Service. Mr. Murrain wanted
to know if this was the premises of a church.

"It's our *house*." Peter addressed Sammy rather than the
stranger. He was standing before them wrapped in a big dirty
blue blanket that dragged the floor, naked beneath it. The costume lent him authority in this doorway causing Sammy
humbly to take off his deputy's cap. Sammy said, "Is your mom
home, Peter?"

Beyond, on the lawn, two movers were carrying something
dreamily familiar: it was a big oak wardrobe, topped by carved
pineapple finials he'd always disliked. It had always stood in
the kitchen, over the years grown sticky and velvety. Good-bye.
Goodbye to disliking those pineapple finials.

"Nobody is here but Wendy and I. You can come in if you
want."

They hesitated. They were a mismatched pair on the
doorstep. Sammy said, with a glance at Mr. Murrain, "Just tell
us, Peter. Has Dean been around here?"

"Dean?"

"Dean Houlihan," the government man clarified blandly.
Peter didn't like this man. He had the complete invincibility of
the disinterested.

"He's probably in town. Did you check the usual places? The General Store, the beach . . ."

"He's not around," said Sammy.

"You won't find him but you're free to inspect," Peter said and he swung backward. "Come on in."

Sammy looked at the IRS man. The IRS man handed Peter a business card. "I have an appointment with Mr. Ness here, later this afternoon."

Sammy said, "I could go in. *Un*officially. I've known Dean for years. In fact maybe I better."

The IRS man thought about it. "Your only job would be to tell him to make himself available for an interview."

Peter said, "He's really not here, Sammy. Come in and look."

He pulled his blanket high over his shoulders, turned away, and swept back to the living room leaving the front door open. Wendy was hiding inside, glaring at him. He lowered his voice to a whisper upstage, "They'll never find him. That big sign hides the whole doorway."

She was creeping around, toward a window. "Is the other guy going to leave?"

"Relax, Wendy."

Sammy came in—alone—and he said, "Now, Peter? Wendy? This is strictly unofficial. I want to just talk to him."

Peter settled himself on the living room couch, in a lotus position naked under the tent of his blanket. This situation Sammy seemed to find also intimidating. Standing before the couch, he took off his cap and started revolving its rim by degrees through measuring pinches. He said, "They're the Internal Revenue Service, you guys. It's possible that Dean is in some kind of trouble."

"He's not here, Sammy."

He looked down at his shoes in a forced smile, wincing. "It's not that I don't believe you, Peter."

"Go ahead and look. Start at the top, work your way down. You won't find him."

"Do you know when your mom will be back?" He had started to turn toward the rear staircase.

"Don't *worry* about it, Sammy. Go ahead. She's not home."

"I'll just take these stairs." He had the waddle of a lost football. At the landing, he looked up the one set of stairs, down the other, and then chose the downward route, recapping his head as he descended. Peter watched him go. Wendy was hoisting herself up on the purple piano, to lower her rear-end onto the keyboard slowly, without sounding a note. She grumbled, "You're responsible."

Mr. Murrain's business card lay in his hand: *Criminal Investigations Division, United States Internal Revenue Service.*

"What is this 'church'?" he said.

She didn't respond. These were the last few days. Soon the big vans would leave for the auction house or for "dead storage," as they called it. And yet neither of them had begun packing. The hundred peacock-feather eyes embedded in the piano's paint went on always watching everything everywhere, with never a blink. On the piano keys, Wendy budged: a deep ominous chord rose and bracketed their conversation and then hung there. Its gradual dying took forever, isolating them together in a space of timelessness in their living room—in the middle of which Wendy finally spoke—"I hate this family"— quietly, lovingly.

Unclothed under his blanket, he was still shining with sleepiness, a state which has its own peculiar dignity and pomp. This was the kind of thing she was always coming up with, unanswerable whines and complaints.

She went on, "You think you're committing suicide. I'm committing suicide. I'm doing it first."

It was slightly unbelievable that she'd said it. There was a paralysis and a black flutter in the vision.

"If you commit suicide," she said further, "I'm putting a big booger on your nose in your coffin. Just because you were the one who always thought anything to do with boogers was hilarious. That's your legacy. It'll say that on your gravestone: He Thought Boogers Were Funny."

He spoke at last. "You are such an asshole," the sentence fluted high in a papery chamber of his brain, the body is such a frail reed.

"What are you going to do?" she said. "There's only a few days left."

He drew his blanket up higher.

She said, "Are you going to go live in Oregon?"

Under the blanket, his shoulders and arms were hard with protectiveness. The more he thought of it, of her mockery, the worse it was. Everybody had always seen how stupid his poetry was, it was famous, like the diagrammed *headache* in the TV aspirin commercial where a transparent statue has an ugly blue gland pulsing through its skull. Ever since that Stanford thing, a new unmentionability had surrounded it, a new holiness of embarrassment. He answered her question, "I'm waiting for the rest of you people to get out of this fucking house, so I can do some work." Staying on here, he would be *strengthened* by people's disrespect.

She was looking at him, perhaps in envy of his staying here. Because then she said, "I'm going to live at Rachel Feinman's house, in her garage."

He turned on his cushion. "You aren't going to Oregon?"

She didn't answer, just picked at a toe.

He said, "Rachel Feinman is beautiful: why would she have anything to do with you?"

After a minute she said, "Mm," distantly. And then with more presence she said, "Really, Peter. Did you see that jar of Tang? I'm asking you."

"What jar of Tang?"

"I *mentioned* a jar of Tang."

"No, I didn't see your jar of Tang." Wanting miscellaneously to be angry, feeling the need as a surge, he said, "You know what I think? I think Ed 'Pease' is hopeless. It's like, how could we even be related? All he cares about is that casino in Nevada. Have you ever tried to talk to him about anything? He's incapable of talking. I mean verbally. He has this weird way of phrasing things. I think there's some *problem* there."

He watched Wendy. She chewed on a wisp of hair plugged into the corner of her mouth. Took it out and looked at it. Plugged it back in and chewed on it some more.

She said, "At least he's not a phony." She was developing a disrespectful way of contradicting people casually. He said, "Well, don't you think he's slightly materialistic? Have you noticed a slight materialism problem?" His voice in the room sounded like an actor's, testing lines on a bare stage.

Sammy was coming back. The sound of his feet came down the staircase from the upper floor. When he came into view he said, "How did I get back here? Whoops." He was rubbing his nose allergically. He turned on the landing to head downstairs again toward the main cellars, rubbing his nose.

As his footsteps sank, Wendy went on, saying something about Ed.

But Peter wasn't listening and he sighed and said, in general, "Oh, I don't know." His lungs emptied. Personal sadness was a secretion in the brain-stem. A ringing in the ears came to draw an outline around him separating him from all life. It felt exactly *logical*, to consider the possibility of his absence, his personal death. It had an ecological neatness, or an economy, the prospect of spending himself to redeem himself, now before he'd wasted any more. Looking into the long, darkening corridor, which Wendy couldn't see from where she was, he heard her voice coming back from the present, as shiny as reflections wrapped around a Christmas-tree ornament: "At least Nevada isn't Marin. At least it wouldn't be perfect."

Louis B. Jones

Secretly inside, Wendy had amazed herself. Saying the words had made Nevada imaginable—simply because it was hot and empty there, *wrong* reasons like that, like because her skin would be less oily there, or because the desert would have an interesting quality of absolute silence extending in all directions. She rolled down on her elbow and laid herself out on the too-short piano bench on her back. Her head hung off the end and her skull started filling with fluid as she looked, upside-down, at the familiar furnishings of the living room—the fake Louise Nevelson, the French horn spray-painted red, Shel Silverstein's tin water pistol hanging on a nail on the wall, the poster of Che Guevara looking beautiful in his beret, the daily chart of her mother's vaginal mucus consistency from *clear* to *milky*—and she repeated, as a way of prolonging the experiment:

"*At least Nevada wouldn't be perfect.*" In her upside-down throat her voice was like one of those criminal voices electronically garbled for anonymity. She had crossed her distant feet at the ankles. Her arms hung straight out on both sides of the bench so her rib cage was pulled flat, slain, but filled with a just calm, the calm of the incorrigible girl admitting she doesn't *want* to go to heaven. Last night she lay awake on the bed, her body sprung in a question mark, mentally rehearsing foggy sexual predicaments in sharp close detail, with Baelthon, with Faro. This house's old post-explosion mist of guilt had found a place to condense: her new body, all sexily aswarm with it. And that, sexiness, would give her the strength, the lithe strength, the buoyancy, to go off on her own, eventually to live in an apartment somewhere, with a bed and a fridge and a stereo, a job at a record store like Tower Records. Baelthon would be standing by dependably. His Volkswagen Bug could move her to Rachel's garage. The new voice in her pinched-off throat spoke again, upside-down, "I'll sneak into the undertaker's office where you're lying in state, and I'll pull down your pants and write on your buns. I'll write 'Bad Poet' on your buns with a permanent marking pen."

Peter didn't say anything.

"And in the funeral I'll accidentally bump into your coffin, so your corpse falls out and everybody will see it says 'Bad Poet' on your Big White Buns."

He whispered sadly, "You asshole."

"'Poet' on the right bun, 'Bad' on the left bun. Or maybe I should write 'Good Poet.' Would that be better?"

He was not answering.

"Or 'Excellent Poet.' Or how about 'Sensitive Misunderstood Poet.'"

He sighed at last.

"You think there's enough room on your left bun for 'Sensitive Misunderstood'?"

Sammy was coming down the stairs again, in his heavy black shoes. She slid her upside-down eye to see him. He stopped on the landing, pointed downstairs, and said, with a little anger, "I'm trying to get to the basement." How strange to think she would miss even Sammy, that she had loved even him, from her afterlife vantage-point in the Feinmans' suburban garage. With his chubby man's daintiness, he dipped his toe in the basement staircase and ventured down to be churned through the house again. That UNGRY I sign completely hid the passageway down there. He would never find Merlin. Peter had been right of course. He was always right, with his legendary I.Q., an I.Q. so high he had turned away from the entire world, turned toward the infinite spaces of poetry, where his fiat could be executed at the speed of light, where he could leave everybody behind instantly.

Lying on the piano bench, she opened her upside-down eyelids to see (in farewell!) the underside of the piano, where old varnish showed through in spots under the purple paint-job, the peacock feathers stuck in the paint like psychedelic eyes. Her erotic body—throat flung open, distant toes pointed in flight, arms outstretched to the sides in crucifixion, breasts mounded uppermost on her rib cage, nipples beginning to bite inward at the thought—was offered to Faro too, not just to Baelthon, her body the theological origin of evil, the crawling inner tunnel of sensation. At Tower Records, there are back-room jobs among stacks of anesthetic-brown cardboard boxes, stacked up close around your ears, where you never have to greet the public, never have to dress up. She could do that for years.

Creaks on the main staircase—a murmurous struggle on the landing—the auctioneer's movers were carrying something heavy. She folded her arms over her own cadaver. Across the theater of the arched doorway, two men carried a table between them, level on the slow river that was carrying everything out the front door. It was the writing-table from the cupola, where her father's blood had been spilled beside his "KJAZ" coffee cup and his ashtray and his green thesaurus absorbent as a sponge: its stack of pages had fattened in height with pink ruffles of corrugation; and then it dried like that; she remembered it. The table passed on out the front door between the two bearers. Against the fading murmur and shuffle, Peter said, "In that case, it's safe to tell you. Nobody really wants you on the Ranch. They've been hoping you'd find a way to live by yourself." He shrugged. "So everything works out for the best."

She had hurt his feelings, and now he was trying to lash back. But he just wasn't very skilled at it. He was good-hearted. He was dedicated to his poetry. "You should get a publisher," she said. "You really should be published by now."

He stood up fast, and turned. He drew his blanket tighter around himself. "You . . . ," he said, ". . . cunt," pausing at the worst word. A pimple showed blue in his throat.

"What'd I say?" She began raising her upside-down head by the drawbridge-cords in her neck, with difficulty, sitting up dizzy. "All I said was you should be published. You should be." For once she had said something nice.

"Yeah, fuck you. You have no fucking idea."

"I'm not criticizing, Peter. It's true. It's a shame you're not published."

"It's a shame you're fat and ugly." His voice had become sad; that was the murderous part about this. He wasn't angry, he was cold. Footsteps sounded in the kitchen. It would be Faro. A sound of objects on the kitchen table. They both shut up, listening.

Faro came into the room and said, "I notice now there's a police car out front. I guess the jig is up."

She had thrust her gaze down in her own lap, sitting down. He stood beaming over them.

Her brother said, "Have you been here all this time?"

"I've been helping pack. I'm in that strange little parlor through the library."

"A man from the Internal Revenue Service was here," Peter said. "The deputy sheriff is in the house looking for Dean right now. We let him in to look around. Here," he handed over the business card. "He said he has an appointment with you this afternoon."

Faro looked at the card. "Hail to thee, Arthur W. Murrain." He distributed a meaningless smile between them. She was a little bit relieved: his attitude would be that nothing had happened last night, a bluff so perfect it created a truth. In the light of it, she could almost think her own memory a fantasy or a misunderstanding! Or maybe that's how it always was with men, they have a happy doggy ability to forget and trot onward. Male faithlessness is perhaps a blessing to the female, in that way. A fortunate gift to her equilibrium: he was less handsome in person than in recollection—his turkey's-breastbone nose showing its stretched-shiny skin in the light, his blue eyes shallow in the mornings with a wino's paleness, his spine poised in the sprain of an elderly lower-lumbar delicacy. She could preserve a certain scorn of him. Yet alone last night she was able to imagine herself yielding to him, all the more for his cheerful tiredness, for his being shrunken and shrunken by her mother's nightly servings of magic stew. Sitting on the piano bench, she pulled her knees up, to withdraw her body from presence, obscurely stuck to everything here in a million ways: the unpopular cold piano, the books on the floor, the single andiron in the fireplace, the empty picture frames leaning in the corner, the promiscuousness and infidelity of everything. Peter said, ". . . We told him to look for Dean all he wants. He won't find him." He rattled his Geronimo blanket about himself and he shuffled around toward sitting down again on the couch.

"What makes you sure he won't find him?"

"Oh . . . this house. . ." He sat down on the same spot he'd risen from, in the midst of the house, the defeating house, obviously unable to express its huge novelistic connections with everything. He drew his blanket up high around his ears. Its nap was grimy, covered evenly with the small blue maggots of its pilled fuzz. He lifted his face and gazed off, seeing his distant poem on its snowy peak; she watched him with admiration; he was so lucky; his poem would always rescue him.

More steps were coming down the main staircase. That would be Baelthon now, inevitably. She hugged her knees. Baelthon and Faro were the two who had lifted her darting body to visibility, by a first male glance beneath the watery surface people's detached faces float upon. And now they would both be in the same room standing on either side of her; she would keep her eyes down and not move at all. Her chin rested on her kneecap. He came in carrying a heavy box and he told Faro, "I found this."

It was cardboard: "Almadén Mountain Chablis, (6) 1.5 LITER." He set it down heavily on the floor beside Faro's chair. On top were the words *AN+END+TO+ALL+WAR*, in White-Out erasure fluid, obviously written with the little brush inside the cap.

"It seems like a novel," Baelthon said. This was—rather disappointingly—the object of Merlin's quest: merely the old unfinished novel. She had forgotten that was its title. Baelthon didn't try to look at Wendy.

California's Over

"By your father? Really?"

"He never finished it," Wendy said but then shut up. In speaking, she'd called attention to herself and she knew she looked terrible, her hair escaping everywhere, her T-shirt's neck all stretched out. The orphaned feeling she was coming into now was an attraction to Baelthon. Last night after Peter's big scene at dinner, he caught her eye with a look of concern, which had turned out to be memorable, all night. Seeing him now, she loved his misguided seriousness, his big janitorial presence here, his soft bulk, his inertia, which amounted to repose. Or else maybe she was latching onto the feeling of being his girlfriend simply because it would save her from Faro. Faro's fingers had gone under the boxtop flaps. "A novel! Are you joking? Maybe it *is* something." Up came a handful of paper: fine onionskin typed fuzzily in carbon-copy, a few legal-size yellow pages, with pencil-notes in James Farmican's dead script, Hammurabic in its irrelevancy to everything now. Faro was flipping through them. ". . . I thought he didn't believe in novels."

"Wendy likes novels." Peter's lips came to a spitting hardness. "Novels are a bourgeois art form. Novels are a female art form."

"You people have had this manuscript sitting up there all this time? Aren't you being a little nonchalant about it?"

Peter shrugged. "It was never finished." But Faro was probably right. They should have pulled it out and at least read it.

"This could actually *be* something." He crouched and hugged the box. "I'll put it upstairs so it can't get confused with the rest of this junk." He got it as far as the main staircase, where he dropped it on the bottom step, while Baelthon hovered and made polite guessing motions toward being helpful. Faro was saying, "This box may be the one interesting relic in all this old crap."

Her brother said, "Hey. So Faro"—using the first name easily—"are you going to find out whether that casino is still operating?"

"Fwish, the casino"—he came back to his wing chair clapping dust off his palms, and he sat down, lacing his fingers in a low seat-belt across his waist and looking down at his stockinged toes, which started to twiddle. "Believe me, the last thing I desire is a casino," he said, as a prelude.

Baelthon was still standing there. He had been presenting to Wendy a profile, not trying to make eye-contact. Which was good. Yet on the other hand it wasn't completely likable.

But then he seized a small moment, glanced, and glanced away, and started to repress pride, to be soldierly severe. He truly felt not-entitled to his feelings. She'd never seen that in anyone. He was scowling, actually trying, not just to hide happiness, but to completely deny it. Then suddenly he belonged to her. She was all water. There was no rational logic to this feeling of hers. But yet there he was: standing there distrusting his own good heart.

He said to Faro, "Excuse me. This is a bill of lots. They took another truckload. I hope it's okay if I signed for it." He was holding some pages from *Butterfield & Butterfield, Auctioneers and Appraisers*. He said, ". . . And lunch is on."

"Lunch!" Peter complained bitterly.

Baelthon told Peter, with some hopefulness, "It's cioppino again."

He pulled his blanket higher, up around his ears. "Is it already noon?"

"This all looks perfectly fine," Faro said, holding up the receipts to read them, sliding down on the small of his back, his knees lolling apart.

Peter said, "Why are they made out to a church? It says 'church.'"

"Where?" said Faro, flipping back to the top page.

"Is this the church that's buying the house?"

A door banged in the kitchen, and her mother's voice rose with a harsh call, "This soup is hot. I'm putting lunch on the table."

Faro stood up, saying, "The church is what Mr. Murrain the Tax Man will want to talk about. Which way is lunch, Baelthon? The dining room?"

"Is the church actually 'buying' the house?"

"The Church of Bread and Wine . . ." Faro stood by the wide doorway embracing the whole room, shepherding people. Wendy got up but lurked at a distance, to go around the narrow way, through the kitchen, escaping Faro's great voice that opened spaces ahead of him in the tomb. "The Church of Bread and Wine is part of your personal family history. Tax avoidance is one of the ways Jefferson and the Founding Fathers designed the Constitution. All governments tend naturally toward fascism. That was the Founding Fathers' view. So, the theory is, a certain kind of civil disobedience has been built into the institution of government. Remember that play *The Night Thoreau Spent in Jail?* Did you see that play?"

Wendy had gone around the other way because she wanted to corner her mother in the kitchen and ask her point-blank about the missing ashes. She was building a stack of bowls on the drainboard and Wendy plunged in without prologue: "Mom?" She cleared her throat. The kitchen held its own peculiar silence far from Faro's lecture. "Mom, listen now," she said. It was the voice of a girl about to leave the family, the voice of a girl who was attractive to her mother's new husband.

"Here," her mother lifted the stack. "Would you put one at each place?"

"Mom, wait." She accepted the bowls. "Where did that jar go? I'm asking you."

At the moment of truth, lifting her eyes, her mother looked merely confused and irritated. She obviously didn't know. It was probably stupid to care so much about it in the first place, it was only ashes, only ashes. "The Tang jar, I'm talking about."

"Honey, I don't know," her mother said, and she lifted the big heavy soup tureen for the trip to the dining room. "Why don't you ask your brother. Is this the same jar you were looking for last night? Come on, bring those bowls."

"Mom, really."

Her mother set down the soup tureen and faced her. "Honey"—she reached out to the spiderwebs Bic-penned into the skin of her wrist, and she laid an ointmenty finger upon them. "I hardly think Baelthon is going to notice you if you disfigure yourself."

Then all of a sudden she was in one of those mysterious warped-gravity zones where excess anger is a possibility, which is a little bit pleasant in a perverted sort of way. "Is that all you care about? Attaching yourself to a male?" Her mother's feminism had always been so phony. Let *her* be not-so-exquisite-looking for a while and see how *she* likes equality. She had widened her beautiful eyes, and Wendy had the sensation of falling away, as if she'd backed off a cliff, watching her mother's facial expression chill toward objectivity. "If you're referring to Faro," her mother's voice sank lower, "just imagine life without him."

She couldn't believe it. She felt slimy and she lifted her shoulders. She had to get out of this family, but for a paradoxical reason: to cede this shrinking province to her mother, the queen, ever more vindictive as she gets weaker. With her stack of bowls, she turned away and walked out into the dining room. It would be possible never to look into her mother's eyes again, and putting off grief, she started limping around the table setting down bowls one-by-one, involuntarily eliminating suspects as she went: *No, not him . . . No, not him . . .* She would never find out. The disappearance of the ashes would be just one more strangeness in this place, her own home, making it that much easier to leave. They were all behaving with an innocence that couldn't be faked. Faro was saying happily as he drew his napkin over his knee, "The separation of church and state is very clear in the plan of American government. It's an important experiment, if you think about it. See, it's arguable

that church and state *can't ever* be separated, not by human be-
ings so constituted . . ." Faro was so earnest about everything.
She set a bowl at his place, her elbow in his vicinity a secret
lover's, then moved on. In the back inventory rooms at Tower
Records nobody would see her all day, walled-in among stacks
of cardboard boxes, whose brown fragrance tapes over the
senses. Thank God for record-store jobs, the one small peaceful
graveyard within capitalism, where you can wear jeans and you
don't have to put on makeup or tie your hair back or wear a
hair-net. The pale immortals at Wherehouse Records in San
Rafael were allowed to go barefoot sometimes, in violation of
health code rules, and they wore holey jeans and ripped sweat-
shirts; and at Tower Records there was the freckled Rastafarian
zombie with a delicate nose ring.

She sat down across from Baelthon. He'd been glancing at
her, his mouth hanging open in an easily hurt grin. He said,
across the table to her, "Want me to help you move that pile of
Free Store merchandise? We could put it in the garage."

She made a pleat at the corner of her mouth. Which was
yes. It was a tryst. It's easy, what other girls have. It always
looked harder.

Faro was saying, ". . . Something like *sixty* cents of every tax
dollar goes to the military . . ." but his voice had shrunk in distraction as he prodded around in his bowl. "Doesn't this soup
keep getting darker? Honey?"

Her mother woke from thought and turned on her sunshine. "It's that old black miso paste. I found it in the pantry,
sitting there mysteriously all by itself on the lavabo. The things
you unearth!"

"Mm, it's good," said Faro. "It's bacon-y. It's like smoked.
Isn't it like bacon? Mmm, tastes mushroomy."

Outside, the Mercedes' clinking engine pulled up. It was
Ed. Nobody mentioned it or exchanged glances, but they'd
heard. A place was already set for him.

"Tell me," Faro said, and he chewed. "Julie. Do you know

anything about an unpublished manuscript called 'An End to All War'?"

It seemed for a minute she wasn't going to answer, then she said, tiredly, "Yes, that was their . . . father," making a sprinkling motion with her fingers. It was a disposal-of-ashes gesture in Wendy's eye, and the actual nightmarish filth of the whole deep-rooted situation clung all over her for a minute.

◉　◉　◉

The missing jar of crematory ashes was never brought up again in that house. Even during the ensuing time in the desert, Wendy may still have considered the loss too intimate to mention, or maybe just too trivial in others' eyes. Now, before the issue is lost to history, I should insert that I myself was the one who moved it, but without realizing what I was handling. On my first day working around the place, I came across it in the upstairs servants' closet and decided it should go out with the recyclable glass. I tore off the paper sheath, not noticing or caring that it was a Tang label, and I put the unlabeled jar downstairs in the kitchen pantry among a collection of other old glass jars on the marble-topped lavabo.

And then I never gave it another thought, protected from alertness by my teenage male's abiding deep guilty stupor. Even when Wendy brought it up, I didn't think of it. All I had on my mind then was my joy in being there at all, in that house, holding onto the rim of that dinner table among people of heroic dimensions, myself wishing to swell to fit any use the Farmican family could have for me, in Oregon or anywhere. I never did sleep in my rented room again. We only stopped there on the way out of town so I could get my checkbook, toothbrush, clothes, a few cassette tapes. Within two days we were far in the desert, hot wind in our hair, windows all rolled down, arguing over which radio station to listen to, Wendy leaning beside me, the box marked "McGuffin" riding under Peter's feet on the passenger side in the shroud of a pillowcase. That box contained James Farmican's missing suicide note, the last page of his unpublished manuscript: it described a safe-deposit box in San Francisco where a new will was laid away, bequeathing his estate to his grandchildren. Nobody had ever read that suicide note, because no one in the family had ever gotten very far in the manuscript.

At one point during my four days in the house, I myself had laid eyes on that note, though without knowing what it was. That selfsame note, not a reproduction but the actual page (I remember clearly the archaic typewriter-letters on onionskin, the ink-clotted Os), will be produced by Wendy's lawyers in the Marin County Circuit Court, sometime next spring, as evidence that James Farmican intended to pass on his estate to his family. Wendy was here at my house tonight. Tomorrow is the official beginning of our cohabitation as man and wife. In an effort at cordiality I think, she came to the house for a friendly visit and sat in the kitchen with me, trying not to look around at everything, at the bicycle leaning against the wall in the same slouch untouched since probably 1985, the sliding patio doors all Live-Rite homes have, whose heavy iron frames tend to rust through the paint, the Paul Newman spaghetti-sauce jar filled with cigarette butts, the collapsed-cardboard-box doormat, the dust on the telephone, all scary stuff to a female, in her trench coat with her belted, cinched warmth, her hair fluffier than when we were in the desert, thicker, lighter-colored, but her eyes the same, her mouth the same. She came over for a drink, I suppose to make this arrangement seem less legalistic, to make tomorrow morning (the U-HAUL truck in the driveway!) seem friendlier. She's making an effort.

I hadn't seen her since I said those idiotic things at the airport, and suddenly I find I'm tired of the whole project of making myself likable. I was honest: I warned her that I will be busy, either with my academic duties or else with my futile, benighted career as a writer in my bedroom, and I won't have the leisure for little domestic pleasures like, say, cooking meals together or other such convivial inefficiencies, though if *she* wants to have fresh-ground coffee or fresh vegetables or tough bread, or all the other indispensibles our generation has brought into the marketplace, she is perfectly welcome. Independence will be our byword here in this house and we'll get along fine. If she likes, during this brief time, I could even put up a little partition inside the refrigerator, of cardboard and tape, in case like college roommates we are completely babyish about the separation in our fortunes. I intend to feel free, as always, to leave a carton of kimchee unlidded. It won't kill anybody.

Her response was "I understand perfectly. We're flexible," establishing artfully the relationship of vulnerable sweet victim to insensitive Nazi; a characterization that will probably serve us well. I have to keep commanding my eyes to stay away: her mouth the same mouth as twenty-five years ago, her jawline softer than twenty-five years ago, her hair changed, cut shorter, feathery and thick. "This is nice here. Do you have anything? A glass of wine?" she said, because she was still standing on the doormat in her trench coat. "Red? White? Either is fine." She was the one who brought it up, not me, which provides a good start to this marriage, because the popular, stretch-to-fit, one-size-fits-all word "alcoholic" applies all too easily to me in this sour decade of diagnosis, when our every peculiarity is supposed to be a symptom of some defect, something to be ashamed of, rather than something to use. It's not a popular insight, but a little wine in the evenings can be *useful* for someone naturally ambitious or impatient, in a historical time and place when ambition and impatience will obviously never have any fruitful result in the world except for discomfort. I went to the old cupboard where the sacrament gets more numb and meaningless as the years go on, and stood in my old pissing stance to hoist the bottle, my eyes the rubbed-valueless nickels that portend the beginning of relaxation, and I told her, "Just as one example" (that is, as one example of the kind of clutter I intend to combat during their stay here), "I unplugged that sculpture."

"The sculpture."

"He set it up in the living room and plugged it in."

"Oh, no. Was it Nixon and Kennedy?"

"I think now I've been sufficiently edified by that thing. Just one glance sufficed, to shock me out of my philistine complacencies. So we can unplug it."

"He wants to impress you. He said you'd met and had a drink. It was a big experience for him."

"This is not how to impress me."

"He's going to be courting your notice. He's making a new hologram for you. For *us* really. He's using our family history as a subject. He says it's his magnum opus. I would be prepared for anything."

"He's making a sculpture about us?"

"Well, in fact, it's about Dean Houlihan. It's Dean in heaven. Dean beatified, he says. But it shows . . . he says it shows Dean on a cloud in the afterlife. Actually he's urinating on everybody down below."

"Fine. Excellent."

"But do pretend to be surprised. It's supposed to be a surprise."

"Why do you suppose Dean is portrayed in that particular way?"

"It's some idea he got from archives in storage in family files. He's been rattling around."

"Let me tell you. I'm *so* glad I'm not an artist." I set her glass in front of her and sat down and closed my eyes within my own beatific smile. "The whole *world* of art has been so thoroughly ruined, by marketing and fraud and attitudinizing and terrible, *terrible* ideas that make money, or get grants, or merely get attention. Now only the sludge rises. Only the absolute slimiest sludge floats. If I were a real artist—I mean like a real '*artist*'— I would be one sad and confused and disappointed person. You will have noticed. The culture is reduced. And a good man is punished."

I didn't look at her. I'm a reactionary now. Or in any case, I was setting a certain tone for our cohabitation. This is my way of addressing my stupid remark in the airport. When I've been bad, I get worse.

In fact, Gabriel's magnum opus does not involve urination. I happen to know because, since she left, I've been snooping in the pile of notebooks he put in the spare bedroom with his first load of luggage. In a big sketchbook, he seems to have developed a series of ideas involving Dean in heaven, and many of the early sketches do involve urination from the clouds. But what he settled on as a final version was simply a lifted hand-gesture, of benign benediction. It's his tamest idea so far. Some of the other sketchbooks are filled with ideas for appalling mutations and celebrities engaged in sex, violence, and plastic surgery, which I won't describe.

Wendy had sat a minute staring at her wineglass, then said, "You never know. He might get an education at this school in Ohio."

"Fat chance. You haven't been near a college campus lately." I'd already had some wine when she arrived.

"Oh. I should tell you this. He does want your help on something." She lifted her glass and sipped. I thought, either she is *forgiving* me my incredible insult in the airport, or else it's something we'll get around to later. "Gabe has to take an entrance exam. He's going to one of those preparation programs that help you get ready for standardized tests. And an essay is required. He's going to write about that Salinger book, *Catcher in the Rye.*"

"And he wants my editorial help. Sorry. I do that for a living. I don't do it in my free time. He can fix his own writing." This in a flippant tone. I'm sorry. Oh, I'm so sorry, my sorriness flows out in rivers through space and time, future and past. This Second Honeymoon is going to be easy for Wendy. Or at least she seems to find it possible. It's not possible for me. Instead I have this numbness of the face, this insult of nicotine, ache in the jaw, dimmed vision, repressed arm-jerk.

"It would be just grammatical help, of course. Gabe would do the actual writing."

"Has he read the book?" As a matter of fact, Salinger's *Catcher in the Rye* is not only my favorite book, but also happens to be the intrinsically greatest novel of our time. It is also a book I have particular insights into. Salinger actually *improved on* Huckleberry Finn's first-person narrative technique. And that's saying a lot. Compared to *Catcher*, Mark Twain's book pales. History will show. I lit a cigarette and exhaled smoke largely. She doesn't smoke.

"Well, I presume he's read the book," she scoffed.

"Oh you'd be surprised. A whole new generation is using only the 'Cliff's Notes' version of life. And they do just fine with it. Happy hollow people. They're lighter and more maneuverable than we are. Than we were."

She made a little effort to smile, a little flip of the lip, as I think she began to see, or realize more deeply, how hard this was going to be. How eloquent I am on these topics. I pitied her, from my diminished perspective here in the distant unimaginable pitiless future, even "loved" her in a cramp, but then, pitilessly, got right to the point: "I don't intend for your residency here to change my life at all. You see that. I have a pretty sane life."

She took a minute to answer. Her fingers were spindling the stem of her wineglass and I could see her eyes were glistening, and she said, "I understand this thing may *be* terrible, but we don't need to focus on that." She was speaking deliberately, as if reading the words in the rim of her glass as she revolved it. "It's obvious what you'd prefer. It was obvious what you wanted twenty years ago when you left Reno. I'm not trying to deny that or change anything. But if we are *going* to go through this period, let's do it with as much . . . " She nodded her head, off toward the rest of her unfinished sentence: as much civility as possible.

I'm somebody whose responses tend to be delayed. I need reflection time alone for the meanings of things to sink in. What she said didn't hit me at first. She seems to think I made a personal *decision* to leave her in Reno. She thinks I *wanted* things to work out as they did. She thinks I deserted her. It's what she clearly implied. But at that minute in my glaze of I suppose anger, I didn't think about any of that and just changed the subject. "Will you be bringing furniture from your mother's house too?"

"My mother didn't have any furniture. She lived with us."

"She did? She didn't have her own place?" In a Novato free-way-side apartment, there's scarcely room for Julia Farmican's expansive kimono-sleeved arm-gestures.

"Ever since Reno, we lived together. Except for brief periods."

"All these years?"

"We had to be realistic. Gabe was an infant when I got a job, so she took care of him. And then when she got a job too, my hours were always the night shift. So we could trade off the time with Gabriel."

"She had a job? Your mother? What did she do?"

"Oh. Different things. For the last ten or fifteen years she worked at the Novato Public Library. It was the best she could do, you know, as a genteel lady, with no experience, and with some sense of her own . . . specialness. At first she got work through friends, but it wasn't real work. Her friends. Dad's old friends. But that was always awkward."

Julia Farmican had a job. I had to literally shift in my chair. Julia Farmican had pushed a squeaky cart full of books along the aisles, reshelving them, checking the call-numbers. "Were you working at the bookstore then?"

In reminiscence her gaze turned a soft angle. I love her. It's the same as always.

California's Over

She said, "You know Bay Convalescent? I turned and washed old people. I did that for a long time."

"Wendy," I said, as the world kept veering. The elapsed quarter-century in flying apart leaves me merely chilled and alone.

"It was the job I could get. I'm a high school drop-out remember. *And* with a child. It's actually amazing—and I'm a little proud—that I'm getting to be an editor at a publishing house without the formal education. But you know, I loved that job at that convalescent hospital. Do you believe that?" She had had some time to drink her wine too, and I had the first feeling our thoughts had begun moving together in lubrication, our lips having both kissed the same red source in its separate stemmed globes. It is an illusion it's possible to get, with wine.

"I stayed at that job four years," she said, in a kind of fuzzy amazement she sometimes still has. "I was just going from one bed to the next, washing these dying, sort-of-dotty old people, turning them and washing them"—her hands made a gentle motion like pushing canoes off a shore. "The job saved me. Because after Nevada, I was . . . disoriented. And just simply young. Also, I loved the old *people*. You know? I even liked their crazy old bodies. It only paid three dollars an hour but . . . " She shrugged. "I did that for four years," she repeated herself. The span of time was important to her. "And then I started at City Lights. I've done that forever now. They love me there. It doesn't matter that I have no formal education. I started in sales but now I'm working with authors and texts. And as I told you, I go downstairs to the store and face Dad's books out on the shelves." I was looking at the whole idea of her. She pleated her mouth in the old way she used to, and said, "There's something I should tell you about that time. About the time I was at Ecstasy."

"You had to. I don't blame you. Peter was in trouble. You had no alternative. Breece got you into it."

She said, "Do you remember him? Breece?"

237

"How could I forget." My sight shortened in this situation. I kept inhaling the fumes of my wine. My habit, when I drink even socially, is to keep stroking the rim of my glass against my chin, to keep my whole muzzle within the hoop of solvent ether. She looked at me for a minute gauging the distance between our lives now. "No, Breece didn't talk me into it, no. It wasn't exactly true that, as you say, I had no alternative. People have alternatives. Even those mean girls in those ranches have choices. People choose things. At the time, we did get some money. If you remember, my family's bank accounts were under audit, but Faro nevertheless found a friend to give us money. I think I was willing to do it because I was sixteen and it was . . . research into life." She looked at me with a quizzical smile, as if she was trying to decide what she might have meant by that.

"Research into life," I confirmed. Because it was a funny idea but I knew what she meant.

"Also I think I wanted to be responsible. I was sixteen. You know me. None of it scared me. When you're young you're . . . you can do things you'd never do. And everything at that point seemed so wrecked."

"I waited there, you know," I said. "I waited at the campsite. And then I went around town searching."

She was looking—through me—into the past. "I wanted Gabriel, I guess. I just wanted to be a mother. And even then, I knew I'd never be a person of your—what—aspirations or talent or whatever. Maybe I'm just unambitious. Or I'm just . . . happy I guess," she finished in defeat. Happiness being a weakness of character.

I stood up for more wine. Turned away. Slid the door in its groove. All old Live-Rite homes from the fifties have these cabinet doors, sliding rectangles of Masonite, painted originally in enamel colors of orange and yellow and purple, with fingerholes rather than knobs. Mine are still the original colors but dirty. The kiss-and-pop of the Sebastiani cork. The buoyant gurgle in the tilted bottleneck.

She said, "Anyway, I thought I should say all that. Some people would consider it a pretty scandalous . . . skeleton in my closet." There was fear in her voice, and she picked up her wineglass and drank.

"I knew," I said. "I've known." There was "forgiveness" in my voice. I sat down all hooded, bringing the bottle with me.

"Well, in fact, to be honest, I sort of knew you would already know. Otherwise I might easily have tried to keep it a secret. No kidding. You know? Bury it? Leave well enough alone?"

"I'm not judging, if that's what's worrying you. I don't see it as immoral. I'm not at all *bothered* by it," I said.

"Well, it was a quarter-century ago. It only lasted three weeks. And the whole thing was totally hygienic and, sort of, *nursy*. Really, *nurses* is the feeling. It was like a clinic." She was pleading, but trying to make it seem light.

I said, "Did you have sex with a lot of men? During that three-week time? Fifty?"

She made a tiny breath of amusement, to treat it as a joke. Therefore I persisted. "I mean, do they pack in a lot of customers per hour? Or do they give you a break? Certainly for meals you get a break."

She didn't look up. She can tell what she is up against, in this house, in me, and she made a superb maneuver of evasion. "Do you want to know what was the most degrading thing? I'll tell you. It's not what you'd think. Breece and his woman-friend took me to the county sheriff's office to get registered."

"'Dana'? Was that Breece's woman-friend's name?"

"Yes, 'Dana,' yes. Did you meet her?"

"So what was the most degrading thing?"

She made a flickering sad smile. "Well, you have to *register* in Nevada. I mean, when you work on those ranches. They

make you go to a doctor. But then you have to have your fin-
gerprints on file and your photograph taken. And I sat there in
this jail office, this was in Carson City, and the cop took my picture for the file. And then he turned my picture over and wrote
'PROSTITUTE' on the back of it. He liked doing that. You
could tell. I've thought about it since. He didn't need to write
that word on there. It was *going* in the file of registered sex
workers. It was the little grin he gave me then. He just liked
doing it. I was sixteen and it looked like a high school yearbook
photo. Mother-of-pearl background. Cute girl. And then he
writes that word on the back. It was a very strange feeling. He
knew exactly what he was doing."

"It's just a word, Wendy. You can choose to let that word
define you, or not. It's just a cruel old word from twenty-five
years ago." I was wearing the mask of kindness and wisdom
again.

"Still," she said, ". . . when you see that word on your own
picture."

"Well." I closed my eyes. "Let us say it puts us in a world
where there's no possibility of love, or disillusionment now.
Most people go through whole *marriages* totally mechanically."
I tilted my glass around at the surrounding neighborhood of
"marriages" installed in tract houses. Where in fact, I'm probably wrong: there probably *does* exist something like love, or at
least stability, which is saying a lot, because stability has its own
kind of ardor, I can see that much as an observer.

Nevertheless, I went on. Because wrecking possiblities be-
forehand provides its own peculiar success and security. "It's
good this came up. One might feel it's contaminating. It's something to get out in the open."

Looking down, she was rubbing a temple with her fingers,
smiling.

I said, "So! When's our court hearing?" I inclined the bottle
in her direction, being hospitable.

California's Over

"Our court hearing," she said dimly. "No thanks. I'm still working on this glass."

"Aren't we supposed to have a hearing? When we stand up in front of a judge and claim we've always considered ourselves married all these years?"

It's remarkable how much older a woman can look, suddenly. She lifted her glass, still keeping her eyes down. "The hearing has been set back. Everything has been rescheduled. Because now Ed's *corporate* lawyers are taking over the case . . ." She stretched her neck. I had really made her uncomfortable, and my heart went out to her, watching her move into a grim tiredness. She breathed, and dragged up around her the net of Farmican family legal trouble. "Here's what happened. Our legal case is falling apart. It looks like Faro's argument might be airtight: in 1973 everything was legally, formally, donated to that church. Everything absolutely." She hugged herself in her trench coat, looking, here in my home, like a woman waiting in an auto mechanic's garage. She focused her mind on the legal dilemma. "The reasoning runs like this: If Dean Houlihan's old imaginary church is what validates our marriage, then it *is* a real church. And then it *does* deserve to keep all its old tax-exempt contributions. You see. Catch-22. It's problematic. And Faro's lawyers for the Open Foundation are very high-powered. Ed had his company, CornucopiaCorp, buy the proceeds of James Farmican's estate. So *his* lawyers can work on the case."

"CornucopiaCorp?"

"Mm." She drank and shivered.

"What is CornucopiaCorp?"

"Oh. You know. Remember how he was driving around in the desert hammering pipes into the ground to stake claims everywhere? And we just told him it was nothing but dust? Well, it *is* dust, and the dust is all gypsum or something. He's in the Sheetrock business. CornucopiaCorp is all gypsum mines.

It makes most of the Sheetrock for the western U.S. He got the mineral rights to all that, by driving around staking claims, remember? He was squatting everywhere? And we thought he was crazy? Don't you remember that whole idea of squatter's rights?"

◉ ◉ ◉

"Squatter's rights is great" was Peter's reaction when Ed first brought it up, and he sat up taller at the table in his dirty blue blanket, naked beneath it, his bowl of cioppino untouched in front of him. He knew he was forgetting his dignity, here at the place where he had slit his wrist the night before, but he happened to know about squatter's rights so he couldn't help explaining, "You can just take land just by being on it. Nobody cares. Everything in Nevada is wide open. Prostitution is legal there too. Guns are legal. They don't have any speed limits either. You can drive two hundred and twenty miles an hour. You can just drive right off the road. They don't have any fences. It's all wide open."

A silence—which felt like accumulated general skepticism—gathered at the end of this speech. "Well!" Faro said. "You make Nevada sound like paradise."

"You go out and just *live* on the land, and it becomes yours legally. You just go out there and squat on it."

The expression made his sister crack up.

"It's true," he told her. "Squatting is the method. Once you've squatted on it, it belongs to you."

She stopped snickering. "After *you've* squatted on it, who would want it?"

Cheered fraternally by this insult, Peter wished for a riposte, but Faro interrupted.

"I think probably what you mean," he addressed Ed rather

than Peter, "is that you can *occupy* some land that's being ignored, and then *register* a claim with the authorities, and then *advertise* your claim, and then *spend* a specified amount of time waiting to see if the real owner objects, and then *hire* a lawyer to sue for ownership . . ."

Ed was buttering his bread. He said, "Whatever." His knife sculpted the butter. "This is in case the actual Cornucopia Casino no longer possesses any real property."

Faro looked at his wife. He raised his eyebrows.

"Is this what you've been out doing this morning?" said his mother. "Researching Nevada?"

"I spent the morning in a card room in San Rafael, to acquire experience of the various ins and outs of playing blackjack."

That put the table in a new odor. Amidst it, Ed sat there looking immovable. He was wearing his plaid sports coat again, and now in Peter's eyes, Ed locked together all the more tightly into a solid figure who would never grow or learn any more. Life had already made him too dense. He was perfect as a casino owner, his sports coat a lantern in that superstitious darkness regularly flash-lit by smothered revelations, men crouching over the tiny stained-glass windows in their hands, where—face-up, face-down—two revolving blades carve the universe.

"I'm anticipating to make an exploratory trip there as soon as possible," Ed said, and he glanced—darkly! with relish!—at Peter and Wendy. He wanted them to come along. "I believe it's an asset to develop."

Peter leaned and whispered to Wendy, "They have whorehouses," with a lascivious shudder. "You'll like that." He made his lips swell. She tried good-naturedly to make the sick smile of being joshed, but really her mind was elsewhere. She didn't even look up.

Faro said, "You'll find most of Nevada is owned by the BLM, Ed. Or else somebody will have an old mining claim.

That's pretty much the case all over the West. The government would be your adversary there."

Ed looked belligerent. He took a minute to answer. Then he said, testingly, "You can take government land. You can take government land with squatter's rights."

"I don't think so."

"You should be able to. It's a right." Ed rose straighter in his chair, in a pulpit, because he seemed to sense some mortal truth at stake here. "Don't they know what land *is?*" he said, his hands holding up a swatch of space, a model of this rectangle of wasteland out there he'd never seen.

Faro said, "Okay, what is land?"

"Land is . . ." His fingers grasped. "Land is what we're *given,*" he said like an Indian chief in the movies. This obviously didn't mean much; so he shrugged in failure and said, "Well, whatever," and picked up the butter knife. Then he put down the butter knife and he looked back and forth along the table. "I'll tell you what. You say we can't do it. But I'll tell you what. We're going to."

So, Peter knew one thing now: he knew *he*'d never go to Nevada. Seeing the light in Ed's eyes, the whole thing was doomed. Or, worse, it might succeed. And then there *he*'d be, stuck on all that terrible carpeting, *red* carpeting, probably wearing a tuxedo, greeting customers and standing next to a big chrome cash register, under a chandelier made of golden plastic whose papery gold curls off; big wall mirrors with merengue frames; he could imagine it all so completely, even the imaginary desert air-conditioning made him cold, and he drew his blanket up higher over his shoulders in larval filth back home here in the present, in reality. One bare knee rose under the blanket and he set his chin on it and looked into the black sulfur-tasting mud at the bottom of his broth. He started again spooning it into his mouth. It tasted like burnt matches. Here at the scene of last night's symbolic death, he would earn his way to dignity in silence, eating, digging his way back.

Faro called along the table, "So! Baelthon! How's it going down there?"

Shrinking and smiling, Baelthon looked up. "Fine! Fine thank you."

"In the basement, I mean. How's all *that* going?"

Interrogated, Baelthon got very grave and set down his eating utensils. "I haven't found any church minutes yet, but I think I know where they are."

"Are you having fun? Are you finding interesting stuff?"

Wendy lifted her face to whine, "What is this *church*?" Suddenly she had grown to be beautiful, that little cat-chested girl who was better than him at tree-climbing and mutiplication tables and manipulating grown-ups. But still she obviously had no idea. There it was: beauty's immediate authority, the inner flame she was completely unaware of, it could make you profoundly envious if you let yourself think about it.

Faro answered. "I was just explaining that. The church is a tax dodge. Long ago, your father and his friend Dean started the church for this purpose. And now we're putting it to use, in a rather major way."

"Dean's church isn't a real church."

"True, yes. The government knows that too. It's a successful *replica* of a church. Which is what they all are, of course."

"What are the church 'minutes'?"

Faro sighed. "Your father and Dean kept minutes of their meetings. They did it because the tax code requires it. You're not a church if you don't have meetings. The IRS needs some documentary proof."

Ed had been watching with a growingly gypped look. "Was this ever a real church?" He was so tiresome. This was all new to him and would have to be re-explained. "What does it have to *say* in the minutes?"

◎   ◎   ◎

Louis B. Jones

+Hello Internal Revenue Service. We greet you at the begining of a long and fruitful relationship+++september 12, 1962 Jim makes Motion to begin meeting+
+Motion seconded: Me.+
+Any old Bunsiness? Any NEW bunsiness?+
+U.S. Restaraunt on Colombus Avenue reduces size of wine glass+
+SEPTEMBER 12, 1962, Buena Vista+
+++THE FOLLOWING CHURCH OFFICERS HEREBY ELECTED
+Pastor & Hagiographer = Jim Pharmacon
+Secretary = Dean Houlihan, moi même
+Treasurer = Illuminated Larry, in absentia,
+Minutes minutes minutes, seconds seconds seconds. bla bla bla bla bla bla Jesus loves me this I now cause the bible tells me so. We are the First Church of the Drty Ndrtkng. Church of the Necessary Evil. Empty Shopping Cart fallen by a freeway exit, Broken Shoes Standing empty on a Thrift Shop shelf, Dusty Old China Cup on Janitor's Sink, Saucer on railing filling with rain. (dirty saucer, clean rain) Old Sock in gutter stiff/gray w/carbon monoxide. Everything you're NOT thinking right now. MR I.R.S., We Are The Church Of Everything You Don'T Think About. At this moment only Judas is out there taking responsability for the starry machinery of night, Allen. Jesus he gone, Jesus gone to heaven. Judas, HE is still hangin hangin on his tree where nobody visit all eternity. Official Prayer, to be repeated four times a day, facing east, or facing back-bar mirror: "Bottoms up, Judas!"
+Girl with groovy hair alone at table on your left+
+Jim moves that these notes be amended or destroyed+
+Threatens schism, dont give fuck bout Judas+
+Compromise is reached: I shall promise never to mention a certain J-person again, which is fine, He's unmentionable, always was+
+Aforsaid compromise to be called in history The Diet of Buena Vista+

246

+Is this enough?

+Hello out there, Internal Revenue Service: we wiggle our bad parts at thee+

+Jim moves as follows: we all take vows of poverty sponge off church+

+Larry seconds motion in absentia+

+Motion is carried+

++++ CELLAR TO BE CHURCH SANCTUARY

++++ LARRY'S VEHICLE CHURCH PROPERTY DO-NATION

++++ ALL INCOME HERAFTER TO BE DONATED DI-RECTLY TO CHURCH

++++ VOWS OF POVERTY ++++

++++ ANY LITERARY ROYALTIES GO DIRECT TO CHURCH TREASURY

+All motions carry unanymously. Girl NOT impressed. We are ruining her afternoon. She was having a perfectly nice day Shopping At Union Square

Avowed Purpose of the One True Church: To Get To Portland! To stand Idly By! To stand Idly By while skinny white boys and electrified gitars take what belongs to the African the American negro, "First Church of Bread and Wine" shall have the following Rituals and Ceremonies:— Twice-Daily Wiggling of the Bad Parts in the direction of the IRS, Ogden Utah, east-northeast—Frequent Parties a Romona's—Every Friday, get together and find some negative space, such as viaduct underpass railroad siding et cetera, where we shall smash a beer bottle in observance. Strand rusty barbwire stapled to a rusty concrete post.

+++ amen +++

1 — James Farmican
2 — Larry in absentia
3 — moi même
September 12, 1962
+++ December 18, 1962 +++

Louis B. Jones

+Hello Internal Revenue Service, its us again, the First Church of Rendering Unto Caesar. We have meetings. This is a meeting. When we get audited you can take all this shit home in your briefcase dickhead. We've taken Vows of Poverty and piss on you from our cloud above. Or wld you like to Swing on a Star? At the Moment Now We're on the ferry going to MDK's house in Mill Valley to meet the Actual Babs Gonzales in person the Actual Oscar Brown Junior and assorted other holywood people, with !!!The Inevitable Edipus Rexroth!!! presiding as Master of Ceremonies which is all such an uncool trap I will ditch to hang with bikers at depot but Jim insists on this, because he's ambitious. I accuse him of ambition. Jim Farmacology, I accuse thee of ambition. The Church of bread and Wine punishes ambition by REWARDING it So look out! +

+ Larry makes a motion that these minutes should be simplified and "More Realistic," oh, but I see you, young bureaucrat with haircut and briefcase, last example of faith in america, and I want to provide you with a Real church. MOTION NOT CARRIED +++ Acording to Larry the IRS doesnt want theology but the IRS is going to get theology whether they like it or not. This boat is jumping 'round too much in choppy water past Alcaltraz.

+++ So, I.R.S. Man. You who are my only auditor now, my only listener, the Only One who will ever read this. It's years later. Hearken unto me, Hear Me O Taxman: I don't despise you, I love you too, even thee, even the tax collector. More my friend than the ambitious poet who pretends to despise thee, and hops into the dependable old Entertainment industry. For Thou, Tax Man thou survivest, Thou containest all things. The "poet" experiences only his own exaltation above Thee and me. He "Protesteth."

+++ I prophesy Thy Coming, O lowly bureacrat tax man. I proclaim thee, O Bodhisattva of Ogden Utah, Middletown Ohio, Golden Colorado, Muncie Indiana, O Avatar. This scripture is for thee alone. the sacramental Kool-Aid and Baloney for thee tonight in the back yard by a lazy bend in the freeway +++

+Secretery (me): motion to end meeting #2 of church of Blood and Wine.

248

California's Over

+motion seconded: Larry
+motion thirded: Jim
+motion carried
+If Rexroth brings his camera, I'm out the door. Never entering.
See that pop of FLASHBULB, Watch old Merlin Vanish +

President and pastor: Jim Farmican
Secretary: me
Spectator and Critic: Larry
December 18, 1962

Mill valley stinson beach Exit
onto Miller Ave.
Left at stop sign (2AM Club) onto Montford
Stay on Montford, 1 mi
Rt. at Tamalpais
park by mailboxes
go up past garbage cans
dirt path up thru big trees

November 19, 1963

+++ Chrch minutes, 3rd meeting, Enrico's
+ Bla-bla-bla-bla-bla-bla-bla-bla-minutes minutes minutes +
+ I declare this church is a bad idea +
+ THE FAINTEST IDEA WHAT "DHARMA" MEANS
anymore +
+ your actions are seperate from the fruit of your actions +
+ Did not the Lord Krishna enjoin the young Arjuna, NOT to
expect $ or The Steve Allen Show or $10 bottles of wine or cameos
in Antonioni movies or even royaltys, Be thou like unto yr old pal
the Kahuna: When I do landscaping work for rich people in Sausal-

249

*ito for two dollars an hour, my mind is on THAT DANDELION,
most important and complete thing in the world. Then the next
dandelion, then the next dandelion, then the next dandelion, then
the next dandelion, then the next dandelion. What'll happen to you
buster is youll get what your looking for, and that lites the way unto
darkness. When Miles hits that fat first punchy note in "Kind of
Blue" THAT is The Next Dandelion. Miles is always on the Next
Dandelion Only. This Holy Church was not founded for any purpose except To Pay Attention To The Next Dandelion and To Get
To Portland So you say these are unintentional results but nothing
is unintentional, the girl, the distractions, Being at Enricos at all on
an elseways beautiful day. These are church minutes you'll never
see, Buster, because the church is hereby exomminicating you
because you got the bad smell now, when we could be at 5th
and Howard with Jose and Pepito and Ramona and Julie I love
them all so much never change or grow old or go anywhere else but
here, because the vision is clearer for the hungry, everybody knows
that.*

enrico's, Nov. 19

"Isn't that illegal?" Ed said, using one knuckle to push aside
his bowl, leaning forward with a leer of—obviously!—admiration. Beat, Peter dropped back from his own bowl, that black
miso paste was so filling, you quickly felt sick with nutrition.
Deep inside him an artifact was rotting: his "poem," his stomach always working, always strangling something. This house,
its plaster walls and rooms, had always—ever since the flash of
a solitary gunshot—enclosed spaces of imprintable twilight,
every empty doorframe a square of old Polaroid gray. Now
these halls and doorways, the many telescoping gray rectangles,

had become suddenly more profound, because of the intrusion of this noisy brother, the kiss of fresh modern air in the catacombs. Peter looked down at the limited tools of life laid out before him—spoon, bowl, butter knife—and he felt hopeless, expecting some unimaginable miracle, living by his own weightlessness, on surface tension, not breaking through.

"It's legal," Faro answered. "And not only that, it's ethical. I believe I'm obeying higher laws than the state. Don't imagine I haven't thought about it a lot, Ed. As a matter of fact, we're *re*submitting *revised* 1040 forms for your mother, covering the past ten tax years, to get back a lot of the money the government owes. She hasn't been claiming donations to the church she could have been."

"But you have to have some ceremonies. Or beliefs. Or something."

"The Supreme Court has dealt with that, twice, specifically with tax-avoidance churches. And they simply can't touch 'em. However, we do have to recover the scripture! Ah, yes! Baelthon, were you aware that a man from the Internal Revenue Service is coming today? This afternoon? So if you could please locate all the church files."

"I know where they are."

Ed wouldn't stop complaining, "But you don't have a . . ." he swam ". . . church."

Faro's arms lifted through space—"You are *in* the temple"—levitating the whole building into an effective church all around them.

Squatting under his blanket and staring at his soup, Peter found himself sinking with admiration. What would they have done if Faro hadn't come along?

"That ranch in Oregon"—Ed was making a sneer of new respect. "It was purchased in the church's name, wasn't it."

Faro shrugged, looking down.

"Are *you* the pastor? How do you get the appropriate . . . ?"

"You pay twenty dollars plus postage and handling, and you

get a piece of paper that says 'Doctorate of Divinity' with your name. It's the same way your father and Dean Houlihan got to be ministers. It's a piece of paper."

Ed sat still. But he was plainly impatient. "Well, but it's so obviously phony anyway." He lowered his head. "I'm sorry, but that's what it is."

"If you mean it's 'illegal,' you're just wrong. But if you're speaking of a *moral* question—"

"No, the whole thing. That 'ranch.'" He started looking ashamed of himself. "Nobody believes. Nobody believes you'll create this *place*, where everybody's nice and good and creative and non-judgmental."

To this direct insult, Faro responded with gladness: "I'm so relieved somebody else besides me is thinking that. Are you saying it's impossible to get outside society's traditional values? Is that what you mean?"

"No, it's just a power trip. It's *your* power trip."

"In what sense?"

"Don't do this psychiatrist thing. Of *seeming* open-minded."

Faro stopped, honestly set back by this, and then he leaned aside applying his point of view at a new angle, "A power trip is exactly what I want it *not* to be. As a wealthy white male WASP in this society—and, you're right, as a shrink, too—I *have* got power. What I want is to abdicate. If you can tell me some way I can make the Ranch an area of freedom and equality . . ." In a gesture like shirt-opening, he looked happily around the table. "Just somebody gimme the knife and I'll impale myself and fall off the throne."

Ed just sighed and started adjusting his silverware arrangement. He was one of those people who, in defeat, simply toughens and clings. At last he grumbled, "I suppose no TV will be allowed."

Everybody shifted, seeing how hopeless he was.

"Edward, it's not supposed to be heaven on earth. What I

want up there is skeptical, thoughtful people, like you. You seem to think I want only idealistic, sycophantic . . ."

"I'm not thoughtful. I'm not skeptical. I'm going to Nevada." He lifted a piece of bread, looked at it, and then took a bite. It was like he was trying to eat as much as he could before leaving.

"Edward, Nevada is out of the question. As a matter of fact, we aren't absolutely required to turn over the Deed to you."

"I can just *get* the Deed. It's right there in the medicine cabinet."

"Julie? Is that right? It's in the bathroom? Is that where the Deed is kept?"

"Oh, Faro, it's only a casino. Who wants a casino? I'm sure it's defunct."

"Why is the Deed of Ownership in the medicine cabinet?"

"I'll go get it after lunch," Ed said, his eyes downcast so resolutely as to look crossed.

"Julie," Faro pleaded.

She sighed, "Edward Male Live Birth," blessing him with a wave of her spoon.

And so Peter's heart snapped shut against Ed. He would go away and take over a probably ruined casino. Let him.

But then his mother, beside him, expanded and drew all the air of the table into herself, and Peter had the necromantic feeling she was publicly inhaling, too, his last-night's performance. Her palms were held up juggler-like. "Now, listen, all my people," she sang, her vision tangential to him. "We have the movers and appraisers here for only three more days. It's time to face the music. I want people to begin the Great Sorting now."

Peter stood up from his chair and drew the shroud high around his neck and went off toward the kitchen, heading downstairs, nobly toward extinction, a spooky patient in his blue blanket sweeping the dirty floor.

Then Faro picked up a couple of soup bowls and stood up, following him. His mother would be catching Faro's eye, as a cue. Peter should have foreseen this encounter. Faro would overtake him before he could get to the basement door.

"Are you going poem-ward?"

"No," he answered abruptly, just because he hated for people to *know*, poetry was such a private and personal friction.

"Well, listen. Wait a minute. Before you get away. Listen. I won't hold you here forever." Faro joined his hands and bowed his head. "I want you to know—just think about this—that there is such a thing as a 'conspiracy of the good.' Okay? We all kind-of *save* each other. It's actually pretty hard to get lost. You have to make a real long-term concerted effort, if you want to get lost."

Peter watched the drip from the kitchen faucet and only wanted to get downstairs.

"And if you ever want to '*talk*.'" The idea of "talk" was illustrated by an airy basketball in Faro's hands. Peter's eyes had gone dull. The air around Faro was always so extraordinarily clear and high-pressure, he himself fogged over. That cardboard box was still standing there on the rim of the washing machine, the word McGUFFIN on all four sides. "*Farmican*" was written in script on its top, naming the contents. Nobody had moved it. Those cinders had been his father, his great skinny, loping, hunchbacked, woman-haired father, smelling of cigarettes, pioneer of American literature, distantly amused by everything, including his children, his ass a great saddle, his books in every bookstore. Peter never knew him.

Faro dodged into his zone of attention holding the invisible basketball up. "In the meantime, here's something for you to chew on. Picture this: cars don't have internal-combustion engines. They have big clocksprings under the hood. What do you think? Too weird?"

Peter shifted his weight, trying to refocus. He was taller than Faro, and slower.

"Solar is a long way off. Here, let me draw you a picture."
He started slapping his pockets, revolving.

Trigonometry was unimaginable. At Shambhala Academy,
all they ever did was discuss *Zen and the Art of Motorcycle Main-*
tenance without anyone's having read it. Or else they took field
trips. The one attempt at a math class had deteriorated again
into philosophizing, and then the usual anarchy while the
teachers clowned and cowered.

". . . Maybe you get a hundred miles per winding. And
when you want to wind it up again, you back your car into a
gantry. Then a weight is dropped, and that winds up your
spring. And do you know how the weight gets lifted? Draft animals! Oxen on a treadmill! With a windlass! You get energy-
transfer with minimal entropy! Nobody who's looking at the
post-petroleum era has thought much about draft animals.
They're a biological energy source. Not only that, they're a relationship"—he was making sorry little motions of embracing
nothingness while Peter edged away toward the basement.

◉　◉　◉

But then a minute later, he was stalled on the staircase, because
he had decided to do something sneaky—and a little bit peculiar—he had decided to take the McGuffin box for himself. A
week from now, he would be here all by himself, and then his
impossible black opera would swallow him. And then, forever
after, Swanson's frozen spinach soufflés, in their crimped-foil
trays: day after day his favorite food. No one would be here to
make him eat otherwise. He still had the one good idea to cling
to—an opera where actual cannibalism takes place right onstage. Right in front of the audience, people eating flesh. That
was foolproof. He had to remember that: it was foolproof.

He rewrapped his blanket. He had lingered on the stair because of the box of ashes. If he didn't do something about it, nobody else would. Or his sister would bury it in the garden, ludicrously like a pet. James Farmican would lie beside a clay tombstone from a ceramics class, inscribed "Flubber," with a speckly pink glaze dumped over it like Thousand Island Dressing.

But what would he do with it? Nothing. Put it on the floor along with everything else in his room. His room was still intact, down to the last apple core, down to the cigarette ash fallen long ago on the stereo turntable beside the tone-arm, its tiny gray castle undisturbed there. Auctioneer's movers were burrowing everywhere else, audibly.

At least it would be, for a moment, an activity. So he started climbing back up the steps under the majestic burden of his blanket covered all over with grubby blue rice. The box was there. He could have just picked it up, without any superstitious hesitation or ceremony: it was merely a purified mineral residue.

But Faro's footstep was approaching in the hall. He dropped back to the top step behind the partition, not at all "ashamed" to be taking care of the urn, but feeling nevertheless slightly occult about it. Faro came down the passageway. Under his arm was a stack of typed pages: it was his father's unfinished novel, pulled from the big carton in the front room. He swept into the pantry with the deafness of a man in a hurry, and he plopped the heavy manuscript down on the dryer. Then he addressed himself to the very McGuffin box! He reached into the box to lift out the urn itself—a cheap-looking shiny tin! with a tin lid to be frisbeed!—and he walked away with the empty box. As he went, he slipped the manuscript into the box.

The can stood alone now, smudgily reflective. Peter watched it. Around the corner, he could hear Faro pick up the telephone: *"Okay. I've got it. It fits in this box. I haven't looked at it, but it's obviously a novel. The front page says 'An End to All*

*War.' And then it says, 'A novel by James Farmican.' And you flip
around inside and it's a novel. It's obviously a Farmican novel. I
guess the family thought it's an unfinished book so why bother. It
sure looks unfinished, but then everything he wrote was like that.
Oh, I see. You would deal with* his *agent. And then that agent
would take a commission too. . . . Sure, of course, I'm happy to.
Great, okay, but Harris? Do me a favor. Address any correspondence to 'The Church of Bread and Wine.' It has to do with a tax
deduction. The proceeds of Farmican's estate are owned by a non-
profit. I'm in no hurry, but it's somewhat scary: I feel like I'm in
possession of a brick of enriched uranium here. Bye. Yes. So long."*
He hung up and went down the corridor and up the main
stairs.

He was simply acting in his usual role, making things grow,
bringing things to light. Why should it bother Peter? It ought
to be published, even if it is unfinished. Who knows, it might
generate income. But Peter's jealous heart was always rubbing,
rubbing. From his hidden spot beyond the basement doorway
he looked at the urn. He was unqualified to lift it, that was the
feeling. Fire in the chamber had turned and turned the last
hard cinders, it couldn't be personal anymore, it was inorganic
matter, inhospitable to life, it was alkaline poison, it was the
surface of the moon, it was the desert. He walked right over
and lifted it—it was light—and he went down the basement
stairs embracing it under his blanket, a thin wall of shiny tin
protecting his bare chest from its holy lye.

A noise came from the kitchen, just as he reached the
bottom.

"Peter?" It was his mother. He stopped. But he didn't turn
completely, because he didn't want her to guess about the can
hidden in the blanket. She was standing above in the kitchen
door. She didn't say anything for a minute but stood there sil-
houetted, rubbing her ear with one hand.

"Peter, when you're living here by yourself . . . ," she said, but she didn't seem to know how to go on. "I suppose you'll be working on your poetry," she said.

"Jesus Christ, will nobody ever listen to me?" He let his voice get loud, as his breath immediately started flipping and flipping, "Maybe the rest of you have no sympathy with the idea of poetry, but . . ." He took strength from the ashes. "Just see what happens when you try to put down an artist, put down an artist, who actually does have a vision. Just see what happens . . . "

"No, Peter, wait . . . "

"You want to say it's impractical. You want to say it's stupid. You think everything is stupid. I don't care how it seems. It probably is stupid. Okay? Is that what people want to hear? Me admit my poetry is stupid? I don't have any excuses or reasons. I don't have anything."

"All I want to say, is that Faro has an old school friend who is a very powerful literary agent. I just wanted to offer the idea"—she paused, her voice was weakening—"that when you get some material together, Faro could get it published. That's all I wanted to say." She drew a big breath but didn't sigh. Then did sigh. "I just wanted to say there's plenty of hope."

The opening of a door felt like the closing of a door. He turned and walked hard down the basement corridor with his too-light burden.

A torn-out car radio; a glass mayonnaise jar holding a Bic pen cap; a Mr. Coffee machine minus its beaker; a cardboard six-pack of antique Sprite bottles of heavy green glass, their waists engraved with a girdle of golf-ball-surface dimples; the tall English riding boots for the horse she never got; a styrofoam cone with a few sequins pinned to its surface; a handful of thumbtacks cupped in a flower of Kleenex; a plastic strap with the word "Wham-O" stamped into it; a box of eight-track tapes; a yellow plastic box of compartmental drawers, affixed with a daisy decal; *Future Shock, I'm OK, You're OK*, road maps, *Horton Hears a Who, The Boston Strangler, Why Are We in Vietnam?, My Name José Jimenez*; a stack of *SKI* and *downbeat* and *LOOK* magazines; a shallow plastic soft-margarine tub decorated with printed asterisks; a slippery pile of clothes in plaid or polka-dot or ugly colors; a bound book of wallpaper samples; a paper Dixie-cup containing a card with the admonition *INHERITANCE TAX! PAY $500*; a crumbling potato of dried clay clutched in balled-up foil; and a spool of paper tickets reading "Admit One."

The pile of Free Store merchandise was worse than she could have predicted. Wendy rose from her crouch and stood over it with Baelthon at her side, and the futility of it wedded them, or so it felt for a minute. She even had the strange picture of him putting an arm around her shoulder. But he, as if to slip the closing noose of her idea, crouched down and reached to loosen from the pile a paperback book whose cover was hidden—*More Weird and Unexplainable Events*, by Hans Holzer—and he said, "This is interesting."

That was the moment when she named this as a "relationship" of some sort, maybe more in her mind than in his. For she found herself insulted and dependent, standing above at a cooler altitude, insulted by his unconsciousness. He was unconscious. And males' unconsciousness prejudices the whole universe in their favor. He was the one who wanted to move this stuff. But in preparation *she* had changed into her one pair of jeans that fit, and she had brushed her teeth and put a barrette in her hair, despising herself for it: it's such a terrible cliché: all that effort results in making the female burdensome and over-sensitive. She stood there folding her arms tight, returning to her usual state, of misogyny, as her mother's consciousness-raising group would call it—because, face it, it *is* misogyny, it's simply better to be a boy, the whole setup is unfair, she doesn't *want* to be weak or peeved or wily, she doesn't want this responsibility of seeing so much more sharply and deeply. Baelthon stood up and edged closer and, with a look over his shoulder, whispered:

"So. That was *it*."

"What was what?"

"'An End to All War.'"

"Oh. Yes."

"It's his *novel!*" Baelthon pointed out.

"I forgot that was the title."

He looked at her. He was amazed that she wasn't awed. "Did you ever read it?"

"He was working on it, at the end."

"Why did Dean want us to find it? It's interesting. Don't you think?" He seemed to find this topic, like everything else, a prelude to sex. She had to admit, something magnetic in his bones did call out to her and turn her all to candy—and despite the watchfulness of every empty doorway, she was perfectly willing to try kissing him. In a way, being caught kissing Baelthon would end the confusion Faro had caused by speaking of desire. He came closer, sucking back saliva, antecedent to a kiss. She backed up a step.

Behind them was Ed, clonking up the hallway loudly in his lustrous penny-loafers. For a minute she'd thought it was Faro and panicked. "Hi," Ed said.

She stood apart. Baelthon was sagging.

Ed said, "I want to talk to you now while I've got both of you."

"About what?" She shifted a little, uncomfortably within the area where the word *both* applied. He was wearing his plaid blazer and slacks, this time blue, which must be his gambling costume. He was definitely James Farmican's son, with James Farmican's unfinished quality, the raw big mouth that looked like it had been eating, the shapeless shoulders and trunk, the energy of dissatisfaction. He said, "First I want to ascertain about Peter."

"You're talking about his wrist-slashing. He loves doing that."

He looked at her blankly. "I mean, is he . . . 'okay'?" His fingers lifted to flutter around that word.

"Suicidal tendencies are inherited," she said, which was slightly witty, but the two boys just stood there. Briskly she asked, "Was that what you wanted to talk about?"

"Well, I won't beat around the bush, I'll lay it on the line. I want to make a case for you both to help me with the casino —and come to Nevada instead of going to that commune in Oregon."

"It's not a 'commune.'"

He was peeking at all the merchandise on the floor, which she stood in front of. "If it's not a commune, what is it?" he said.

"The word commune has connotations."

"He's . . ." Ed made a circling gesture behind him, toward the whirlpool of trouble that was Faro Ness. She finished for him, "He's idealistic," which was true.

"Fine, but I'm going to Nevada. I believe you have to hitch your wagon to something real. I want to leave soon. Actually, I want to leave tomorrow or the day after. The address of the casino doesn't answer any letters, so the only thing to do is personally go out there and evaluate. It looks like an eight-hour drive to this place. Wendy, are you knowledgeable that this casino has definitely been bequested? And that it might be a formidable element?"

"Oh . . ." Her lungs expanded against inner stitches. "I don't really—" *care* was the word she would have finished with, but it wasn't anything she was proud of. Other people had a lot of energy, to care about their specific lives, to work at making themselves happy, whereas her own moments of miscellaneous irrelevant happiness seemed to arise from small passing things like the weather, or drinking milk from the carton when she came home, or having her shoes laced up tight walking down the driveway. It was the saving weakness of her character, her secret weapon: she didn't care about anything, whether she ever got married, where she lived, whether she had nice clothes, whether she had any friends. She could probably even embrace her mother's new husband, or even lie down with him, or else with Baelthon; and it wouldn't matter, except to other people, like her mother and everybody, and the whole world.

Which somebody like Ed would never understand. He cared about things. It was likable in him. He was energetic, trustworthy, good-hearted, and she just wanted to keep out of his way. With his penny-loafer's toe, he nudged the car radio and griped, ". . . What is all this stuff?"

It would never get to the poor. It was just Faro, coccooning people to store them aside.

"Just some stuff," she said.

Then she turned. Dean Houlihan had materialized in the door from the kitchen, behind them. His body had Charley the Tuna's beat slouch leaning in the doorway. He'd been there for some time, incompletely sketched-in by her consciousness. The old hinges hung empty there. "Hello, people," he said. Baelthon and Ed turned.

"Merlin, they're looking for you," she said. "They need you to sign something."

"Me?" He was rubbing his belly and chest.

"They need you to sign some documents."

"I only write on my surfboard anymore. They know that perfectly well." He began addressing Ed, with a wink: "They like to keep testing me. It's the burden of leadership. You probably don't remember me, but we met on the road when you were first coming into town."

Ed told him, "You live in a cave on the beach." It was an accusation.

"That's a romantic legend. In truth, I live in rich people's au pair cottages. I'll tell you who I've been, Ed," raising his voice toward the W. C. Fields level. "I've been the Kahuna, the original authentic Kahuna. And that's been some responsibility. It's why I've called you all together here today. To provide a little bit of pre-Cana counseling to a certain happy couple. But tell me—" he had begun to slide down against the door jamb until he was squatting—"how is the Exodus progressing? Why aren't people beginning to gird their loins? You people have to start looking about yourselves. You have to start putting together things you can *use* out there. Take what you can use. That's a good rule of thumb. And don't take what you won't use."

Ed said, "We only want what's ours."

Dean made a frown that Wendy alone would recognize as affectionate. "Edward, you are a lot like your father. Jim Farmican was a friend of mine. You ought to know that. These documents I'm supposed to sign: I can't really see them from this side of the tapestry—" he was closing his eyes, pressing a wrist to his forehead. "Were these church documents, by any chance?"

Baelthon—he'd been growing silently taller beside Wendy—sang out, "They're outside in the tent. I can go get them."

Dean turned his attention on him. "Your name is Baelthon," he said, his eye gathering to clutch the dark gleam; it was his 'Merlin' mask and it made Wendy nervous. His W. C. Fields voice swung in, "Now listen to me, you two. This is a most holy sacrament. By marriage you save not only yourselves but the tribe around you. Not only that, but property descends along lines of birth and marriage. Birth and marriage, yass."

"What marriage?" Wendy said.

He pushed himself up to his feet again. "Do you suppose you would be inclined to take Wendy to be your lawful wedded wife?"

Baelthon was grinning worriedly. Wendy said, "Merlin, that wouldn't be funny."

"You two fellows," Dean called out the open front door

where two furniture movers were packing boxes on the lawn. "We need you in here for just a minute."

"Merlin, please. They don't want to come in here." In one of his ceremonies, by humiliation alone she and Baelthon would be welded together.

"Come on in here," Dean called again. He turned to Baelthon. "What is your real name? The name on your birth certificate. The name your parents call you."

Baelthon's eyes slid under pressure and he said, "Steve." She was ashamed for him. A decent covering had fallen away between them and they stood before Merlin as mortal creatures in error. Two big furniture movers came up the corridor, jostling in the door's backlight, their hands hanging in readiness to move anything they were told.

"Now watch this, gentlemen, please," Merlin told them. "Steve, do you take this woman to be your wife? Just say 'I do,' Steve. Go ahead. All you have to say is 'I do.'"

With a grinning scowl, he looked at Wendy, and he asked, "I do?"

Merlin turned to Wendy. She blurted out *I do* in an effort to stop the rest of his ritual, but he went on, "Wendy, do you take this man to be your husband?"

"Merlin, sheesh. I do."

"Then by the powers vested in me, I now pronounce you man and wife."

Both movers shifted uneasily on their feet. Merlin told them, "Gentlemen, we'll need your names."

Ed asked, "Does he do this to everybody?"

Part
◉ 3 ◉

S o that was the historic legal moment. A bona fide marriage ceremony. As for me, I supposed Dean's sacrament would have no real effect, but I had an idea it
might allow me to stand nearer to her and monopolize more of
her attention. It had become the knack of living in that house,
merely to stand around in the right place at the right time, to
get dubbed with a new role and then expand tauter to fill it.
Dean had melted back somewhere toward the basement, while
Wendy and I stood side-by-side in the outer archway under the
east porte cochere (the red bricks of the mossy disused side-
driveway, smell of rain, the grommets of my canvas shoes, the
shiny shoulder-seam of her old suede jacket, pencil-eraser smell
of my own palm), she hugging a pillowcase full of clothes, I a
cardboard box where a glass mayonnaise jar clinked against the
torn-out car radio—and as rain started to fall, we were isolated
together with the ancient grief of our different genders. All
morning oceans of white air had churned above the far hills
across the San Andreas Fault where the muddy mountains of
West Marin are thrown up in the rocky flood of earth-against-
earth. Then as we stood on the threshold, hot air poured in
from the south with a rustle everywhere, we felt its moving
wall arrive, and then we were *inside* a warm, forming rain-
cloud. Our clothes were damp with it, and our skin under our

267

clothes. Our shoulders were touching and—this was the crucial excess—we were allowing them to remain in contact. At last she provided an excuse for going back inside (to sort through more old objects, in a far attic, while it rained), and we clambered up through back staircases and rooms together without looking at each other directly, but with the corners of our vision lit up to each other, as if hoods had been freshly removed, our napes impressionable to each other's movements. Took a wrong turn and almost bumped into each other. Brushed wrists. Finally we found our way to a far room where we could kneel over some pile—or maybe some box—of forgotten old stuff, one more trough of miscellaneous heirlooms and trinkets, a river she knelt by to stir, her hair a curtain. Our knees kept touching. Through a series of brushes and alignments we revolved toward an embrace, then lay on the carpet closing our eyes. And in a far room of the doorless house, deafness and blindness gave us privacy, dark mounds rose around us, until at last in the generous swallowing motions that carried us, Wendy lost self-consciousness, forcing upward the latch of the unopenable purse of ancient greed, which to rub and rub is not to open. But then she had a way of, at lowest points, stiffening, like a woman being held down underwater. Her eyes had opened. Seen a ghost. I rose on one elbow. She was looking away above me—then at me.

And then lying with her in the warm shallows at that dim noon, I ran a finger down her breastbone between her breasts, slowly, but with pressure. My other hand supported her arched back. She looked at me and I opened my hand and set my palm against her heart. I could feel there where it beat. I said, "What will we do?" The question expanded after I spoke it. It seemed to roll out into the future in a silent impact-wave. She said, "Take me to Nevada," the strangest, dreamiest thing she could have said. Her eyes, in surprise, deepened. In imagination I skimmed over Nevada, over the bleached-out masking-tape colors of the desert, where you can live in an abandoned shack on white ground like hard-packed detergent that poisons all life and all healthy filth, except for immortal hard thorns that survive through millennia by the trick of staying forever near-dead, Ed's casino a dark gaudy mosque on the horizon, where Wendy would stand above a revolving roulette wheel wearing a spangled dress, holding a white baton for some reason, perhaps to push chips around on the tabletop, or to tap a white plastic ball hopping in the wheel as it slowly turned.

But I would have to write novels then. She was looking up at a novelist, so she thought. I foresaw a card table holding a small gray manual typewriter, in a motel room of painted cement-block walls, an ashtray, a stack of white paper, something toxic in the vicinity like a glass of Scotch, a twisted wire of cigarette smoke. It was a dust-jacket photo. And my heart felt steep and brave because such a picture didn't seem the least bit implausible! That day I had begun to imagine myself with a new courage easier than I'd thought. That morning, when I found Farmican's unfinished manuscript, I sat down alone with it in a stairwell, just to read a page or two. Reading a page of "An End to All War"—this one from the end—I could see how brave and easy writing ought to be.

First of all, All Is Forgiven. Mine was the way of absolute bliss and truth and spontaneity not everybody can follow. You lived in the OPPOSITE of bliss-truth-spontaneity (worry-compromise-selfdeception-materialism-adjusting-considering). Magician will arrive soon with the pistolettes d'honneur. You may not realize it but RIGHT NOW your listening for the bang. This is the comment upon my own demise you will have been seeking. I have put on my clown suit, one last time to stand on the corpse, defend it. Well, you'll see when you read the will. It's in the safe deposit box in the bank on Geary

in SF. Gelman will get copy automatically. As your all
going to see, I've taken measures against materialism.
You'll see when you read the will: whatevers left will go
into trust for second generation, nothing to wife or children. Because that will be your way out of lies, faked,
compromised, artificial small worried world of Normal,
the force of the American Economic Machine right here
in the kitchen, the bedroom, all this commercial noise. It
shows in all the little things:

a) interrupt poet when he speaks, with trivial concerns.
   I'm dead now. Go ahead. The floor is yours. From
   Now On. This emptiness? This silence? is for you to
   take the responsibility of speaking in.
b) the scene at Enrico's is a perfect example: the room
   gradually clears. Hundreds millions of people do
   RESPECT POET BELIEVE IT OR NOT
c) Children will always be too young to remember:
   turned poet into this coward, but once i was a real
   poet and never did compromise or lie and tried to
   raise even you to truth and spontaneity, the economic
   heart of woman's vanity destroying planet, considered normal and healthy. I'm only telling you this so
   you'll know, America, America in the form of my
   wife . . .

That was the page I read, and I could see that, obviously,
such a novel wasn't to be "understood" in any traditional way,
lacking plot, character, setting, or even the slightest effort to be
comprehensible. Which was why it was so liberating, the contempt for the reader almost thrilling. Writing was a more reck-
less thing than I'd thought, and now I could begin it: she had
knighted me. She was herself surprised by what she'd said
about Nevada. As I held her, she was looking up at me, as if I'd

caught her back from falling. I was the weighted-down end of a see-saw.

Baelthon? Are you here? Where are you?

Faro Ness's voice rose through the walls. Wendy and I in our room lifted our heads together—and Nevada, the great useless tan hinge on the map, became all the more real.

"What does he want?" she whispered.

He wanted the church documents. The Internal Revenue Service investigator, Mr. Murrain, had arrived. He was standing at the foot of the main staircase in the foyer, tapping the edge of a manila folder against a lower lip fattened in disapproval of the rotten splendor all around him being packed up in cardboard boxes and wooden caissons, while I galloped down the main stairs and limped past, beneath Faro's introduction, "This is *Baelthon*, Mr. Murrain. He's just going outside. *Baelthon* has been working for us here. He's been organizing all the church archives, and he'll be able to put his hands on exactly what you need. Or at least I hope he will."

I jogged out the door, crippled by my lying with Wendy, through an interval of rain, into the big green tent. As soon as I entered that crowded space under the patter of raindrops on canvas, my eye picked out the cardboard GENUINE FRYE BOOTS box. Inside it—along with a dried-out ink-pad and a rubber stamp and a chrome key for tightening a drumhead—the envelope marked "Church/Tax" came up to my hands, all in the immediacy of dream-time, I had grown so intimate with that house, with juggling its rebus of objects. During those few days of climbing through the cataract I had become infallible, finding handholds and footholds without paying attention. I brought the "Church/Tax" envelope back inside, to hand it over and then go straight back upstairs and find Wendy.

But she was in the living room. She was following Faro and the IRS auditor, who had gone to the far corner of the room. I gave the envelope to the IRS man, just as Faro reached and made a motion of interception. I should have given it to Faro, but it was too late. The IRS man was unfolding it and reading.

"Who is Illuminated Larry?" he said right away. "Is Illuminated Larry a church officer?"

"Oh, well, let's see." Faro was trying to edge into reading distance, arching an eyebrow. It was an old yellow legal-pad page, long ago folded down to pocket-size, creased into eight panels. The tax man went on reading without a change in expression. At one point he sighed. Of course I recognized him: he was the same man who had intruded on Little Tom's.

He went on reading.

In suspense, Faro looked at his wife. She smiled. Everybody stayed on their feet. No one sat down. Wendy was over on one side. She paid no attention to me. She shifted her weight, shook her hair back over her shoulder, and lifted a hand to nibble on her thumbnail, her lips parted. Holding one elbow. The tilt of her head.

Mr. Murrain's voice came up off the sheet of unfolded paper, ". . . 'Avowed purpose of the one true church: to get to Portland.'"

"May I see?" Faro was edging in, and he was able to gently unstick one page from the fingers of the IRS man. He had hardly started to read but, looking worried, he said, "Mr. Murrain, I have to refer all specific questions to my lawyers."

"Are these the church minutes? Are you representing these to be the church minutes?" He was flipping over the other papers.

"I know what you're thinking," said Faro, while his eyes moved on his page. "You're thinking these look . . . rather facetious. Heh." He turned the paper and perused the back side. For a while the room was quiet as both men read the minutes. "You have to understand, I've only *just* taken over pastorship of this church."

Mrs. Farmican spoke. "Would somebody please go get Dean?"

California's Over

"No, honey. He isn't relevant here."

Mr. Murrain said, "That would be Dean Houlihan. He is named as church secretary on your Form SS-8 and your Form 4631?"

"He's really not relevant to this. In fact, he's very busy. He's extremely busy. He might not even be here. He might be out and about—ministering to his fellow man." Faro smiled a little.

"Mr. Ness, all church records must be producible on church premises and must be complete. These minutes are not valid unless they've been signed by the officers, but Mr. Houlihan's signature appears only as *'moi-même'* here on some of these. On this one not at all."

Faro turned on me in my corner. "Baelthon? Is that all you found? Was there anything else? Mr. Murrain, I have to refer all these questions to my lawyers and my tax accountant. We'll provide whatever documentation you need and cooperate completely. I have no intention of doing anything illegal. We'll act on your office's advice on all these matters."

Mr. Murrain held a ballpoint pen upright before him in the manner of a jouster, and he began a speech. "I specialize in tax investigations of clergy and other religious workers. Your application is the largest individual estate ever to be exempted in vows of poverty. It's been assigned to the CID for that reason. Now"—he inclined his pen—"of the original founders of this church, from the pre-1968 period, only the secretary is still living. If these are the original church minutes, they're not valid unless they've been signed by the secretary. I'll tell you something, Mr. Ness. Yours is not the only church that files in this manner. But it's by far the largest ever."

Faro thought for a minute, looking at the tax man, and said, "This might be all we have, as documentation." He was holding up the old yellow legal page. "You understand that."

"I understand that."

Faro seemed to be reevaluating Mr. Murrain. Speaking

273

without removing his eyes, like a man being held at gunpoint, he said, "Would you guys go get Dean?"

Wendy and I looked at each other.

"We can wait," Faro said, and sat down. "Go find him, it won't take long. He can sign these minutes right now."

◎　◎　◎

We couldn't find him. He wasn't in his room. We started looking all over the house, calling his name. His separate cellar didn't communicate with the rest of the basement, so we had to come back up to the kitchen, then go back down the flagstone stairs to the main basement. Peter's room was empty. But a tink-tink noise was coming from farther in. There was another small room beyond, lit by a lightbulb hanging on an extension cord.

Peter was in there. He had been taking apart an old hand-crank Victrola. Its turntable had been pried off to disclose a wound-up inner spring, and he was using pliers to grip the spindle and wind the spring tighter. On a bench beside him was an out-of-date-looking encyclopedia, open to the page reading "Trigonometry."

"Peter, what are you doing?"

"Yeah, fuck you."

"You broke that old record player."

He went on straining with the pliers, tightening the spiral to the breaking point.

Wendy said, "Peter, have you seen Merlin?"

The spring leaped. A tornado of metal bands rose and whipped around and settled on the floor clattering, while Peter jumped back. He had hurt his finger. His mouth began to form the f-word and he started sucking on his knuckle.

Wendy said, "What are you *doing?*"

His eyebrows sank. "Don't get involved with her, Baelthon. She's a secret snarfer. She's got a bag of greasy shit in her closet, and she goes in there at night and stuffs her face so she can't even breathe." He started sucking on his knuckle again.

Wendy's mouth flattened, and she turned and walked out. Then she stopped by his bed. "Is this your stupid poem? Here, I'll read it."

"No you won't."

"*O, sickness and insanity. Go ahead and eat me,*" she declaimed—and then she looked up at him with an incredulous, outsmarted look, on the brink of a smile.

"Give me that," he said, but he just stood there. He was like a boy with polio, lifting a weak paw.

"'Eat me'?" She forced a little cough of scorn and then read on, while Peter started hobbling after her, as she dodged. "*O, eat me, you insane Americans! You selfish fiends with cars and houses. / Cut a big juicy glob out of my stomach. What pleasure it arouses.*"

She gave him a cracked expression, not real mirth but a mask. "Peter, this *rhymes!*"

She went on, walking around the room through open spaces in the clutter:

> "*Indigenous peoples weren't the usual mediocre shit.*
> "*But destruction of innocence is the national spir-it.*"

He had stopped following her and instead was picking up sheets of paper and pressing them to his chest in a growing messy sheaf.

"You write *rhyming* poems."

"It's not a poem." He took the sheet from her hand.

"Why isn't it a poem?"

He paused to digest the tiniest bit of satisfaction. "—It's an opera." He knelt on the floor, snatching together pages, revolving the whole sheaf to tap it together into a neater pile.

"An opera. Sure. It's an opera." She seemed to only half-believe him.

He straightened up. "It's an op-er-a."

She tilted her head in something like amusement, but tears were forming. She looked down and walked for the door. But then she stopped at the door and said, while her voice rose into a higher song of sadness, "You only pick something like an opera because it's impossible. You want to pretend everything is over everybody's head. You'll never commit suicide."

Peter's upper lip swelled—it was supposed to be a sort of smile—and he said, "That's a bizarre comment, Wendy."

"I'm not going to Oregon," she said. "You just everybody go there and be cool."

She left.

Peter looked at me with a sigh. "Sorry," he said. "Weird family."

I would have followed her but I wasn't sure I had the right, not yet, being still just her sexual pesterer. Then while her footsteps ran up the flagstone staircase, Dean appeared in the doorway. He said, in W. C. Fields twang, "That's no kind of behavior for a new bride."

I put my hands in my pockets. Peter was sitting with pages in his lap, putting them in the right order.

Dean said, "I been hearing voices."

I said, "They want you upstairs in the living room." In the far depths of the basement, a sound of a power tool became audible—someone on the appraisers' crew was dismantling something.

"Here." Dean held out in both hands a paperback book. It was *Worlds in Collision*, by Immanuel Velikovsky. "Peter, I want you to keep this, so you can have it to refer to in the days to come. You're going to be out there." A Mosaic hand lifted in the direction of Out There.

I started to slip away, intending to go find Wendy. Dean said, "What exactly do they want upstairs?"

"They want you to sign something."

"Ah, well, you can tell them I can't sign anything."

"I think it might be important."

"I'm non compos mentis. They know that."

"There's a man up there from the Internal Revenue Service."

Dean, still holding *Worlds in Collision*, pressed the book to his heart and bowed his head. His eyes were closed. He was blocking the doorway. Peter and I watched him sway. He started snoring and then gave a shudder and, chin on chest, he murmured, "The Internal Revenue Service is here now."

"He's waiting up there."

"You found 'An End to All War.'" He looked at me.

"Yes. I'm going to read it," I said, standing taller. Humoring Dean's delusions was a local custom one entered into easily. His eyes weighed me.

"Yass yass, it's an amazing thing, when you children grow up you'll find in life"—he was squinting into a distance—"how the very gravest matters depend on utter artificial silly crap like this." He plucked the fabric of his costume. "Okay, lead me to 'em."

◎ ◎ ◎

"Oh, Dean," Faro called out with a lifted arm. I hung back at the edge of the room.

"Dean, this is Mr. Murrain. Mr. Murrain is from the Internal Revenue Service. And this, here, is Dean Houlihan. Dean is the secretary of the Church of Bread and Wine. Has been since nineteen-sixty-something."

Dean closed his eyes and swayed, pressing his two thumb-knuckles to his lips.

"The oldest living church officer." Faro's hand almost

touched Dean's shoulder, then dropped. "Isn't that right, Dean?" he said. He handed him the few yellow legal-size pages. The top page had been folded to the size of Dean's own hip pocket in 1962, its central crease-cross worn through, almost to soft incisions.

Julia Farmican was in the room too. Everyone was there except Ed. Ed was always somewhere else.

Dean, reading the page he'd written long ago, breathed deep in happiness. "Julie, have you read this?" he said. "We were wonderful." His W. C. Fields affectation had gone. "The part about how your vision is always clearer when you're hungry—that's Jim's poem." He looked at Mrs. Farmican, whose eyes shone. She said, "I remember."

"About going to the museum with an empty stomach, and being able to see the pictures better. Oh, look at us now, babe. Our stomachs are always full."

"What we need to do now"—Faro started mincing his way into Dean's reading-space—"is just sign this now with your name. It doesn't have your actual signature there at the bottom."

"Can't. Sorry. I've taken a vow of illiteracy." He went back to reading. He seemed to take up extra space, perhaps because of his hair. The tax man was doing a good job of pretending there was nothing unusual about him.

"Dean, this is a legal situation. It has to do with the non-profit tax status of the church."

Dean lowered the page and told the tax man, "In 1963, I vowed that I would not pick up my pen until the white man lays down the electric guitar. I have not wielded a writing implement since then."

"Well, Dean, you like to joke around. But this is serious. Mr. Murrain is going to think we're not a real church."

"No," said Mr. Murrain. "That's not how we deal with situations like this. We don't question the legitimacy of a church's beliefs." He spoke with blandness.

"'Situations like this?'"

"Even in the case of a patently frivolous church"—he gestured slightly around—"the Internal Revenue Service does not get involved in religious doctrine." His head had a peculiar shape: flat-faced, and also flattened on the back side.

Faro looked at him with a tentative new honesty, making his shoulders relax and then glancing around. "In that case, how does your investigation proceed?"

"We monitor church bank accounts for violations of IRS code."

"What code?"

"Sections 501b and 7611 of the Internal Revenue Code. You may donate as much as you like to this church of yours, and you may claim all donations as tax deductions. That's the law as it's written. However, we will regularly audit the church's expenditures and the personal expenditures of church officers. If we find that the salaries and perquisites of church directors are excessive, the church will be in violation. For example, the property in Oregon. You've claimed it as a church retreat for meditation and study and fellowship. The CID says, Do all the meditating you want."

"The CID?"

"Criminal Investigation Division."

Faro looked at Mr. Murrain thoughtfully, and he said, "Well, I'll tell you. We intend to spend church money on research. And scholarship. And publication."

Mr. Murrain just stood there, possibly not understanding that Faro was asking a question.

"Are research and scholarship and publication considered frivolous expenditures?"

"No, those are legitimate, but I'm a field officer, I don't adjudicate cases. I'm only here to look at this document. And now I have. If the secretary will just sign it."

Dean was still holding the old yellow pages. He had closed his eyes and pressed his forearm to a chakra between his brows, and he lifted his warbling baritone. "Faro Ness, you're going to have to acknowledge my spiritual authority here . . . " With a backward stagger, his free hand drifted out to accept the pen.

Faro was exasperated, even disgusted, and he looked at his wife, blaming her. "Of course! Dean! You're the patriarch! Of the Church of Bread and Wine!" He remarked levelly to the IRS man, "You see what one does. To keep the world going round on its axis."

The IRS man's stony face seemed for a moment almost appreciative; a deep facet had shifted, with a buried glimmer. I had the impression the two enemies esteemed each other, across their necessary barrier, but then his eyes were hooded again and it could have been my imagination. He held the pen out to Dean.

Dean thumb-popped the end-button a few times. He peered up into it telescope-wise. "This is missing the ink-thing." It was a cheap maroon ballpoint with SKILCRAFT: *U.S. Government* printed on its barrel.

"I've got another one in my car," said Mr. Murrain.

"We've got a pen somewhere."

I myself spoke up—"I know where there's one"—and went out through the hall. Across in the library, I'd left a row of unpacked objects. On the study desk was a clear-plastic cube holding a single pen in a central hole. I tried to pull it out, but it wouldn't come—I realized it had been thrust into the Lucite block and stuck there permanently to function as a paperweight—but then it came free, an old-fashioned heavy fountain pen, surprisingly leaden in my hand, as warm and filled-up-feeling as lead. I tried it, and it made a few strokes on a piece of paper. It still worked. I brought it back to the living room and gave it to Dean so he could sign the page that would establish all this as holy ground.

But then he didn't. He looked at it, then he pressed the yellow pages to his breast. He let his head hang down and closed his eyes, his body drifting off vertical. Glances flickered around the room. At last he grumbled, "Julie, I'm going to think about this for a while." He began shuffling in a stagy sleep-walk, and he said as he drifted, with eyes squeezed shut, "Right now I'm going to my chambers. I shall issue my ex cathedra opinion via the usual bull." With caresses he was folding the old pages.

Faro looked to his wife, who did nothing but watch him go. He let out a breath he'd been holding, with resolve, to show her he didn't intend to be toyed with forever by someone who was merely playing self-dramatizing games. It was clear he didn't believe Dean was "non compos mentis" at all, but rather considered him a formidable manipulator, a personality self-created of deceptive glints.

The IRS man, who did think Dean was crazy, said gently, "Mr. Ness, I can understand the circumstances you have. My only job here is to complete your file. At the moment, this church has no documentation. *That* paper has to be signed by *that* person." He added, "I realize . . . ," and rolled a shoulder.

"Dean? How long do you plan to think about this?" said Faro, though Dean was long gone.

"Sorry, Julie. Can't hear any of you. I'm already over on this side of the tapestry."

◎   ◎   ◎

Late that night, Wendy came barefoot downstairs to the kitchen. She had been lying awake again. In bed her *body* always lifted and carried her worries, in local floats and cramps, grinds of the hip or shoulder, while in her mind she let the worst ideas grow, like for example the likelihood—the virtual certainty—that Rachel Feinman was too popular and busy to *want* her to stay in her garage, and so that whole plan would be out of the question and she should have realized it long ago. Or how stupid she'd been to even mention Nevada to Baelthon. At the moment she said it, she saw the topaz light enter his eyes. Now she would have to talk him out of it.

When she got downstairs Faro was there. He was in the kitchen in his robe, leaning one elbow heavily on the counter, downcast in a prizefighter's vulnerable exhaustion looking into an empty milk glass. It was his weight she'd heard on the main stairs. The kitchen was thrown into silhouettes by a bulb in the next-door pantry: this was a meeting backstage. He glanced up with a weak smile, as if she were a stranger, his eyes swimming senilely up from a bath, and dropped his gaze back down into his glass without having quite focused it. Expecting her. His collarbone's brave crux showed at the open lapels of his robe.

"Couldn't sleep," she told him. She tightened her own robe and did her best to aim a shoulder at him as she walked around his zone toward the refrigerator. The carpets were all gone now, exposing flagstones dim with having been unseen for years. She had been thinking of ice cream but now instead reached for a cupboard door, and the first thing that came to hand was a box of Saltines. She ran her thumbnail under the Nabisco emblem.

"Me neither," said Faro. His glass's rim tapped the bronze surface between his lapels. "Couldn't sleep." She kept her eyes away and answered with just a broken hum, biting on a cracker, her mouth full of its unleavened dust, a fugitive here already, opening the refrigerator. She was still, on this night, entitled to anything in this refrigerator. She lifted the milk carton out and left the refrigerator door hanging open because it seemed—its chill, its clinical light—to prevent intimacy in the room.

Faro said, "Late." He stared into the fathom of his empty glass where light was trapped. "Well, shoof, I suppose I'm a bad guy now." He nodded toward the living room, where the encounter with the IRS had taken place.

"Why?"

He didn't answer for a minute.

". . . In addition to scaring *you* so completely last night, you'll probably never come up to the Ranch," he said, with a rather amazing lack of foreplay. "You know something?" he said. "If the whole world sometimes seems morally ambiguous—which of course it is—well then you have to keep thinking you're following this one little thread. The little thread of the right thing. And hang on to it."

All too complicated. "Why are you the bad guy?"

He tilted his head, again, toward the living room scene where the IRS had been hoodwinked: "Today."

He recrossed his ankles and started tapping the rim of his glass on his chin. She turned aside with her milk carton, feeling herself contemplated, in her robe. But that was just her imagination; he continued, "I am quite aware of how I seem to be playing the role of corrupt—acquisitive—materialistic—et cetera. It really does look to you as if this whole thing is all about property and money. Doesn't it."

"Oh! . . ." The merry scowl stuck on her face. She kept pouring milk.

"You don't have to pretend."

"Well, Faro," she said, using his first name, like a girlfriend. "You must admit, you don't *believe* it's a church."

". . . 'Believe' . . ." He smiled a little and bumped softly within his moorings at the counter. "My family was Catholic. And one nice thing sticks with you from Catholicism, about mortal creatures, and what their minds make them think they 'believe' . . . " But then he didn't follow that thought. "I could *tell* you what I *think* I believe: I 'believe' that the Open Ranch deserves to be tax exempt. Because the government is corrupt and I'm not. That's what I believe. I'm above all the governments. Does that all sound vainglorious? Yes."

He had thought this all out, in insomniac times like these, while her mother slept. She felt she was seeing the dark side of a planet. His downcast face had gone vacant. Maybe he had sensed the trap around him here, unable to fill the role of the dead king in these chambers. The light of the pantry bulb behind him sharpened his jaw. He changed the subject, cheerily, "But so your brother Ed. He really wants to get control of that casino. He's going to *go* out there. So, great." He toasted Ed's ambition, with the limpest lift of his empty glass.

She pulled out another Saltine and took a bite of it, mouth too dry. "That Ed," she scoffed. "There'll always be somebody who's cynical." Intended as a sort of comfort, it felt in her bosom like a wifely remark.

He looked up at her. "Hey, it's not as if *I'm* immune to cynicism. We're all, always, teetering on the brink of cynicism." What was remarkable about Faro was right there in his eyes: his sharp specific expectancy.

"Yeah well, my mother, she's the cynical one." Too much anger was in her voice.

"Your mom?"

She didn't want to get into it—the words had shot from an inner sac that must have been filling harder for a long time—how could she explain—it was such a mean-spirited notion—that everything in this house had always been controlled by inclinations of her mother's wooden ladle, by adjustments in the slant of her mother's beautiful eyes. To come out and say so was merely to poison herself inwardly, because in fact *she* was the cynical one. All she wanted was to be alone. Out of this house. In Rachel Feinman's garage, the pine smell of exposed 2 x 4s against Sheetrock would cause a cleanness in the lungs, she would get more homework done, and she would eat less, far from this huge old refrigerator here. In some disgust, she picked up her glass of milk and went to the threshold of the back staircase. So long, good-bye. She wouldn't begin to explain herself.

"Wendy, nobody's evil or guilty," Faro said, in his prescient way. "Your mom isn't 'guilty' of your father. She's right when she says it was his own responsibility to be happy. And in a similar way, I'm not 'guilty' of . . . of *you*"—he nodded upward, toward her bed upstairs, toward incest. "I mean I *would* feel guilty if *I* prevented you from coming to the Ranch. The only evil in the world is bad communication." He lifted his gaze over her head and was obviously going to go on talking, fists driven into his robe pockets, swaying beside the counter, his eyes fixed parallel in a distant focus on some utopian point where honesty and passion and integrity all converge, a theoretical point visible to *him*, maybe in Oregon on his Ranch. Up in his tower, he was able to struggle alone with all his moral questions only because he had no idea: how weak everybody was, how weak *she* was, she was in the generation of no principles or scruples anymore, because the future had already been used-up, or mysteriously *bought*-up like real estate, or like the way they buy next year's wheat crop on the stock exchange. It was almost interesting to stand there toying with the, of course horrible, idea of opening her robe, and thus making it immediately impossible for him to keep his faith. He made her feel like a gift to be unwrapped, in her robe, all aglow beneath it.

"Well, Faro, you're being very thoughtful about me, and I appreciate that."

"About you? Thoughtful?" That troubled him. It seemed a belittling remark, but she hadn't meant that. He said, "No, the truth is I'm just thinking of myself. As usual." He put his glass in the sink and started shuffling off toward the front corridor.

"Protecting me from . . ." Her head bobbed. "As if I'm a little girl."

He stopped before her. "I'm protecting myself too." He smiled sorrily and let his head fall forward, and slipped his forearms into a tight knot at his chest: a yet further way of protecting her. "I personally don't picture myself like a kind of Daddy-Long-Legs by lamplight. Creeping around here in my—*slippers* like Humbert Humbert." Imagining him tiptoeing from bedroom to bedroom, she could have laughed. Her hand came up to cover an altogether wrong twitch at her mouth.

"In a satin smoking-jacket," he complained, yet it wasn't very amusing to him. He was sinking into a stony sadness all his own, a throat-muscle pulsing. She let herself laugh, in a little breath. He looked at her. The picture of him lurking in a smoking-jacket was funny, and he did repress one grin, with a glance aside. "What a fate. Out in the hall with my big . . . bumbling hard-on. Sheesh."

With a painful wateriness all in her midsection, she could see now, how he had always been unloved in some profound way, and would always be, how that was one thing they had in common in the household of Julia Farmican, in the shadow of a back staircase. Unable to be held by him while they were both visible, she drew back deeper into the dark doorway, and found he too had fallen into the same distortion in space, his hands on her waist, her own hand resting on his shoulder implying he had permission, her milk glass balanced upright. Now she was out of this family for good. His rather hard lips closed on a spot on her neck. A very nice deep male Graham-cracker smell rose through her. He wasn't like Baelthon, whose clogged nose whistled. He lifted his mouth and whispered, "Wendy—this is complicated." It didn't feel like a warning but rather a proposal. Her mother would never find out. This would never go any further than one kiss, so that they could both see that they were capable of this; and that would be enough; after this, the kiss would fall as a bar separating them. His tongue had started picking between her lips, and that was so very strange, so much against the rules, and really so disgusting, she found her whole body falling into belief in him, despite how wrong this was. She hadn't expected that. It was strange how his hand cupped her hip in a way that implied deeper anatomy, sculpting curves whose radial centers were inward, so that she had never felt so mammalian, her thigh wanting to move. In the darkness all around her, a new wealth of lies shimmered in a new-opened canyon of diamonds she was sinking through. Or she herself *was* that canyon of lies. Her hip could feel his hard nuzzling attachment, the second to be forced on her in one fateful day. A penis is simplicity itself, simplicity incarnate. She decided—in an irrelevant etymological reflection in her cloven mind—that *simplicity* and *duplicity* were obviously related words. Her thigh had moved now of its own will.

"Well, Wendy," he said softly. Then his arms lifted away, and the old cold brine rushed between them again and she was standing there with the knowledge that she was probably capable of anything, faith is such a delicate invention. He took a little stab at grinning and touched her hair, and he turned and escaped through the kitchen and up the hallway toward the front staircase, the way to the queen's chamber. He did have faith. Whereas her mother's faith was more like the Catholic Church, all based on spectacle and authority, all based on covering up, plastering over and forgetting the old central story.

◉　◉　◉

The next morning Wendy came downstairs and bumped into Faro himself, in the kitchen, just escaping for his morning swim, in his squeaky wetsuit a frog. He ran away wordlessly, and the look he gave her as he went out—rueful, bug-eyed—was an apology: she knew right away, he had told her mother about the kiss. He had told. He was actually being true to his implausible belief in total honesty. Well, good for him. She stood still in the house. Her mother was packing boxes in the corridor by the front stairs. Her usual sexy *"Good morning Wendy"* seemed bent.

In an impulse of hiding, she opened the refrigerator. There was the same old collection of esoteric, unlabeled condiments, all crushed aside by the central pot of fish soup smelling of sulfur and brimstone. Which it would be her fate to eat again at lunch. Unless she packed up and moved to Rachel's garage today. Now. She closed the refrigerator. She wouldn't eat breakfast. From the basement stairs rose the scholarly murmur of auction-house restorers. All yesterday afternoon they'd been circling the mural of the People's Park's battle, discussing, like archaeologists, how to remove it intact. Outside the window a corner of a temporary new fence was visible, loose-knitted steel, its upright pipe-posts sunk in disks of concrete. She'd been aware of the sounds of its installation all the day before, the clang of metal and the remarks of men. The side door opened. By its swing and bang it was Peter. His voice lifted generally to anybody: *"Where's Ed?"*

"Your brother Ed . . . ," said her mother, in the hall toiling over cardboard boxes that baffled her words. "I want you to hear this too, Wendy"—her offstage voice rose to project through the doorways. "Brother Ed is making preparations to drive to Nevada in his car. He thinks a visit to the putative casino shouldn't be put off any longer and he's leaving tomorrow, and I have no doubt he wants everyone to come with him."

"There's a letter for him. It's from Nevada." Peter came in carrying the mail, and he asked Wendy, "Do you think we should open it?"

"What time is it," Wendy said, sitting down at the table, imitating the sleepy irritable regal innocence of one who was still entitled to be a daughter in this house, hidden within these same old clothes she'd put on, which had been mopping around all week ankle-deep on her bedroom floor, her jeans as cold and waxy as the floorboards. She reached for the pile of letters. As usual, it was all for her father: the *Authors Guild Bulletin*, a publicity card from Zoetrope Studios, a postcard from a publisher announcing a poetry anthology, a leaflet advertising a Japanese film festival in Los Angeles, addressed to James Formican, a misspelling that recurred often as mailing lists multiplied and deteriorated out there. Peter said, "Let's just open it. It's from the Nevada Business Registry, so it's partly for us, too."

"You can't open people's mail."

"The casino is ours too." His finger was digging under the flap.

"What does it say?"

He pulled out the letter to start reading it, and he tossed across a brochure. It was printed a decade ago, in that decade's cheap inks of liver and mustard. "WELCOME TO THE WORLD OF LEISURE GAMING—*Nevada Style!*" At the bottom, in italics imitating a businessman's efficient script, were the words *The Western Growth Industry of the Future!* A photograph depicted a mixed group gathered around a roulette wheel: a James Bond sophisticate in a tuxedo, a showgirl-type delighted by her winnings, one nondescript couple representing the norm, one fool in a fisherman's vest and crushed hat covered with lures. Wendy hated them all. Peter was reading, "It says the casino is worth sixteen thousand dollars! The last time they appraised it, it was worth that. The last time they checked was 1943. It's probably gone up in value by now. Things do that. They go up."

"Lemme see." She reached.

He dropped back out of her reach and started reading aloud, "'Transfer of ownership may be officially recorded by remitting a fee of twenty-six dollars, a facsimile of the Deed of Ownership or other document of sale, and a Note of Transfer from the Claim and Title Bureau of Bowden County containing a legal description of the property, along with the enclosed form. It is not necessary . . .' Blah blah blah. . . 'until such time as the casino is placed on active status. In addition, you requested information on the appraised value of the property. The State of Nevada does not conduct such tax appraisals except consequent to sale. The Cornucopia Casino was last on active status in 1943, at which time the value of all assets was given as \$16,212.08 . . . .' Wow,

Wendy! . . . blah blah blah 'please contact our office if we can be of any further service to you.'"

"How is the letter addressed?"

"Wow, Wendy," he said again, shuffling the papers, narrowing his eyes as he scanned. "Sixteen thousand is a lot."

"Is it addressed to Ed Pease or Ed Farmican?"

Peter flipped to the first page and smiled. "Farmican." Across the table they shared an awed fraternal look, of amazement at the whole idea of Ed Farmican. Peter raised his voice—*"Ed?"*—while his eyes still held Wendy's—*"Hey! Ed!"*

He got up from the table and went out to the foot of the main staircase. There was a spot at the bottom of the stairs where the notes of a voice could rise up through the house, and he planted himself there. *"Hey. Ed. We got a letter."*

Wendy almost followed him but her mother was out there on her knees among stacked dishes and empty cardboard boxes crumpling sheets of newspaper around things.

"Wendy? Would you come here? Would you help me?"

She turned and, in a rather surprising blackout, walked back through the kitchen, her body able to tightrope-walk in blindness. Her voice was cheerful: "Just a second, Mom. I can't right now." She was headed for the basement steps. Through the pantry, past the back door, she passed the spot where the marble lavabo had always stood. But now it too was gone, leaving only a high-tide mark on the wall, so her hand could no longer brush it in passing. Her mother was following—empty cardboard boxes banging a doorframe—"Wait, Wendy darling."

"I don't have to deal with this." She went down the stairs but stopped at the bottom.

"Wendy, wait."

It was a mistake not to flee but this basement corridor led nowhere, just to a series of digestive dead-ends. Beside her on the wall was the Boronovska mural of the Liberation of People's Park. She laid a palm against its sweat-and-flour surface, and she stood there hanging her head. Underfoot, the flagstones drifted westward, toward the ocean, cheese growing in the gaps, here where the floor was damp year-round near the rumor of an old spring. Her mother had come down the steps. She said, "Let's just talk." Wendy's neck pounded. She had no idea what her mother would do.

First, she sat down on a stair. There was a long pause—it would have been, in a musical comedy, the inevitable song coming on—and then she began, slowly, at the low end of her register, "I've always known that I'm not very good at all this 'mother' stuff. We wanted you kids to grow up without all the nonsense we got. To be free. To *have* your sexuality. And then also *be* whatever you want and avoid the get-married-have-kids trap. That was my mother, and *her* generation. She *died* of niceness." It was true, Wendy was the first girl in history not to have those expectations laid on her. Her gratitude for that, of course, her mother would make the basis of any conversation. Thus she always set herself up on the high ground.

For a minute she sat there on her stair and seemed to think. "Faro—" she clucked. "He's really so sweet, he's such a wonderful person"—somehow, for her, an expression of contempt. "Now he's on this campaign about 'hypocrisy' and being dead-honest all the time, as if *that* would solve anything. Well, you see what it does," gesturing at Wendy's body. "In a way, his indiscretions are a good thing. Because you do need an ego boost, love, and even inappropriate attention is flattering."

She decided she had been insulted. But she had always lived under a steady drizzle of her mother's judgments. All she had to do was stand up here until the speech was over.

"We always treated you as an adult. You've always made your own choices, and we didn't interfere. The result, I find, is that I respect you! I'm almost afraid of you, really. Does that sound strange? That I should be afraid of your opinion?"

No, it made sense: her mother had always hoped for others' opinions, a soprano unable to see into the darkness beyond her own personal glamor. She looked straight at Wendy: "I assume you won't sleep with him." (This was the whitewater-rapids part, where she only had to hang on.) "Not that there would be anything intrinsically *wrong* about sleeping with him. It's not incest. He is an attractive man. And it's not that I judge you or blame you. But just think of it, Wendy, everything would be so impractical." She smiled sadly and then looked down. "I think Faro feels he missed out on the sexual revolution. Ah. And so he did, poor man." Her mother's hands were so fine, so small. Wendy's were big and flat and white, like James Farmican's, with a dimple on each knuckle. As her mother picked idly at a cuticle, her fingers made delicate spidery motions in air, lyre-plucking. She lifted her eyes to catch Wendy admiring them, and her face got serious.

"Wendy, I don't want you to feel 'responsible' about what happened between you and Faro," she said in her clichéd, buttery voice from the sixties. Wendy was squeezing one hand with the other, hating the *miniaturization* that happened to people who listened to her mother long enough. She said in almost a quiet soft melody, "I just hate this." She should have turned and walked away, but stubborn love made her stay, love that gave her hope and made her weak and hopeless.

"Honey, wait, wait. Can we talk about these things one-at-a-time?"

"No. The whole *system* of talking about things in this house is . . . fucked." Footsteps sounded in the kitchen, so she lowered her voice. "I don't want to have to explain myself and defend myself. And defend myself and defend myself and defend myself."

"First of all, Wendy," with wide eyes. "Faro . . . ," she began with contempt, but then stopped herself. Then it was visible: Faro would never redeem himself. "Wendy"—she made a gesture of throwing him easily away—"he's a wonderful man. He's got many rare qualities. He's great. But he *is* to blame, if he puts you in that position."

"People don't put each other in positions. People don't put each other in positions. You know what? I feel sorry for Faro. I do."

Her mother didn't get it. She wasn't listening. She was never really listening. She took a big breath to start talking again, so Wendy jumped without forethought into the middle of the fire: "Wouldn't you be depressed? If somebody was marrying you just for your money?" Her two hands rubbed up and down on her hips.

"Oh, Wendy."

"Obviously Dad's royalty checks aren't so huge."

"Wendy, sit down. Seriously, I'm your mother now."

"I don't want to sit down."

"Wendy, sit down, just please."

"Everything is such a big joke. Everything is so perfect."

"Please just sit down."

Aflame with anger she did sit down on the bottom step, though weightlessly. Put her forehead on her knee. Once again, her mother was defeating her, bringing her to confusion. But she preferred her confusion. Her confusion was righteous. Her confusion would boil her up out of this trap. She would only have to trust her confusion.

"Honey, listen. I know that Faro . . . I know that there is something *unshaped* about him. I don't want you to think I'm *modeling* him into some sort of *thing*. I'll tell you. Men are fragile, more so than us. I know they have to seem big and brutal and confident. A man's ego is like an erection. Which obviously is an analogy you will understand when you are older. In fact, I'll tell you: Faro's money does matter. A man needn't be rich. Poor or rich: doesn't matter. He just has to be solvent. I'm speaking as your mother now. Because this 'money' thing is a mysterious substance nobody will tell you about. Love and money are the two things in life nobody comes out and *tells* you how to handle. They're very much alike, how you handle them, whether you're stingy or generous. Whether you make investments. For you,

you just have to learn as you go. Now, the main thing about men is that they work. They do. Because they love it. Or if they're fortunate they do. I'm talking about work, not a 'job.' They're more obsessive and narrow than we are, and less flexible. They're a little bit crazy that way. Your father *had* work. Unlike Faro. Wendy, are you paying attention?"

Her head was on her knee. She sighed to indicate she was listening. In fact she was fascinated, morbidly. It was almost calming to see. Her mother seemed to be coming apart before her eyes.

"They're all a little bit crazy. Each one. They're impossible. It's generally just a big mess. I'm telling you that now. It's not perfect. The reason *Faro* is out of sorts and being an ass right now—I think the reason he's seducing you right now—I'm sorry, I don't mean to be unflattering, but this is what I think— is that he doesn't have any work. It's hard for a man who inherits. But this wind-powered ranch is going to make him happy. These clocksprings."

"Is that," Wendy said, lifting her face, aware that her lip twitched, "is that what you did to Dad?"

"What."

"Treat his books as, just, therapeutic little *things* to keep him happy?" Her ears rang. She was talking in a vacuum. And the vacuum was history, this corridor.

Her mother gathered herself together on her stair-seat and bowed her head over Wendy's evil outburst. At last she said, "It was not our job to keep him happy. It was his own job. I'll tell you about your father, dear. He was meant to be a very happy-go-lucky man. He was very fun and charming. He was wonderful. In fact, he wouldn't have been capable of committing suicide. He was the love of my life, I want you to know that. As a writer, he was just, you know, happily scribbling along, he and all his friends. But when the damn fucking Endicott committee called, that was the start. From that moment on, I suppose he'd always had this inner fault-line. The rest of us started to be outside his bubble. Adulation was replacing love. All that supposedly 'anti-establishment' . . ." She manufactured one of her icky shudders. "As if there ever *is* such a thing as an 'establishment.' "

Wendy felt herself wakened, lightened: her mother had been this malevolent all these years, always this unfaithful; so that now she could be unfaithful after his death. "Mom, they don't give the Endicott to just anybody," she chided in a fakey tone.

"Oh *Conquistador*! Wait till you're older and read it again, honey. There are a few things he loved in there. He did really love a few things, accidentally."

"Accidentally?"

"What he *meant* to write was all the down-with-society stuff, which is just for children really. But accidentally he talks about a gas station in Sacramento? Remember?"

"I don't remember," said Wendy listening now despite herself in espionage.

"It was the inside of a gas station, where there was an old-fashioned candy machine, where you put in a dime and pull a lever. And how the morning sun falls on the candy machine. And he talks about a cold morning and walking to the corner store to buy milk. He gets it exactly right. How it feels to have the sun on your wrist. Just that. Just sun on your wrist. Those are the things people can use. Those are things you carry to your grave. Oh, he was the real thing. . . ." She looked away. She had rhapsodized a little, and now she frowned downward and refolded her hands: amen.

"It's an example of how wrong you can be: you know what the most important thing in your father's life was? And he didn't know it? Not writing. *You.* You and Peter. Were the best things that ever happened to him. You love your father, and that's good. But he got so angry later. There were really two Jim Farmicans. The Before version and the After version. He was going around with those guns. You kids and I had gone to

Morocco. Your safety was in question, because he was going around *announcing* that your safety was in question. So one of the things to preserve, too, was his memory in posterity, the image of the happy, wild . . . " In her mist her gaze condensed on a shining lost minute, and she aimed her voice out at the past. "When your father and I said good-bye at the airport, we both knew. We said good-bye on the curb, and he actually looked at me, right in my eyes. He hadn't done that in a long time—he hadn't been *sober* in a long time—and it was like we both knew he had a job to do, but didn't have the strength for, even then—shoof!" —there was that new little expulsion of air, which she'd adopted from her new man. "Oh Wendy, don't give me that wide-eyed look like I'm Lady Macbeth. I just don't happen to believe in suttee—where the wife has to kill *her*self, too, and throw herself on the husband's pyre. I believe in surviving. Get used to it, Wendy. You may want to be a survivor yourself one day. I hope so." She was kneading the tendons in one bony hand, a habit Wendy decided now she'd always found disgusting. "Though of course, he'd been threatening suicide for years."

"He was?"

"Oh, honey, you don't have any concept. Suicide was a big . . . *theme*." She chuckled.

Wendy didn't have much to pack. She could go upstairs right now and start putting clothes together. Her mother kept on talking but Wendy wasn't listening, the sound track was off now, she was watching her mother with a new detachment as if Julia Farmican Ness were a rubbery monster of a special-effects laboratory, just an arm's-reach away, an animated effigy, with visible new mouth-wrinkles, her stair a throne.

California's Over

That morning in the front library, Wendy sat beside Peter on the remaining couch, while Ed stood before them rattling the Nevada letter in his hand and saying, "First of all, we know the casino exists and it belongs to us, *and* we know we can initialize its operations by just remitting a fee. However, after that point, everything might be insurmountable when we get there." He was obviously self-entranced by the role of corporate president, which he had settled into with furious serenity. "Don't operate under any illusions. The different variables are potentially insurmountable."

Peter had begun listing to one side, eyes closed, beside her with folded arms. He hummed, "The desert is a place where the mind is cleansed." When he felt good, he had a way of radiating happiness that was distinctly aggressive, so that Wendy wanted to move away from him. Ed focused on him. "Don't operate under any illusions. *If* the casino is in existence at all anymore, it will be hard work. The Gaming Control Board informed me that they did have a telephone number for the Cornucopia Casino, but it was from twenty *years* ago. She said Bowden County out there is chocked full of abandoned casinos. So don't operate under any illusions. There's a lot of work and a lot of risk. We'll probably have to begin with extensive marketing studies. Basically, what the lady in the office told me was, all we've got is a piece of paper but in Nevada you can get a long way on a piece of paper."

A flapping and slapping in the side entryway, she knew, would be Baelthon, coming back from town. He entered the room damp and breathless. "The wiring is totally ruined," he proclaimed, of his car, as if it were good news, and Wendy's heart sank with loyalty and devotion. "The mechanic at the garage said it wouldn't be worth the cost of having it towed away. But I got my jacket at Little Tom's. It was hanging on the same peg." He held up one of those fake-sheepskin jackets with outer velour made to look like suede, carbon-monoxide-colored. He was heroic because he was mentally undivided, in a way that would always make him lucky and strong.

"So anyway," Ed said, summarily, "desert conditions. Lots of physical work. It might be just a ruined old building in the desert. In fact *probably*."

"Couldn't we leave now?" Wendy said, recklessly. "We could leave today."

"Mmm, car camp!" Peter moaned, his eyes still closed. His self-pleasure had grown fatter while Ed was painting an ever more painful picture of life in the desert. "Sleep on the ground by the road. Live off the land. We could make the border before nightfall."

"Today? Now? After lunch?"

Baelthon looked around and said in approving awe, "Whoa."

Ed folded his arms. "You have to understand. It's abandoned. The climate is harsh. It's not comfortable. It's not like this. It's the desert."

◎   ◎   ◎

The ladle's heel made a granular sand-crunch against the bottom of the tureen. "We're down to the best part now," Mrs. Farmican chuckled low as she stirred in the column of steam. "There's plenty left. That old miso is so potent, we could go on stretching this soup forever."

Everybody looked across the table at everybody else, silenced by the appearance, one by one, of bowls of ever darker soup, its salty flaring-match smell. Today, on that same spot of ground where the dining room was, a vigorous stand of bay laurel is getting a start, its hard poles rising out of the earth, its fumes cleaning the air, its leaves the same fresh uniform almond shape as in the laurel garlands awarded to Classical poets. In the dirt are bits of masonry, a nylon-tipped drumstick, a knob labeled BALANCE, soaked old plaster, an elastic string ending in a staple, a champagne cork, all blackening with the digestion of soil warmed by rot to the temperature of incubation, ground so soft underfoot you expect almost to fall through a fluffy hole. The only sound is the distant thud of the beach below, the clatter of bay leaves, a foghorn from San Francisco when the wind is right. The razed area of flat ground is surprisingly small, for a house once so confusing and vast. One monument of masonry is still standing, tilted a little: the seven brick steps that led up to the front door, the same staircase Julia Farmican stood at the top of when I first met her and she told me I'd come to save them all. Of course I hadn't. Everything that passed in that house escaped me, a lot more than a vessel of funerary ashes.

". . . So you'll come back in a week or so." Faro provided this information as a kind of query, while he accepted his bowl of black soup. "Either to here or to the Ranch in Oregon. Depending. After you've had a good look at 'Void.'"

Nobody answered. Over my lifted spoon I spied on everybody. Wendy wouldn't raise her eyes to me at all, or to anybody. She was impatient, full of held breath. Her brass-green hair hung as a curtain over her face. Mrs. Farmican seemed to keep an eye on her as she stirred the huge tureen. I stayed quiet, out of a sense that I was getting away with a sort of abduction. Out front, the car was packed.

Peter asked, "Where would we sleep in Oregon? What kind of place would people live in?"

"There's a trailer, but it's small. Your mother and I will be there. I think you should camp. The weather's mild. The cows won't bother you. The point is, you're free to build anything you like, for any *purpose* you like. The funds will be there if you propose something."

"The cows?"

"The land is leased to a rancher for grazing. It's interesting." He chewed. "Waking up with a cow standing over you. Gives you some perspective."

Ed wasn't entering in. He just buttered his bread. When we'd been packing the car he was ready to go within five minutes, his plaid suitcases stowed. Then he stood aside and watched Peter's possessions fill the trunk: an electric guitar, the IBM Selectric trailing its cord, a plastic garbage bag of clothes. Wendy by contrast packed like a boy, skimpily, in two paper grocery bags. I tried to persuade her she ought to bring more— clothes or books or something, because I suppose I thought it would give mass and swing to our elopement, bringing luggage.

"Hey, this ranch is not a vacation," Faro warned. "Every one of you Marin County faeries is going to have to work. Like I should think what most interests *you*, Peter, would be the *Open Journal*." His words were partly blotted out by hot soup revolving in his mouth. With his spoon he sketched around Peter's outline: "Being literary."

Peter raised his eyebrows, open-minded, groggy.

Faro went on, "Getting the printing press up and running. 'Cause eventually I want to publish distinguished intellectuals and writers, but the first issue could just be a journal of impressions. Would you like to do something like that? And then picture it: your own writing studio: a table, a chair, a stack of paper, a window. Close the door on the world and have all eternity with your blank pages. What else is civilization *for?*"

Peter sat there picturing it, his wrists on the table, looking handcuffed.

"If you want, your meals could be brought to you. You wouldn't even have to stir from your chair. It would be just you and an infinite supply of blank pages. And a doorway with a real door on it."

Peter never did involve himself with the Open Ranch's publishing. He still writes, but only for his weekly community-access TV talk show in San Diego, of which he is the host. The Open Ranch did publish a magazine for some years. It was called *Open Journal: essays, criticism, resources,* and it became rather widely known during the seventies. Its articles, written by Distinguished Guests of the Ranch, concerned everything from kitchen-garden composting to interstellar space exploration; political commentary; a design for an innovative waterless toilet like a cabinet that produced, as an end product, not sewage but small green bouillon cubes to be tossed in the garden; new windmill-vane designs; the coming global computer link-up. It usually contained photographs and etchings and drawings, and always a few poems, but never any poetry of Peter's. Still today you can find a copy or two of the *Open Journal* at the bottom of used-bookstores' bins or barrels, handsomely printed on expensive recycled paper, still hard and fresh and cold. Faro said, reaching for the loaf of bread in the middle of the table, "But first we have to build a fence. A real fence. A solid fence all around."

"I thought it was all fenced off."

"Nope. Not yet. Cows all over. And when the infrastructure starts breaking down"—his lips made a soft wind. "Oil is at what per barrel now? Gas is getting up toward two dollars a gallon? Detroit keeps building bigger cars? Arable land prices *tripled* the last decade? Factories going overseas to third world countries? All these things are straws in the wind. *Il faut cultiver notre jardin*: you gotta cultivate your own little garden," he said, making a little strangling motion with his hands to indicate the decent size of one's garden. "You gotta save the world."

"This soup is awful," Wendy said. She put down her spoon.

People looked at her.

She said, "I've had enough of this soup." She directed the remark at her mother.

Her mother looked, eyes shining, in Wendy's direction, and said, "You don't have to eat it, dear."

Wendy looked down and said, "In that case, I'll go." But then she didn't move but just sat there looking defeated.

Faro took in breath, held it, and then said, "I honestly still don't see what the hurry is." He was speaking to his wife.

Nobody answered him.

"You know there won't be much of a casino left. Or even if there is a little bit of an asset there, you'll decide that being even halfway successful in business is really too compromising, frankly. You know what? Making money is boring. You have to *love* what you do. I think you should all come straight back up to the Ranch and we'll kill the fatted calf. It's nothing but capitalism out there."

"Capitalism is reality," Ed said, the ready-to-launch remark sprung by a catch. It was the first thing he'd said. He stuffed his mouth with bread.

Faro seemed slightly startled. Then, thinking about it, he began in a reasonable tone: "There are various realities. There isn't just one over-arching reality. A lot of our economic reality," he nodded inland, "is truly based on war and racism and sexism and injustice and a class system. That's what you're going out into. That's what you'll be cooperating with."

"Yup," said Ed.

"They think selfishness is a virtue. Out there it's like you're stupid if you're *not* selfish. Ed, I've *been through* that whole enlightened self-interest philosophy—where people who get fucked over are supposed to take responsibility for their own lives; and a class system is a good thing because then you get such a thing as 'excellence.' I know what a coherent worldview that all is." Faro breathed and looked away for a minute, then he looked back. "I'm just ashamed and tired. That's all."

That seemed to be the end of it. Faro's capitulation. But then he spoke again. "In fact, Edward?" He put his hands in his lap. He looked pained. "Listen, we're keeping the Deed of Transfer here, your mother and I. You've *said* this was just an exploratory trip."

"What do you mean?"

"We're not giving you the Deed, not just yet. You would need to describe your venture a little more specifically—"

Ed looked almost delighted with amazement. "You can't do that."

"You don't want it out there in the desert. It will be perfectly safe here with us. It's only a piece of paper. Plus, you might be tempted to get rashly *involved* out there. Because, be honest. Ed. You don't know much about business. Especially *that* particular exotic business. So we moved it to the safe."

"It was given to us legally."

"Fine. So take a few days, go out to the desert, have a look. Operating a business is a big thing. You'll find it involves you in compromises which, you don't realize how permanent they are."

Ed didn't say anything, but sat back, looking downward.

"You're still young, Ed. That's a *good* thing, being young."

Mrs. Farmican said, "Excuse me," with a businesslike little smile, and she set her napkin aside and stood up. Faro watched her go out of the room.

Ed started mumbling as if to himself, "We'll go to the desert now. And then we'll sue you, I guess"—he sighed—"to get the Deed."

Faro's clasped hands flew apart. "I can't believe you guys *want* to go," but really he had swung to address Wendy personally. "You hardly know this 'Baelthon.'" (I stopped chewing and swallowed and tried to look solid.) "You know almost nothing about him. You've been acquainted with him for about three days."

"Now dear, you *are* sounding square," said Mrs. Farmican. She was coming back into the room. She sat down and put a white envelope beside Ed's plate. "Here. This is the Deed. I give it to you."

"Julie? Really?"

Ed Farmican, formerly Ed Pease, accepted the award by

simply looking at the stuffed fat envelope where it lay on the table, his hands lying in his lap. Faro accelerated himself slowly back against his chair, looking at the wife who had betrayed him.

"They'll be fine," she said.

"I was trying to create a *place*, honey," he said. "Does anybody perceive the purity of what is being offered here? And the usefulness? I mean the utility? Is there something faulty in my *conception* of it? Or have I perhaps done a poor job of *describing* it?"

◉ ◉ ◉

Peter stood perfectly still in an upstairs doorway and listened for motions anywhere else upstairs or down. The cardboard box sat by itself on a chair, McGUFFIN printed on all four sides in red letters; "*J. Farmican*" written on top in script. Inside, the top page said, "An End to All War, a novel, by James Farmican." He closed the boxtop flaps over the title page's impassive face. Lucky that he should find it in a public space, out here in a corridor rather than, say, on Faro's bedside table. This way, he wouldn't have to feel exactly like a thief.

He tucked it under his arm and tiptoed away by the servants' corridor and down the back stairs. Nobody had seen. He had the manuscript. It would slip nicely into a pillowcase, and then ride under the seat of the car. Down in his room, he sat down cross-legged on the floor and settled the box in his lap and looked at the lid: *J. Farmican*. He didn't have the will to lift aside the title page and read even a few lines. Good-bye. He slipped the box inside a pillowcase. He would read it later, in the desert.

Also, before leaving this place, he was going to indulge one more inner necessity, just as illicit: he was going to bury the ashes. It was probably a sentimental or sacral thing to do. But he was going out into the world as a "poet," for better or worse; and a poet's duty would always be the care of the sacred, the slighted. Nobody else cared about it. It was on the floor under his rolltop desk. Its imponderable contents. Along the basement corridor, a cellar door would lead him up a flight of cement stairs onto the back lawn. Then he could run around behind the garage with the urn tucked under his arm—and make his way out to the highway. And he would bury it by the Seawall turn-off, in the tender ground beneath a willow tree by a fence post. Suicides belong not in the sheltered churchyard, alongside the complacent and the lied-to, but out in open country at the crossroads under the wind. He picked up the cookie-tin. It was like fluffy sand in there, you could tell by the samba sound as he moved. Funny: burial involves a necessary kind of absolute disrespect, actually putting something in the ground. Disposal it is indeed. There was a line from one of his father's early poems, "Bury me by the roadside. Always loved the cold, and public places, the 24-hr Dunkin' Donuts, my cheek on the curbstone." There was an actual Dunkin' Donuts, Peter remembered it well. It was in North Beach. His father lay there snot-chinned on the floor—the white floor blindingly lit and shining: it had just been mopped with sugary-smelling soap—at two in the morning, while Peter—maybe he was nine or ten years old—sat beside him on one of those molded-plastic yellow seats bolted to the floor. They had been across the street in Tosca, and he'd been shouting that they should turn off the juke box so he could say something important. And because it was James Farmican, they did turn off the music—it was opera—and right away everyone was embarrassed, because James Farmican was crying as he explained why the Ring Cycle was a great work: because *he himself* was a little Hobbit just like everybody else, but there really is a trade-off between love and power in the world: if you go for the one, you're missing out on the other, and the Ring of Dark Power had finally fallen to *him* and *he* had been the one to melt it down at last and throw it away, *he* had been the one little Hobbit brave enough to end the eternal curse, and that's why all the other little fucking Hobbits couldn't forgive him, because now history was changed and the Ring of Power had been melted down and thrown back in the water, and *they'd* never have a chance at it. Peter followed quietly, and nobody noticed him—he was a little child then, and slipped through things like a minnow—while James Farmican was escorted out the door by some friends, who then didn't know what to do with him. So they left James Farmican there in the Dunkin' Donuts across the street, where the night manager was a shy Chinese man speaking only broken English, uncertain what to do with the big long-haired man on the floor, his chin shiny with tears, his ten-year-old son beside him dry-eyed—and he tucked the tinny urn high up under his arm, its inner dune sliding, and when he got up the cellar stairs and out into the bright day on the level lawn, his body asked to lift into a jog as he rounded the grassy stretch to run behind the garage and head for the spot of ground by the roadside under a willow tree at the coast highway turn-off.

Wendy passed through the front door for the last time. Outside, the new temporary chain-link fence cut off the driveway. Its steel posts were still powdered with the talc of the foundry. The county building inspector's Day-Glo orange sign was already wired to the steel mesh: DANGER. The long green tent was still there on the lawn, fattening on the house; it was like the book-cover of one of those Arthurian futuristic-fantasy novels, an immense green conquering worm-dragon. All four doors of the Mercedes-Benz stood open. The trunk lid was up and the hood was raised. Everybody else was milling around the car. She slipped through the gap in the fence and went out there too.

Faro had folded his arms high: "Energy crisis out there. Fifteen years of petroleum reserves"—he flipped his fingers toward the gas-guzzling car. His mysterious wife treated the
remark like a kind of admiration. Wendy could see she was beginning now to dispose of Faro. He had erred. He was standing
there in happy confidence, little knowing.

He was right, though. This was a stupid car to be traveling
in. In the open trunk she put her paper bag of clothes. She had
to move Ed's plaid suitcase to make room. It was unbelievably
heavy. Its latch was broken, and she could see that, inside, it
was filled with canned food: Campbell's Cream of Mushroom
Soup, Chef Boy-R-Dee Ravioli, Dinty Moore Beef Stew, Kraft
Macaroni Dinner.

She said, "This is full of food!"

Ed looked around and saw that everyone was watching him
and said, "It's an investment." He was holding up the radiator
cap, in an oily rag.

"Okay. I keep some of my cash in the form of non-perish-
able food. Inflation is at six percent now. In a normal savings
account, the bank wouldn't be giving me any interest. That's an
investment at six percent."

People couldn't take their eyes off him, sizing him up.
In fact, Wendy found herself impressed, weirdly. At least,
somebody that flat-footed, you could trust. Solvency is next
to integrity. So her mother would say. Among all her other
philosophizing. About how time isn't real and experience is
imaginary.

Then Merlin of course appeared, beside the house, leaning
to one side as he walked, with his horsey way of tossing his
head, and instantly she knew she would get emotional. And of
course he would insist on hugging everybody. He actually got
Ed to stand still—for an embrace, a clap on the back—though
Ed visibly hardened himself.

"Ed, listen now," he said. "You're going to find out something over the years: that your father was a great poet. He

wrote a few great poems, and that's the most important thing anyone can do. You don't believe it now, but you'll see," he told him, while Ed only backed away and went back under the hood.

When he came to her, he closed his heavy arms over her and hung there for a minute, and then whispered in her ear, "Oh, my dear Wendy-girl, look for the comet out there. It will be easy to see in the desert nights. You have to be watching for the end of the world 'cause people tend to miss it. And here, I've got this." He had an envelope. He put it in her hands, then wrapped her fingers around it to latch them. "Secret documents for you. Use them when the time comes. You'll need both of them." Then in a flourish, stretching his neck tall, he turned to Baelthon. He told him simply, "Young man,"and he awarded him a firm grip on the shoulder and shook his hand before turning away. "Congratulations to all of you, direct from the original Kahuna." "Peter will be along soon."

"Where's Peter?"

"He's coming."

"Oh great! Peter's not here."

"Here he comes."

He was walking up the long driveway from the road.

"Where were you?"

"I'm all packed," he said across the distance. He skipped, to start trotting. "Just a second, I have to get one more thing." He was heading into the house.

"Now, Faro," Dean said. "Now they've got the Deed. And I have a number of things *you* will want." From within slashes in his garments he was juggling up the pages of original church minutes on yellow legal paper. In his other hand he had the same pen Baelthon gave him yesterday. "I'm going to sign this now, Julie." He was shambling over to the car to use its fender as a writing surface. "Here I shall found a mighty edifice," he sang in monotone as he wrote. He straightened up and presented the pages to Faro. "You are *in* the Church of Bread and

Wine now. You're coming into a responsibility here. And there are some other things. Young fellow, run back into that tent there and find a box that says 'Original Frye Boots.' Bring it here to me." Baelthon did as he was told and went to the tent.

Peter came out of the house, swung off-balance by a heavy duffel bag. He was also carrying a box in a pillowcase. He and the duffel bag slipped through the gap in the new fence. As he passed, Dean's fist nicked his shoulder in farewell, and he stowed his bag and his shrouded box on the floor of the passenger seat—"Good work, Peter Farmican"—and then Peter hung himself before Dean to be embraced. Dean rubbed his back as he hugged him, and then he released him and backed away. "You do your best, Peter. You take care of all these people."

"Here, Ed," Faro said to his new stepson. "Why don't you take this along with you," and he handed over a Standard Oil credit card. "Just in case of emergency."

Ed accepted it, but it was clear he intended never to use it. That evasion was visible in his manner of turning away and pocketing it. Wendy liked him for it, and felt a little like his sister.

Dean said, "Good, yass, inside there you'll find a stamp," for Baelthon had come back with the box from the tent. He lifted the lid and held the box up: Wendy looked inside and tapped around among the mixed-up contents—to come up with a rubber stamp. It said *For Deposit Only, I.R.S. #53-4721723.*

She handed it to Dean. And then Dean made a little ceremony of passing it across to Faro, with both hands. Faro said, "Oh. Thanks. Yes." He looked at the seal, picked at its rubber face with a fingernail, and looked around in tired patience: "Excellent, Dean. Wonderful."

And then Wendy could see it again: her mother looked away from Faro with the quietest decision in her beautiful eyes. Faro was treating Merlin with disrespect. His sarcasm, and a lot of other things, were adding up. Wendy didn't feel as guilty as she ought to, for having let Faro kiss her. It was as if mother and daughter had *conspired*, accidentally, to rub a brassy spot on Faro Ness. At that moment, watching her mother, she could see she was lifting her blessing from him—just as she could reinvent James Farmican disloyally in memory, just as she could lightly explode the entire landscape instantly in a cloud of whirled free-way-litter, simply by departing for Oregon. She was that Hindu goddess, what's-her-name, bare-breasted dancer in a hoop, both creator and blithe destroyer of worlds. It was a little bit chilling, seeing the exercise of power, in one who was so lenient. All un-witting beside her, Faro took a grave poke at the Mercedes' tire with his toe: "Pretty soft shock absorbers there, Edward."

Ed was holding up an oily dipstick. It was true. The bag-gage was heavy, especially Peter's. The car looked like a beast driven to its knees. Ignoring Faro's remark, Ed ducked under the hood with the dipstick and stood on tiptoe to make a final matador's-thrust into the engine.

Then kisses and hugs. A general shuffling and milling. The waltz-like dream of it. All *already* in memory, even as it was hap-pening. Six slams, including the trunk and the hood. The skin already waxed by the traveler's numbness. No good-byes. A few practical admonitions. Faro was behind his new chain-link fence. Her mother had climbed the seven steps, to set herself up as a silhouette in the door's arch. Merlin fading on his own sepa-rate historical island. The floor-smell of motor oil they'd have to get used to. The old parking-permit decal they'd have to get used to, bleached to irrelevancy on the windshield. The engine started quickly and sounded strong. Premonition of carsickness. The coffin-lid upholstery on the ceiling.

These would be their fixed places now, Ed and Peter in front, she and Baelthon in back. The car began to wallow down the driveway and nobody spoke while they rolled downhill onto the new, other, tectonic plate. She sat sunken by her win-dow against her door, an invisible tide of trouble rising in the world as they came into the actual 1973. The marsh skimmed past the window. From his end of the seat, Baelthon was eyeing her, disappointed and ardent. She took a big breath, with a sort of resolve, and then—self-conscious of her own being desired, pleasantly like water gripping her body all around—she rose and drifted against him, put one arm around the small of his back and laid her head against his chest, with an undulant nudge of her hip—so that he of course inflated uncomfortably. They were making a public declaration. It felt exactly fine, pinning herself to him.

In front was the McGuffin box! She could see the word. Peter had brought it along, badly disguised inside a pillowcase: McGuffin showed plainly through the thin fabric. He would never have any idea it was full of orange Tang powder. He thought he was sneaking the ashes out, sentimentally. She would certainly never tell him. Let him go on believing. Let him never know that James Farmican's ashes were lost, through some mistake. Probably Baelthon's. No doubt Baelthon had thrown them out but didn't know it. Peter tossed their desert guidebook *Worlds in Collision* up on the dashboard (dashboard they'd have to get used to, hot-dog-colored hard rubber, soon to be split by Nevada sun), and he started playing with the radio dials. The checkerboard lay at Wendy's feet on the floor, its disks taped down under Scotch-tape crosses. Her eye rested on it, and the game rose up to her in a new configuration: *she* had been arranging for *him* to win. Her own black pieces were lining up to let the red jump them. She'd forgotten that, how happy he was while they played checkers. She'd always had the power of his happiness. That was also something she had forgotten: that she'd always been responsible, even as a little child, she'd always been like a mother to him. And now on this trip too, she would be the responsible one. She knew that. On this one day of confusion, everything felt flipped-up, orbiting, juggled in a gravity-free zodiac: the McGuffin box filled with Tang, the lost jar of ashes, the checkers game, everything revolving for this one day as pieces of an unsolved puzzle.

Baelthon—his real name was Steve!—said, "I'm hungry."

She shifted her head against his chest and aimed her voice vaguely, "Is Burger King the one with Whoppers?" She was so tired of tofu and cauliflower and rice and all that yinny food administered by her mother over the years as medicine against the yanginess of everything. Peter gasped and spun and clutched his belly with a strangled look in his eyes. "Burger King!" He flopped back to face forward, whimpering with desire, "I want a Whopper." Everything was possible, and her thighs clamped. The Whopper would be an opulent trash-heap almost too big for her to enmouth, as they sat in the Burger King parking lot, while the radio played "Song Sung Blue," then "Brandy, You're a Fine Girl," then "I Can See Clearly Now, The Rain Is Gone," and the freeway roared next to their table leading to the Interstate. She had not turned around to see the house's turret sink, the last dark pines going down beyond the churchyard. Baelthon's arm around her cinched tighter while Point Cuidad fell away. The fog broke. Blasts of sunlight began to flash on seat-backs, shoulders, laps. Sun lay on the skin of her own refrigerated wrist.

Ed said, "What's the best way to Interstate 80?" and Peter, feet on the dashboard, moaned happily, "Oh-whoa, people are gonna be consciously unevolved out there."

This observation went unremarked, and after a minute, Peter went on, "The last decent cup of coffee will be Sacramento."

Brother Ed kept his eyes on the road. A corner of his mouth gently lifted.

She laid her head on Baelthon again; he was made more substantial by it. In the last glimpse she'd had of her home, the green tent was feeding on the house, free to gorge itself now. Ed's shoulder, under its new stripe of sun, mounded up in turning the wheel as the car rounded the corner at the Seawall turn-off, beside the stump of the latest sawn-off sign, and headed up and east toward Interstate 80.

Merlin's sealed envelope was still in her hand. Her fingers

were still closed exactly as Merlin had latched them. She quietly tore it, and in the shelter of her shoulder she pulled out the two official forms inside. None of the blanks were filled in. They were both duplicates of the same form:

County of Marin
PETITION
for
CIRCUIT COURT HEARING,
in Testimony to
FACT of MARRIAGE

*Date on which Ceremony Occurred*_____;

Witnesses Present, if any: _____ . . .

Epilogue

I always thought you had to take out a marriage license first, and have blood tests. It turns out you can be legally married without all that. You don't need the signature of the presiding minister, you don't need witnesses, you only have to show you've believed you were married all these years. That's the legal criterion: belief. The lawyers say it will be easy. They say it will be routine. However, also, they say it won't accomplish anything. Our being married won't necessarily win any money away from Faro Ness and his Open Foundation.

Nevertheless, she and Gabriel moved in three days ago. They live here now. I keep to my room a lot. Sometimes I stand at my door listening. I suspect they do the same kind of thing, standing beside a sensitive wall trying to determine *my* motions. A lot of silences. The faint chirping of Gabriel's Walkman headphones somewhere. A general avoidance of the living room area, where one of Gabriel's holograms is always on display. A lot goes undiscussed. I've taken to grading my essays in bed rather than at the kitchen table, so they won't be forced constantly to *see* how things have turned out. They know I've compromised with life, but they needn't be constantly exposed to the sight of me correcting grammar errors on fifty essays a night. Getting eye fatigue, and a cramp in the shoulder where the pedagogic anger abides. For the first few nights, I brought my Tap Ramen in here to eat it in front of my computer.

317

Louis B. Jones

Tonight for the first time, we ate together in the kitchen. It's Gabriel's birthday.

He's twenty-four. I can't sing the Happy Birthday song because I find I'm all stopped up. I just sit there while Wendy's voice carries the tune and Gabriel watches the candle on his cake, makes a wish, blows it out. I am aware that you don't have to be stupid to be happy. Nevertheless, I'm too old for this. Happiness is a heart attack. I walk through the rooms, through this our cohabitation, with a jarredness like a man on the brink of an epileptic seizure. When she came over for a visit and a glass of wine the other night, I could hardly look at her. A certain wince contains me. I keep reaching for another smoke. I've already said enough, to insult her and mutilate myself and mutilate this whole situation. Yet this happened too: when she got up to leave the other night, she put her arms around me—and I around her—and our bodies were so perfectly puzzled together, I'm sure she felt it too, because she didn't want to unstick herself too fast. A kind of supremacy, or confidence, has come over her in this house. Tonight at the dinner table, she looked calmly straight at me, while she asked Gabriel what he wished for in blowing out his candle. I didn't speak. I tend to sit here getting glassier in this kiln. Gabriel told her he'd wished for two things, rather than just one. She said, "You may not want to tell us your wishes," taking her eyes from me and applying them to her plate, "because if you don't keep them a secret, they won't come to pass." She has a certain tone, which she inherits from her mother, an ability to diffuse meaning sidewise, an eclipse of radiance.

"They'll come to pass," Gabriel grumbled. Sitting here at my table, he was sucking frosting off a candle. He is arrogant, which I find I'm impressed by and stand out of the way of. He does resemble me, a little. He said, "Here's what my two wishes are. First of all, this person has to help me do the *Catcher in the Rye* essay."

"We've talked about that," I said.

318

California's Over

"You have no choice, 'Dad.' You have to confront your guilt *and* get me into that scholarship money." He never bothers to look at me when he talks. The grommets have been removed: purple scabs at the eyebrow and earlobe. But still, he is psychologically a wreck. He hasn't had a real father figure to kick around, just the usual series of casual friends passing through Wendy's life over the years, agreeable guys under the reign of the Birth Control Pill, clever and handsome and inoffensive and talented and evasive, I can picture them all, they're my generation, they're just different versions of me. Now that Gabriel has an actual father, he's wasting no time. Within a day of moving in, he got the word that I was disgusted by his idiotic, pretentious, shitty, insulting sculpture of Nixon and Kennedy, which actually was driving all of us out of that whole corner of the house—so he "put in a new crystal." Now the equipment projects a big 3-D image (supposedly less obnoxious) of Charles Manson and the child actress Shirley Temple. This is what "art" has become these days. Charles Manson, with his famous decorative swastika carved into the skin in his brow, is sprawled facedown on the floor gnashing his teeth, wearing a yellow sheath cocktail dress, bound at the wrists by duct tape, while a curly-locked Shirley Temple holds him down by setting a foot on his neck: she waves, sunnily, jauntily in victory, with a prosthetic stainless-steel hook instead of a hand.

What is that supposed to *mean*? How is that supposed to *reward* contemplation? Is it supposed to convey some nifty message? "It doesn't mean anything, it's just supposed to get your attention," says Gabriel. "The definition of art is anything man-made that gets your attention."

I unplugged this one too. I did it this morning. So far no one has mentioned it. It's as if the two of them are *amused* by my slinking around the house, the misanthrope, the Excavated Father. When their U-HAUL truck arrived on the first night, it was late, they were way behind schedule, and I had had a lot of wine and I just sat in the kitchen chair while they carried things past me—all their possessions are cheap shit, a plastic end table, a chrome-framed poster, a dusty stereo in pieces; all of which will harmonize perfectly in this old tract home with its hard cold push, under the heel, of a concrete-pad foundation. I sat there watching this procession of furnishings go past, and I told Gabriel as he went by, "Let me get your attention for just one minute." This kitchen chair of mine, handily, swivels on an axis. He stopped and devoted to me a certain polite attention which made me see myself as sloppy-drunk. It was distinctly impolite of him. He was holding a futon in his muscular hug. The grommets had recently been removed, and a square of thready white gauze was taped over one eyebrow. I said, "I have every hope that you will get into the college of your choice. But I need to lay to rest any idea that I might 'help' you write an essay about *Catcher in the Rye*. To do so would be plagiarism. It's called plagiarism. If your generation is really going to be stupid—as if stupidity were desirable, like some big life-long vacation—well then, you should suffer the consequences of being stupid, and just go ahead and *have* an empty life." The futon was a slippery seal that kept pouring out of his embrace. He said, "Just a minute, there, Dad," and dragged it off. The conversation was never resumed, but I was sure he got the point, and I swiveled back around, like one of those big guns on a battleship.

Yet tonight he had the temerity to bring it up again: *This person has to help me do the* Catcher in the Rye *essay*. I said, "All right, what's your thesis?" Because, as a matter of fact, I happen to be a little bit of an expert on the topic of that greatest American book since Huck Finn. My idea was to kill Gabriel's idea by simply exposing it to light. Ideas wither and die under any close inspection. That's been my experience as a professional English tutor.

"Thesis? I don't know. Shit. Thesis," he sniffed, and bobbled his head, "I have to have a 'thesis.'"

California's Over

"Thesis. Yes. Like, 'Holden Caulfield and Huck Finn: The Attack on Society.' Or 'Holden Caulfield, The Victim of Phoniness.' A thesis."

When I'm conceding a little generosity, I can sometimes seem cross. It's how I am. Also, as a matter of fact, this was a big concession I was making, and I wasn't sure he appreciated it. My time is important. I don't have time to waste helping illiterates cheat on essays. I might be more generous if *he* weren't so insolent. I started eating again. But he went on looking at me. He seemed confused. He said, "Holden Caulfield is not the victim of phoniness."

Anyone who has looked into Salinger's book knows that the narrator uses the word phony on almost every page in describing the adult society around him. I pointed that out.

Gabriel said, before I could even finish, "No, *he's* the phony."

A remark like that—that Holden Caulfield is a phony— raised the ever-likelier possibility that he hadn't read the book at all, or at least not very well, and I said so.

Regally at my table, he was carving up his own birthday cake. He stopped that, picked up *my* wine bottle and refilled my glass for me, and said, "Here you go, Dad. Time for a little more of this."

A panel of darkness falls across my mind when I'm refraining from regrettable impulse. Anger has a way of *freezing* me, in a state of waiting. Waiting for what? To be released by a touch, as in the childhood game of statues. But even a touch would bring on the blinded arm-jerk reaction. Gabriel, having served cake to everyone, took a big forkful in his mouth and said, "I made a new crystal."

More long silence. Wendy and I, the two adults at the table, were sharing, silently by telepathy, the observation that Gabriel was practicing terrorism here in the house, successfully. She said, "We saw it, honey. Everyone saw it."

"No, it's not Shirley and Charlie. It's my masterpiece. It's my birthday gift to '*Dad*.'" Whenever he uses that word, it arrives from a two-decade journey as a rebuke to me—in my cardboard cowboy boots on the sunny streets of Reno, loitering alone in front of Dr. Tulip's office on an afternoon in 1974 when we failed to keep an appointment. Sitting on a concrete tire-stop because my boots hurt too much. Waiting for the bus out of town, smoking cigarette after cigarette as I walked in front of the casinos' open doors, each with its own separate seashore sound offering immediate contact with the infinite. Inside, men crowded around the rail of a craps table like drowners around a rescue dory. No comfort for me was in there. My shadow sharp on the noon Nevada pavement, in my pocket the eight hundred-dollar bills in a hard cylinder that would get me started again in San Francisco.

Wendy set her fork down on her plate and said, "Gabriel? Couldn't you just relax? Not everything has to happen all at once."

"Here, I'll show you." He took another big forkful and stood up to go get something. "What I did was, I've been going to the storage lockers in Sausalito. I wanted to use a relic from the time before I was born. Something from when I was just a gleam in my mother's eye."

He was standing behind me. I sat there not eating this wedge of cake in front of me. He said as he turned to go to his room, "So I found *this*."

She lowered her voice and told me, "This would be the portrait of Dean on a cloud in heaven."

"I'll tell you something," I said volubly in a nice loud normal tone of voice. "Just because they've discovered a gimmick with laser light, that doesn't mean there's anything artistically redeeming about it. Are we aware of that? It doesn't increase its merit as art, just because it exploits an interesting new technology that came along. If you gave Vermeer a twig to draw in the dust, he'd figure something out." I find lately, my very *body* keeps getting shrunken hard back into the form of an angry adolescent. The adolescent body is pithier.

Wendy picked up her fork and said in resignation, "Well, this is going to go on for a while."

Gabriel came back with a wooden case. From it he was pulling a gun.

"Gabe!"

"Don't worry, it isn't loaded. It hasn't been fired in . . . thirty years? Twenty-seven years?"

In the wooden case was a second, identical gun, cushioned in satin. They were matched dueling pistols. He set the gun on the table. By the clunk, it was heavy. From a string on its trigger hung a tin-rimmed cardboard disk bearing the words, in stamped fading blue ink: *Marin County Sheriff Department*. Inside the case, the second gun lay in its bed. The words + *Not This One* + were written on its barrel in White-Out erasure fluid.

"I got this out of storage, and I scanned it into the new crystal." Gabriel made a wink toward me. "I'm exploiting as much as possible the famous name."

I was watching the gun. The runic White-Out crosses, bracketing the words, were troubling to the memory. I could see myself at the age of seventeen, in that dark, cold-sweat basement, pulling these guns from a trunk, wondering whether they should go to the auction house. Tonight I could see that the writing on the barrel belonged to Dean, the family's guardian angel.

"Well," Gabriel said, "I can see this idea is pretty depressing to everybody." He picked the gun up and slipped it in the case.

"I'll take those," said Wendy, holding out her hand. Under the surface of Gabriel's snotty personality lurks an Obedient Boy, which his mother can bring out, but not I. He handed the gun case across.

She said, "I'll put them back in storage."

"Fine. I'm done with 'em. Thanks." He picked up some cake in his fingers, knocked it back into his mouth, and went around the partition to the living room—to start plugging in his new masterpiece. No one has the heart to tell him what a dead-end idea "3-D laser art" is. Wendy and I looked at each other. Does all parenthood feel like this? Like being held hostage? The kitchen and living room are separated by a half-partition: sounds came from the other side, of Gabriel plugging in the equipment, the soft *ding* of the computer's hello, the tiny electronic voice in a thimble saying *"Welcome to Adobe Sculp-tureShop."* We went on listening: the laser projector's cooling-fan. Somehow I'm enjoying this game of skittles in this house, the spinning of the top, the pins still standing. I took a bite of cake. The general assumption around this house is that I am weak. Wendy saw my weakness again the other night when I said that the possibility of love was contaminated.

She leaned across the table and lowered her voice beneath the whir of the projection equipment: "Let's not go to court."

I must have looked confused, because she rephrased it, "Let's not fight it. We don't need money."

For some reason I picked up my fork and started demolishing the wedge of cake on my plate, leveling it to crumbs without eating any. Something irrelevant popped into my mind, and I started talking about it, though dizzy: "But Wendy, I was thinking. Your mom was Faro's ex-wife. Shouldn't she have gotten half his property? Did she legally divorce him? Because she would get half his property."

"Faro and my mother were never legally married."

"Dean married them."

"He did?"

"Yes. Out on the lawn. I think it was the second day I was there on the place. We were talking about an old leather drum Faro wanted to give to the poor."

"I remember that conversation about the drum."

"And Dean said, 'I now pronounce you man and wife,' and he made them both say, 'I do.' You were there too."

"I remember the day, but I don't remember that. But then who knows," she said fondly. "Plenty of things happen."

"There were witnesses. An appraiser from the auction house was standing there."

"Well, I suppose if Dean *had* performed one of his marriages, you might say they have been legally married. But I was there. I remember we just went inside."

"I'm positive. Dean made first your mother say 'I do,' then Faro. And then on the day we left for Nevada, he gave you those forms to claim you've been married."

"Yes, those forms."

"Peter was there. He'll remember."

She picked at frosting on her plate. "Memory is such a funny thing."

Gabriel's voice in the next room said, "Are you coming?"

So we pushed back our chairs and stood up and went around the corner. I wanted to hold her hand. I just felt like it. But I didn't.

In its cylinder of dusk, the new eidolon was projected high overhead near the ceiling. For some technical reason, a laser is able to project a single figure better than a plurality of figures. So this image—Dean Houlihan on a cloud—is the most substantial-looking of Peter's spectres I've seen so far. This house of mine, like all the others on Idylberry, has a living room ceiling that slopes up toward the rear wall; realtors call it cathedral; so there was room for Gabriel to float this hallucination on high.

Dean Houlihan is suspended on a cloud. Let me see if my description can do it justice. It looks, at first glance, like a local section of the Sistine Chapel ceiling. It's got the Sistine Chapel's colors and churning weather, Michelangelo's distinctive glow and muscular flow of drapery and cumulo-nimbus. He got his computer to reproduce those same Renaissance colors and shades and brilliancies, but in three dimensions. I think he may have copied a particular section of the Sistine ceiling—called 'The Last Judgment,' maybe?—a section where angels or souls, or whatever, are tumbling in mid-heaven on their windy up-drafts and downdrafts. From that section, he's taken the central, Jehovan figure. But rather than Jehovah, it's the 1973 version of Dean Houlihan. Dean transfigured in bliss—in his purple-striped pants and his crocheted vest, lifting a soft hand in a sign of benediction. In his other hand, hanging down in repose, is the pistol with its white cardboard tag on the trigger. He looks mild and merciful and saturated with joy.

But here's what happened. Wendy looked at it for one second, as if it were a real person in the room, then she turned and went straight out. She made a little gasp of keeping grief silent.

This wasn't what Gabriel was expecting. What he said was, "Oh," with his eyes on me. He looked remorseful, and that was a good thing to see.

"You took out the pissing part," I told him.

He obviously felt unforgivable. I left him there and followed her outside. All these houses have a sliding side door off the kitchen, leading out to a pad of old concrete, now in this decade crumbling to aggregate pebbles. While I followed, she kept on walking—around the carport and into the front yard.

I was able to halt her by following close enough. She folded her arms to repel me and she said in explanation, "I never saw him happy."

"Who?"

"Dean. I never did see him smile, or be . . . happy." Her forearms in a ropy twist tightened hard at her chest. "He never *was* happy. He's . . . ," she gestured toward the image inside, ". . . happy!" By a trick of computer imaging, Dean's face has been reconceived: now he's so radiant with inner joy he illuminates the heart of the beholder. In his life, Dean's features were always crushed hard together in his constant focus on The

California's Over

Next Dandelion. But here tonight in Gabriel's reincarnation, he looks like a man who has learned in heaven that there was never any reason to worry about anything.

Dean Houlihan, in actual fact, died of exposure in the winter of 1990. Wendy told me about this. He died on the piers of San Francisco alone, holding up a Styrofoam cup filled with rainwater, wearing a nylon parka that had once belonged to James Farmican. After a point he had stopped taking care of himself, and resisted others' care, living on the San Francisco streets barefoot in his greasy parka. He always loved the cold windy piers below North Beach, and he loved the rail yards south of Market. At the end, his zone of habitation mostly dwindled to a stretch of sidewalk on Colombus Avenue between an automatic teller machine and a Häagen-Dazs ice cream parlor. Also, the zone of his intellect shrank. As he got more addled, his conversation was limited to the words *Only the Pure of Heart*, his old greeting from the days when he patrolled the main road to Seawall. Wendy says that if you spoke to him, he would listen in a rapture of complete incomprehension, and then he'd bring back up those words, as if he were remembering fondly something that had slipped his mind.

He never went back to Seawall after a certain point. The Free Box was still there—it's still there today, in fact—but the Veritas closed its doors in the mid-seventies, and Angelo Parinesi moved back to New York. Humper's Bar has been sold to some new people who have been turning it into a bed-&-breakfast. Seawall has been changing, but also staying the same. The Bubble Gum Tree and the Soda Water Fountain are still there. And some of the same people are still there. And the Seawall Sign Wars continue to this day. Indeed, the town seems to have won. A few years ago, Cal-Trans gave up trying to mark the turn-off. So the Seawall Border Patrol has widened its theater of operations to include the coast road north and south of the turn-off: during the night, they take down NO PARKING signs which are considered to disfigure the roadside along the marshes, south toward Stinson Beach and north as far as Point Reyes. And the turn-off itself remains forever unmarked. Still today, if you want to take that turn, you have to know the signal stretch of sleepy oak woods, the willow tree, the falling fence post.

To explain her emotions about Dean, Wendy said at last, "He was taking care of us."

I said, "Well, . . . and me too," which caused her to lift her eyes to me for one mistrustful second and then sheathe her gaze again in the blinded zone beyond my shoulder: the world.

I've had this insight as I get older. Women, after a certain age, never look at you anymore with absolute faith showing in their eyes. Those candles are for children. Rather, paradoxically, when a woman is beginning to have faith in you, she eyes you with *doubt*, as if she were weighing you in as trustworthy, but against her better judgment. That moment of wariness and dubiety is what you're looking for, rather than unfiltered radiance. At this moment she's fine, she's sleeping at my back while I work, and faith is certainly a condition of sleep. But for a long time after seeing the portrait of Dean Houlihan as a happy man, she was weakened, in a way that comes to me as a responsibility. It was an odd moment. We were standing together in the front yard, which is really just a dust-square bordered by sunken 2 x 4s. Dark was coming on and it was blue everywhere, and I was holding her in my arms. It didn't feel strange at all, holding her. I suppose I just felt lucky and still unworthy. Same old thing. But now it's here at 555 Idylberry. There isn't much traffic in these side streets, and a dinner-hour quiet extends to hearing's furthest edge, which is the freeway. From the front window came the aurora borealis of Gabriel's, I suppose basically well-intentioned, hologram.

That's when everything suddenly started to seem very simple. It was strange. A car was coming past, up Idylberry, and together we felt interrupted. Its headlights rose and took our picture. We both lifted our heads to look into the blaze and be

California's Over

covered in it. Then it went on around the curve of Idylberry and disappeared, the kiss of tires on asphalt on an autumn evening. In the quiet of this whole neighborhood, that suburban sound of a single subsiding car—that washing, gliding *shoom*-sound I know so well from living where I do—grew smaller and smaller and shrank to a single little point that hung essentially in the distance like a star, the first star of evening. All the usual things were all around, the far-away rising moon of an old basketball backboard eclipsed by a garage roof, the velvet dew on the windshield of my neighbor's Camaro, the profound deep dark squares of lawns at night, where somewhere a cricket sings. To that passing driver, we would have looked simply like two people standing in their front yard. That was all. And the interesting thing is that that's right. That's exactly right. There's a certain kind of freedom, a blessing in the totally indifferent glance of a stranger going past. You're just two people on the front lawn. Of course—yes—people also have particular lives with a lot of particular worries and hopes and plans, and requirements for particular meaning. But it's also true that, at a given moment, you're just two people out front; you could be anybody; you could be anyplace.